# THE
# SEVENTH
# MESSAGE

## A NOVEL BY

# WILLIAM T. JOHNSTONE

# THE SEVENTH MESSAGE

An Ashley Kohen Thriller

Copyright © 2017 William T. Johnstone

This is a work of fiction. All characters, names, incidents, organizations and dialogue in this novel are either products of the author's imagination being used fictitiously, or are a matter of public record.

ISBN – 13:978-1541162204

ISBN – 10: 154116220X

Book Cover Design by Mariah Sinclair

T

This book is dedicated to my wife

**Judy Johnstone**

Who I share my life with now and forever.

# THE SEVENTH MESSAGE

# Acknowledgements

This novel is the result of a promise I made to myself, many years ago, to write a novel upon retirement. Up until that point, my writing was of a technical nature. The Seventh Message was a lot of fun to write and a great challenge for the author. It started with an idea for a character with dedication and motivation to save others from the evil side of human nature. From that concept the story grew toward the fulfillment of the ultimate triumph over malevolence. Getting to that end required a great deal of imagination, research and help from those willing to expend their time and knowledge on my behalf.

My thanks to Weldon L. Kennedy, author of *On Scene Commander*, who introduce me to the culture of the FBI. His true life experiences gave me insight into the day to day workings of a Federal agency important to public safety and national security. I also appreciate the technical review of piloting procedures offered by Donald E. Anderson, and to the Federal Aviation Administration that employed me long enough to gain insight into their flight management system and their ridged determination to maintain flight safety procedures.

No writer writes alone. He or she must rely on others to see what is invisible to the author. Those with keener eyesight then mine include Elaine Jordan, Chris Hoy, Sandy Nelson and Susan Lanning who reviewed the draft manuscript and made if better.

I want to thank the Monday Readers Group for their diplomatic, penetrating and resourceful critique of my weekly scribblings. Without input from Ed Gates, Judith March Davis, Dougal Reeves, Patricia Batta and Mary Ann Clark this work of fiction would never have reached a successful conclusion. Thank you for suffering though the drafts and tolerating my revisions.

Finally, I want to recognize my wife's ability to spell better than me and her willingness to not comment on her superior skills.

# THE SEVENTH MESSAGE

# PROLOGUE

IN A SUBTERRANEAN CHAMBER with walls of limestone blocks six men stood around a stone table of inlaid jasper, jade and malachite. Two men dressed in flowing Arab wear, faced four others in western business suits. Pale light from the stone fireplace reflected on their faces. The cobbled floor, rutted by centuries of wear, felt uneven underfoot.

The Arab wearing a checkered headscarf spoke. "I am the Supreme Leader and have met your demands. My inspectors tell me all is ready." His companion, a large bearded man in black robes and a white scarf, nodded agreement, and then added, "It has taken my Supreme Leader months to assemble the gold and melt it into uniform ingots."

The Russian and his translator confronted them across the table. Two bodyguards stood in the darkened corners of the chamber. The Russian, dressed in a tailored black suit, challenged the Arabs. "Months of negotiations mean nothing to you." He spit out the words. "My auditors tell me you are short ten million U.S. dollars. Your actions are intolerable." He spoke in his native language. His interpreter, standing beside him, translated in Arabic.

The Supreme Leader raised his head in disbelief. "That is not possible. My Chief Disciple has supervised our efforts personally. You demanded payment in a manner untraceable through established banking procedures, and I have complied. I calculated our payment using the value of gold we agreed to earlier. My inspectors weighed the bars many time to ensure everything is in order. They assure me there are 3,676.5 pounds of gold bars at our transfer point, as you demanded."

The Russian eyed the Arab and sneered. "Our deal is $100 million in pure gold. Pure gold is 24 karats, as you must know. Hundreds of samples reveal the gold is on average 21.5 karats: contaminated with 2.5 karats of worthless base metals. You are not dealing with a fool. I have sold arms to countless factions, who conduct coups, revolts, political uprisings and wars around the globe. You seek to buy a most unique weapon." In a loud and angry voice he shouted, "Do you think you can cheat me?"

The interpreter, an American, translated the question.

Humbled, the bearded Arab bowed his head, knelt beside the Supreme Leader, and clutched his gold embroidered robes. "Forgive me my most holy descendant of the Prophet Mohammad. Their auditors told our inspectors of this error minutes before this meeting. I will arrange to deliver 367.5 pounds of pure 24 karat gold worth 10 million dollars by week's end. May Allah the Magnificent testify to my innocence, as I speak" The interpreter quickly told the Russian of their promise. "Tell them I will accept their gold. I am suspicious of their explanation, but I have invested too much time in these negotiations to walk away."

Both Arabs exchanged hurried words. The big man, visibly humiliated, stared at the stone floor, head bowed. The Leader ordered him to put wood on the fire, then spoke to the Russian. "I will correct this oversight. You should have no further concern. What is of concern to me is a guarantee you have what you say you have to sell. I need proof."

As if he expected that demand, the Russian pulled documents from a briefcase and spread them on the table on top of the *End User Certificates*. He explained. "These are secret drawings. The notes are in Russian, as you would expect. The photographs are both old and new, some with a digital date. This should confirm your research. A team of our experts will train your people when you are ready. That's part of our deal."

The Supreme Leader listened to the translation and studied the documents. "You must guarantee that my purchase will be set before me in a timely manner. Are you prepared to meet my demand?"

The Russian countered. "Here is what I propose: you will name the point of transfer. If I agree, we will each appoint observers to oversee the transfer." He leaned forward, placed his hands flat on the stone table, and stared directly into the eyes of the Supreme Leader. "Before any work begins we will exchange ten male hostages to be held in a secure and secret place of our choice. You will appoint an armed guard to watch my hostages, and I will appoint an armed guard to watch yours. You and I will make daily contact with our transfer observers. If either side reports the trade is compromised, the other side will kill one hostage a day until the problem is resolved." He moved his face within inches of the Supreme Leader, his jaw muscles flexed, "I pay my hostages well and have never lost one." He offered a thin smile. "I suspect you have martyrs to serve as your hostages?"

The translator explained this complex arrangement in detail. The Supreme Leader listened and conferred briefly with the bearded man. "I agree. I name this chamber as our final exchange point. The item I am buying from you, and the gold I am paying you, will be moved here. Agreed?"

The Russian responded. "Yes. You need only sign the two *End User Certificates* laid out on this table to consummate our deal. You must know, these certificates describe procedures recognized internationally. We will sign both documents and each of us will keep one."

The Arab ordered his companion to bring him a pen. With no further words, he and the Russian hunched over the ancient table and added their signatures to the documents. No one spoke, until the Russian said, "Everything is in order. This deal is done."

The Russian retrieved his copy of the agreement, stepped back, and leered at the Supreme Leader. "I will watch the future with interest. You have at your disposal a unique opportunity never before available to anyone. Properly carried out your actions will be felt around the world." With a smile he added, "The future will be changed forever."

# THE SEVENTH MESSAGE

# ONE

SERGEANT ASHLEY KOHEN faced five uniformed police officers seated as an Initial Board of Inquiry in the headquarters conference room. An electric fan moved the hot and humid air, but didn't eliminate the smell of body sweat. Her back ached as she sat at attention and wondered how much more of this crap she'd have to take.

Captain Flynn continued, "Then what did you do?"

"I called dispatch and reported officer down."

"Did you render aid and assistance?"

"Yes, but I couldn't revive Officer Saviano."

"Was he dead?"

Sergeant Kohen hesitated. She must now repeat the obvious results of the shooting, yet again. "Yes sir, he was dead. Three shots in the center mass at close range. Dead. Not moving. Not breathing. Lifeless, like not alive anymore."

"Calm down, Sergeant. We're about done here." Captain Flynn turned to the other four officers on the board. "Any more questions?"

A lieutenant at the end of the table nodded. "Sergeant, you say there was a witness to this incident?"

Ashley Kohen recalled the vivid image of the frightened store owner's thin body slammed against a wall by Saviano's big fist. The officer's other hand, clutching a wad of money, pounding the shopkeeper's bloody face again and again.

"Yes, sir. Like I already said. While on my way to work I heard dispatch make the call, and I responded because I was in the vicinity." Ashley strained to keep her composure "The store owner, Mr. Lee Chan, called in the robbery before Officer Saviano arrived. He said the officer would rob him. It had happened before. Mr. Chan gave a statement to the Professional Standards Unit explaining the entire incident."

Captain Flynn picked up the digital recorder lying on the table in front of Ashley. "If there are no further questions, I call this Initial Board of Inquiry adjourned." He snapped the recorder off.

Sergeant Kohen felt a release of tension in her body. She could go home, sort out what happened, and get on with her life. The last time she'd felt this tormented she was a little girl in school. Because the boys bullied her on the playground, she came home crying every day. Her mother told her, "Ashley, when they knock you down and kick you, reach up and grab their foot and twist it until it hurts." Ashley never forgot her advice.

She hesitated in front of the windows of the conference room. Down below the night-lights of Chicago outlined the buildings and lit the constant movement of life on the streets. It had been a rough day for her in the Windy City.

Captain Flynn remained after the others left. With his head down, he moved close and whispered, "My boss, Commander Morgan, is outside. Sorry, I can't help you."

Commander Morgan, a square-shouldered man with a protruding belly straining the gold button of his uniform, stood blocking her exit from the room. "Kohen, the Chief wants to see you upstairs. Right now."

"See me, tonight, this late?"

"That's what I said, sergeant." Morgan glanced at her breasts, and shook his head. "Such a pity. With so many men crowded together at headquarters, a good-looking woman was a tasty diversion."

Ashley straightened and took a deep breath. "What do you mean 'was'?"

"I mean Saviano wasn't the greatest cop working the streets, but he was one of us, and one of the Chief's oldest friends."

"Meaning?"

"Meaning you've had a good run. Too bad it has to end."

Ashley's voice hardened. "Armed robbery and assault is a crime, even if the perpetrator wears a uniform and works for the Chicago Police Department. I did what every cop is sworn to do."

Morgan scowled. "The Chief's waiting. Follow me."

Captain Flynn, helpless to intervene, watched as the two disappeared down the hallway.

12

# TWO

THE WALNUT PANELED WALLS of Chief of Police Marvin Danforth's office held rows of mounted animal heads snarling into the room. Interspersed between the hunting trophies hung photographs of Danforth at various times during his checkered career.

Danforth stood up when Sergeant Kohen entered his office, but not to be polite. He brushed by her, slammed the door, and then turned and glared at her with that pissed off expression he wore when things didn't go his way. Ashley braced herself for a confrontation. The smell of stale cigarette smoke filled the room.

"Okay, Kohen. What the fuck happened out there?"

Ashley stood at attention. "I've reported everything to Professional Standards, sir. You should have their report."

"I have it. Answer my question."

"Yes, sir. Last night I worked late and parked the police car in a secured place. On my way to work this morning I heard dispatch report a robbery in progress at the corner of Cicero and Prospect, a retail shoe store only two minutes away. I answered the call and proceeded to that location."

"Standard procedure. Get on with it."

"Yes, sir. As I drove up, I saw Officer Saviano stroll into the store. I assumed he didn't know he was going into a dangerous situation–a robbery in progress. I parked in the alley behind the store and entered the unlocked back door of the building. I did this so I could approach unobserved and stop any harm coming to a fellow officer. With my gun drawn, I passed through the storage room and heard shouting up-front. When I entered the store I saw Officer Saviano holding Mr. Chan against the wall by the shirtfront and punching him. He yelled he wanted more money. They were alone in the store."

"What did you do?'

Ashley suspected the Chief had not read the report. He should know all of this. "I holstered my weapon and asked Saviano what was going on."

"What did he say?"

"He screamed at me. Told me this wasn't my territory, and to fuck off. His words, not mine, sir."

"What then?"

"Mr. Chan begged me to help him. He said he reported a robbery because he knew Saviano would come by and steal his money. Like he always did."

Chief Danforth edged forward, his eyes fixed on her. "That's bullshit."

Ashley stepped back. "It's not bullshit, sir. Officer Saviano assaulted the store owner right in front of me. Saviano had a fist full of money in his right hand with the cash register drawer open. I had probable cause."

"Probable cause to do what?'

"Arrest Saviano, sir."

"You tried to arrest a fellow cop?"

Ashley took another step back. "Yes, sir. I again drew my weapon and ordered him to get down on the floor, hands on his head. That's when he pulled his gun and shot at me."

"I don't believe you. Joe Saviano didn't do that."

"The fingerprints on his gun are his. The On Scene Investigator dug his bullet out of the wall and bagged it. Ballistics will prove it came from Saviano's gun."

"More bullshit. If he shot at you, you'd be dead."

Ashley took one more step back. She felt the wall behind her. "Have you ever tried to fire a Glock with a hand full of cash, Chief? We don't train with that handicap. And I don't stand still when someone reaches for a gun. I move fast and return fire."

Chief Danforth got in her face. "You killed Joe Saviano." He poked his finger against her chest hard. "Joe Saviano was my friend." Another poke with the finger. "We served together." One more poke, harder this time.

"Don't touch me again."

"Or what?"

Her body tightened. She worked out the moves she'd take to put this flabby red-faced piece of crap on the floor. With her years of martial arts training, he'd fall in seconds. Then she relaxed. Stayed in control. "I'll twist your foot."

Danforth blinked. "You'll twist my foot?" He laughed, stepped back and then moved behind his massive hand-carved desk which occupied one end of the room. "I'll tell you what you'll do. You'll put your badge and gun right here." He pointed at the center of his desk. "Right now."

"Are you firing me?"

"What the hell do you think?"

"I have spent my life preparing for this job. To carry out a mission."

He sneered. "What mission?"

"To stop those who would hurt innocent people." Her expression grew solemn. "Evil people bent on senseless acts of violence."

"So you want to wipeout organized crime all by yourself?"

Frowning, Ashley shook her head. "Something like that."

"Well, you won't do it as a member of this department. I want your gun and badge right here, right now."

Released from the need to be respectful, Ashley moved to the desk and confronted the Chief. "You've watched too many movies, Danforth. That's not the way it works. First I go before a Review Board of my peers for a hearing. Then the Professional Standards Unit makes a recommendation. They will find I acted in self-defense, and in fear of my life. Saviano assaulted me with deadly force while committing a felony. I will be cleared, and you know it."

"Professional Standards will do whatever the hell I tell them to do. Badge and gun." He banged his fist down on the desk. "Right here!"

Ashley didn't move.

"Maybe you don't get it, girlie. Commander Morgan is right outside. If I tell him to arrest you for the murder of Officer Joe Saviano, he will do it. You have ten seconds, before I open that door. Last chance, badge and gun, now."

Ashley unclipped her badge and removed her gun from the holster. She centered both on the desk, and then locked eyes with Danforth. "You made one mistake."

"I don't make mistakes."

Ashley spoke with new confidence. "Last year you took me off the streets and assigned me to records, making me an administrator–a glorified secretary."

"Yea, so what. You're a woman, aren't you?"

Ashley ignored the affront. "When you transferred me last year, you screwed yourself big time. There will be no arrest today, at least not of me."

Danforth narrowed his eyes.

She continued. "You will accept my resignation with regret, and have one of your more intelligent flunkies write a glowing letter of recommendation for me. If you can't find someone smart enough to write it, I'll dictate one."

"You're out of your mind, Kohen. That won't happen. But I can tell you what will happen, and you' won't like it."

"Not before I tell you a story. A true crime story, and you are the star of the show."

Danforth pulled back, clearly shocked at her impudence.

Ashley put both hands on the desk between them, and spoke in a cold level voice, "Last year when you assigned me to records I controlled data for the whole department including the Intelligence Unit. A fancy name for your personal spy club. I heard rumors about you and how you bent the rules to suit your needs. I watched you manipulate this department so you can stay in office."

Danforth, his fists clenched, shouted, "You're out of line. I'm going to..."

"You're the one out of line. Under your written orders you have conducted illegal wiretaps on innocent people–some famous. You've ordered shakedown operations to fund election campaign donations for public officials, and carried out 'services' for your friends and political cronies. I have copies of your activities spanning the past ten years." Ashley drew breath and got in Danforth's face. "And I have your *Vendetta Files*."

"You what? My personal files? I'll have your ass on a plate, this..."

Ashley cut him off, again. "The only ass hanging out around here is yours." She straightened and crossed her arms. "Those files hold all the dirty little secrets you used to blackmail your enemies and threaten your friends if they don't do your bidding. I also have the files you've collected on your commanders and most of the division heads of the Chicago PD. Wouldn't they like to know what a paranoid bastard you are?"

"How did you get your hands on those files?"

Ashley tilted her head to the side, "Don't you remember? You put me in charge of records." She had him off balance and relished the feeling.

Chief Marvin Danforth fell silent. His eyes darted about the room. "You don't know what you're getting yourself into Kohen. I have dealt with this 'holier than thou' shit before. No one fucks with Marvin Danforth and lives."

16

"You mean like those two street cops you had killed–Morris and O'Neil," she gestured with air quotes, "in the line of duty?" Everyone in the department knows about that, only they can't prove it." She leaned into his face. "But I can."

Danforth stood silent for a moment. A bead of sweat formed on his upper lip. "So you think you got me by the balls. Think again."

"That's what I do. I think. I think about those two honest cops. I think about why they died and what they didn't do to stay alive."

"What are you talking about?"

"Ever hear of Skyscope?"

"What?"

"Skyscope is a virtual data bank in the Cloud. It's not on my computer or any computer. It's deep in the digital universe–in its own special cloud. I have an account. It's coded. I have transferred all of your records to my Skyscope account. Every dark secret protecting your career is in my account. Did I say it's coded? So a dumb-ass like you can understand what I'm saying, I'll lay it out for you in simple terms. It's called biometrics. Only a scan of my eye will open it; it's not a password your cronies can hack. And get this; if I don't check in periodically, the data dumps. Do you get my drift?"

Danforth's knuckles turned white as he gripped the desk.

"The data dumps right in the lap of the Illinois State Attorney's Office. Also the Chicago Field Office of the FBI, and just in case no one is paying attention, I have arranged for an email service to send hard copies to every newspaper in three states." She paused for a moment, with a glint in her eyes. "Do you feel a little tug on your testes, Marvin?"

His face drained of color and became covered with sweat. He stared back at her, but not with the glare of anger she saw before.

In silence, they studied each other for a long moment. Finally, Danforth spoke. "If you turn me in, you lose your edge, and I'll get you. You'll be dead meat."

Ashley knew he'd do it or have someone do it for him. "That's a given, but you and your buddies will rot in prison for life, and one of the scumbags you sent away will make you his whore. That's also a given."

Danforth proposed an alternative. "If you don't turn me in and give me the files, you're free. No arrest," he said with a straight face.

"Am I supposed to not notice 'give me the files'? You've been dealing with Neanderthals too long. No, deal old buddy, but you can count on this;

I'm going on paid administrative leave as long as it takes to get my head together. You will award me a *Commendation for Valor* and great letters of reference when I resign."

Danforth frowned, shifted his weight, but nodded agreement.

"One more thing. No reports on the Brady List. Nothing!"

"The Law Enforcement Integrity List?"

"I'm surprised you know anything about a list with the word 'integrity' in it." Ashley picked up her badge and gun, and moved closer. "Think of Skyscope as a shotgun aimed at your ass. I control the trigger because my eye-scan is on file." She paused. "I have only one question for you."

His arms hung limp, his shoulders sagged. "What?'

"Did I twist your foot, yet?"

Danforth rocked back. He didn't laugh this time.

Ashley knew she had more than twisted his foot, she had humbled him. Yes, she had lost her job, but she had protected herself from one of the most powerful politicians in the state. A man who could have snuffed out her life and her mission to protect the innocent. A mission that would change her life, and the lives of many others in the not too distant future.

# THREE

WALTER KENT, FBI SPECIAL Agent in Charge, stood before the large dry erase board mounted in his office. His brown eyes squinted at the tiny names and numbers scrawled across the board's white expanse. One hand held a well-used felt eraser, and the other a nearly spent felt-tip marker.

Son of a bitch! There's no way to make this work.

At the top of the board the surnames of twenty-nine Special Agents assigned to the Albuquerque Field Office headed a column of listed case numbers and crime categories currently under investigation. On average each agent worked twenty or more active cases. The FBI's *Target Staffing Level Manual* set a goal of fifteen active cases for each agent, and no more than fifteen back-burner or cold cases. Walter Kent frowned, ran his fingers through his thick black hair, and figured the boys in Washington had lost touch with workload assignments in the field.

Three days earlier he had placed a call to Henry Michael, of the Special Agent Transfer Unit in Washington. Henry, known as the Transfer Man, held a key position in matters concerning personnel, and almost never answered a direct call from the field.

Kent stepped back from the board, and with an athletic stride, walked across the carpeted office floor. At his desk, he pressed the intercom button and asked Administrative Assistant Dorothy Hogan to place another call to the Transfer Unit in Washington.

"To Mr. Michael?" she asked.

"Yes."

"How strange, Mr. Michael just called, he's on line two. Can you take it Mr. Kent?

"Sure."

Special Agents in Charge, always referred to as SAC's, ran the day-to-day field operations. They were considered the supreme authority within their assigned geographic areas, but they did not control personnel matters outside their office.

Kent hesitated a moment, took a deep breath, then punched the speakerphone button. "Henry, I was just thinking of you. Thanks for returning my call."

"Good morning Walt, sorry it took so long. I serve fifty-six field offices. That keeps me busy."

"I suspect your workload is heavy all the time."

"You're right. What can I do for you today?"

"I've completed the Field Office Annual Survey of Activities, as directed by our manual. Based on my caseload, I'm way understaffed. I need at least three street agents if I'm going to keep all the bases covered."

"What's your caseload, Walt?"

"Almost two thousand when you count the cold cases and follow-ups." Kent fudged a little on the numbers, but what the hell.

"Active cases?"

"Five hundred and eighty, but remember we're a border state with time consuming interagency coordination."

Michael cut him off, "I don't have to tell you, Walt, I'm real limited as to what I can do. If I transfer one agent out of an office, that leaves a vacancy which I have to fill, which means I move another agent, and on and on. It's a shell game all the time."

"Do you see anything on the immediate horizon?"

"No, its budget time and no one is moving."

Kent hoped to receive a positive response to his next question. "What about Quantico?"

"The Academy? A class graduated last week. Most of the graduates are placed. Let me check availability."

Kent knew his best chance to add to the staff would be a graduate from the Academy. He preferred an experienced agent, but a green recruit was better than nobody.

"Walt, I have six candidate available. Five are specialized analysts."

"I don't need analysis, I need active investigators."

"That leaves one candidate."

"What's his background?"

"Damn good. A licensed flight instructor certified in both single and multiengine aircraft. Awarded a full scholarship to Ohio State University. Majored in criminology with a little public administration thrown in.

20

Earned a Bachelor of Science, with honors, in only three years. Took a job with the Chicago PD. Got a reputation for catching terrorists. Has a knowledge of Middle Eastern culture. Stayed with them five years and made sergeant before accepted into our Academy five months ago. Finished in the top three percent of the class and honored as a top achiever in academics. Impressive.

"How old is he?

"Old? Let's see." Some paper shuffling. "She's twenty-eight."

"Did you say she?"

"Yes, a young woman named Ashley Kohen, with a "K". Notations in her file by supervisors and trainers say she is remarkable. Also says she's a real looker." He paused a second. "That shouldn't be in the file. I'll strike it out."

"Henry, I don't need added support staff, I need shoes on the sidewalk. Real street agents to work cases."

"Sure. Sure, I understand. I'm checking her personnel file. I see police commendations and glowing references from Chicago." He paused. "Walt, I have a call on the other line I have to take. Stay with me, I'll be back. I promise."

Kent prided himself on being politically correct. He had three female agents on staff. He assigned them to cases he felt would not endanger their safety. But right now he needed tough street cops to do dangerous work, something he was reluctant to assign to a young woman.

Henry came back again. "Okay, Walter. What do you think?"

"I'm not sure. Good stats, good recommendations, but will she meet my current needs, Henry?"

"Tell you what. I'll send you her file on our secure line. Give it a look-see. Get back to me tomorrow at the latest. I understand your concern, but she will not be available for long. Good talking to you, Walt. Got to go."

# FOUR

ED NAILER, A SCRAWNY man with thick eyeglasses and shaggy gray hair, held a degree in petroleum engineering and part ownership in the Fanning Land and Exploration Company. For almost a century his company, and others, had explored for oil in the New Mexico portion of the Permian Basin with phenomenal success. Using new technology the basin now resembled a tangled forest of pump-jacks, drilling platforms and work-over rigs standing side by side.

For half a dozen years Nailer had tinkered with a plan to drill north of the established oil patch on the land south of the town of Tatum where no production existed. Before work could begin he needed site clearance from the Bureau of Land Management in Roswell. Nailer started with a call to Joe Halverson, Minerals Specialist in the BLM's District Office.

"Joe, Ed Nailer here, how's it hanging?"

"Busy as a big buck in the rutting season, Ed. What's up?"

"I'm planning a little drilling action on lease 9870 about twenty miles southwest of Tatum. I'll email you the coordinates. Wonder if you guys could check it out. The lease is getting older than a broke-down mare. I need to get this project going now. What do'ya say?"

"Damn, Ed. We're knee-deep in a habitat study out there–endangered species stuff."

"Stuff? What stuff?"

"Prairie chickens."

"Shit Joe, there ain't no prairie chickens out there. You're lucky to find a rattlesnake or a prairie dog"

"Don't say that, Ed. Prairie dogs might be next on the list."

"I know you all have a job to do, but Joe, we're talking *oil*, now. I got an opportunity that could dry up tomorrow. You need to cut me some slack, old buddy."

Any BLM environmental project chugged along at the speed of an arthritic sloth–especially habitat studies promoted by environmental interests. The agency's policy encouraged multiple-use on public lands, in other words; they tried to please everybody all the time with limited staff and funding.

"Let me check with the team, Ed. Maybe I can work something out. I'll get back to you. Might be a few weeks."

"Sure Joe, I know I can trust you to do the right thing, can't I?"

"You bet, I'll get right on it."

When the conversation ended, Nailer tossed his phone across the desk. It smacked into *The Sally One*, a 12 inch bronze oil derrick perched on the corner of his desk–a replica of their first big strike years ago. He imagined Halverson scribbling down a note to inspect lease Number 9870 at some time in the distant future.

"Damn bureaucrats. I don't have time to fart around with their rules and regulations," he muttered as he searched his computer to find the name of the current director. His voice rose as his frustration mounted. "Who the hell is the director, now? They change so damn fast I can't keep track of 'em. Hey, Maggie, get your butt in here."

Maggie Rodriquez was the Executive Assistant to President Nailer. Over the years she had developed the ability to deal with her boss, who had an unpredictable and sometimes explosive personality. Nailer demanded she get the name of the District Manager in Roswell.

Maggie called, got the manager's name, and learned a bit of background on what might be the best way to approach him on leasing problems. When ready, she rehearsed her speech as she prepared to enter the lion's den.

"I have the name of the BLM manager you wanted." She pushed a sheet of paper across the desk. "His name is Tim McKruger. He's been here two years. Before, he worked in the State Office. Got an Annual Award for signing the most oil leases on public land. He's well-thought-of around the State."

"Oil leases? Could be worse. Could be a damn environmentalist."

"Can I get anything else for you, Ed?"

"No, Maggie. I'll give him a call." He reached for the phone.

A cheerful voice answered. "Good morning, Roswell District Office, may I help you?"

"Sure, this is Ed Nailer of Fanning Oil. Is McKruger in?"

"I believe he is. I'll transfer you to his office."

Ed drummed his fingers on the desk and waited. He glanced at the ceiling and noticed one of the florescent lights had burned-out.

"Good morning, this is Tim McKruger. How can I help you today?"

"Yes, well, I'm calling about a lease we hold southwest of Tatum. I talked with your staff guy this morning about a land clearance survey. Joe Halverson. He seemed busy with other matters."

"Joe is a key member of our staff, Mr. Nailer. He stays involved."

"Well, this is a crisis. Our lease term expires in ten months. Lease 9870. To make the deadline I signed a contract with Blackgold Drilling to start work in 60 days. I'm lucky to get 'em. Most rig operators are booked through this year into next."

"Yes, there is more production in the district now."

"Right." Ed continued with more urgency. "I'll have to cut twenty miles of road to get to the site before I can start drilling, which means clearing fences and putting in cattle guards—the whole nine yards. It'll take about six months to explore the lower Permian formation with horizontal drilling techniques. Maybe longer.

"Always a risky business, Mr. Nailer, but you know that better than I do."

Of course he knew it better than this agency speed bump, but he let it pass. "If you add it all up, I'm at eight months. If everything works out, I only have two months to file for a Found Lease. Not much time."

"A Found Lease application does take a while to process since it runs the life of production."

"Right. So you see I can't wait for a land clearance survey to happen in a couple of month."

"Did Halverson give you a date?"

"No. That's the problem. Said he was busy with prairie chickens and stuff."

"Hold the line, Mr. Nailer, I'll check with him."

Ed's frustration level climbed as his thoughts raced. Why all these regulation? Damn it, I'm exploring for oil. What's more important than that? This guy acts friendly, but he's still a goddamn bureaucrat.

"Mr. Nailer."

"Yes."

"I've checked with Halverson on your land clearance survey. Considering your timeline, I've asked him to move your survey up. He will get his team together and schedule you for next Monday morning. Joe will call this afternoon for any information he may need to speed this job along."

Ed blinked, and for a moment couldn't speak. Son of a bitch, this guy must have worked in the private sector. "That will be just fine, Mr. McKruger. Yep, just fine."

"Feel free to call anytime, Ed. We're here to help."

McKruger hung up leaving Ed staring at his phone. Both elated and confused, a feeling of satisfaction crept into his being as if a locked door suddenly popped open, allowing him passage into the future. Bureaucrats, he thought, were like tug boats. Most of the time they pulled your barge forward barely faster than the speed of the current. Not this time. This time he might make his deadline.

# FIVE

BITTY SMITH FELT EXCITEMENT as he prepared for a new and wonderful life. This would be the most important Saturday night of his twenty-one years. His expectations swelled like a flower bursting into full bloom in a stop-action video.

Standing before a cracked bathroom mirror, Bitty stretched on his toes to get a better view at himself. He parted his hair with care and adjusted the rolled collar of his polyester sweater. Cheap aftershave lotion stung his face, and a swish of mouthwash left his breath fresh.

Ready for the ninety minute drive, he grabbed a duffle bag with all of his possessions stuffed inside, and snapped up a bundle of papers crammed into a file folder. Slinging his jeans jacket over his shoulder, he headed for the front door of his shabby two-room apartment. He shut the door behind him for the last time.

As long as he could remember, loneliness shadowed his daily existence. Though a woman bore him, one of twins, he had no mother, only a wretch who couldn't afford an abortion or so he imagined. The State of New Mexico became his, and his brother's, protector, and foster care their extended family. He hoped to put all of that behind him as he began a new and promising future.

His five foot three inch frame slipped into the ancient 1969 VW Bug. After miles of deserted county roads, he grew bored and let his mind wander. His memories of childhood were vague–a kind of day care existence among strangers. At age six, separated from his brother, he was placed with foster parents who argued often, drank too much, and mostly ignored him. The State paid them five hundred dollars a month for his upkeep until the man ran over an elderly woman on the street, got arrested for DUI, and went to jail for vehicular homicide.

The second family to accept him consisted of a stern father, an overly affectionate mother and six other foster kids ranging in age from two months to sixteen years. The seven dependents netted the family a monthly

26

income of $3,500. In this environment he got the name Bitty because of his less than magnificent size. He learned about child abuse when the woman bathed him daily for hours at a time. He didn't know the name for what she did to him, but he knew he didn't like it.

An oncoming car flashed its bright lights and dashed by with horn blaring. He must pay attention to his driving. This was no time to change his luck, which had turned good two weeks ago when he met beautiful Allen Lee. So handsome with dark consoling eyes, jet-black hair, skin with a constant tan, strong hands and shoulders–oh my, those shoulders!

Allen Lee became his friend and he hoped tonight more than a friend, and why not? Didn't he pay attention to him? Wasn't he fascinated by his life and loves, ordinary as they might be? For hours they talked, and Allen asked all kinds of questions while taking notes on his laptop computer and sometimes speaking into a recorder in a strange language he promised would protect Bitty's privacy. Allen wanted to know everything about his years in foster care, his two former boyfriends (one brutish, the other slovenly), where he had worked, and on and on. No detail was too trivial or ordinary.

Allen Lee had explained that his interviews with Bitty supported his research into the success or weakness of foster care. As a writer his work had to be grounded in true-life experiences. But Bitty knew this relationship had become more than a writing assignment. This was something wonderful. Something Bitty had dreamed of all his life. He sensed the warm glow of affection that grew each time they met. Sometimes Allen Lee would express sympathy for the hardships of his youth, and touch his hand, holding it for a longtime. Those were moments of splendor. When Allen urged him to vacate his apartment and move in with him, he knew he would never be lonely again. He knew the companionship, support, and yes, love, he had yearned for all of his life would finally be his.

As Bitty entered the driveway, he noticed the glow of light from the living room window and imagined Allen eagerly waiting by the door.

EVERYTHING WAS READY for Smith. Much time, thought and careful planning had been put into this romantic liaison. It was now time to harvest the benefits of this charade.

When the headlights of the little car flashed by the front window of his rented ranch house, Allen knew Bitty had arrived five minutes early. If

Bitty Smith was anything, he was punctual. Within seconds, a knock sounded at the door. He waited until the third knock before greeting his visitor. Pretending a warm greeting, he turned the doorknob.

"Bitty, I've been waiting for you. Come in."

Bitty looked both nervous and elated as he entered carrying the dog-eared bundle of papers he dropped on the first chair in the living room. Allen fingered the paper file, purposely ignoring his guest. As the minutes passed, he saw Bitty glancing at him, his face flushed with growing excitement.

"How was the traffic?"

"Okay. Not a lot this time of night." He turned to see Allen sorting through the paper files. "Everything you asked for is there." In the yellow light of the table lamp Allen's sexy muscles flexed under a tight T-shirt.

"Good. Did you stop the newspaper, cancel phone and mail service?"

"Sure, I did everything just like you said. I paid the rent with the money you gave me and quit my job. It felt good to put all that behind me." He moved tentatively forward. "I want you to know how happy I am to be here with you." Closer now. "Being with you is all I can think about." Making body contact, Bitty reached up and encircling his lover's neck. "Oh Allen, I've come home."

Allen's powerful arms reached around him and they kissed, softly at first, and then Allen Lee consumed Bitty's lips clamping down hard with his teeth, while shoving a six-inch blade of Damascus steel into his back. At that instant Allen felt shock waves of what he knew was agonizing pain flood through Bitty. Held tight by Allen's arms, the little man's feet lifted off the floor and his scream choked back against his tongue. His body trembled as if it were a rag doll shaken by a vicious dog. Allen Lee's cold eyes stared into Bitty's face, as he watched life dim, then fade away.

HE HAD LIBERATED Russell (Bitty) Smith's soul for the greater good of Allah, Praised Be His Holly Name, but he was stuck with the body. Given the advances in forensic science, disposal had to be carefully thought out. Cremation would need specialized containment facilities not available, and decomposition in acid posed liquid disposal problems. Given his geographic location in a semi-arid land, his plan was simple: remote burial in the vast Chihuahua Desert.

He carried the small limp body, facedown, into the bedroom and laid it on the tile floor. The handle of the stiletto remained upright, serving as a cork in Bitty's back. Cutting the shirt from the body he removed the stiletto, then slapped the wound with a piece of moleskin effectively sealing off escaping blood. He put the knife aside for cleaning later. A small purple mole on the right shoulder, a birthmark that might serve as identification, attracted his attention. He burned it off with a butane lighter. Removing the teeth needed a greater effort. Using a pair of pliers and a screwdriver, he ripped out the teeth, piling them in the bathroom sink. Facial features are the most common way to identify a body. A few dozen swipes of his knife resulted in an unrecognizable corpse. Then, Allen carefully placed each hand of the body in a bowl of acid long enough to dissolve the fingerprints. When done, he removed all clothing with gloved hands, and starting at the head, cleaned Bitty with household bleach. As he worked, he solemnly bowed his head and repeated a prayer for the spirit of his sacrificial offering–an American infidel.

"For Bitty Smith, I bear witness there is no God but Allah the Magnificent and Muhammad his messenger."

Between each repetition he bowed and touched his forehead on the floor facing east toward Mecca. When finished with the ceremonial washing, he rolled Mr. Smith in a white linen sheet, neatly aligning the arms and legs. He then turned the ends of the cloth over and tucked them inside the folds of the cloth, as required by tradition.

"For Bitty Smith, may the peace, mercy and blessings of Allah the All Worthy be upon you."

He rose from the floor no longer Allen Lee, but, as Russell Smith: Social Security Number 333-45-9942, Birth date: August 1, 1995, a registered voter in Lea County, New Mexico.

# SIX

LATE SUNDAY MORNING, Abdullah al Jamal loaded the linen wrapped body of Russell "Bitty" Smith into the back of his old four-wheel drive pickup in preparation for informal interment. The truck, provided to him by his handler in El Paso, blended into the drab desert earth tones as if camouflaged intentionally.

In the truck he unfolded a BLM map of southeastern New Mexico. He spread it out on the seat beside him, and searched it to determine the locations of public and privately owned desert lands. The rugged jeep trails, that appeared to end with no clear destination, were of greatest interest to him. With a highlighter he marked the route he would take through thousands of undulating uninhabited acres. Since he would stay on public land he had no fear of trespass law, but would watch for ranchers.

As roads went from gravel to dirt and finally no road at all, his progress slowed. On sparsely vegetated rangeland, devoid of anything but scattered clumps of brittle grass and thirsty desert shrubs, he bumped along on uneven land noting a distant cow or two and an occasional galvanized metal water tank fed by a spinning windmill. After five miles from the nearest trail, he stopped at a desolate patch of ground. A visual search revealed the location to be surrounded by higher elevations. He reasoned high ground would be the best burial site, since it would be less subject to water erosion. With shovel in hand, and the little body of Bitty Smith flopping over his shoulder, he trudged uphill until he found what looked like a perfect spot. Dumping the body on the ground, he began to dig.

He encountered hard packed soil, not unlike the deserts around his home on the Arabian Peninsula near Dhahran. Each shovel of dirt required tremendous effort and no little pounding with his foot. His sweat evaporated almost as soon as it appeared on his skin. A half hour later, his muscles sore, he had chiseled through the top twelve inches of the sun baked soil. He drank from a dented canteen and sprinkled a little water on his head.

Work progressed as the temperature edged up. He paused to catch his breath. It was hot, but not as hot as the last time he dug a grave in desert heat. Abdullah jammed the shovel into the hard ground, rested on the handle and remembered his family's disgrace.

Ten years before he bury his sister Nadia, one of three siblings. The labor performed that summer day restored his family's honor. As one of six thousand members of the Royal Family, Abdullah's father, Prince Abeer Jamal, enjoyed the wealth and privileges that went with the title, and the requirement that honor be preserved in the name of Allah, the Lord of the World.

On a hot day in August the *Brotherhood of the Defiant* kidnapped Nadia, and held her for twenty days before accepting a fraction of the original ransom demanded for her release. At the hospital, the doctors found that her hymen had been ruptured which brought dishonor to the family. The loss of her virginity, even against her will, meant she was a disgraced woman and could never be married. She became a liability to the family and, therefore expendable.

Family prayers preceded the taking of her life. In deference to her membership in a royal family, she experienced a peaceful death by lethal injection administered by her father. This spared her the agony of stoning, strangulation or a slashed throat. Prince Jamal ordered that Abdullah, his oldest male child, hide their shame in the scorched sand dunes of the Persian Gulf south of Dhahran. Abdullah's brothers, little more than babies, remained at home.

Abdullah regretted the loss of Nadia. If his younger brother had been kidnapped, none of this would have happened. Every member of the *Brotherhood of the Defiant* would have been hunted down and hung from light poles in the city streets. But, she was a woman, and the Will of Allah the Majestic must be served. In a strange way, this experience strengthened Abdullah's determination to serve his God.

"I must not think of that time," he muttered, still standing before the future grave of Bitty Smith. "I have work to do."

By mid-afternoon he had created a hole in the ground one meter deep, two meters long and one wide. Good enough for the likes of Bitty Smith. He rolled the wrapped body into the hole. As he filled the grave with rock-like soil Bitty disappeared. After each shovelful he tamped the ground

31

using a booted foot to pack it down. When finished he scattered the excess soil, in an effort to restore a natural look to the surface.

Satisfied, Abdullah stepped back to admire the results of his landscaping. Bitty is now a seed in the earth. Given his sexual perversion this may be his only opportunity to nourish new life. This idea caused him to chuckle.

He returned to his truck, tossed the shovel in the back, sucked down a long satisfying drink of water, and prepared for the drive back to his remote desert home.

As the truck bumped from one uneven surface to another he contemplated his next move. Tomorrow, in the name of Russel Smith, he'd open an account at the Bank of America, and, of course apply to the U. S. State Department for a passport.

# SEVEN

AT 5:00 A.M. OF HER first day on the job, Ashley Kohen's alarm clock erupted in the silence of her bedroom. To turn it off she must get out of bed, and walk across the cold tile floor. She reasoned once on her feet, guilt would prevent her from returning to bed. It always worked.

Her routine seldom varied. In her tiny bathroom she splashed cold water on her face, brushed her teeth, and swept her hair into a ponytail. Then she dressed in a black sweat suit that covered her trim figure, jammed her feet into running shoes, and headed out for a five-mile jog. This morning her run would feel more like ten miles, since Albuquerque's 5,000-foot elevation would put greater demands on her than the sea level air of Quantico. Ashley's body would adjust. In fact she knew many adjustments, lay ahead for her in this new physical and social environment.

She drove to the University of New Mexico campus, only a mile south and west of her small rented apartment. She found college campuses a safe place to run in the early morning. After leg and back stretches, she started slow at first, then faster as her body adjusted. Her gait assumed a steady rhythm that allowed her mind to consider the hours ahead.

This would be her first day as a special agent in a field office of the FBI. Rigorous and demanding instruction at the Academy had prepared her. She knew she could meet the high standards of the Bureau. She also knew being a woman may reduce opportunities, and the nature of future assignments–even in this age of gender equality. She had dealt with all of that in Chicago, and before as a flight instructor working to supplement college expenses.

At the Chicago PD, Ashley had proven herself more than competent. She fought her way up the ranks to become a detective sergeant. She earned the respect of her peers and most of her supervisors. Rough, often crude, and at times an undisciplined work environment taught her how to protect her mental stability and physical being, both on and off the job. She had survived a corrupt system that compromised her duty to reveal political decay within the department leadership; a compromise that saved her life. The dichotomy between her moral duty to expose crime and her need to avoid execution by a corrupt chief of police, festered in her mind.

Midway through her run she recalled how for two months she had remained on paid administrative leave while the Saviano case played out in the newspapers and on television. Chief Danforth promised a full investigation of the shooting and after a time cleared her and publicly awarded her commendations, claiming she represented the high standards held by his department. She remembered her resignation went unnoticed by everyone except Captain Flynn, one of the many good cops serving the Windy City. When Flynn contacted her the first time, she suspected Danforth had recruited him, but discovered Flynn represented a coalition of officers ready to take down the old bastard. They reasoned, correctly, she survived only because she had something on the chief that might help them clean up the department. They asked for her help. She gave them the details of how Danforth had Officers Morris and O'Neil killed two years earlier. Staying in the background, Flynn had already prompted inquiries that made headlines daily. Ashley figured it may take months or years, but Danforth would fall.

She finished her run at 7:00 a.m. right on time. Driving back to her apartment she prepared herself to meet whatever came her way at the FBI. The formal and complex workings of the Bureau would hold challenges for her. She thought of her mother. Her jaw muscles tightened. Damn it, I'm going to do this

# EIGHT

MONDAY MORNING STARTED out like any day in June, hot and dry. Rainfall for the first six months of the year totaled less than two inches, and the monsoon season held little promise of relief. Not happy to be outside in the god-awful heat, the BLM's Field Survey Crew cursed the air-conditioner that didn't work in the District's only four-wheel-drive passenger van. Repairs had been put off due to budget cuts.

Alice Kabunsky, the District's archaeologist, had begged team leader Joe Halverson to start work an hour early to avoid the heat of the late morning sun. The rest of the team, composed of a realty specialist, a biologist, and a range manager, agreed to this early departure if they had lunch at the Ranchland Cafe in Tatum near the Texas border. Joe maneuvered the van out of the district's storage yard and onto Highway 380 heading east. At mile marker 48 they left the highway.

Getting around New Mexico is easy, until you leave the paved roads and cross into the great desert lands that appeared much the same mile after mile. Fanning's oil Lease 9870 covered forty desolate acres about twenty miles south of Highway 380. To get there, the white van zigzagged around desert obstacles for over thirty rock-hard miles. Many of the team dozed off during the trip, but Alice stayed alert, not wanting to miss anything that might be of special note. They arrived on-site at 9:15, and everyone piled out of the van. There was little enthusiasm for the task ahead.

Not so for Alice. She kept detailed records of each field survey conducted so she could later transfer any useful findings into the District's Archaeology Database. Today she felt like a squirrel about to find last winter's cache of carefully hidden nuts. If she found nothing, that meant there were no signs of past human life or culture on that tract of land. If she discovered even a small shard of pottery or rock tool, it added another piece to the historical puzzle of the living past.

Joe instructed everyone to walk a thirty yard pattern starting from north to south, and then switch directions and walk the track again. Everyone carried a two-way radio, making communication between the team members possible.

The crew formed a line with the proper distance between each person, and began to march south. Forty acres driving a tractor is manageable, but forty acres on foot is like swimming a mile–it looks easy until you do it. At the end of the first tract, they reformed and started over, Alice called to the other members of the crew on her two-way radio. "Keep an eye open for bits of pottery or other things of a suspicious nature. Sing out if you see anything. I'll come to you and check it out."

Howard Duran, the range manager, couldn't resist a comment. "How about antelope droppings, if there're old?"

"Not funny," she answered.

By 11 o'clock they had covered half of the tract as the temperature inched up. Alice studied the ground with a trained eye. She seldom missed even the slightest clue to the past. As she approached an abrupt rise in the terrain she noticed the ground surface was different. Disturbed. The hardpan, a gray colored impervious layer of soil located inches under the surface was scattered over the surface. Two steps further she knelt down for a close inspection. Something's been digging here. Probably coyotes. She moved forward and flicked on her radio. "I'm not sure what this is, but it's strange." Alice pulled her metal trowel out of her back pocket and began to probe the ground.

Halverson radioed back. "Did you find something, Alice? A big old chunk of pottery?" No answer. "What do you see that's strange?" Still no answer.

Then, Alice's voice burst from everyone's pocket radios. "Damn. You better come over here. Right now. I mean everybody. Jesus Christ! I don't believe this!"

# NINE

THE SECRETARY FOR THE BLM's district manager poked her head around the edge of the doorway. "Mr. McKruger, Joe Halverson on line one. It sounds serious." Tim nodded a thank you, and reached for the phone.

"Joe, what's up?"

"Alice found a dead body. Mostly buried."

"A body? A human body?"

"Yes, sir."

"Where?"

"On the Fanning mineral lease. Just stumbled over it. She's real upset."

"Are you on the lease now?"

"I'm about ten miles south of the highway. Had to drive back to get a signal on my phone."

"Where's the crew?"

"They're with me."

"Stay where you are. I'll call you back."

"Yes, sir."

McKruger had never experienced finding a dead body on public land. Plenty of dead cows, deer, horses, and maybe a drunk cowhand, but not a buried human. He dialed 911.

"Emergency Assistance, may I have your name?"

"I've received a report from my field supervisor. They found a body."

"Your name please, and address?"

"I'm Tim McKruger. Manager of the Roswell BLM. 1010 West 2nd Street."

"Will medical assistance be required for the victim?"

"No, my supervisor said it's a dead body."

"Where is the victim located?"

"It's on an oil lease southwest of Tatum near the Texas border. I can give you a phone number of Joe Halverson. He can direct you."

"His number, please. "McKruger gave her the number. "I'll get back to you."


DEPUTY SERGEANT Johnny Gallaher answered his phone. "Lea County Sheriff's office, Gallaher speaking."

"This is the Emergency Call Center. I have a report of a dead body southwest of Tatum. I'm connecting you with someone who has the location of the victim." Sergeant Gallaher grabbed a pencil and paper. The 911 operator continued. "I have Mr. Joe Halverson with the BLM on the line. This will be a three way conversation."

A man's voice came on. "Hello, this is Halverson. We found a dead body an hour ago."

Gallaher held his pencil at the ready. "Where are you, Mr. Halverson?"

"South of Highway 380.

"Are you with the body?"

"No, but I have the longitude and latitude. Are you ready?"

"Yes." Sergeant Gallaher noted the location. "What can you tell me about this incident?"

"We were surveying a tract of land for cultural artifacts when our archeologist found a burial site. Actually disturbed ground with a foot wrapped in white cloth sticking up. Probably a coyote uncovered it."

"Mr. Halverson, I want you to go to where you found the body. Do you have any flares with you?"

"Yes."

"When you see a helicopter, set one off."

"Yes sir." Halverson wiped sweat from his chin. "How long do we have to stay out here? It's hot."

"Until I release you. I'll arrange for a flight to your location. I'll get to you as fast as I can."

Johnny Gallaher held the title of Investigative Sergeant with the Lea County Sheriff's Office in Lovington, New Mexico. In a more populated county he would head a team of experts numbering six or more, but in rural Lea County the team consisted of him alone.

At this point he didn't know if it was a crime scene, but accidental death rarely wrapped itself in a white sheet. He pulled his checklist out and went to work. First he called Cisco Ortega's Helicopter Service. Cisco owned the only available helicopter in the county. Next, he called Doc Henry, a local pediatrician who served as the county's part-time medical examiner. He left word his services might be needed. With some dread, he called the Sheriff to tell him of the dead body found in their county.

When Gallaher's call rang on Wendell Hardgrave's desk, he dropped a copy of *American Sportsman* and answered the phone. "Sheriff Hardgrave, can I help ya."

"Sheriff, this is Sergeant Gallaher."

"Who?"

"Gallaher, sir. Investigative Unit."

"Right. Right. What's up?"

"I received a report a few minutes ago of a dead body out on the prairie north of here. I talked to Mike and he's fueled and ready to fly. I'll need a couple of deputies on this one."

Gallaher knew Sheriff Hardgrave, recently elected as the *Get things done Sheriff*, didn't have any interest in dead bodies in the desert, because they didn't vote. He also lacked any experience in police work. Politics yes, but law enforcement, no.

"Sergeant Gallaher, we're a little short on manpower, and the Centennial Celebration is underway. I can't spare nobody right now."

"Yes sir. I understand, but this doesn't sound like an accident, I need help with this one."

He drawled. "Where is this here dead body?"

"Southwest of Tatum about twenty miles."

"Isn't that on public land?"

"Why, yes sir, I think it is. Why?'

"Public land is Federal land. The Federal Government has a hell of a lot more time and money to investigate what happens on their land than we do. Let 'em handle it."

Sergeant Gallaher didn't know how to respond to the idea of the Federal government's involvement in a local matter. They lacked jurisdiction. "Sir, I'm not sure they would bother with this case."

"Well, you won't know until you give them a chance, will you, sonny? Call 'em up."

"Who should I call?"

"Hell, I don't know. Call the CIA."

"The CIA is a spy outfit."

"Okay, call the FBI. Check in the phone book. Keep me posted."

The Sheriff hung up, and continued reading his copy of the *American Sportsman*.

# TEN

ASHLEY KOHEN GAVE herself plenty of time to find the Albuquerque Field Office on her first day of work. Being late would not be the best way to start a Federal career. When she approached the imposing three-story red brick building on Luecking Parkway, she noticed it sat isolated in a dense network of city life, as if it were an island guarded by a perimeter of neatly trimmed shrubs. A public parking lot and a wide walkway led to large wooden doors intended for use by the public. Around back, Ashley found a fenced and guarded employee parking lot with a sign that read: *Warning: Staff Only*.

Showing her identification at the gate, she parked and followed other agency workers into the building. A receptionist on the first floor, with a grim expression, directed Ashley to the office of the Special Agent in Charge–the SAC, room 300, top floor.

In keeping with his importance as head of a field office, Ashley expected the outer office of Walter Kent to be large and impressive, instead she entered a small room with six hardback chairs and a gray metal desk backed by a wall of four-drawer file cabinets. All neat, functional, and ordinary. Not ordinary was the young and attractive woman standing behind the desk. Her nameplate read, Ms. Dorothy Hogan–Executive Assistant. Dressed in a tailored pants suit, much like the one Ashley wore, she made a handsome impression. "Good morning, you must be Ashley Kohen, from Quantico."

"Yes, I am. I'm reporting for duty."

Ms. Hogan presented a friendly smile. "First up, we have to get you processed and registered. It won't take long, well, only most of this morning. When finished, please come back here." She smiled again and handed Ashley a sheet of paper with directions of where to go and who to see.

41

Ashley spent the morning following instructions that would prepare her to become an official member of the Albuquerque Field Office. As if to prove she had joined one of the largest bureaucracies in Federal service, she had to fill out forms asking for information already on file in Washington.

At the Academy she had been issued a semi-automatic 9 mm Glock 17L handgun, and locking holster used during firearms training. Today, at the Quartermaster's Supply Depot, she picked up the rest of the gear assigned to every new agent: an Advanced M26-C Taser gun with three rechargeable cartridges, handcuffs, two leather belts, a shoulder holster, a bulletproof vest, an outer vest and coat with big yellow FBI letters on the back, a field investigators uniform, pepper spray, ammunition clip holders, and a portable two-way radio transmitter with a pin-on-mike.

The man behind the counter suggested she buy a small handgun and ankle holster and always wear it. He explained they were not Government Issue, but all the agents carried one. He gave her a black duffle bag to carry everything. She signed for each item.

At one o'clock, Ashley arrived back at the SAC's office lugging all her stuff in the black bag. Ms. Hogan greeted her with another expression of friendliness. "Be seated, Ms. Kohen, Mr. Kent will be with you shortly."

Ashley perched on the edge of a straight backed chair. There were no magazines or newspapers to read. No ashtrays or any form of office decoration. Smiling photographs of the President, Vice President and the Agency Director hung on the opposite wall. This office had all of the necessities and nothing more.

She waited. Would her associates be friendly like Ms. Hogan or sour like the downstairs receptionist? It didn't matter. I'm here to do a job. That's what this is all about. She heard voices in the SAC's office. He must have an open-door policy.

"You can go in now, Ms. Kohen. Sorry for the wait." Ashley rose, smoothed the front of her navy blue pants suit and thanked Ms. Hogan. She entered the office and was confronted by a stern looking man who motioned her inside, and introduced her to her new boss. "I'd like you to meet Special Agent in Charge, Mr. Walter Kent."

The well-groomed man behind the desk stood and offered his hand. His mouth curved upward slightly. "Good afternoon Ms. Kohen, welcome. This is my assistant, Marcos Ramirez. Have a seat."

Ashley noticed Agent Ramirez ogled her as if he were bidding on prime beef at the farmer's auction. While continuing his appraisal, he pointing to a metal chair. "Sit here, Ms. Kohen."

Kent settled into the chair. "Henry Michael at headquarters had good things to say about you. I'm pleased to have you join our team. Have you found suitable living quarters?"

"Yes, sir. Near the university. Not too far from here. Thank you."

"Well, I'm pleased to hear that. I've arranged office space for you. You will work in the bullpen on open assignment. A free agent for now"

"Free agent, sir?"

"Yes. I'm working on a staffing realignment plan. We'll get you properly placed, don't worry," he said, "So let's get on with it. To be official, I will swear you in to our Field Office. Marcos, get Ms. Kohen the bible."

"I'm already sworn in, sir. I took my oath at the Academy."

Ramirez handed her a small leather bound book. "We do things our way here, Ms. Kohen. It not a bible. It's the FBI's *Manual on Personnel Conduct*. Our bible."

Ashley noticed Ramirez continued to admire her figure, his gaze fixed on her breasts. "Yes, I know what you mean. Agent Ramirez," making direct eye contact. "I'm sure you live by these rules of decent conduct all the time. Don't you?"

Walter Kent glanced back and forth between the two sensing some hostility, then began reading the oath administered to every agent new to this office. Ashley stood at attention and responded as needed. When he finished Kent walked around his desk and shook her hand. "Welcome, Agent Kohen." She felt a wave of emotion come over her, something she didn't expect.

Dorothy Hogan knocked on the open office door, and entered. "Mr. Kent, sorry to interrupt, but you might want to take this call. It's from the Lea County's Sheriff's office in Lovington. It's about an alleged murder there. They want us to investigate. I told them it's not our jurisdiction, but he insists on speaking with you."

"That's okay, Dorothy. Thanks. I'll take it here." Kent turned to Ramirez. "Stay, Mark. I want you to hear this for the record. I'm putting it on speakerphone." He pushed the phone button. "This is Special Agent in Charge Walter Kent."

The hollow sound of the tiny speaker filled the room. "Good morning Mr. Kent, I'm Sergeant Johnny Gallaher of the Lea County Sheriff's Office. Sheriff Hargraves asked me to call. We have a situation here and need your help."

"What kind of help do you have in mind, Sergeant?"

"Well, we just got this call about a dead body wrapped in a white linen sheet buried in the middle of nowhere twenty miles from Tatum. The BLM found it earlier this morning and called it in. It's on public land. I thought you ought to know. We aren't prepared to handle something like this, and would like you to investigate."

"Sergeant Gallaher, I appreciate you calling; however, local authorities handle these matters. We are restricted from interfering."

"Yes, sir. Your secretary said as much, but since it's on Federal land, I thought you might want to check it out."

In an effort to get his attention, Ashley leaned over and scratched a quick note, and tentatively pushed it forward. Her face wore an expression of urgency.

Kent peeked at the note. "Hold the phone a minute, sergeant." Switching the speakerphone to mute, he frowned at Ashley. "What's this about?"

She hesitated, then spoke. "I apologize for this intrusion, sir. I know this is awkward, my first day and all, but I'm alarmed at what the good sergeant is telling you. I think we need to find out more. If invited we could conduct a joint effort."

Irritated, Kent asked, "What are you talking about? This isn't our business."

Ashley continued. "I understand we don't deal in local matters, but I know terrorism is our agency's first priority."

Puzzled by her forceful response, Kent switched the speaker back on. "Sergeant Gallaher, let me call you back. I have to check something first."

Agent Ramirez stepped forward. "Listen lady, this doesn't concern you. You're new here."

Ashley turned and fixed a glare on Ramirez. "I'm not a lady, Agent Ramirez, as of two weeks ago, I'm a Special Agent of the FBI, and unless you have changed the primary mission of this Bureau, terrorism is our business."

Walter Kent stood and motioned Ramirez to back off, then turned to Ashley. "I'm not sure what to make of you, Ms. Kohen, but I think you're out of line. Please explain yourself."

Ashley stepped back and tried to remain composed. She knew this didn't look good. The new girl pushing herself in without an invitation. "First, I want to apologize for being abrupt, but I hope you will understand why in a few minutes." She took a deep breath. "May I sit?"

"Of course. We all need to calm down." Kent eyeballed Ramirez. Ashley began. "In Chicago, as a detective, I dealt with cases that involved narcotics, homicides, and terrorism. I worked on half a dozen cases involving national security, and helped the FBI on two cases that preventing terrorist bombings. I learned a lot about the Muslim culture and their religious practices."

Ramirez interrupted. "What's this have to do with Muslims?" Ashley ignored him.

"As is true of all religions, most Muslims are good, law-abiding citizens and trustworthy members of their faith. Also true, is the fact there are certain rituals obeyed by all Muslims worldwide. One is ceremonial burials that follow a well-established practice. The first rule is to clean the body. The second is to wrap it in white cloth. The finest cloth available to them. It's done throughout the Muslim world."

"You're suggesting the body in a white sheet is connected to a Muslim burial?" Asked Kent.

"No, not a Muslim burial, but a burial by a Muslim."

"I don't understand."

"The third rule is to bury the person in sanctified ground. If the body in Lea County is not buried in ground designated for that purpose. The body is not of the Muslim faith, but was buried by a believer following traditional practices."

Walter Kent nodded. "I see what you are getting at, Ms. Kohen. I'm not aware of a significant Muslim presence in this state, outside Gallup and Albuquerque. A proper burial most likely would occur in northern New Mexico, not down south."

"Yes. This burial sounds more like hiding a criminal act by a Muslim than a proper interment. With all due respect, I think we should consider Sergeant Gallaher's request to take part in the investigation in Lea County."

Ashley watched Walter Kent lean back in his leather chair and consider the proposal made by his newest member of the staff. "Okay, Agent Kohen, since the Bureau has been asked to take part, I agree we should check into this matter, but only as observers. Normally I would assign an on-scene investigator to assist you, but no one is available right now, and officially you're not investigating anything."

"Yes sir. I understand. I'll do my best, sir."

"I'll call Sergeant Gallaher and tell him you are on your way."

"Do I have your permission to requisition necessary equipment and transport?"

"Of course. See Ms. Hogan for contact information." Kent glanced at Ashley with a hint of skepticism. "You represent Uncle Sam, now, Agent Kohen. Try to stay out of trouble, you hear?"

# ELEVEN

READY FOR HER TRIP to Lea County, Ashley Kohen stood in the underground garage of the field office. The motor pool manager handed her the keys to a white unmarked Chevy Suburban parked at the exit gate. "When did you last service it?" She asked.

With an ugly twist of his mouth, the manager spoke slowly to emphasize each word. "Yesterday. I topped everything off, too. By that I mean the gas tank is full and I checked all fluids."

Ashley kept a blank expression. "Four-wheel drive?"

"All our vans and SUV's are four-wheel drive." He rolled his eyes upward. "And it's equipped with emergency flashers, radio communication units and GPS. That stands for Global Positioning System"

Ashley gave him a hard smile. "How informative. You're missing one thing."

"What's that?"

"It's listed on my order request." She pointed to the paper he held in his hand. "I'll need two five-gallon reserved tanks mounted in the rear. One with gas and the other with water–if it's not too much trouble."

The manager dipped his head. "My crew must have missed that. I'll tend to it right away. Do you need a hand with your stuff?"

"No, thanks, I'll manage." Her stuff consisted of the black bag from the Supply Depot, a Crime Scene Examiners Field Kit, granola bars bought in the cafeteria, and half a dozen bottles of water. On her way to the motor pool, Ashley had stopped in the rest room, changed her clothes, and clipped her badge on her belt.

With reserve tanks locked into place and everything tossed into the suburban, she punched Roswell into the onboard GPS. Then she buckled up, started the engine, adjusted the rearview mirror, and flipped on the flashing emergency red and blue lights. The tires squealed as she climbed the underground ramp and entered the public street.

To preserve evidence, she wanted to get to the body in the desert as fast as possible. Two hundred miles of four lane highway lay ahead. A four-hour trip she intended to make in fewer than three.

The busy forty-five mile stretch of I-40 leading to the junction with Highway 285 at Clines Corner's needed her full attention. The Suburban hurtled down the pavement as if it were an NASCAR entrant on steroids.

Finally, the road signs announced Clines Corner's on the horizon and Ashley eased up on the gas as she exited the Interstate south. The traffic volume on 285 was nonexistent. This gave her a chance to make some necessary calls. First she called Sergeant Gallaher in Lea County and learned he had been delayed by helicopter problems but was now on his way to the crime scene. Next she called the BLM District Manager Tim McKruger, who promised to meet her in Roswell at the north side Wal-Mart parking lot. He would escort her to Joe Halverson's location east of town.

At 3:15 p. m. Ashley turned off the flashing lights and pulled into the Wal-Mart parking lot with McKruger on her phone explaining his exact location. She spotted him standing beside a BLM truck. She ran the passenger side window down and lurched to a stop a few feet away.

"Good afternoon Mr. McKruger. Hop in." She noted surprise on his face. "I know, you planned to lead me to the burial site, but if you come with me, we'll get there faster. The body is slowly cooking vital evidence under the hot sun. Time is important." Ashley gave him one of her "pretty" smiles, and he went for the bait.

"Straight south on Main Street?" she asked as McKruger buckled-up. "Yes, make a left when I tell you. It's about thirty miles east."

Main Street was like most main streets in rural America. Everyone used it–frequent stoplights and slow moving traffic. The left turn she made onto Highway 380 downtown, gave her hope of an open road.

"Straight ahead," said McKruger. "My field crew is waiting. There are no roads to the site. Four-wheel drive?" Ashley gave him a thumbs-up sign. At the edge of town, she switched on the flashers and concentrated on the two lane road.

Twenty minutes later, McKruger pointed. "There, on the side of the road." Ashley slowed and pulled alongside the BLM white van. All the doors were open and five sweaty faces confronted her. A man slipped out of the driver's seat. "That's Joe Halverson." McKruger and Ashley jumped

48

out of the suburban. Before the two men exchanged greetings, Ashley asked, "Has Sergeant Gallaher arrived yet?"

"Uh, yes." he stammered, "about an hour ago. Two of them, a pilot and the deputy."

Ashley noted the crew was ready to pack it in and go home. Not the best way to spend an afternoon. "Who found the body?"

Halverson pointed over at the van. Kabunsky nodded her head and raised her hand. "That's Alice, she's our archaeologist. She found it."

Ashley stepped over to the van. "Alice, I'm sorry, but you need to come back to the site with me."

Alice shook her head. "I don't want to go back there."

Ashley paused a moment. "Alice, this is a police investigation. You must cooperate. It won't take long. I need to document your discovery."

McKruger agreed. "You have to do this, Alice. Sorry." He placed a hand on her shoulder.

Ashley continued, "I have an air-conditioned Suburban, with water and snacks."

Alice perked up. "Air-conditioned?"

Joe, and Alice prepared to go with Ashley to the site. McKruger and the others would take the van back to the District office. Ashley heard McKruger tell the others, "Okay guys, you're done for the day. Police work is not in your job descriptions."

He glanced at Ashley. "Take care of Alice." A long pause. "You must be dedicated to do this kind of work."

Ashley knitted her brow. "If you only knew."

49

# TWELVE

WHILE HEADING BACK to the crime scene, Ashley paid no attention to the oppressive heat, the cactus that scraped along the side of the Suburban, the black-barked mesquite bushes that dotted the land or buried rocks in the hard packed desert soil.

Finally, the car crested a low-lying hill and skidded to a stop. A Robertson R44 helicopter sat silent below them on a flat area. Joe said, "The body is over there below that small ridge." Two men stood next to the ridge. "That's Sergeant Gallaher and his pilot, Cisco."

Ashley reached for the Field Investigator's Kit and exited the Suburban. She headed for the men, one wearing a deputy sheriff's uniform. "Good afternoon. I'm Agent Kohen, FBI." She showed her ID, offered her hand to Deputy Gallaher, who shook it, and then to Cisco.

"I've been on-site about an hour," said Gallaher. "The victim is over there. I've covered it with a body bag to keep the sun off. I haven't disturbed the scene, like you asked. The corpse has been in the ground a day, maybe."

"Why do you say that?"

"A portion of the victim's foot is uncovered. The skin is pale, not green, and it feels like traces of rigor mortis remain in the muscles."

Ashley nodded. "That suggests death occurred within 24 to 36 hours. What about the temperature?"

"Oh, I didn't get the temperature, the body is wrapped tight and buried"

"I mean the atmospheric temperature."

"Oh, of course. Aboveground it's a 105 degrees, but that doesn't apply to the body. At twelve to fifteen inches below the surface, the earth keeps a constant 56 to 58 degrees. That's why the creatures around here, live in holes during the day."

Not knowing desert conditions, Ashley had to accept Gallaher's statement. It made sense, and she welcomed the news. This big piece of evidence, buried a few feet away, might be in better condition than she thought possible.

Deputy Gallaher, it's important that we reclaim the body with minimum site disturbance. I have with me an anthropologist from the BLM. I'd like her assistance in unearthing the body. Do you have any objections?" Sergeant Gallaher shook his head.

Ashley motioned to Alice to come over. "I need your help." She impressed upon Alice the importance of preserving the 'evidence' and likened it to the recovery of ancient bones. "I want you to approach the job with the same professionalism needed at any archaeological excavation." Alice squared her shoulders and raised her chin. "Yes, ma'am I'll do my best."

Ashley asked Gallaher about approach paths to the investigation scene. "Have you discovered any shoe prints or tire marks?"

"I found one set of each. I've taken photographs with shadows that show strong ridge patterns of both shoe and tire prints, approaching and leaving the site. To determine scale, I put a bright penny in each shot."

Ashley gave him a nod of approval. A quick view of the LCD frame on the back of his camera displayed a series of well-defined impressions. An analysis of the footprints would result in an estimate of the height and weight of the subject.

Alice Kabunsky, using her tools, removed soil that crumbled away from around the wrapped body. After thirty minutes of careful digging, the corpse lay exposed in the grave. Before moving it aboveground, Ashley inspected the body's positioning. The head pointed south and faced east. The body lay on its right side. She found flat rocks under the head, chin area, and right shoulder. Except for smudges of dirt on the linen covering, it was clean and had a sweet smell of lilacs. She asked Gallaher to photograph every detail.

Kneeling beside the body, Ashley examined the white shroud. She noted the neat folds and the snug wrappings that showed the outline of a small body, possibly a child. If the burial preparation was performed by a murderer, it had been meticulously executed. Victims are seldom treated with such respect by their killer. Why this one?

On a positive note the careful preparation and handling of the corpse guarantied the body to be in nearly pristine condition. A skillful autopsy and a professional forensic study should yield significant clues. To guarantee a fast, accurate, and expert examination, the FBI had to employ the services of a forensic professional.

She had three immediate tasks to perform; gain approval from her field office to accept jurisdiction in this case, secure agreement by Lea County authorities to surrender jurisdiction, and arrange transport of the body.

Ashley asked Gallaher, "How long have you lived in this part of New Mexico?"

"All my life."

"Then you know the people and the local culture around here?"

"Sure."

"Are there any mosques in the area attended by people of the Islamic faith?"

"You mean like terrorists?"

"No, sergeant, I mean Muslims. People who practice that religion."

Gallaher thought for a moment. "No, Agent Kohen. I don't think so. This is small-town America. Everybody knows everyone. If any Muslims lived around here I'd know."

"Now, tell me about the medical examiner in Lea County, and your forensic capabilities."

"The M. E. is part-time. We collect fingerprints and send them to you guys. Lab studies are all done by the state in Albuquerque."

"What's your turn-around time for analysis of hair and fiber evidence?"

"Hard to say. A couple of weeks. Maybe a month if there's a backlog."

"You asked for the Bureau to review this case. How serious is your sheriff about our involvement?"

"Real serious."

"Would he sign an MOU between his office and ours?"

"A what?"

"A Memo of Understanding, giving the FBI jurisdiction as the lead investigative agency in this specific case."

"I don't know, but I think he would."

"Thank you, sergeant."

Ashley walked back to the Suburban and called her office on the satellite relay radio. The late afternoon heat caused perspiration to sprout on her forehead. Dorothy Hogan answered. "Ms. Hogan, this is Agent Kohen, is Mr. Kent in his office?"

"Yes, he's free. I'll connect you."

After a moment of silence, "Kent here. Where are you, Kohen?"

"Good afternoon, Mr. Kent. I'm on scene in Lea County. I will make a written report, but right now I need your approval to have the FBI take jurisdiction." She braced herself for a negative response.

"I sent you there as an observer, Kohen, not to drum up business for the Bureau."

With an uneasy feeling in her stomach, she said, "Yes, sir. I understand. Let me share my observations with you, then you decide."

"Okay, I'm listening."

"I don't have hard evidence, but I have strong indications the circumstance surrounding this incident needs further inquiry. First, the way the body was prepared for burial is in conformance with Islamic tradition. The corpse is on its right side with supports under the head, chin and shoulder. The grave is perpendicular to Mecca and the white linen cloth has a sweet smell. These are all Islamic customs, unlike anything we normally see in this country. Second, the body is hidden in a remote area suggesting a crime had been committed. Third, there are no Mosques anywhere near here and no Muslim populations in this part of the state. Fourth, signs indicate this killing occurred fewer than thirty-six hours ago, meaning potential evidence may remain intact if we act quickly. Finally, advanced forensic techniques in Lea County are nonexistent, and the local sheriff's office wants nothing to do with this case."

Walter Kent listened to Ashley's oral report. "When you boil it down, Kohen, it's a hunch, not a solid basis for assuming jurisdiction. It sounds vague, mighty vague."

"Yes sir. It probably does, but..." Ashley decided to take a chance, one that might affect her fledgling career in the FBI. "...you probably remember a few years back two Islamic men took flight lessons in Florida to learn how to fly a commercial jet plane. Nobody wondered why two men wanted to fly an aircraft they couldn't afford to buy. Nobody got suspicious. No one figured they might put that knowledge to some horrific use, like flying an airplane into a building in downtown New York City. It would have sounded like a vague notion. Mighty vague," she said, swallowing hard.

There was a long pause on the line. Ashley clenched her teeth, and waited. Had she just screwed her career? Had she offended the one person she needed on her side? She waited, gripping the phone hard enough to feel pain.

"They used to call that a sucker punch, Kohen."

"I know."

"You've got guts, I'll give you that."

"I think this is important."

Ashley wondered what was going through Walter Kent's mind. She hoped he would consider the likelihood that this might turn out to be a case involving a terrorist. Would Kent be willing to ignore a situation that might lead to a future terrorist attack? Ashley was betting that he wouldn't take that chance, no matter how remote the possibility.

"What the hell. Okay, Kohen, go for it."

Ashley felt a release of tension in her body followed by a wave of gratitude. "Am I allowed to incur necessary expenses?"

"Of course. Within reason."

"Thank you, Mr. Kent."

"Not necessary, Agent Kohen. You're doing your job. Keep me advised." He disconnected.

It took a few seconds for her to compose herself. She had gambled and won, which prompted her next action. Motioning Deputy Gallaher over to the Suburban, she offered to dictate a binding MOU. Using the Suburban's radio Gallaher checked with Sheriff Hargraves who agreed to the arrangement, and put his secretary on the line. Thirty minutes later the letter was signed and faxed to the Albuquerque Field Office for the SEC's approval. Finally, Ashley questioned the pilot of Cisco's Helicopter Service.

"What's the flight range for your aircraft?"

"About 300 miles, if the wind is right," answered Cisco.

"Weight limits?'

"With passengers eight hundred pounds, give or take."

"Flight time to Albuquerque?"

"Couple of hours."

"Hourly rate?"

"Three fifty an hour."

"Get real, Cisco. Two-hundred plus gas is top dollar. That's all I'm authorized to pay. What do you say?"

Cisco checked Agent Kohen. She didn't blink. "Deal," he said.

"Where's the closest source of ice?

"Ice?"

"We are going to keep our little passenger cool for the same reason you put steaks in the refrigerator–preservation."

"That would be the Roswell Industrial Airport. We can get gas, too."

Joe Halverson agreed to drive Sergeant Gallaher back to Lovington, then take Kabunsky home and leave the white Suburban at the FBI's satellite office in Roswell. With the body bag zipped and loaded on board, Agent Kohen took her place next to Cisco who reviewed his checklist, started the engine, and headed for the nearest supply of bagged ice.

Once airborne Ashley watched the late afternoon sun stretch long shadows across the land. Many questions raced through her mind–all without answers.

# THIRTEEN

ABDULLAH AL-JAMAL TRAVELED east from his house in rural Maljamar to Artesia, New Mexico, the nearest town with access to the Internet. As his source he selected Starbucks, with its Wi-Fi connection and international coffee.

After buying a latte and settling in a secluded corner, he reviewed his recent accomplishments. Could it be eight weeks since he entered the United States? It felt more like eight days.

Abdullah opened his computer and inserted the thumb drive Bashir, his American handler, had given him the day he crossed over from Mexico into America. He loaded the encryption software he would use to communicate with his contact in Rome. Bashir had explained the procedures necessary to operate the program, and made Abdullah repeat the instructions aloud until he had memorized them.

Bashir had cautioned him to write nothing down, and to guard the thumb drive with his life. "This portable drive contains a unique code that changes in a randomly prescribed routine matched only by your contact in Rome," he said. "The use of this drive is your only safe means of communication. Allow this program to fall into the hands of the American authorities, and you will die, I will see to it." The threat was unnecessary. The thumb drive would never leave Abdullah's protection. If cornered by the enemy he would destroy it before his martyrdom.

Abdullah sipped his coffee as he consulted his Islamic calendar, and entered the date followed by the Gregorian equivalent which launched the coded program. This would be his first report to his primary handler in Rome whose identity he did not know. His contact would forward Abdullah's report to Caliph Abd al-Ghayb, a descendant of the Prophet Muhammad, and a well-known leader within their secret society.

In this report he wanted to boast of his cleverly planned arrival in America. Using a forged passport Abdullah had flown from Riyadh to Mexico City, and then taken a bus to Juarez. In a public rest room he changed into a Hard Rock Café T-shirt, shorts and sandals. Then he walked to the nearby Lincoln Dental Clinic one block south of the Mexican border with the United States. The clinic attracted U. S. citizens by offering dental care at a fraction of the U. S. cost. As often as six times a day the clinic hauled van loads of Americans back across the bridge that spanned the Rio Grande River. Abdullah secured safe passage to America by blending into one load of departing clients.

At the border, American immigration agents conducted a cursory inspection of the routine trips back and forth. The vans entered El Paso, dropped off customers at parking garages, motels and hotels and then returned to Mexico.

At a predetermined time and place in downtown El Paso Abdullah met Bashir who gave him $12,000 in cash, and two sets of clothes, followed by a crash course on being in the land of the western crusaders. Abdullah didn't need Bashir's lecture having studied aeronautical engineering as a graduate student at Oklahoma University three years earlier while on a student visa. So as not to offend Bashir, his only link to sponsors at home, he had listened attentively.

Abdullah composed his report in great detail. He included all the glorious achievements. Testing his discipline as a warrior of Islam he reluctantly shortened the number of words with each of five revisions. Finally satisfied with the last rewrite, he reviewed his account of the past two months.

*Gracious and Dear Brother in the Jihad,*

*The thought of Allah the Almighty shields me while I am amid the crusaders who spread the seeds of Satan. I serve Allah in this epic battle between Islam, the Judeo-Christian infidels and all unbelievers.*

*On my entrance into the United States, I secured the use of an American truck provided to me by my appointed contact. Posing as a legal immigrant from Mexico, I secured a driver's license in a place called Alamogordo, where the American crusader armies train to kill Allah's lambs around the world. I then traveled to a remote village in an arid region of southeastern New Mexico called Maljamar. I became a tenant of a house far from the hard roads.*

*My research of records made public in several jurisdictions allowed me to identify organizations catering to beggars, orphans, sexual deviants, and homeless infidels. (The Americans have no shame and proudly display detailed records of their misfits and criminals.) Access to these records led me to many potential martyrs.*

*Posing as a journalist, a profession believed worthy here, I interviewed many candidates and discovered a perfect subject–an orphaned homosexual too worthless to gather friends. Although insignificant, his loss will honor Allah the Great God of Islam and all his prophets.*

*By assuming his identity. I am now believed to be a native born American with all the civil rights and privileges allowed by their government's constitution. I have applied for a passport, am registered as a voter in Lea County and have joined a Methodist Church of Christians who sing much and pray little. Next year I will pay money to the government in the form of taxation on the earnings of Russell Smith, my new identity.*

*I await your instructions as to the transfer of funds to expand my undertakings. I prefer a contact within our Hauula network of money dealers. Many exist to support the illegal migrants of the region.*

*Since my first contact in El Paso, I have communicated with no one. It is my plan to work independent of all others. As a vanguard of the jihad, my files steadily grow with photographs, maps and descriptions of civilian and military populations ripe for destruction. I await your call to action.*

*In the name of Allah the Exalted, I remain your loyal soldier for the cause. Praise be to God, and blessings upon the Messenger, his family, his companions, and all those Believers who follow Him.*

*The Sword*

After a final review, Abdullah transferred the report into the coded program and hit "send." Within seconds it would be available to his primary handler in Rome. By matching the lunar and solar dates on his report, Rome's source code would recognize a multilayered encryption. In the unlikely event a cryptologist at the National Security Agency would convert the code, he would be confronted with a second encryption.

Abdullah closed his laptop, confident in his ability to function unobserved while surrounded by secular dogs–Jews, their pawns the Christians, and all nonbelievers. Had he not been commanded by the Mullah of the Holy Mosque in Makkah, the holiest city of Islam? Did he not hear the words, "Go forth and take the fight to the enemy, and he shall quake in fear of you." Yes, they must quake in fear–a worthy goal.

# FOURTEEN

ASSOCIATE PROFESSOR RASHID al Youris, entered his private second story office overlooking the central campus of McClellan University in Virginia. A blinking light on his answering machine, barely visible amid a stack of term papers on each end of his desk, attracted his attention. He hung his worn tweed jacket with less than fashionable leather elbow pads on an ancient swivel chair that matched the desk.

The caller ID displayed the name *Johansson Plumbing,* but Rashid knew the caller's plumbing experience didn't exceed flushing a toilet. He wondered why Mike Johansson, nicknamed the Big Swede, wanted to invade his comfortable work space in the Office of Middle Eastern Studies. The identity of the caller aroused both suspicion and curiosity.

Even five years after Rashid's retirement from the FBI the bright eyed, rounded face, and white haired image of Mike remained vivid in his memory. During the early days of Rashid's Federal career he served as an interpreter for Mike when they worked for the International Response Cadre coordinating with INTERPOL. As partners, they bounced around the "Stans" on undercover duty assignments for six years. Each assignment made them adapt to new conditions and confront different enemies. No sooner had they mastered the challenges in Kazakhstan, they were thrust into a new and more dangerous environment in neighboring Uzbekistan. Later, as operatives in Pakistan, their professional relationship resulted in a close friendship. While their cultural and educational backgrounds were different, the dangers they faced united them.

Six years of conducting stressful assignments brought them both to the edge of burn-out. When two openings in the Office of Domestic Counterterrorism (ODC) came out on the FBI bid sheet, they agreed the time had come to move on. Each applied for a position, resulting in their selection and subsequent appointments.

Rashid leaned back in his chair and clasped his hands behind his head, bronze tinted hands colored by heritage, not by the sun. He remembered that after their assignments in the Middle East, they worked stateside on many projects for almost twenty years. Unlike now, in those early days counterterrorism was a backburner operation, low on the list of agency priorities.

Professor Youris reached for the play button on the answering machine, and wondered why this sudden interest in an old comrade in arms? Mike was not the type to call and share war stories. Nothing good could come of this.

He moved his finger over to the erase button.

If he's going to ask me to do a job, even a little one, I'm not interested. I have a comfortable retirement from Federal service and am working toward tenure at McClellan.

His finger hovered.

Rashid remembered Mike had recommended him to head-up the Bureau's Division of Analytical Standards and probably pulled a few strings to make it happen.

The finger strayed back to the play button.

As if to rationalize his decision, he figured he would listen to whatever Mike had to say, but would show no interest in any proposition proposed. Rashid tapped the play button and the room filled with the robust recorded voice of the Big Swede.

*"Hey, Rashid. Sorry I missed you. I need a little of your time. Everything is different in the Bureau now. I'm leaving for London and will be back tomorrow afternoon. How about a late dinner at Calwoods–my treat. They've moved to K Street. Maggie's got a reservation for us and will send you directions. See you then. You know the number."*

Calwoods–baked trout almandine came to mind. Rashid felt manipulated. Mike knew his love of their baked trout. There is something fishy about this. He smiled at the unintended pun. So he wants a little of my time, does he? Well, a little of my time is all he's going to get. Anything more and I'm not interested. Definitely not interested.

# FIFTEEN

DOROTHY HOGAN SAT at her desk outside Walter Kent's office, her left shoulder hunched holding a phone against her ear. Her right hand scribbled notes on a sheet of paper. "Yes. Thank you, I have it. Ten this morning? I'm not sure, at least three. Yes, if they are available. I'll confirm. Goodbye." Dorothy scanned her notes, and added a few words to clarify their meaning.

As soon as the weekly Narcotics Task Force briefing ended, she planned to tell Mr. Kent about the call. She knew that would be soon because of Kent's open-door policy. When the Narc Team left, she entered. "Mr. Kent, I received a call from the State Office of the Medical Investigator–the OMI. They are ready with a report on John Doe 136."

"John Doe 136?"

"You remember, Agent Kohen's case."

"Oh, yes. When do we go over?"

"Doctor Zumbeck's assistant says he has taken a special interest in this case and will brief us today at ten o'clock, if that's convenient."

"The MI will head the briefing? Interesting. Get Agents Ramirez and Kohen and ask them to come to my office, and Dorothy, please come along and take notes. I know they will send a written report, but that takes days."

"Yes sir, right away."

Because she knew how important this briefing would be to Ashley, Dorothy called her first. "Agent Kohen, the OMI has prepared a briefing on your guy in about ninety minutes. Walter wants you and Ramirez in his office."

"Oh my God, finally. They have me doing security clearance interviews. Marching around trying to find dirt on people who seldom have more than a parking ticket."

"Part of the job. Everything can't be as exciting as the office annual picnic, you know," Dorothy laughed and heard a smile in Ashley's voice as she asked, "What about the OMI, are they any good?"

"Oh yes. They're nationally known for their forensic pathology skills. We're lucky to have them."

"That's good to know. I'm on my way."

THE FIELD OFFICE team of Kent, Ramirez, Kohen and Hogan entered the MI's office building early and followed a receptionist to a conference room on the second floor. The room, lined with windows on one side, was bright with polished furniture neatly arranged.

Dr. Bob Zumbeck, managing forensic pathologist, and one assistant, were waiting. Dorothy marveled at the doctor's impeccable neatness: sharply creased white pants, starched white shirt, red bow tie and a carefully groomed mustache and goatee.

"Good morning, Agent Kent. I see you've brought your team of bodyguards with you," Zumbeck said with a chuckle. "Get comfortable. This shouldn't take long."

Dorothy and the others took seats on one side of the oval table. The OMI people sat on the opposite side. Zumbeck began. "I would like to go through our findings in the death investigation of John Doe 136, and answer your questions. There will be an official report including a description of the Reconciliation of Exhibits: histology, toxicology and serology in your office in three days or fewer. At least that's the plan." He adjusted his wire-rimmed glasses. "We are waiting on a few items, namely DNA analysis of the victim and some organ tissue studies. I can tell you no proximal diseases were found based on the tissue sample analysis completed."

Dorothy Hogan begin taking notes. She saw Ashley sitting upright at rapt attention.

"Before I begin, I would like to compliment Agent Kohen. We usually don't receive bodies in such good shape. Icing down John Doe 136 made our job a bit easier and not so, shall I say, fragrant." Zumbeck winked at Ashley.

"Okay. Let's begin. *Subject Description*: a male Caucasian, age twenty to twenty-four year, weight 110 pounds, height five-foot three inches. *Time of Death*: estimated at 36 hours before admittance in the OMI June, 15th at twenty hundred hours. *Cause of Death*: penetration wound inflicted by sharp object–a stabbing. *Manner of Death*: homicide, caused by the penetration of an object into the back of the body below the left shoulder blade. The object pierced the heart causing massive internal bleeding and shock," Zumbeck paused. "We have made a wound-casing of the object that shows it in a three-dimensional view; a six-inch double-edged knife blade with at least a two inch hilt. We have photographs." He laid his report on the table. "Okay, that covers the preliminaries. Any questions before I cover the forensic items?"

Ashley asked, "How do you know the knife had a two inch hilt?"

"The external examination, brought this to my attention. Pushing and holding the knife in the body needed great force. The hilt left bruised marks."

Walter Kent. "When you say homicide, what do you mean?"

"Manner of death is limited to five circumstances: natural death, homicide, suicide, therapeutic implications and unknown causes. Toxicology results show no medical conditions or treatments that could cause death. That rules out therapeutic implications. The stab wound rules out natural and unknown causes. It is unlikely anyone would fall on a knife that penetrated at this angle and depth and stay in that position. That rules out suicide and suggests homicide as the manner of death. Any other questions?"

Dorothy Hogan noted there were no further questions.

"Now for the forensic study. I have taken a particular interest in this case because of the unusual circumstances we encountered. I feel this homicide was premeditated. Zumbeck stopped long enough to check his notes, "I say premeditated because someone took extraordinary pains to prevent identification of John Doe 136. First, the fingerprints were burned off with acid. Second, the teeth were removed preventing orthodontic identification. Finally, the cleaning of the body with household bleach from head to toe removed any foreign hair or fiber evidence."

Silent until now, Agent Ramirez commented. "Definitely premeditated murder."

"Was there an odor of lilac flowers?" Ashley asked.

"Yes. The white shroud that wrapped the body held that odor. Toxicology confirmed it. Speaking of the shroud, it was made of a linen weave of a cotton and flax fiber: a tablecloth sold by Wal-Mart Stores–a common brand. Our investigation revealed bite marks around the mouth of the deceased. A reconstruction of the bite pattern is underway. Since no one can bite themselves on the face, the bite pattern may prove useful in identifying the killer, as soon as you folks catch him or her. Due to the body cleaning, we could not recover DNA for testing."

The forensic pathologist paused, and glanced down at his report, and then back up, his eyes bright with a glint of humor. "But we did have some luck. We found several strands of black hair four inch long in the cloth wrappings. John Doe had brown hair. I have sent the hair sample to your lab for DNA analysis."

Walter Kent's expression brightened. "Finally something."

Zumbeck nodded agreement. "There's more. We found an impressed thumbprint."

"But I thought there were no fingerprints on the body," said Ramirez.

"That's right. This print wasn't on the body, I found it on the underside of a piece of moleskin used to stop bleeding from the inflicted wound. A beautiful print preserved in the adhesive."

"We can run that through our database," said Ashley. "Did you find any identifying marks on the body, like a birthmark?"

Dr. Zumbeck took a deep breath. "I believe we did, but it won't help you. On the right shoulder we found a burn mark inflicted after death. The burn probably removed what you have suggested, a birthmark or an identifying scar."

The Medical Investigator stood. He stared into the eyes of his guests. "A combing of the pubic region revealed no foreign substances,"... his voice trailed off for a moment... "but we found a tattoo in a not so obvious place on the body."

Dorothy Hogan stopped taking notes, and became aware of total silence in the room. She observed Ashley's expression, a mixture of surprise and elation. Ashley shifted her position and leaned forward. "A tattoo?"

"Yes, but I can't take credit for that discovery. Medical Assistant Morrison, found it." Zumbeck then turned to his assistant seated next to him. "I'll let her explain."

Dorothy Hogan had paid little attention to the doctor's assistant, but now saw a petite, middle-aged woman in a white lab coat wearing glasses halfway down her nose.

Ms. Morrison stood, and cleared her throat. "I worked with Doctor Zumbeck during the full work-up of our forensic autopsy. From my vantage point I noticed a tiny patch of skin tissue that appeared to be a skin rash or abrasion. At first I didn't think much about it, then I realized the color was not in keeping with the normal gray-white skin color of a male Caucasian. I moved closer to view this anomaly." She shifted from foot to foot, and cleared her throat again. "I performed a manual reorientation of the tissue to discover the cause of the discoloration. Based on this examination I found the color was the result of a partially exposed red tattoo."

Ramirez asked, "What was the tattoo?"

"A rosebud. A red rosebud."

"It must have been small?"

"It was three centimeters, about an inch in diameter, bright red."

Dorothy Hogan looked up from her notepad and saw an expression of confusion on Walter Kent's face. She knew he would ask the question on everyone's mind.

"Why did the killer, so careful to hide the identity of his victim, miss such an obvious marking?"

Doctor Zumbeck began to pace. "The killer did not see the tattoo, Agent Kent, because it was not obvious. It was, in a sense, well hidden in plain view." He faced them. "It would have been obvious had the victim been circumcised."

Everyone took a few seconds to process this information. Agent Kent remained stoic. Ramirez laughed, and Ashley kept her composure. Dorothy bowed her head, and continued writing.

Kent asked, "Do you have a photograph of this tattoo?"

"Yes. Ms. Morrison had our staff forensic photographer take several shots."

"Color photographs?" asked Ramirez, not trying to hide his grin.

"Rest assured, Agent Ramirez, the color saturated photos are in sharp focus and most revealing." The doctor took his seat. "We have prepared three sets of these images. One set for our records, one for the report and one you may take with you today. I have included a picture of the victim's face, but the features are mutilated–useless for identification."

Dr. Zumbeck snapped his report folder shut. "If there are no questions I have one for you. To whom shall I release the body?"

Dorothy Hogan summarized the discussion that followed. She wrote the body of John Doe 136 would be assigned by the OMI to the Kirk Funeral Home, embalmed and returned to the State and placed in storage for a period of time not to exceed six months. If not claimed by the next of kin, a burial would occur at the expense of the State of New Mexico.

Damn, she thought. There are rules for everything.

# SIXTEEN

RASHID AL YOURIS ARRIVED at eight o'clock and greeted Mike Johansson with a vigorous handshake. The waiter escorted them to a private alcove off the main serving area of Calwood's International Cuisine. Their table, set with fine china and crystal, stood enclosed by walls on three sides leaving one access point for service personnel. A small chandelier sparkled overhead. The scent of garlic flavored the air.

They ordered without reference to the menu, and small talk followed. Mike asked Rashid about his wife Hessa, and her adjustment to the kids growing up and leaving the family nest. Had she recovered from her cancer treatment? Did Rashid enjoy teaching at the University?

Rashid countered with inquiries about Mike's daughter and the grandchildren, careful to avoid any mention of his wife who'd recently passed away.

When the food arrived the conversation turned to food and wine. After dinner, during coffee service, the Big Swede's expression turned serious. "What do you think of our Commander in Chief?"

Rashid glanced up from his coffee. "Still in training."

"What about the jihadist Caliph Abd al-Ghayb hiding out on the Pakistan border, in Iran or maybe Manhattan?"

"He's an ass, but dangerous."

Mike laughed. "Remind me not to ask you to write any lengthy obituaries."

"There are a few obituaries I would like to write, but that wouldn't solve America's predicament. My students ask why we are in such a mess in the Middle East. Is it our leadership? Is it religious fundamentalism or is it an unavoidable clash of culture? I tell them it is all of that, and much more."

"That must confuse the hell out of them."

"Yes, they are confused. So are the political and religious leaders around the globe. Everyone has lost sight of the underlying cause of the conflict.

Mike arched an eyebrow. "And that is?"

"Greed and a lust for power."

"Not unique in history. Today nuclear technology and oil money prompts cultural conflict and war. Not long ago economic and political ideology underwrote the Cold War, and before that, in the thirties and forties, it was racial superiority and extreme nationalism."

"Yes, yes." Rashid said, with a touch of excitement. "History is full of madness and always will be, but that is no reason to accept it much less to tolerate it."

"You're right. We must not excuse it. We must, however, deal with the madness. Good or bad policy is in the hands of politicians. That's the domain of leaders the world over. Whether they are right or wrong, and it's a little of both, there will always be consequences. Dealing with these consequences is what it's all about."

Rashid assumed a skeptical expression. He knew Mike to be pragmatic, but never this earnest. The Big Swede was leading up to something. He suspected the trout almandine had been the bait, and that an attempt to set the hook would soon follow.

"As you know, Rashid, conflict with Islamic radicals has been brewing a longtime, but no one considered it a major problem until 9-11. That day we woke to a dangerous enemy."

"You're preaching to the choir, Mike. What's your point?"

"The threat of terrorists' activity, inside and outside of the United States, is real. The intelligence community has a monumental job to do. Unlike years ago, the current FBI's domestic counter terrorism program is the primary mission of the agency, and it's big."

"Again I ask, what's your point?"

"My point is, I need you back."

Rashid clamped his teeth together and glared at Mike. He needs me back? He must be insane. Going back after even a few years would be like starting over. And there is my work at McClellan University.

"Before you say no, hear me out. You and I have been through a dozen governmental reorganizations. It goes on all the time, but it's usually only a change in name or a shuffling of personnel, not a change of function or a new mission. Well, it's different this time." Mike faced Rashid. "The changes are genuine and significant. To say it's a new ball game is an understatement. It's a new sport."

Rashid had never seen Mike this energized before.

"Everyone knows about the creation of Homeland Security, and the National Intelligence Director's appointment years ago. Not reported is the staggering burden these changes have put on the intelligence community." Mike stopped and faced Rashid. "Imagine the challenge of coordinating fifteen highly classified and independent organizations."

Rashid's reaction was immediate. "Why should I believe it's any different now than in the past? All the changes are on paper. Nothing will change. Never has, never will."

"Rashid, you're not listening. It has changed. The wall of silence between agencies has crumbled. Sure some organizations are slow to come around, but most act as a unified community working together to track down the bad guys."

Rashid shifted in his chair and fidgeted with his tweed sport coat. "All right, I'll take your word for it. What's that have to do with me?"

Mike resumed his seat. "The Director of National Intelligence, who controls all our budgets and sets the program goals, has created a new clearinghouse called the Terrorism Threat and Investigation Center. This organization, T-TIC, will consist of representatives from each of the fifteen intelligence agencies. The center will streamline all the intelligence gathered in the war on terror. It will be the dot connector."

"The what?"

"They will connect the widely dispersed dots of information needed for rapid response. The information collected by the clearinghouse will pass directly to the Secretary of Homeland Security and the National Security Council that advises the President.

Rashid nodded. "T-TIC is a direct link to the Commander in Chief?"

"That's right. Each of the agencies must appoint an Agency Ambassador, and organize an in-house task force to feed T-TIC."

"That *is* new, Mike."

"Yes, it's the government's answer to the ongoing changes in technology and the enemy's growing sophistication in the digital world. As a newly appointed Assistant Deputy Director of the FBI, I am responsible for selecting the Ambassador to represent us, and creating the in-house task force I call the JTTF teams."

"What's a JTTF team?"

"To beef up the FBI's response, I will form Joint Terrorism Task Forces–teams of highly trained specialists. These mobile forces will serve any of the fifty-six Field Offices around the country when a threat is identified. They will be a cross between a SWAT team and a Military Special Ops Unit."

"Congratulations Mike, I'm impressed. That's a big job advancement. Who will be the bureau's Agency Ambassador, anyone I know?"

Mike leaned back, looked Rashid directly in the eyes, beamed broadly, and allowed a long pause to linger.

"You're crazy, Mike. Out of your mind!"

"You have to be to survive in my job. Our old outfit, the Office of Domestic Counterterrorism, had a small handful of experienced people. The ODC no longer exists, and most of its people have retired or died off. The new people are just that–new and inexperienced. They will develop over time, but we can't wait for that to happen."

"What you're asking is unfair to me and my family."

"Perhaps, but necessary. You are a rare commodity, Rashid; you speak five languages, you understand the Muslim culture and history and you have thirty years of agency experience. Plus, I can't think of anyone I trust more that you."

"I've worked hard to get ahead at McClellan University," Rashid explained. "If I leave I will lose my position and a chance at tenure, not to mention the income. I can't turn my back on that. Hessa would never forgive me."

"There's something you should know."

"What?"

"Last week I met with Chancellor Henderson and Dean Oliver of the College of Social Studies at McClellan University."

"You what?"

"Hear me out. Without getting into classified information, I explained the situation. They agreed to maintain your faculty position. You will assume the duties of a tenured professor with full pay right on schedule. You can arrange your classes to consist of assigned outside readings and let your graduate students handle most of the day-to-day stuff. You will appear in class twice a semester. The rest of the time you will be granted research leave."

"This takes spying to a new level or perhaps a new low."

"Finally," Mike continued.

"There's more?"

"Yes. I phoned Hessa this morning. At first she was hesitant to have you come back to the Bureau. But when I explained the dangers we face and why we need a person of your skill and experience, she understood why I'm making you this offer. She agreed you should take it for the country and for the American Muslim community. If you decide to take the job, she'll support you 100 percent. She confesses she likes the idea of going back to Georgetown and seeing her old friends again."

"What are you talking about?"

"I am authorized to provide housing and incidental expenses for special assignment personnel critical to the mission. I can't think of anyone that fits that description better than you. I've leased a colonial townhouse with a view. I think she'll like it."

"You old bastard!"

"Just say yes, Rashid. Just say yes."

# SEVENTEEN

THE MEDICAL INVESTIGATOR's briefing on John Doe 136 ended shortly before noon. When the field office crew returned, Walter Kent ordered a meeting in his office at one o'clock to plan a case strategy.

Ashley skipped lunch. Food held no interest for her. She propped the picture of the red rosebud tattoo against her desk phone, and stared at it. What a lucky discovery, she thought, a real lead to the identity of the victim.

She couldn't help but be amused by the photograph. Why would anyone want a tattoo on the penis? And why a rosebud? Did that have any significance? She imagined the etching process. Indelible ink forced into the dermis layer of skin with an oscillating tattoo machine. She wondered if he had undergone a general anesthetic.

Two agents walked by her desk in conversation. Ashley quickly tipped the picture face down. She didn't want to become the subject of lurid humor around the office. Instead, she wanted to come up with an investigation procedure that would put her case in high gear. She snapped on her computer and started searching. A plan formed in her mind.

DOROTHY HOGAN and Ashley entered Walter Kent's office a few minutes before the one o'clock meeting. Kent acknowledged them. "Come in, have a seat. Ramirez will be here shortly. He's completing a meeting with the press on crime statistics." Kent stretched his arms over his head. "I feel our meeting this morning may shed some light on the Mummy Case." Ashley winced when she heard Kent use the name given to her assignment by Ramirez. It had caught on around the office. She hated that name because it showed disrespect.

Kent caught Dorothy's eye. "I'd like you to type your notes on the briefing today. We won't get the OMI's official report for days."

71

"Yes, sir. I'll get on it."

Agent Ramirez entered and sat next to Ashley. "Sorry to be late, Walter. Media update, you know."

"I understand." Kent stood, and began pacing behind his desk. "I'd like to resolve this matter quickly. If the case supports our mission, fine. If not, I'll forward our findings to Lea County, and get on with other business." He stopped and observed Ashley. "Agent Kohen, this is your case. Based on what we know so far, what do you think?"

Ashley leaned forward. "It might take some leg work, but we'll learn the identity of John Doe from the tattoo."

Ramirez looked at the ceiling, then at Kohen "All we have is the tattoo. That's it. The hair and the thumbprint belong to someone else."

Ashley snapped back. "Short of a positive ID, I can't think of a more unique marking than that tattoo."

Kent stopped pacing. "It may be a one-of-a-kind, I'll grant you that."

Ashley continued. "Tattooing is an art form. It's not a do-it-yourself skill. It's also become a heath issue because of the increase of HIV and hepatitis infections. The State of New Mexico licenses the tattooing business. I already have a list of the State's license holders. In case there are some Mom and Pop Shops not licensed, I'll run a cross-reference with the yellow pages and Craigslist online."

Ramirez nodded approval. "A good start."

Ashley continued. "I have a plan. I call it the concentric circle search."

Walter Kent sat down and crossed his arms. "Never heard of it. Is this something you dreamed up?"

"Starting with the burial site, I will select a four county region on the assumption the victim lived in that area. I will map the location of each tattoo shop." Ashley stood and walked to the dry erase board mounted on the sidewall. She drew a small circle, then another until her drawing resembled a bullseye of circles. "I'll superimpose these circles over the map of the county region centering the smallest circle in the most dense location pattern, which is Roswell. I'll work my way out in all directions."

"An interesting approach," Ramirez said

Walter Kent nodded. "I like your plan, Ashley. I hope you and your partner have early success."

"My partner? I don't need a partner to conduct this search."

"Yes you do. That's the way we work in the Bureau. I never send an agent into the field alone. This is your case, Ashley. You're the lead. Ramirez will be your partner for now."

"But Ramirez is your second in command. I can't imagine why you would pick him as my partner. He is far too valuable to this Field Office to spend his time on a case that's not high profile." Ashley hoped her true feelings didn't show on her face.

"Mark requested the assignment. He will be your mentor."

AFTER THE MEETING, Ramirez asked Ashley to follow him. As Assistant Special Agent in Charge (ASAC) he had an office on the same floor as Walter Kent, smaller, but private. His supervisory position made him one of Ashley's many bosses. "Have a seat, Agent Kohen. We need to talk." She wondered where he planned to go with this meeting. They hadn't agreed on much. Based on comments around the office, most people didn't like him.

He started. "I asked Walter to assign me as your partner on this case. He agreed for several reasons. First, our staff is swamped with work. No one is available right now. I can take some time for fieldwork, if I have to. Also, the Mummy Case is a dead end, in my view, and won't take much of my time." Ashley's expression hardened. "I don't mean to denigrate your efforts here. I know you are sincere, but that's my opinion. If the case does develop, I'm 100 percent behind it. Okay?"

"Sure. Whatever you say."

"Another reason is mentoring. I know you bring knowledge and experience to this agency, but you are new to the FBI. Trust me, you have a lot to learn. All of our new agents in this field office go through orientation and mentoring, even seasoned personnel who are reassigned."

Ashley agreed. "Yes. I understand. If I seem a little pushy, it's because I want to do a good job." She figured being the new kid on the block always had a downside. She would live through the 'mentoring' period and survive it.

"Ambition is good, but it has to be channeled to get the greatest benefit. I think you have potential. My job is to help you realize that potential."

Ashley shifted in her chair and consciously forced her limbs to relax.

"Yes, great potential," he repeated. The conversation paused for a moment. "Now about our being partners. You know the routine. We protect our partner's back, and work as a team. Each of us will respect the efforts of the other. When in the field we are two agents doing our job. We become united, so to speak." Ramirez paused, peered at Ashley and grinned in a lustful way. "Understand what I'm saying?"

Ashley had faced this situation many times before. At age twelve she learned that men liked to consider her in a funny way. Her mother cautioned her about inappropriate touching and body language. "You're a pretty girl Ashley, and that's just fine, but you have to be careful. Some people may try to take advantage of you."

"Yes, Agent Ramirez, I understand perfectly. I want you to know I have learned how to take care of myself on and off the job. You can ask any of my former partners." She tilted her head to the side, flicked a restrained smile at him while thinking–let the games begin.

# EIGHTEEN

.

VIEWING HIS LAPTOP, Abdullah read the reply from his handler in Rome with both elation and astonishment. Elation because the encryption had performed as designed, and resulted in a quick response. Astonished because his mission, not yet defined, would soon be known to him in a face-to-face meeting in Rome. The details of the meeting were specific: Albani Hotel, 45 Via Adda, Rome, Italy in five days, at 10 a.m.

He faced a problem. His application to the U. S. State Department for a passport in Russel Smith's name had not been processed. Abdullah had hired an online passport service provider to speed the paperwork with no success to date.

How strange that his handler made no mention of a passport or of transport arrangements, only that Abdullah must appear as directed. He considered this an oversight, then determined it was not an oversight. It was a test of his resourcefulness. If he could not deal with a simple matter of transport, how could he be trusted to carry out more complicated and worthy assignments?

Abdullah devised a plan. He would reverse the procedure he followed to enter America by using the forged passport that allowed him to pass through the border with ease. Bashir, his contact in El Paso, would be a starting point. He would call him and set a meeting at their prearranged location. He made the call, and packed a suitcase.

ABDULLA PARKED his pickup next to the Motel 6 on Gateway Boulevard in downtown El Paso, where he had reservations for the night. This motel was unpretentious, and would draw no attention to their meeting. He and Bashir had agreed to meet at five o'clock. Abdullah arrived early and waited in his truck with the air-conditioner running.

Twenty minutes later he entered his ground floor room with Bashir in tow, shut the door and turned the security lock. Facing each other, both men bowed their heads, then extended a hand in friendship.

Abdullah spoke first. "Have a seat, brother. I have good news. Rome has summoned me to define my mission." Bashir nodded his approval, and sat on one of the queen beds across from him. "So soon. Are you ready?"

Abdullah shrugged his shoulders. "I am always ready to serve the jihad and the will of Allah, the Mighty." Both observed a moment of silence. "I will meet with my superior in five days. I must arrange a flight to Rome. My American passport has not arrived. I will use my original passport. It is my hope that you will assist me in this matter."

Bashir didn't hesitate. "I have a contact in Mexico. He is trustworthy. For a price he will arrange everything, including transport from the border to Benito Juarez International Airport outside Mexico City. Security is less strict there. A direct flight to Rome is no problem. Prepare to travel, my brother."

Abdullah raised both hands high over his head and gazed upward. "I am a servant of the Great One. Let His will be my command."

TRAVEL TO MEXICO CITY took three long, hot days. The means of transportation varied from a series of taxies to a rickety bus and at one point a two-mile hike to reach the airport because of monumental traffic congestion.

Over 450 passengers crowded the Boeing 747's flight to Rome. Abdullah found the seating cramped and the food unappetizing. The cabin temperature varied between sweaty hot and a damp cold. During a miserable eighteen hour transit, with one stopover in Miami for fuel, Abdullah slept, walked the aisles, urinated, and repeated the cycle many times. Now, as his plane entered the approach pattern for landing at Fiumicino Airport near Rome, he calculated the time change and estimated the hours before his meeting. He anticipated the Albani Hotel, a hot shower, and a few hours to settle his mind and prepare himself for what may prove to be the most important meeting of his life.

REFRESHED FROM HIS difficult flight, and calmed by an hour of prayer and deep meditation, he dressed in his black suit, white shirt, and bright red tie. At exactly 10 a.m. Abdullah responded to a loud rap on the door of his hotel room. He whispered a brief prayer to Allah, the Exalted, and reached for the doorknob.

A large man stood in the hall scrutinizing him with dark eyes set in a bearded face. He stepped into the room and closed the door. "Confirm your identity. What is your code name?"

"I am the Sword."

"Good morning, my son of Islam. I am Sheikh Hadid Ghamadi, your contact here in Rome." From a solemn expression, his face brightened, showing perfect teeth. He lifted his hand in a traditional salute as did Abdullah. "Follow me. We will meet in private quarters, a place of safety. A short walk from here."

Abdullah followed the big man out of the hotel onto the street. They crossed the corner intersection, walked a block, and entered an apartment building that appeared shabby on the outside, but inside radiated elegance. They took an elevator to the top floor. It opened onto a windowless lobby with one door.

Sheikh Ghamadi entered a code on an electronic keypad, then opened the door and waved Abdullah into a large room decorated with ornately carved Middle Eastern furnishings, polished wooden panels and a glittering chandelier. A stately conference table centered the room. Glass doors that opened onto a balcony formed a background for two desks, one large and one small.

A man in western clothes, wearing a flowing red and white patterned keffiyeh held in place with a braided black egal circling his head, rose from the large desk. He came to greet them with a cordial expression half hidden by a well-manicured gray beard and mustache. Ghamadi bowed before the man, then looked at Abdullah. "This is Caliph Abd al-Ghayb, descendant of the Prophet Muhammad, and Supreme Head of the Society of Rule by Sharia Law."

Abdullah, stunned, stood in place a second and then fell to his knees bowing his head to the floor. "Allah the Majestic is great," he said. "And to Him I give praise." He rocked back and forth several times. Ghamadi, smiled at Caliph al-Ghayb, offered a hand to Abdullah, helped him to stand and lead him to the conference table. Clearly unprepared to meet with the Supreme leader, he stood by the table unsure of his next move.

Caliph Abd al-Ghayb spoke. "Be seated, my son; soldier of the jihad, I have heard much about your training in the camps and your skill dealing with the invader enemy." The Caliph sat across from Abdullah. "You have been recruited for this assignment not only for your ability as an effective agent, but for your devotion to the cause." Abdullah sat at attention. "I am told of your success in the place called New Mexico, your clever acquisition of a local identity and your devotion as an Islamic warrior. I feel you are ideally situated."

Ghamadi left the room briefly, then returned followed by a servant woman carrying a silver tray with spiced tea and cheese.

Abdullah tried to relax, unable to fully comprehend his presence before the Caliph, a true descendant of Muhammad.

Abd al-Ghayb continued. "As you may know, the Society of Rule by Sharia Law is a keystone in the hierarchy of the global jihad that is carried out by our many affiliates–Hamas, The Muslim Brotherhood, Hezbollah, Al-Qaeda, the most famous and least disciplined, and many others. Our ideology of extreme purity, that supports the spread of Islam throughout the world, relies on many strategies, one of which is violence."

The Caliph reached for the spiced tea and filled his cup. "The use of violence is a calculated tool, most effective in a world of nonbelievers. It sows the seeds of chaos, a well-established theory, one that has served us often. Without the chaos of violence, nothing changes. With it, societies react and transformations occur over time. Our enemies regard the jihad as carried out by crazy men, bent on mindless destruction. They are blind to the progress underway." Abd al-Ghayb paused, sipped tea from his cup, tasted the cheese, then dabbed his lips with a linen napkin.

"Our struggle is fought on many fronts. The most troubling interference with our movement is western intervention in the affairs of Islam led by the United States and its allies. Their fanatical belief in democracy and fear of losing control of capital markets cause them to meddle in the affairs of others, particularly the Muslim world. Their paranoia will be their undoing. I look forward to an Islamic America under Sharia law, but that will take time."

His eyes narrowed as he appeared to take stock of Abdullah's reaction to his words. A nod of his head showed approval. "The New York incident– the twin towers–is a perfect example. It cost a little over one million U. S. dollars to take down the World Trade Center buildings. Most of that, $600,000, compensated the families of the brave martyrs who died for the greater good of Allah the Exalted. The balance, about half a million, were operational expenses. A small sum when you tally the results. America, has spent tens of trillions of dollars, disrupted their way of life, and continue to destabilize their economies because of our actions. If analyzed from a cost-benefit standpoint, it was a success beyond imagination. It proves we can drain the blood and treasure of the American government until it crashes to the ground like a water starved camel." Again, he tipped the teacup, drained its contents and refilled it.

Abdullah, fascinated by the words of the Caliph, remained alert and attentive.

Warming to the subject, he continued. "America has the greatest military might in the history of the world. It is protected by two oceans, and surrounded by friendly nations. Direct action is inconceivable, and has rarely been successful in the history of civilization. No, the great powers of the past and the present fail not by military aggression, but by internal decay brought on by their reaction to chaos." His eyes sparkled with excitement.

Sheikh Ghamadi interjected a comment. "These words speak the truth and support the true purpose of this meeting. He reached across the table and touched Abdullah's hand. "We have a plan to advance our cause and stunt American influence."

"Our plan," Abd al-Ghayb continued, "has been in the making since that September day in 2001. If you consider the effect of that attack, you will understand why this current undertaking will dwarf that former success.

"Yes," Ghamadi said, "What we plan will make the September attack pale in comparison."

Abdullah listened while his mind raced to understand the implications of these words. The scope of this thinking–these words excited him, and lit a fiery passion in him.

Abd al-Ghayb, his eyes glistening with enthusiasm leaned forward, clasped his hands tightly on the table, and lowered his voice, "What I am about to tell you is known only by me, Sheikh Ghamadi and a select number of the members of my Majis al Shura Constative Council." Ghamadi placed a copy of the Quran on the table in front of Abdullah. The Caliph stroked his beard, took the hand of the young warrior of Islam, and placed it on the holy book. "You must swear to me on your life, the life of your mother, and the life of your father, Prince Abeer Jamal that you will tell no one what I am about to tell you. That if captured, you will end your life, by whatever means possible, so that this secret dies with you."

Tears of emotion welled up in Abdullah's eyes as he spoke. "As one who surrenders to Allah the Great, to the Society of Rule by Sharia Law, the global jihad for which we fight, and to you Caliph Abd al-Ghayb descendant of the Prophet Mohammed, I swear."

Caliph al-Ghayb studied Abdullah's face, and observed Sheikh Ghamadi who nodded approval. He then sat erect in his chair and waited for the tension in the room to subside. In a whispered voice, he said, "We have secured a small, but powerful nuclear weapon."

# NINTEEN

ON THEIR FIRST DAY as partners Agent Kohen drove south on Highway 285 while Ramirez read through the list of tattoo businesses Ashley had compiled the night before. He noted their location on a map of southeastern New Mexico. "I can't believe some of these names, Ink Bomb Tattoos, Creepy Crawler House of Art, and Fat Zombie Body Etchings. I wonder what they were smoking when they dreamed those up."

Ashley glanced at Ramirez as she approached the city limits of Roswell where their concentric circle search pattern would begin. "Some of the names are strange," Ashley slowed to the posted speed limit. "It's a competitive business. A catchy name helps." She passed Wal-Mart and continued down Main Street. "What's the first name on our list?"

"The Vivid Dragon Tattoo. It's on West Second Street," Ramirez pulled the photograph of the rose tattoo out of his shirt pocket. "What do you say–I show the picture and you ask the questions. Okay?"

That proposal didn't surprise Ashley. Gallantry still lingered in a culture that said a woman should be shielded from embarrassing moments, even by the likes of Ramirez. On some level she appreciated the gesture. "No way Jose," she said. "A potential witness is more likely to talk if knocked out of their comfort zone. A good start is a woman showing them a picture of a guy's genitals in one hand, and an FBI badge in the other."

Displaying a wide grin, Agent Ramirez shook his head. "Okay, I'll remain the strong silent type."

The Vivid Dragon Tattoo shop shared walls with a thrift shop and an auto parts store on the west edge of town. The wood frame building with faded orange trim needed repair. A weathered painting of a giant green dragon breathing fire covered the front window. When Agents Kohen and Ramirez opened the front door, the jingle of a tiny bell announced their arrival. From behind a beat-up wood and glass display case that served as a counter, a man wearing black leather pants, a vest and no shirt raised his head. He offered a grin displaying several missing teeth. His face turned sour when Ashley flipped open her ID.

"Good morning, I'm Agent Kohen and this is Agent Ramirez with the FBI. We're investigating a missing person and have a few questions." She noticed a barbed wire tattoo around the man's wrist and assorted red, green and blue designs decorating each muscular arms. "What's your name, please?"

"Sam. Samuel Jones. I don't know nothing about no missing person."

Ashley remained positive. "I'm told you are the best tattoo artist in town, and we thought you might be able to help us. Have you been in operation long?"

"Sure. Well, for a while. I have a state license." He pointed to a crooked frame hanging on the wall. "I been in body art for years. I run a clean business. No complaints from nobody."

Ramirez leaned on the glass display case. "As Agent Kohen says, we're seeking a missing person. We need your cooperation." He made direct eye contact with Sam.

Sam nodded. "Okay. Is it a guy or a gal?"

Ashley slipped the photograph out of her pocket. "Will this help you identify this person?" She placed the photo on the counter.

Sam squinted at the picture, his eyebrows pinched together. "I don't do private parts. That's sick and a piss-poor job, too. I'm professional."

"I'm sure you're are," Ashley said. "This is a unique tattoo in an uncommon location. We are searching for the identity of its owner." She pulled the photo back and started to pocket it.

"Wait a minute. Let's see that again." Sam took a magnifying glass from under-the-counter and studied the picture. "That's done freehand. Nobody does that any more. It's all done with electric tattoo machines that are fast, safe and clean."

Hoping to shorten their list of interviews, Ashley asked, "Who does this work by hand?"

"Nobody in Roswell, that's for damn sure."

"Are you saying someone without a license did this work?'"

Frowning, Sam paused and tilted his head from side to side. "I know all the artists around here, and none of them would touch this job or those people, if you know what I mean." The corners of his mouth turned down. "I don't mean no disrespect to you all, but this is a queer job."

"You mean a strange job?" asked Ramirez, knowing exactly what Jones meant.

"No. I mean only a fairy would get a rosebud tattoo on the end of his dick." Sam hesitated and stepped back. "I guess that ain't a politically correct way to put it these days, but it's true. I know all about faggots and I got no tolerance for that way of life."

Ashley ignored the crude language. "I appreciate your candor Sam, and you have a right to your opinion, but it doesn't answer our question. Who did this work?"

Sam leaned against the wall behind him. "It's not like I talk to the cops all that much, but when it comes to homos, well that's different." Ashley raised an eyebrow at Ramirez, who winked back at her. "There's a place in the mountains that does crotch jobs for a price. They ain't licensed, neither."

"Mountains?" Ramirez asked. "There are many mountains west of here. Can you be more specific?"

"Mayhill."

"Mayhill?"

"Yea, it's a little town west outa Artesia. It's behind the general store, in the woods. Low-Down Tattoo they call it. Two guys run it. A big one and a little one. There're real good 'friends' if you know what I mean." He smirked. "Little guy does the work. Big guy, well, you gotta watch him."

Ashley put the picture back in her pocket. "What do you mean by 'got to watch him', Mr. Jones?"

"He's big, dumb and mean as a rabid dog in heat. Not nobody you want a mess with. Everybody goes there with cash and nobody gets off the table till the jobs done."

"Do you have a name for us?"

The artist clamped his mouth shut.

Ramirez placed his hand on the counter. "We'd like to know what we're getting into. You'll be protecting us so we can continue to protect you."

Jones thought about that a moment. "Butch Cassidy."

"You're serious?"

"Butch is what he goes by. George is his real name. George Cassidy. His picture is in the newspapers a lot. Bar fights and the like. Enough said."

MAYHILL WAS IN the foothills of the Sacramento Mountains. Barely a town, it straddled Highway 82 with a general store, a gas station, a small well-appointed post office, and several broken-down structures in serious need of repair. Most people traveled to the area to enjoy the cool summer air and three RV parks nearby.

Ashley felt a man should ask for directions to the tattoo shop considering their usual cliental. In the car Ramirez removed his coat, shoulder holster and necktie before climbing the well-worn wooden steps that led to the front door of the Mayhill Cafe and General Store.

A gray haired woman stood behind a counter and greeted the stranger with a grumpy expression. She held an ice cream scoop in her hand. Two kids sat at a nearby table licking cones. The air smelled of fried food.

"Good morning. I'm new to these parts. I hear there's a tattoo shop here in Mayhill. Wonder if you could direct me?" The women put the scoop down and stepped back distancing herself from the outsider.

"Yea, we got a tattoo place for certain people." She gave Ramirez a probing gaze. "County Road 69 back that away." She pointed east. "Take a left. It's about two miles in the woods. They got a sign. Can't miss it if that's what you want."

Ramirez thanked the woman. The two kids with ice cream cones giggled as he passed. He crossed the highway and climbed into the car. "No problem finding out about the Low-Down Tattoo. It's well-known around here." He adjusted his shoulder holster and coat.

Ashley nodded. "Little town. Everyone knows everybody's business. Which way?"

They took a left onto County Road 69. After 200 feet, it turned into a rutted dirt path barely wide enough for two cars to pass. Their tires created a plume of dust as they bumped along at twenty miles an hour, steadily climbing uphill. The few cabins they passed appeared deserted.

Before leaving Roswell, Ashley had checked the onboard computer for priors on "Butch" George Cassidy in Chaves and Otero Counties. Cassidy had a string of aggravated assault charges and two DUI's. No jail time.

Ashley pointed, "There's a tattoo sign on the left. I'm going to drive by to get a feel for the surroundings." A shabby two story wood frame house served as the shop and living quarters. Ashley remembered the warning about the 'big guy' and wished she had bought an ankle holster and revolver last week. She promised herself to do it when she got back to Albuquerque.

After passing the house they turned around and parked the car near a rusty pickup truck in the driveway. As they approached, Ashley saw a curtain move in the front window. "We're being watched."

Ramirez unbuttoned his coat. In a low voice he answered, "By the numbers."

Ashley knocked on the door, then stepped to the side. Ramirez stood back three feet at an opposite angle. No answer. She knocked again, and waited. She saw Ramirez rock from one foot to the other. "Mr. Cassidy, we are the FBI," she shouted. "We want to ask you about one of your customers." She heard hurried talk on the other side of the door.

The latch clicked and the door opened an inch. An eye appeared. "Whatcha want?" The voice sounded like a woman.

"Someone told us you may be able to help us in a missing person investigation. We have a few questions," The door opened wider and a short man peeked out.

"Who told you what?" The man, no more than five feet tall wore a T-shirt with a faded peace sign on the front, worn-out jeans and no shoes. The shape of a large man loomed behind him in the shadows of the room.

Ashley advanced to the threshold. "We believe one of your clients is missing. I need to identify him. May we come in?"

"Sure. Okay, I guess for a minute." Over his shoulder he asked, "Is that all right, Butch?"

Before the man could answer, Agents Kohen and Ramirez stepped into the room. Ashley addressed the small man. "This will save us both time. No search warrant. No state police." Ashley then turned to the big man. "You're George Cassidy, what's your friend's name?"

Before Cassidy spoke, the little man answered for him, "My name is Barry. Barry Malinowski."

Cassidy stepped into the light. A spider tattoo covered his thick neck which supported a shaven head. He held an enormous hunting knife in his beefy fist. Ramirez dodged to the side. "Edge weapon," he shouted and drew his gun. "Drop the knife, now!"

"You gonna shoot me, asshole?"

"If I do you won't know about it after the first slug rips a hole in your chest."

Malinowski started to cry. "Don't hurt Butch, he's my friend."

Ashley moved next to Barry while staying out of the line of fire. "Don't be stupid, Cassidy. Technically you are about to assault a Federal Agent. That's jail time. Drop the knife. We just want a few answers to some questions, and we'll go. You're scaring your friend."

The 9 millimeter gun held steady. The knife clunked when it hit the wood floor.

Ramirez kicked the knife away and shouted, "Hands on your head. Sit on the floor. Do it!"

Cassidy didn't move. Barry pleaded with him. "Do what he says, Butch. I don't want a go to jail." With a scowl on his face Cassidy got down. Ramirez walked over and stood behind him, holstered his weapon and said, "Stay put."

Ashley went to Malinowski. "It's all right, Barry. Butch will be okay. Calm down." She scanned the dingy room. A sofa with sagging cushions divided it in half. She went to it. "Sit over here, Barry. A couple of questions and we're gone." She patted the cushion next to her. He joined her.

"We are trying to identify a missing person. We know this person has a tattoo. We have a picture I'm going to show you. Tell me what you know about it." Ashley handed the photograph to Malinowski.

"Don't tell 'em nothin," Cassidy growled.

Ramirez slapped him on the bald head. "Shut up."

Malinowski looked at the picture and started to cry again. He dropped the photograph on the floor and buried his face in both hands. Overwhelmed he sobbed, hardly able to breathe. "No," he wailed, rocking back and forth. "No."

Ashley put a hand on his shoulder. "Barry, what's the matter. Do you know something we should know?"

In a high-pitched voice he screamed. "That's my brother!"

# TWENTY

TELLING SOMEONE THEIR PET is a victim of a hit and run is a distasteful chore. Telling them their friend or loved one is dead is far worse, but that's what police officers have to do. Ashley faced this situation twice in her law enforcement career and knew it could be handled only one way. Just say it straight out, and wait for the reaction. That's what she did.

"Barry, based on your identification of the rose tattoo we must inform you your brother is dead. We found him buried in the desert. We are investigating his homicide."

Shock, followed by denial leading to overwhelming sorrow registered on Barry Malinowski's face. The sound of anguished sobbing filled the shabby living room of the remote Mayhill house. Moved by his friend's emotion, Butch Cassidy got up, stood next to him, and placed a hand on his shoulder. Agents Kohen and Ramirez stepped into the shadows of the room, and waited.

After a proper length of time, Ashley approached Barry and set about convincing him, and Cassidy, that they needed to go with them to Roswell. Her gut instinct told her she would get better results if she asked questions on neutral ground away from Barry's psychological haven in the mountains. She also suspected that Barry's primary support came from Cassidy, who should stay nearby.

In a calm reassuring voice, Ashley addressed Butch. "This is a difficult situation. It's better for Barry if we go to our office in Roswell where I have access to agency support. We need to make it as easy as possible for him. Agent Ramirez will arrange for you and Barry to stay at the Holiday Inn." Cassidy nodded as if he realized the gravity of the unfolding events. "Please take your friend and follow us in your pickup truck."

He agreed without hesitation. "Yes, ma'am. I'll take care of him."

Ramirez drove a moderate speed back to Roswell. He appeared agitated. "Finally we have a chance to make some headway in the Mummy

Case. When we interrogate this little guy its good cop, bad cop." He shrugged his shoulders. "I'll be the bad cop, of course."

Ashley tightened her expression, but didn't respond.

"That Holiday Inn offer was a smart move," he grinned broadly, "and we'll only have to pay for one room."

Ashley held back as long as she possible, but that last remark pushed her over the edge. "A few days ago you agreed this is my case. That you would not pull rank, even though you are way up the food chain from me. You gave me your word."

Ramirez frowned, "That's right."

"I know when a Special Agent gives his word, especially a veteran agent, it's as if Moses delivered the ten-commandments. You can take it as truth. It's as good as an oath in a court of law."

"What are you getting at?"

"What I'm getting at is that Barry Malinowski is not a perpetrator, not a suspect, not a person of interest, not a witness to a crime, and not under arrest. At best he may be a victim of a sad and useless killing." She took a breath. "My second point is that he will not be interrogated. He will be interviewed. Point three, we will not play good cop bad cop or any other stupid game."

Ramirez gripped the steering wheel.

"Barry will be treated with respect. That's the only approach that will give us accurate and reliable information. I will work with him while you watch over Cassidy. Barry must not be intimidated. He needs support." Easing off a bit, she concluded, "Finally, unless they request something different, we will reserve two rooms at the Holiday Inn."

Ramirez stared at the road ahead and said nothing.

They cleared security at the front door of the Federal Building in Roswell, and climbed the stairs to the second floor. The FBI's satellite office had three rooms all painted a pale green: a reception area, an office for the rotating Special Agent assigned, and a small interrogation room with a one way glass window. Barry sat in this room with bent shoulders and head down. Ashley, her back to the one-way window, placed a small audio recorder on the table between them. "I want to thank you for this chance to ask you questions, Barry. I know this is not easy for you. Our conversation will be recorded."

Barry looked up with red rimmed eyes and didn't speak.

"Would you like a cup of coffee or a cold drink?"

"No, ma'am."

She remained silent for a moment. "Today we need to do two things. We need to identify your brother and confirm that he is the victim in the case we are investigating. Only then can we begin to catch the person who did this terrible thing."

"Okay, whatever you say."

"Describe your brother, please. What did he look like?"

"He's bigger than me. About five foot three inches tall. Brown hair. Kind a skinny. About hundred pounds."

"Any special markings or scars?"

"Yes. That tattoo you showed me and a small birthmark."

Ashley wrote on a notepad. "Describe the birthmark and its location."

"Little purple mole high on his right shoulder. He keeps it covered cause it's ugly." Barry choked as he added, "He always wears a nice smile, too."

Ashley noted Barry referred to his brother in the present tense. "I'm sure he did. Do you know his birth date?"

"He's a year older than me. Born on December 3rd." Barry stiffened. "Where is he?"

"Where is he?"

"Yes, my brother. Where do you have him?

"By State Law unclaimed victims are retained by the Medical Investigator for six months. He's in Albuquerque."

"Can I see him?"

"Yes, but first we have to establish identity." She didn't say that John Doe 136 would be unrecognizable. "Tell me your brother's name."

"Can Butch come in here?'

"Butch is right outside with Agent Ramirez. It's better if you and I speak alone. I want you to feel free to talk to me. Anything you say is confidential. Your brother's name, please?"

"Bitty."

"Bitty Malinowski?"

"No, his real name is Russell Smith, he got the name Bitty because he is kind a small, like me."

"Why did he have a different last name?"

Barry bowed down and started to cry, again. He held onto the table for support.

"Take your time, Barry."

Head still down, and in that effeminate voice, he started. "It was me, Bitty and Faye. Bitty is the oldest. My sister Faye is a year younger than me. We were in Child Protective Services back then. I don't know anything that happened before that. I don't remember a Mom or anything. I only know what they told me. We was real young."

"How young, Barry?"

"Like three years old. The Malinowski family adopted me. They was wonderful. Bitty wasn't so lucky. He just moved around from one foster home to another. Faye, too." Barry's expression hardened. "I lost track of him for a long time. Then he showed up a couple of years ago. We got to be good friends.

"Was he married?"

"No. Only Faye got married. She's a nurse down in Carlsbad, where the big cave is."

"Do you have an address for Faye?"

"Yes, I got it in my wallet."

"Barry, I will be contacting your sister in the next couple of days. You have to decide how best to handle this. I mean about telling her."

Barry straightened himself in the chair. "I'm the older brother now. She needs to hear it from me. I'll call her."

Ashley sensed a strength in Barry that surprised her. He would need that strength in the days ahead. "I think that's best. Do you have an address for Bitty?"

"I don't know for sure, but Faye knows. She stays in touch better than me."

"Why don't you know where Bitty lived, if you were good friends with your brother?"

Barry glanced off in the distance. "Bitty was different from me. He had boyfriends." He turned back to Ashley. "Just boyfriends. After he grew up he moved around a lot. But he was my brother and I loved him." He choked and his eyes reddened again. He asked, "Why would anybody want to kill Bitty? He never hurt nobody."

Ashley watched Barry struggle with that question. She pushed her emotions aside so she could stay focused. "That's what I'm here for, Barry. To answer that question and more, much more."

MARK RAMIREZ listened to the interview on the office intercom while he watched though the interrogation room window. Ashley was handling

90

this with skill. His more direct approach would probably not have achieved the same results. He made a mental list of things to do: (1) ask Cassidy and Malinowski to not leave the area without notifying them first, (2) caution them to talk to no one about this case, (3) have them contact Agent Kohen if they remembered anything that might be important for the agency to know, and (4) have a transcript of the audio recording typed and forwarded to the field office. Walter Kent would assign it to a staff analyst right away.

He opened the telephone book and found the number of the Holiday Inn. "I'd like to make a reservation for tonight. I want two of your best rooms, each with a King sized bed."

Ramirez knew tomorrow they would begin to put together the pieces of the Bitty Smith puzzle. A puzzle that would need many answers. He could not know that the answers would lead to a conspiracy that could potentially change the lives of untold thousands of people.

# TWENTY-ONE

IN THE AGENCY PECKING ORDER, an Assistant Deputy Director is near the top. For someone in that position getting an audience with the director of the FBI requires little more than making an informal request. As the newly appointed head of the Joint Terrorism Task Force Division (JTTF), Mike Johansson belonged to that inner circle.

"Since it's your first day on-the-job Rashid, I've made an appointment to introduce you to Director Delong," said Mike. He and Rashid hurried down the corridor to the director's office. "The President appointed him last year. He got a narrow approval by the Senate, but that's politics. He's a good man."

They waited only a few minutes before entering the office. Delong set aside a report he was reading. "Have a seat gentlemen." He pointing to two leather chairs in front of his glass topped desk. FBI Director Edward Delong didn't look like the polished well-groomed government official people expected to see heading a high profile agency. His disorderly brown hair matched his wool sport coat with a frayed lining that hung an inch below the bottom of the jacket. A well chewed cigar he never lit, jutted from the corner of his mouth. "Good to see you, Mike. How's your task force shaping up?"

"We're making rapid progress, Ed. I've started to assemble counterterrorist teams, and I'm currently interviewing lead investigators for each unit." Mike remained standing as did Rashid. "Today, I want you to meet Doctor Rashid al Youris. He will serve as our agency ambassador over at Homeland Security." Rashid extended his arm and shook the director's hand.

Delong held Rashid's hand in a powerful grip. "I read your resume. Impressive. How long have you worked in the private sector?"

"About five years, sir. I'm on leave from McClellen University now"

"Five years." Delong eyeballed Mike Johansson. "Have you checked his security clearance status, Mike?"

"Not a problem, Ed. Rashid and I go way back. I will vouch for him. He is the most trustworthy guy I know."

The Director released Rashid's hand and continued to inspect him. "Agency Ambassador is a sensitive and vital position, Doctor Youris. Interagency communication or a lack of it, affects our capacity to fight terror both in America and abroad."

"Yes, sir. I'm aware of that. I plan to make sure the flow of information from the intelligence community moves freely, into and out of the FBI."

Ed Delong shifted his attention back to Mike. "If there's anything you need, let me know. I'm in complete support of this mission." He moved the cigar to the other side of his mouth. "As for you, Doctor Youris, you have an opportunity to make a difference in this war on terror." He clamped down on the cigar. "Good luck."

"Yes, sir. I plan to work hard."

As soon as Johansson and Youris thanked the Director for his time, and left the office, Edward Delong ordered a security clearance investigation on Rashid al Youris.

# TWENTY-TWO

COMPARED TO THE MISERABLE ATLANTIC crossing before his meeting with Caliph Abd al-Ghayb, Abdullah experienced a comfortable, almost pleasant return home aboard an Air France Boeing 767. The flight gave him an opportunity to relax and consider how much his life had changed in twenty four hours. Never did he think he would meet the Caliph in person, a much-revered holy man or sit before him and counsel with him. How proud his father would be to learn of this honor bestowed on his son. An honor he may never know, at least while Abdullah lived.

Seated by a window, he stared down on an expanse of white clouds that extended to the horizon. Yes, I am the son of a Prince in my country, but that is inconsequential compared to the status of a Caliph, a successor of the Prophet Muhammad; an Imam, not of a mosque, but of a world nation of believers. Through the authority of the Caliph, Allah the Magnificent has blessed me, and has chosen me to do His will. Why would He place a nuclear weapon into my hands if He did not intend for me to use it to glorify Him? I am meant to be His servant–His sword. These thoughts excited him.

After his meeting with the Caliph, Sheik Hadid Ghamadi had taken Abdullah aside and shared details of their plan, starting with the nuclear device. He explained. "The nuclear weapon, referred to as a Suitcase Nuke, originated in the Soviet Union. There were over 250 of these tactical weapons made, each weighing less than sixty pounds. More than a hundred mini-nukes disappeared from the Soviet arsenal after the political dissolution of that country. A cartel of international arms dealers acquired a dozen of the bombs and have kept them in storage under radiation containment for sale. Russia claims none of this is true, but clearly they do exist, because the Society of Rule by Sharia Law bought one." Sheik Ghamadi didn't reveal the cost, only that the purchase came with a team of nuclear experts who would supervise its handling.

He continued. "The next step is in your hands. You will research a suitable target. Your goal is to maximize the effect of this weapon on the Americans. Only then will the western infidels heed the might of our jihad."

Abdullah learned the Society continued to work on details concerned with the transport and storage of the bomb, and that they would keep him informed of their progress. Sheik Ghamadi told him the Caliph would set aside any amount of money needed to carry out the mission, no matter how large the sum. "Your actions should be deliberate," he said, "and you must take whatever time necessary to be successful, but not a minute longer."

AFTER ARRIVING IN Mexico City, Abdullah learned he would return to El Paso on a chartered flight, arranged by Rome. A few thousand pesos here, and a few more there, smoothed his way back home–evidence that his importance had grown.

He got his old truck in El Paso and drove back to his place in Maljamar. The dumpy little house in the middle of the bleak desert depressed him, and because of his newly defined mission, it no longer served his needs. At first, his remote location in an almost nonexistent town gave him time to adjust to his new surroundings in America. It helped him to learn how to navigate from rural to urban settings and assume his new identity. Conditions were different now. He couldn't waste his time driving to town to find a connection to the Internet. He must stay in constant touch with Rome and remain anonymous. With unlimited funds at his disposal, Abdullah was free to make changes.

Every time he ventured out of his desert hiding place he noticed many Americans drove recreational vehicles. Most interesting were the big motor homes common in America. RV parks with hookups were everywhere. Abdullah decided to buy a motor home and tow a car. He would become an American nomad, live well, be mobile and have no permanent address.

Before he carried out this plan there were annoying details to handle. He must contact Bashir in El Paso and arrange the transfer of money through the Hawala system: a global money handling institution based on generations of honor, and no written records. Moving a few thousand dollars would go unnoticed, but a few hundred thousand in cash needed special arrangements.

Bitty Smith, who had lived a life of poverty, should not become wealthy overnight. That would draw attention to a sexually challenged little loser. Abdullah remembered Sheik Ghamadi had suggested he setup a small private company to receive items for storage. He realized that a company could also serve as a repository for money transfers.

Abdullah set about creating Smith Trading Company, specializing in international imports and exports. The new enterprise would have a bank account that could receive deposits and make purchases in the name of the company. His plan included leasing office space in Roswell and hiring a mail forwarding service to transfer funds and link him to the outside world.

Abdullah decided to pay rent on the bleak little place in Maljamar and keep it as a backup location in the event he might need it later. He would store the old truck in the shed behind the house. The title transfer of the truck from Allen Lee, his original false identity, to Russell Smith would need a Bill of Sale–easy enough to do. He sold Bitty's 1969 VW Bug on Craigslist for a few hundred dollars.

All these preparations, the transfer of funds, creation of a company, and his withdrawal from Maljamar were necessary but served as a nagging distraction from his real job of searching for a suitable target and making plans to carry out his mission. Although he felt frustration, Abdullah knew he must proceed with caution. He must remember, no matter how friendly and accommodating the Americans might be, they remained his enemy. They were common people led by wicked evildoers bent on destroying his dream of an Islamic world. Their domination by Sharia rule would be their salvation. And he would become their agent of change–their savior.

# TWENTY-THREE

FAYE ORR, AN EMERGENCY ROOM nurse, dealt with tragedy every day. Over the years she had learned to insulate herself from emotional involvement and concentrate on doing her job as a medical professional. That changed when her brother called to tell her Bitty Smith was dead.

"Bitty? Dead?" she asked before she grasped the full meaning of the words. "What do you mean, Barry?" An ache welled up in her throat as she listened to her brother explain what he knew. With a quiver in his voice he said, "Two people from the FBI wants to help us. They need to talk to you."

"The FBI?"

"Yes. I told them you'd give 'em the information they need."

ASHLEY TURNED INTO the Carlsbad hospital parking lot on West Medical Center Drive with Ramirez next to her. She spotted the Senior Circle sign in front of a converted single family house next to the main hospital building. "Carlsbad Medical Center is a corporation," she explained to Ramirez. "They sponsor organizations like this as a community service. It's only a short distance from where Barry's sister works. Faye Orr thought it would be a good place to meet."

They parked and entered the building. A gray haired woman sitting at a desk greeted them. "Good morning, would you like to register?" She pointed to an open book with names and addresses neatly written on each page.

Ashley noted the woman's hand trembled a bit. "We're here to see Faye Orr. Has she arrived?"

"Why, yes. She's in the conference room in the back."

"Thank you. My friend will sign us in. Down the hall?"

"Yes, straight back and to the left."

The conference room, decorated with photographs of former Senior Circle members, had chairs for eight people. Faye Orr sat in the back corner, her hands on the table clasped in front of her. She had well-groomed brown hair and wore a solemn expression. Ashley went to her side. "Hello, Faye Orr?"

"Yes," she said, surprised at seeing a young woman holding a gold badge.

"My name is Ashley Kohen. I'm with the FBI. My partner, Agent Ramirez, will join us in a moment."

"Barry told me you wanted to ask some questions."

Ashley spoke in a quiet voice. "I'm sorry for your loss, Mrs. Orr."

"Thank you."

"I know this is a difficult time for you. We need to know more about your brother, Russell Smith. This won't take long." Ramirez joined Ashley and they sat across the table from Faye.

Ashley began. "Barry said you were in close contact with your brother."

"I try to stay in touch."

"Do you know if your brother had any enemies that might want to hurt him?"

"Enemies? Oh no. Bitty kept to himself."

"When was the last time you saw Russell?"

"About two months ago. I helped him move into a little apartment in Roswell."

"How did he act? Was he happy?"

"I guess so. He had a job working at the college. Eastern New Mexico University on the south side. Close to where he lived."

"What did he do at the college?"

"He worked in maintenance."

"And you haven't seen him since he moved?"

"That's right, but I called him most every week. I called about two weeks ago. After that his phone was disconnected."

"What did you think about that?"

"Bitty moved around a lot. I figured he would get back to me when he could." Faye looked off to the side and tears welled up. "I guess he can't do that now."

Ashley touched Faye's hands. "The last time you talked, did he say anything unusual?"

Faye wiping away her tears. "No. He said he had a new friend. A reporter or writer or something who showed an interest in him. Asked a lot of questions about his past life in foster care and all."

"Questions about his life?"

"Yes. Said his friend was beautiful. Bitty talked like that."

"Did he tell you anything else about this man?"

"No."

"Do you have Bitty's address in Roswell?"

"I have it. Barry mentioned you might ask. I wrote it down with his phone number." She hesitated, then reached into her pocket. "Here's a picture of Bitty you can have. He was a sweet boy, I loved him."

THE EASTERN NEW MEXICO University, near the Regional Airport on the south side of Roswell, occupied modern buildings and offered both Bachelor and Master degree programs. With a campus map from the Chamber of Commerce, Ashley located the Office of Human Resources on the campus. She asked the receptionist if they might meet with the head of the department. "Of course. Dean Alice Black is in her office. I'll check to see if she's free."

Dean Black appeared remarkably young. "I'm not often visited by the FBI. Please have a seat. How can I help you?"

After introductions, Ramirez led off. "We are conducting an inquiry about a Mr. Russell Smith. We understand Mr. Smith worked here."

Dean Black wore a mystified expression. "Russell Smith?"

"Yes. Here's a picture of Mr. Smith."

"Oh yes. Bitty Smith. Everyone called him Bitty. He worked in the maintenance unit. I'm afraid he is no longer with us. He quit a few weeks ago."

"We need to see his personnel file."

Alice Black paused a moment. "I'm sorry, but those files are confidential."

Ashley leaned forward. "I understand, but our investigation concerns a serious crime."

"Oh my. What did Bitty do?"

"Mr. Smith was the victim of a serious crime. We are searching for a perpetrator. We need your help in this matter. You understand?"

"Well, yes, but university policy..."

Ramirez interrupted. "I can get a court order, Ms. Black. If that's necessary."

Dean Black stepped over to the window and watched students hurrying by on their way to class. "I'm sorry to hear about Bitty. I'll need to make a copy of your identification before I can release those files to you."

"Not a problem," Ashley said, "A copy of everything in the file, please. We'll wait."

# TWENTY-FOUR

AS THE FIRST AGENCY AMBASSADOR appointed by the FBI, Rashid al Youris understood the primary thrust of the job. It consisted of sifting through terrorist related data recovered by the fifteen intelligence agencies who report to the Director of National Security. As a member of the newly formed Terrorism Threat and Investigation Center (T-TIC), he began arranging interviews within the intelligence community.

The National Security Agency (NSA) topped his list of important contacts. After repeated tries, Rashid arranged a joint meeting with Admiral Henry Smithy, Director of NSA, and Norman Miller, head of their Signal Intelligence Unit in McLean, Virginia. To save time, Miller met Rashid at the NSA's Security Entrance and escorted him upstairs.

The Admiral had decorated his spacious quarters with naval artwork depicting vintage ships from both world wars and the most technologically advanced vessels in today's navy.

"Good morning, Doctor Youris. Come in and have a seat," said Admiral Smithy, a broad shouldered man with short cropped gray hair and a chest full of colorful ribbons and awards. "I see you have already met Norman Miller my chief of cryptology. He, like yourself, will serve as our Agency Ambassador to T-TIC." Rashid greeted each man with a cordial handshake.

Smithy settled behind his desk and held a steady, but uncertain smile. "My assistant tells me Homeland Security is behind this creation of yet another layer of bureaucracy. Do you agree?"

"On the contrary, while T-TIC is an added cog in the machinery of government, I consider it more like a lubricant designed to smooth agency liaison." Rashid laid his letter of introduction from Director Ed Delong on the admiral's desk.

Norman Miller twisted the corners of his luxurious mustache and stifled a laugh, "I can tell you are not new to Federal service, Doctor Youris."

"I'm retired with thirty years with the FBI. I've volunteered to help in this initiative because I think it is worthwhile."

The Admiral finished reading the letter. "So we will pass along our findings to T-TIC who will share it with the rest of the intelligence community. How is that different from what I'm already doing?"

Rashid expected that question. "Homeland Security built their in-house Agency Council to track their five point mission which includes: natural disasters, policing cyberspace, immigration law, border security, and terrorism prevention. T-TIC deals specifically with terrorism. It streamlines the antiterrorism program."

Norman Miller interjected, "This supports the government's continued emphasis on terror prevention."

"Exactly, and among all the intelligence agencies I feel NSA's database is most effective in uncovering potential threats to America."

Miller gave his mustache an extra twist. "That's why we exist, Doctor Youris."

Rashid edged forward. "To save your time, I have a few questions for both of you."

"Sure. Fire away," said Admiral Smithy. "Depending on the nature of the questions, I'll answer them."

"Tell me how you isolate terror related information."

Norman Miller straightened. "We intercept 1.7 billion information exchanges every day. Much of that is origin and destination patterns. Certain patterns will trigger closer examination needing review and approval."

"By review and approval, you're referring to the Foreign Intelligence Surveillance Act–FISA?"

"Yes. Emails, phone calls, faxed material, every form of communication is fair game. Without getting too technical, we have a series of multilingual filters using keywords and phrases coupled with geographic markers that allow us to classify information in digital form."

Rashid glanced at the celling. "I'm glad you're not getting too technical, Norman."

"Only a tiny portion of this information deals with national security, and most of that is ready to read."

"By that you mean it's not coded?"

"That's right. The stuff we can't read is the encrypted data. That's where we find the best intelligence and that's when the Signal Intel Unit goes to work–my people."

"How do you deal with encryption?"

"It's analyzed with mathematical algorithms that decode most of these information exchanges without staff intervention. Human eyes review advanced encryptions. Most of the time our experts can decipher, in a few hours, days or weeks these coded items."

"How big a staff do you have to deal with the hands-on decoding?"

"That's classified, but it's enough."

"Okay, what percent of communications can't be decoded by your experts?"

Miller shifted his weight. "Excluding cell phone encryption, most communications we can handle. There are a few we can't. I call those our coconuts because they are hard to crack. I don't think of them as a percentage. It's too small a number."

"How small?"

Admiral Smithy, frowned. "The number is small. That's all you need to know, Doctor Youris."

Rashid turned toward the Admiral. "What I know is that if someone has taken the time and expense to devise a code you can't break, it's for a reason. Those information exchanges are the most dangerous to national security."

Miller agreed. "That's why we employ the best and brightest mathematicians in the world."

"Of course you do." Rashid let a moment pass. "I'm not an expert in cryptography, but I have worked with smart people in the past. I've been able to supplement their work resulting in significant success."

Shaking his head, Admiral asked Rashid to explain.

"I've lived and worked in the Middle East most of my life. I know the culture, the religion and the languages of those people. I know how they think. My knowledge can't be reduced to a mathematical equation. It can, however, complement your skills and get results no logarithm can calculate."

Norman Miller faced the Admiral and nodded his head. "There might be merit in that approach."

Smithy said. "Give me an example of where you achieved a significant success."

"That's easy. During my assignment in Pakistan, our team intercepted encrypted messages flowing between the FIA, Pakistan's equivalent to the NSA, and the Ministry of Intelligence in Iran. Our Cryptology Section in Washington failed to break the code nor could the CIA. The code used a variation of the One-Time-Pad encryption. Both agencies asked that I lend a hand."

"If written correctly, the OTP is damn near impossible to break," the Admiral said.

"Yes, that's right. The author of the Iranian-Pakistan code selected a secret random key. He used the Quran, the Muslim holy book as the basis for the key. That was the first source I urged the analyst to examine. Using the best techniques available, we discovered that the key used the first letter of each of the 114 chapters of the Quran. We broke the code and the world soon learned Iran had made a deal to buy advanced plans to refine weapons-grade plutonium."

The Director leaned back in his chair and nodded his head. "Remarkable. A marriage of science and sociology. I have the feeling you are about to make a proposal."

"With your permission, sir, and the backing of Mr. Miller's staff, I would like to work on those coconuts in my spare time."

The Admiral looked over at Norman Miller, who gave his mustache another twist and winked his approval. Miller turned to Doctor Youris, "You understand nothing leaves this office. We will monitor your work and you will undergo a security search when you enter and leave this facility."

"Of course."

Miller continued, "There will be a trial period of one month. Your agency, the FBI, must approve this experiment in advance–in writing. You cannot reveal anything you learn at NSA outside our approved network.

A flush if excitement swept through Rashid. "I understand. How many coconuts?"

With a shrug of his shoulders Miller answered. "Six, all originate in central Europe."

"Good," Rashid stood. "I'll start the paperwork this afternoon. Thank you for your time, cooperation and trust gentlemen. You won't be disappointed."

Rashid returned to FBI Headquarters with one thought in mind: mission accomplished.

# TWENTY-FIVE

ABDULLAH RECLINED ON THE king-sized bed in the rear of his new diesel powered Class A motor home. Hands clasped behind his head, he stared at the ceiling, lost in thought. He daydreamed about the influence of his mission on Islam. If successful, it would make him a figure of celebrated importance in the Muslin world. Even if he lived, people would speak of him with reverence and respect. The name of Abdullah al-Jamal would forever be a part of his people's history. All true believers would talk about his accomplishment on holy days throughout the Arab world. Future generations would remember the man who cast aside the enemies of Islam, and advanced the spread of Sharia influence in the western world. To rid his people of the malignant influence of the United States and its allies, he must kill many Americans.

The sound of a pickup truck next to his campsite bought him back to reality. The driver gunned his engine as he positioned his rig for utility hookups.

Abdullah, rose from his bed and headed to a makeshift office in the forward living area of his 45-foot home on wheels. At this point in Abdullah's research, he knew if he planned with skill and dedication he could kill thousands of Americans. His nuclear device, while small in weight and size, could produce the explosive energy of six kilotons.

He imagined the size of a single kiloton which is a thousand metric tons of TNT. If he loaded a five ton truck with TNT, he would need 200 trucks to move one kiloton. His bomb was six times that number. To equal the energy of his device he would need 1,200 truckloads of TNT.

Abdullah Googled World War II online. The size of the atomic bombs used on Hiroshima and Nagasaki were sixteen to twenty-one kilotons. He viewed pictures of the aftermath of those cities showing massive damage and loss of life. Although a third of the size of those bombs, his nuclear device, located in the right place at the right time, would inflict enormous destruction.

He set five goals for himself. He must take full advantage of his weapon's power, place it where many people congregate in a small space, hide it, and be able to detonate it remotely at the perfect time.

Abdullah started his search for a suitable target by making a list of places where large numbers of people gathered. He first thought of a church or a revival tent, but dismissed this idea. People might think it was a strike against a particular religion. That would be misleading. His second idea to bomb a political convention or large rally also might be misinterpreted as an attack on a specific political party.

An ideal target would be a dissimilar grouping of Americans. An assembly representing a cross section of this bloated capitalistic society. One that contained a mix of whites, blacks, Asians, Native Americans—people of all ethnic groups, both men and women. He favored mature adults—the most productive members of the population. Abdullah excluded children because American society had not yet tainted them. They were young enough to learn the duties and penalties of Islam as contained in the Quran. He thought of his six-year-old brother still in the age of innocence and with a future as a Prince of Saudi Arabia. Children must be spared. Even children of infidels.

Abdullah heard something hit the side of his motor home with a dull thud, followed by sounds of laughter and shouting. He opened the door. Two young boys jumped back startled, one holding a basketball. The other boy said, "Sorry, Mister," and then both ran off. No discipline. Then it struck him. A sporting event. Yes, that's where Americans go in great numbers. Some type of ball game might fit his criteria.

He settled in front of his computer with new excitement, and searched for 'games of ball'. Baseball, basketball, billiard, football, ping-pong, soccer, and tennis appeared on the screen. Making a list, he had to decide which event would best serve his needs.

Immediately he crossed off ping-pong and billiards. Both played indoors to small audiences. Soccer held limited national interest in America, so he checked that off, too. Since professional basketball is played in a covered building with maybe five to ten thousand fans at professional events he eliminated that sport.

Outdoor sports held the greatest potential. Tennis attracts a few thousand people to major events. Abdullah marked this off the list due to attendance numbers. Major league baseball, the American pastime, is played outside to larger crowds of ten thousand or more fans seated on two or three sides of a playing field. He marked baseball as worthy of consideration.

He then turned his attention to football. For some reason Americans were obsessed with this brutal game of young men smashing into one another with a ball pointed at two ends. Always played outdoors, it attracted large crowds who surround the game on all sides. It is attended by mostly young to middle-aged adults with few or no children. He decided football would meet his criteria.

An online search resulted in a long list of large stadiums around the country. The professional teams played in their own well financed facilities. Abdullah considered the Super Bowl, but scratched that off because of the heavy security such an event attracts. After further study he decided the NFL teams presented too many security risks. That left college football.

The University of Michigan had the largest stadium in America with a capacity of 110,000 seats. Fans usually filled eighty percent of the stadium. Every seat filled when Michigan played Ohio State University. Abdullah went to the Goodyear Blimp site and viewed the huge crowds photographed by this famous airship. As he stared at the photographs of people crowded close together, devoting their attention to a central point of interest, it looked familiar to him. Where had he seen such a crowd before? A crowd of tiny specks that sparkled like a kaleidoscope of many shapes and hues. Where?

Then it came to him. The week of Hajj, the Islamic pilgrimage to Mecca. The largest pilgrimage in the world attracting two million worshipers each year. A journey of faith required of all able bodied Muslims at least once in their lifetime.

As a young man his father, Prince al Jamal took him to western Saudi Arabia's holiest city, the birthplace of the Prophet Mohammad. Because of his father's membership in the Royal Family, Abdullah sat high above the marble floors of the Great Mosque viewing a hundred thousand dedicated believers. A massive congregation of men and women conducted the rituals of faith–all standing, kneeling and bowing shoulder to shoulder. This image remained unforgettable in his memory. From his position high up, the multitude blended into a human sea of devotion. No one individual distinct.

The masses of people in the football stadium in Michigan and the assembly in the Great Mosque in Mecca, looked the same. Abdullah did not want to admit the similarity. "They are not the same!" he shouted aloud, slapping his hand on the table. But the resemblance was inescapable, and he could not ignore that fact.

Okay, he thought, but they are not alike. They are people, but not the same people. My people believe in Allah the Almighty, the one true God. These people believe in many Gods. Some believe in no God, only power and money. He viewed the image of the Michigan stadium. These are Americans. They pay taxes to their government and elect leaders who defile my faith. They support killing innocent Muslim men and women in the name of democracy and their vision of freedom. He again looked at the photograph. Many beliefs? Could there be Muslims in this stadium or innocent visitors from other counties—my homeland?

He deleted the Michigan photograph and the list of college stadiums reappeared on his computer screen. He stared at the capacities of 125 stadiums found around the country, and forced himself to calm down. I must kill many Americans to make a statement, but I do not have to kill the maximum number possible to achieve my goal.

He searched the listings again, this time steering away from large cities where he knew mosques existed. Finally he selected the Aggie Memorial Stadium in Las Cruces, New Mexico. Only a few hours from Roswell, near the border with Mexico, and no mosques listed in the area. A low risk target with minimum or no security concerns. Las Cruces, the City of Crosses, a relatively small urban center with a stadium capacity 30,343. Ten times the number killed on 9-11. He had found the perfect target. Allah the Avenger be praised.

# TWENTY-SIX

"LISTEN UP, EVERYBODY. We have work to do this morning." Walter Kent sat at an oak table centered in the main conference room of the Albuquerque Field Office. Agents Kohen and Ramirez, flanked by Dorothy Hogan and Lead Analyst Bill Johnson, faced him. Other agents with active cases occupied chairs around the table. They contributed to a subtle humidity in the air. Heavy drapes at each window blocked the summer sun.

"We have a dozen items to review this morning." Kent read from a roster of cases. "First is Case Number NM-1056." He dipped his head and turned to Ashley. "You have assembled your team, Agent Kohan, what can you tell us?"

"Thank you Mr. Kent." Ashley stood. "This case is starting to shape up. I and my partner, Agent Ramirez, working with Staff Analyst Bill Johnson, have made good progress in a short period of time."

Ramirez interrupted. "The Mummy Case."

Ashley made a face, then continued. "This is a murder case that involves a male victim found buried in the desert south of Roswell. The killer tried to make identification of the victim difficult: a calculated act by the un-sub–the unknown subject. As a result of a post mortem study we discovered a unique body marking. Using a photograph of this marking we have identified the victim. His name was Russell Smith. "We have Smith's former address, place of work, his Social Security number and insights into his life until his death two weeks ago. We also found the victim's brother and sister. Both are cooperating in this investigation."

Ramirez still seated, exclaimed, "Piece of cake."

"At the crime scene it was discovered the burial of the victim by the killer followed ceremonial rituals associated with a Middle Eastern religion. A terrorist link is possible."

"Ramirez again interrupted, "We don't have any proof of that yet."

Ashley's jawline hardened. Her expression softened when she turned toward Johnson. "You all know Bill is a former field agent with an impressive record and many commendations. He's been hard at work. What can you report today, Bill?" Ashley sat down.

Johnson, an elderly man with wavy white hair, giant eyeglasses, well-hidden hearing aids and bushy eyebrows remained seated. He viewed Ashley with a cheerful expression. "Thank you young lady. Based on the excellent legwork you and your partner over there have performed I can tell you quite a bit." He cut a glance at Ramirez, dropped the smile, and addressed the room. "Russell Smith, like everyone here, drove a car. I checked the New Mexico Department of Motor Vehicles, that agency we have all grown to love and adore, and found that Mr. Smith still lives." He thumped his cane on the floor three times.

Ramirez piped up, "What do you mean old man? He's as dead as a doornail."

"Well if he's a doornail he most certainly would be dead considering doornails are imamate objects." The room exploded into laughter. "Of course he's dead." Johnson glared at Ramirez, and then continued. "Someone assuming his identity traded a VW Bug on a luxury motor home that cost about a quarter of a million bucks and a 4-wheel drive SUV worth another 50K. DMV records show these transactions in detail."

Walter Kent took note. "Do you have an address of the *current* Russell Smith?"

"Yep, Number One, Boring Lane, Maljamar, New Mexico. Little place west of Lovington. There's nothing there but a bunch of pump jacks, a few houses, and a radio relay tower used by the Public Broadcasting System."

"Boring Lane?" Kent raised an eyebrow.

"The name kind a fits the place, don't you think?" Johnson peered at Kent over-the-top of his glasses. "There's more. Russell Smith also owns a 1979 Ford pickup truck recently transferred to his name from an Allen Lee, who has a New Mexico driver's license and the same address as the deceased. Very likely Allen Lee and Russell Smith are one and the same persons."

"That needs a follow up," said Ashley.

"I'm sure you will get on this like flies on..." He searched for an acceptable word. "...manure, my dear." Johnson appeared pleased with his word choice. "But I'm not finished." He flipped a few pages and began again. "The thumbprint discovered on the moleskin patch that covered the victim's wound doesn't match anything recorded in our database. INTERPOL can't get a match either." He paused. "The lock of black hair found in the body wrapping is awaiting DNA analysis. That will take months unless this case gets a top priority rating from Headquarters. Not likely." He eyed the attentive audience. "An analysis of photographic footprints at the site of the burial suggest the un-sub is around 180 pounds and six feet tall, give or take an inch. Background checks on Russell Smith's brother and sister reveal nothing unusual." Johnson slapped his hands together. "For now, that's about it folks."

Ashley again stood. "You've done a great job in a short time, Bill. I need descriptions and license plate numbers for all the vehicles."

"Right here, my dear." he said, holding a sheet of paper. Ashley thought he looked like Santa Claus without a beard. Cute and smart.

"Agent Kohen is right," agreed Kent. "You have done your usual good work, Bill." He turned to Dorothy Hogan. "I will issue an All-Points-Bulletin for the owner of these plates. I want the APB to read *Acquire Do Not Apprehend*. I want it sent to all local jurisdictions, the State Police and appropriate Federal agencies. If we don't make contact in a week, I'll broaden the distribution."

Ramirez jumped up, "Wait a minute. We have this guy by the short and curlies. He lives close to the burial site, he has assumed the victim's name, and stolen his car. We may have a matching thumbprint. We should arrest him on the spot."

Ashley, already on her feet, "We don't know what he's up to, and can only speculate on the danger he poses. We don't have enough proof for an indictment."

Both agents glared at each other.

Kent shook his head in disgust. "Okay. Enough. Sit down both of you." He scratched a note to himself: *Review pairing of Kohen and Ramirez.*

A moment of silence lingered in the room before he spoke. "Based on what we know, it's my judgment that making a move on the un-sub this early in the investigation would be premature. Here's why. First, stealing the victim's identity may *not* be the killer's only purpose for the murder, since the victim didn't have anything else of value to steal. To what use could this stolen identity be put? I need to know the answer to that question. Second, there are Islamic practices linked to facets of this case. The Muslim faith is not practiced in the general area where the crime occurred.

I have to wonder if the un-sub is using this identity as cover, while planning an act of terror. I want to rule out a threat to national security, not leave this question unresolved. The best way to do that is to let this person show us what he is up to. Placing him in custody and using interrogation techniques to find out his mission is a less reliable alternative." Kent glanced over at Ramirez. "Third, where in the hell did this un-sub get close to 300,000 dollars to buy a top of the line RV and car, and why does he need them?"

Ashley surveyed the room and surmised by the body language the audience approved of their boss's logic.

"To sum up. Once we find him, and we will find him, I'll put him under twenty-four hour surveillance while this investigation continues."

"I agree. That's the right thing to do." Ashley blurted, then covered her mouth as if to control herself. She cast a shy glance at Kent.

"I'm pleased you agree," Kent said with a good-natured wink.

For a moment, the room remained quiet, followed by an exchange of knowing looks. Dorothy Hogan bowed her head and smothered a giggle.

# TWENTY-SEVEN

BOREDOM SMOTHERED ABDULLAH'S daily existence. Since his return from Italy he received only two messages from Rome. The first complimented his resolve and promised swift progress. The second hinted at expected developments without details. Neither advanced his ability to act. He must act. His drive, his ambition, his purpose for living, needed to be set free. Instead he was condemned to sit with idle thoughts to fill his mind. When he answered these messages he tried to show restraint and respect, but feared frustration showed.

Many visits to the athletic stadium in Las Cruces had allowed him to compile much data. He gathered information on the physical structure and every possible access point to the facility. Abdullah endured two silly football games of boys crashing into one another while crowds cheered for no obvious reason. Based on this research, he had prepared plans for every possible contingency his imagination could create. He had worked out each detail and noted it in his Master Plan, written in Arabic and well hidden.

Careful investigation before the purchase of a motor home prompted him to buy the perfect vehicle for his purposes. Granted, it was a bit ostentatious with three slide outs, a diesel engine and advanced electronics, but still it had everything he needed to prepare for his mission. The selection of a four-wheel drive tow car, designed to be pulled without a dolly, and therefore quickly detached, had needed research, too.

With great care, Abdullah setup Smith Trading in Roswell. He found a remote 2,000 square foot vacant commercial space on the west side of town. Sandwiched between a vacuum cleaner repair shop and a small ice cream parlor, it became an almost invisible place. A sign reading *Smith Trading* in small letters and *Imports and Exports*, in smaller letters, hung over the glass door he had painted black. The adjacent single pane window he covered with light reflecting film that blocked any view inside.

Eager to carry out his plans, but unable to move forward without further direction from Rome, Abdullah grew more restless each day. He had too much time to think about the comforts of his former life at his father's palace in Dhahran where his every need and desire was attained with ease. Its many pleasures: swimming, games, feasting and women lingered in his memory. Oh yes, the women.

The servant girls were there to serve him at any time. He had his pick of them. His momentary urges were satisfied with a sharp command or a point of a finger. They served the purpose all women served; to meet the needs of a man, be it cleaning the bedroom or lying in its bed for the master's gratification.

But not in America. Women wore tight clothing to show off their bodies and tantalize men. They were allowed to go to school, work beside men and even dominate them. In this unholy place, with no shame, women took their status for granted. In the public media they were all but worshiped.

He tried to ignore the American way of life because it disgusted him. It caused him to cringe inside and yearn for the civilized culture of his homeland. The western world forced him to suffer the loss of the most basic privilege nature intended for men—control over women and sexual enjoyment. These thoughts and overpowering boredom led him to a necessary distraction. He had lured Bitty Smith to serve his purpose, he would now use those same skills to meet his personal and immediate needs.

Abdullah considered what kind of candidate he would select for this new conquest. Maybe a girl, young enough to be free of disease but old enough to be serviceable. Another choice might be a mature women with young children and no husband. Yes, a woman who had undergone medical examinations, given birth in a hospital, but still desirable. Easy enough to find considering the divorce rate in this pagan country.

Ah, finally, something to occupy his time as he waited to make world history.

# TWENTY-EIGHT

THE FIRST TIME, without an official escort, Rashid found the NSA's security inspection qualified as a serious invasion of privacy verging on sexual harassment. He expected the full body scan, endured an intensive pat down, complained about the need to strip some of his clothes off, rendering him damn near naked, and refused an invasion of his 'cavities'.

When the security official balked, Rashid fished his phone out of his pants, lost in a crumpled pile on the floor, and called Norman Miller, Chief of the Signal Intelligence Unit. Released five minutes later, he dressed and took the elevator to the fifth floor.

Like most Federal offices, that floor had five-foot high partitions sectioned off into small cubicles. Each contained a desk, chair, bookcase, computer, and a worker hunched in front of a glowing monitor.

"Sorry about that security check," Chief Miller said as Rashid entered his private office which had a door and a window, amenities reserved for executive status in Federal service. "Since this is your first time unescorted, security can get overly protective," Miller pointed to a chair in front of his desk. "Get comfortable, Doctor Youris."

Rashid decided not to comment on the security debacle. He sat.

Miller continued. "I'm pleased our two agencies agreed to this experiment. It will be interesting to see if you can help us crack a few coconuts and milk them." He grinned at his coconut milk joke and Rashid supported it with a nod. "I'm going to pair you with our top cryptologist, Isaac Gunner. He will fill you in on our operation. Mr. Gunner is your primary contact here in the Signal Intel Unit, as well as myself."

"That'll keep our liaison uncomplicated."

"Yes. We have enough complications in this business without creating new ones." Miller gave his mustache a quick brush with his finger and stood. "Follow me. Mr. Gunner has his own workspace separate from the other members of his team."

As Rashid walked beside Miller, he learned more about the Intel Unit. "Gunner is a cyber specialist. You might say he is our Top Gun," Miller's lips curled up at his aviation analogy. "He deals with our advanced decryption. I think you'll find him bright and colorful." They arrived at a metal door with a digital keypad. Miller swiped his ID card, and the lock clicked open. They entered.

The dimly lit room had no windows. It pulsed with blinking red, yellow and green LED lights. Rashid noticed the back of a huge man in an office chair. He heard him tapping furiously on a keyboard. The man stopped, twirled his chair around and faced them. Even in the lowlight, Rashid saw he had no legs.

"Doctor Youris, this is Chief Cryptologist Isaac Gunner."

Gunner broke into a cordial smile showing white teeth that contrasted against his black skin. "Heard about you, man." He raised a hand for a high-five. "Don't want to hear any of that Isaac crap. Call me Ike, Okay?"

Rashid high-fived him back. "Good to meet you, Ike."

"Excuse me if I don't get up," said Ike, with another grin. "Mr. Miller, here, told me all about you." He worked the lever on his electric scooter and zipped over to a leather chair with rollers, pulled it back next to his desk, and gestured to Rashid. "Have a seat right here."

Miller turned, "I'll leave you two. Don't work him too hard, Ike." He closed the door behind him. The lock snapped shut.

"So you a college professor?"

"Yes, Middle Eastern Studies, but I work for the FBI now."

"I'm gonna call you Prof, okay?"

"My name is Rashid, but you can call me Prof, if you want to."

"Good, I like it that way–nothin' fancy."

Rashid studied this big man. Above his waist he could be a center on any NFL football team. Still, he seemed content in his own skin. "Miller said you would brief me on the operation here."

"Yea, man. I can do that." Ike's expression grew serious. "We got a hell of a set-up here. I call it the big sieve." He flashed a smile, then continued. "We deal with billions of information exchanges from all kind a communication sources from around the world. Ain't possible to actually read 'em, so we screen 'em with filters and keywords."

"Miller touched on that before."

"Sure he did. Well everything gets run though our system or as I said, the big sieve. It's like a pyramid. On the bottom, ninety-nine percent of what we process is chitchat. Just folks a talking to each other. We see it as a bunch of contact points. We calls it metadata. But it's that one percent at the top of the pyramid what keep us busy. Most of those still get processed by the math wizards. Real smart guys and gals that have created code that sifts through all the known ways to screw up the meaning of somethin' on purpose so it don't make no sense. Well that catches most of it. When it gets to the ones the wiz-kids can't crack, they send 'em to me and my team. The coconuts. That's the tip-pity-top of the pyramid. They say, hey Ike, we can't crack these nuts. So I get my nutcrackers out and go to work."

"You practice your special skills?"

"That I do, man. Might take a while, but I git'er done–mostly. The ones I don't get...well that's why you is here, right, Prof?"

"I hope I can add a useful perspective. How many coconuts do you have and how old are they?"

"I only got six now, and they is real new. Oldest is less than a couple a weeks old. So far my software ain't hard enough to make a dent in 'em." He grinned. "Get that, Prof? Software...not hard?" He laughed and slapped the table.

Rashid marveled at the disparity between the simplicity of this man, and the sophistication of the environment he worked in. He noticed Ike looking at him and figured he was reading his thoughts.

"I bet you wonder what the likes of me is doin here?"

"I have the feeling I'm not the first person to wonder that."

"Happens all the time. Don't bother me none. I kind a like it," he laughed, again. "So let's get this outa the way right now. You might a noticed I got no legs. Kind a hard to miss. Afghanistan, that where I left 'em. Weren't my idea, but it happened. Got mustered out the army and had no job, so I learned computers. Kind a home schooled myself with help from some not so honest guys. Hacked into about anything that made me money. Shut down the power grid one time. Pissed everybody off. Got me caught and sent to jail. Then along comes this Admiral guy. Gave me a job soon as I got out a prison. He said he heard bout me and that I had a gift and should serve my country. Damn, I tried that once in the army and it didn't turn out so good, but I say okay. Now I'm makin a difference and a few honest bucks, too."

Rashid stared at Ike. After a long pause, he extended his hand. "That's a hell of a story." They high-fived again. Even though they were different people, Rashid knew he could work with this man.

Gunner explained the ground rules; the parameters that would limit the scope of their work. "We are searching for what the average person would call a password, except it's not a word or a combination of words. The math guys have ruled out those possibilities already. You might say it's a coded key. A key made up of unknown symbols in a unique sequence. That's a mouthful of marbles, ain't it Prof?"

Rashid nodded and shrugged his shoulders.

"By symbol, I mean any letter in all the modern languages on earth, every number or group of numbers in all numbering systems, and any picture image–hieroglyphics. We call it the *key-space universe*, and it's a big mother-fucker. Real big."

Rashid shifted in his chair. "That's almost an infinite number of combinations."

"You got it, Prof," Ike said as he made a wry face. "The tool we use to find this coded sequence is called a Brute Force Attack."

"A Brute Force Attack - sounds fearsome."

"The NSA has the most powerful super computer in the world. At least we don't know of one bigger. It's half a billion dollar baby. I call this contraption Big Mamma. We feed Mamma all the time, so she gets bigger and more powerful by the day. She can process a billion bits of data in a nanosecond. At that rate it would take her about 20,000 years to exhaust the *key-space universe* using Brute Force, our most advanced software tool.

"I don't think we have that much time."

"You got that right, Prof." Ike clasped his hands in front of him. "The NSA has a policy. Even Big Mamma has limits, when you think about the workload placed on her. If Brute Force can't break a code in two days, we terminate the search. That action creates an official coconut." Ike raised his shoulders, threw his hands into the air as if to say–so there you have it.

Rashid scratched his chin. "What's your gut tell you about these encryptions? Are they separate and unique or do you see similarities?"

"The only thing not unique about these coconuts is their style."

"Style?"

Ike's eyes lit up. "It's like Hemingway, the writer. He got a style to his way a writing. Well cryptologists have a style, too. I been in this game enough to know a style when I sees it. The same guy or team of guys built these nuts."

"So the chances are if we crack one, we crack them all?"

"Better hope so, Prof."

# TWENTY-NINE

WITH BRIGHT EYES AND an expression of excitement, Ashley dashed into Walter Kent's office and announced, "They found him."

Kent glanced from his desk and saw an energized Ashley Kohen waving a notepad over her head. "You look like you won the lottery. Who found who?"

"Chavez County Sheriff's Office called. They found our man. The Russell Smith impostor."

"That's good news. Only five days since our APB went out." Kent tried to stop staring at her. Never had he seen her face so flushed and her eyes sparkle as they did at that moment. He forced himself to refocus his attention. "Where did they find him?"

"Downstate in an RV Park south of Roswell. A deputy sheriff went camping on his day off. Parked right next to the suspect's rig. He checked it out when he got back to work. Sure enough, the description matched."

Kent didn't expect to find the un-sub this fast, but had prepared a surveillance team to stand ready for mobilization. Checking his assignment roster he turned to Ashley. "I've ordered Agent Jerry Cebeck and his surveillance team to work with you. As the lead investigator this will give you a chance to watch the un-sub and learn his modus operandi."

"What about Ramirez?"

"I've reassigned him. I need Mark back doing what he does best—helping me with administrative matters. For now, I want you to work with Cebeck." He paused for a moment. "I hope your work with Agent Ramirez has been a learning experience." Kent checked Ashley's response.

"Oh yes. A unique experience, Mr. Kent. One I will remember for many years."

He noticed the corners of her mouth twisted with amusement.

LATER THAT MORNING Ashley met Cebeck in the staging area of the field office motor pool. Florescent lights disclosed gray concrete walls and a dark tire-marked floor. "Hi, Agent Cebeck, I'm Ashley Kohen, the lead on this case. I have a Covert Entry search warrant for the suspect." She handed him a copy of the order. "I can extend the time period, if needed."

Cebeck, a burly guy with watery blue eyes, dirty blond hair and a perpetual two day growth on his face, took the paper. "A Sneak and Peek warrant. We need that. Thank God for the Patriot Act or whatever they call it nowadays." They shook hands. "Surveillance means long hours in close quarters. You can drop the formalities. Call me Jerry." He tucked the paperwork in his back pocket. "You're new to the field office. Have you done this work before?"

She knew Jerry Cebeck had worked surveillance much of his career with the FBI, and did it well. "Sure. I've done my share of stakeouts with the Chicago PD." He acknowledged her with a skeptical nod.

The other team members joined them in the staging area. Ashley counted ten men. Cebeck began the briefing. "The suspect is in an RV park. Our assigned agent on duty in Roswell is watching him as I speak. I've arranged to rent a truck and a camper so we can locate near him tomorrow, Saturday. This will be a 24-hour shadow operation. Under no circumstance will any member of this team allow the subject to become aware of his presence. The subject is about six feet tall and 180 pounds with dark hair. The size of our team will vary based on the subject's movement. If he's idle, the team will consist of two stationary observers and two remote agents ready to move as needed." He snapped on his pointer. A tiny red dot danced across a map of Roswell taped to the concrete wall. "If the subject becomes mobile, the team can grow to half a dozen or more agents using various modes of transport–usually four-wheeled vehicles. I have two bicycles and a motorcycle ready if needed. Each of you have a copy of this map in your file folders. Learn the streets and highways." He studied their faces. "Radio contact will remain constant 24-7. We'll work four hour shifts. Dress code is standard seedy American. I will create a base of operations in the travel trailer on-site. The Bureau's satellite office in downtown Roswell will serve as a backup. Any questions?"

A veteran team member asked, "Will we have tracking receivers?"

Agent Cebeck, besides his role as surveillance team leader, also served as the *Bug Man*. A title given him years ago for good reason. Cebeck's expertise in planting satellite tracking devices matched or exceeded anybody's skill in the Bureau.

"You bet. Every unit will have electronic trackers set to our usual frequency. As soon as we find out the subject's movement pattern, I'll get my gardening tools out and do some planting." A ripple of laughter was heard. "Any other questions?" He heard nothing. "Okay gentlemen tomorrow you start your engines." He gawked at Ashley with a crooked grin. "You too, Agent Kohen."

FOUND ON THE SOUTH side of the city, the Town and Country RV Park occupied a twenty acre rectangular parcel of land with a paved road that looped the interior. A swimming pool centered the loop with camping spaces backing onto it. Across the looped road the remaining sites lined the park boundary. Most sites had a mature tree to provide shade and all offered standard hookups.

In the northeast corner of the park, facing the interior road, a fancy bronze painted 45-foot motor home housed the subject. The impressive rig bristled with slide-outs, and had a satellite antenna mounted on the roof. The thirty foot awning extended over a picnic table and two bright green folding chairs. Next to the table and chairs, a brown SUV faced the road.

Ashley arrived at the Town and Country early Saturday morning and drove the loop. Only a few sites were occupied because of the hot weather. The big motor home stuck out like a circus clown in a church choir. She got a park map at the office and studied it, then called Jerry. "I've found the perfect site. It will view the entrance side of the subject's motor home with an unobstructed view. The site is a pull-though. That puts the large tinted rear window of our trailer facing the subject. He can't see us enter or leave the trailer."

"Sounds great. Rent it."

"Will do. It's site number twelve."

That afternoon Jerry arrived with a twenty-nine foot trailer and a pickup truck. They parked their trailer, and hooked up. To create an authentic appearance, Ashley unfolded a couple of lawn chairs, strung a clothesline and hung two wet towels on it. "Now we look like real campers." She tossed an overnight bag on the foldout sofa.

Cebeck grinned broadly and clapped his hands. "All the comforts of home. Time to get to work." In the rear of the trailer, facing the subject's motor home, Cebeck mounted four computer monitors. Two were attached to tiny wireless surveillance cameras mounted on the roof. One camera viewed the subject's campsite, and the other the park entrance. A third monitor remained available for messaging and general Internet use. The fourth served as a backup unit. A 250 watt radio transmitter bounced a satellite signal back to all mobile units–the chase cars. If a power outage occurred, an onboard portable generator stood ready.

Ashley watched as Cebeck scurried about, much like a caterer making last minute preparations for a big banquet. Impressed with the improvised command center, she asked. "What, no binoculars, Jerry?"

He scarcely looked her way. "Of course. Night vision binoculars." He pulled a pair out of a duffel bag and handed them to her. "This will keep you out of trouble working the night shift." He also handed her an infrared digital camera. "Works well under extreme lowlight. I have other cameras for daytime use." He showed Ashley how to work all the equipment. When finished, he asked, "What do you think?"

Ashley reviewed the procedures. A bit more advanced than her stakeouts in Chicago, but easy enough to handle. "Great setup. Now what?"

Cebeck checked his watch. He flicked on his phone and tapped an app. "It's a new moon tonight. It'll be dark outside."

Ashley nodded. "Great for bug planting, right?"

"Why do you think I dressed in black?"

The story around the office said Jerry would never have to worry about money because if he quit the Bureau he could always make a good living as a cat burglar. A crude joke, but also an implied compliment that recognized his ability to move with stealth. Ashley, using the binoculars, watched his shadowy green form slip through the night planting a miniature satellite tracking device on the SUV and the motor home. It took fewer than five minutes.

Tomorrow would be the first full day of surveillance. She would at last see the killer of Russell Smith. It would also be a day that would turn Ashley's life in a different direction.

# THIRTY

ASHLEY COMPLETED HER SHIFT at midnight and then stretched out on the queen-size bed at the other end of the trailer. Fully clothed, she fell asleep in seconds. A little before five o'clock, she woke to the smell of fried bacon. After splashing cold water on her face, she checked out the kitchen. Jerry was feasting on scrambled eggs, toast, bacon and coffee. "I made some extra. Help yourself."

She dished the food and poured a cup of coffee. "Any action over there?" She pointed her eyes towards the giant motor home. With a mouthful of toast Jerry shook his head no. "You look beat," she said. "Why don't you turn-in? I'll take over."

"Good idea." When finished, he picked up his dishes, dumped them in the sink and headed for the bedroom, closing the folding door behind him. "Thanks," he muttered.

Still dark, Ashley checked the monitors, selected a book entitled, *The Practices of Islam* and began reading. By 6:00 a.m. the sun gradually brightened. She sensed movement on the first monitor. A tall, dark man stepped out of the motor home. As the sun rose, it caused the awning to cast a shadow across the picnic table where the man stood. She adjusted the telephoto feature of the surveillance camera to see him better. Ashley saw his form, but not much detail. She turned on the video recorder.

After a minute, he unrolled a small rug and laid it on the ground, then bowed facing east. He's performing his Morning Prayer ritual–the Five Pillars of Islam. For fifteen minutes the man knelt, bowed, placed his head on the ground and sat in meditation. Then he stood, rolled the rug, and stretched his arms over his head. The sunlight, brighter now, showed a well formed man, lean and muscular. With a clean shaven face, surrounded by black hair, he moved in a deliberate manner as he reentered his motor home.

Absorbed capturing this action on video, Ashley didn't notice her heart thumping or her rapid breathing until seconds later. So that's what the son-of-a- bitch, looks like. A killer who could pass for a male model. Odd, you'd think they would select someone who didn't standout physically.

At eight o'clock Jerry stumbled out of the bedroom, his hair a mess. Ashley showed him the recording. He played it back several times. His only comment, "Scary bastard." Ashley agreed.

The man emerged from his elegant camper at noon. He wore shorts and a T-shirt, common clothes for summer. The subject unlocked his SUV and climbed in.

Jerry picked up the radio microphone. "Unit 1 and Unit 2, the subject is on the move. He's in a brown Lincoln MKX. License number VAK-8909. Copy?" He got an immediate response.

"Unit 2, copy." Then a moment later, "Unit 1, copy. Got him." Both agents assigned to tail the Lincoln waited until the subject moved out of sight. Each tracking screen showed a moving map of street patterns. The satellite device Jerry attached last night blinked rhythmically on their tracking screens. Jerry got the same signal on his monitor.

Ashley watched the slow speed pursuit play out. The subject drove north on highway 285, then turned west zigzagging through the west side of town. At the intersection of Hobbs Street and Union, he turned north onto Union and continued for several blocks.

"Unit 1, reporting. He's turning into a small strip shopping center."

Jerry directed their movement and noted the time. "Unit 1, pass him by. Unit 2, turn in and park away from the subject." He watched his monitor as the flashing dots emitted by his pursuit vehicles complied with his orders. "Keep an eye on him Fred, but don't get out of the car. What can you see?"

Fred, in Unit 2 answered. "This is an old complex. Four shops side by side in one building. He's getting out of his car. He's approaching the door of the second shop on the south end between a vacuum cleaner repair shop and an ice cream parlor. The sign over the door says..." Fred paused. "I can't see it. He's unlocked the door and entered the building."

Jerry thought a moment. "Stay put, Fred. You can read the sign when you leave." He checked the location of Unit 1. Joe had parked one block north on a side street ready to move either north or south on Union. They waited. Fifteen minutes later the subject exited the building and drove out of the parking lot onto Union and turned north. Unit 1 picked him up when he passed by.

"What's the sign over the door say, Fred?"

"Smith Trading. Imports and Export. Can't see inside."

"Good man. Standby."

The subject traveled north, turned east onto Second Street and made a left turn onto Main Street. He didn't stop until he approached Roswell's main shopping center on the north side of town. He turned into the center and drove around back.

"Unit 1. What's he doing, Joe?"

"He's parking. There's big building back here. It's a movie complex. He's getting out of the car. I think he's going to the movies."

"Okay. Joe, park, then buy a ticket and follow him inside. See what feature he's attending. Make sure he goes into a theater." Jerry beamed at Ashley. "This is great. If he goes to a movie we know where he is and how long he'll be in one place. Perfect. Damn perfect."

Five minutes later Joe came online. "He went into theater 3. *Crime Hunter* is playing. Running time two hours and three minutes."

"Okay, gentlemen. Stay on target. Remember there is more than one way to exit a theater. Let me know when he's on the move again." Jerry checked his watch: 1:05 p.m.

"Are you going over?" Ashley asked.

"You bet." He grabbed his tool kit and started for the door. "I have never jimmied a motor home door lock. I hope it's not some offbeat mechanism."

"Why not use a key?"

He stopped at the door. "Because I don't have one."

Ashley slapped down a key on the kitchen counter. "Now you do."

"Where'd you get that?"

"I called the manufacturer and asked for two keys. Gave them the VIN number I got from the DMV. When you're the FBI you can do stuff like that." Her lips curved up. "I'm coming with you."

Jerry slipped the key into his pocket. "No, I need you to stay here. Joe or Fred might call in. You understand?" He arched an eyebrow at her.

"Sure. I'll mind the store. Have fun."

Trying to look like a camper on a casual walk, Jerry approached the metallic colored motor home, and then quickly stepped to the door and unlocked it. Ashley watched. She imagined him searching for the best place to hide each of the listening devices: three, she figured—one at each end and the third in the middle. The time: 1:15.

Twenty minutes passed, and no Jerry. Where is he, she wondered. The bugs are state of the art, and easy to hide. He called them chameleons because when placed they assumed the color of any surface.

At a quarter to two, she prepared to march across the road, when the door to the motor home opened. Jerry stepped out and hurried across to their trailer. "Hey, is the Bug Man losing his touch?" Ashley asked as he entered, "Any problem?"

No answer.

Ashley watched him as he turned away from her, and stored his gear. He moved to the bathroom and shut the door. She waited. Finally he came out. He wore a grim expression. Avoiding her eyes, he said, "I downloaded the contents of a laptop over there. It took a while. I have to go downtown." He started for the door. "I need a secure line to send this download to Bill Johnson at the field office."

On her feet, Ashley blocked the door. "You're not telling me something. What happened over there? Did he set a booby trap?"

"Not exactly."

"What does that mean?"

He backed up, then dropped into an upholstered chair–a vacant look in his eyes. Ashley waited for his answer. Finally it came. "There's someone over there."

"My God, our cover is blown!"

"No. It's not."

"What do you mean?"

"She is blinded with a black bag over her head and is tied up.

"She? A black bag? How can you be sure it's a woman?"

"Because she's naked."

Ashley stepped back to steady herself, a hand on the kitchen counter. "What's her condition?

"She made a sound. Like a moan or a cry, but she isn't aware of anything. I checked her pulse. It's weak." He forced himself to focus on Ashley. "She's a tiny thing tied to a king-size bed. Splayed at both ends. Arms stretched out tight over her head. Feet spread wide and tied to a pipe. She's been there a while."

Ashley tried to piece together the image.

"There are bruises all over her body and plenty of dried blood. The pelvic region has most of the blood." He stared at Ashley, his hands gripped the arms of the chair, his jaw muscle tight. "I think you get the picture."

126

She got the picture. She could see the woman in her mind. A wretched creature being used up little by little until...until....

Jerry stood. "I have to go. You need to stay in contact with Fred and Joe."

Ashley moved forward. "We can't leave her there."

"I don't like this any more than you, but we can't make a move now. Touch that woman and we expose the surveillance. The whole operation blows up."

"She needs help. She needs us."

"I'll talk to the SAC. See what Kent thinks. I got a go." He opened the door and stepped out. "I'm sorry. I've seen a lot over the years, but nothing quite like this." He shut the door.

Seconds later Ashley heard the truck start and pull out of the driveway. Her wristwatch read two minutes past two o'clock.

# THIRTY-ONE

*THERE ARE BRUISES ALL over her body and plenty of dried blood.* Jerry's description, haunted Ashley. She paced the floor, her feelings vacillating between anger, sadness, and deep concern.

Only a few hundred feet away a helpless woman lay brutalized, too weak to speak. A victim of a monster who had already killed a pathetic little man. Now this savage has enslaved a woman for sexual gratification or worse. Without intervention, only death will free her. Death that will come when he finishes with her.

Ashley struggled to deal with the ramifications of any decision she would make. She had the power to free the woman, save a human life, and take her to a hospital for medical treatment. Such an act would have consequences. When this evil man discovers his sex slave is gone he will know someone entered his secret world, cut her loose and carried her away. He will react. If he runs we may lose him, and the case falls apart. Even if we find him and continue the surveillance, he will be more cautious. He will take extraordinary steps to protect himself. If arrested, we can't be sure he's working alone. His mission might be assigned to another terrorist leaving us with a dead end.

Absorbed in thought, Ashley found herself staring at her image in a full-length mirror mounted on the wall. She spoke to a face twisted with distress and filled with anguish. "If I rescue this woman, and he gets away, it will be my fault. I could lose my job, my career and my reason for being."

Ashley turned and faced the motor home across the road. She sat in front of Cebeck's array of electronic gadgets. She thought back to a decision she made long ago. She remembered, as a little girl, she cuddled next to her mother after her first day in school. She cried and told her mom the kids teased her, called her little rich Jew girl, and sometimes hit her when the teacher looked the other way. Frightened, with her hands covering her face, she asked, "What can I do mom?" Her mother kissed her gently, held her close, and told her God would protect her as long as she tried to make the right decisions.

Ashley remembered her Mother's words "You will make many hard choices in your life. Let your heart show you the way and your mind carry you forward. You must decide if you will hide from the scorn and the cruelty of people or be strong and stand your ground because that's the right thing to do." Those words gave her the strength to fight back, and by the end of that school year she earned the respect of her classmates. Remembering those words, Ashley knew only one course of action lay before her today.

She stood, and began packing the tools she would need in the minutes ahead: a box cutter, side cutters, first aid kit, camera, and hand tools. She turned the video recorders on and scratched down a note to Cebeck—leaving it on the kitchen counter. The clock on the wall read 2:15.

Ashley bolted from the trailer, slammed the door behind her and sprinted to her car parked across the road next to the park office. She backed the car and kicked up gravel as she drove the short distance to the motor home, and parked as close to the camper entrance as possible. Once outside she dug in her pocket for the second key and unlocked the door. The electric step slid out. In seconds she entered the motor home, and ran for the bedroom in the back. What she saw sickened her.

In the darkened room, sprawled across the king-sized bed lay an emaciated waif-like form—her arms hung from above, hands curled over at the wrist like dried leaves about to fall. Stretched wide, her legs had no slack to bend at the knees. Like gnarled stumps, two small feet, tightly wrapped with layers of duct tape, jutted up above a PVC pipe. A black bag, pointed at the corners covered her head. Ashley gasped when she saw the crudely performed female genital mutilation now caked with scabs covering partially heeled tissue.

She quickly moved to the side of this pathetic spectacle. Black bruises, some fading into yellow circles covered her body. Smears of dried blood marked her lower torso. On and around her breasts Ashley saw small circled wounds—burn marks from a hot object like a cigarette or a red-hot kitchen utensil. Ashley exploded into blind fury, and started to tear at the woman's bonds, then pulled back. She realized this indescribable horror may not be believed. She must photograph it. It would take only a few seconds, then she would free her.

The camera flash lit the dimly lit room much like a bolt of lightning reveals the damage of a deadly storm. Two, three, four shots at different angles; every gruesome detail recorded. Then she went to work—first the arms. They were fastened to eyebolts screwed into the wall. Ashley snipped the plastic ties that dug into the woman's wrists. When the hands dropped down some of the plastic stayed in the crusted wounds. Using the box cutter she turned her attention to the feet. She carefully sliced through the many layers of tape that trapped her swollen ankles against the plastic pipe. The left foot fell free followed by the right. Now for the black bag hiding her face. Drawn tight, a cord held it in place. She cut it away and pulled the bag off. A once beautiful face looked at her with unseeing eyes. A narrow strip of tape covered her mouth. Ashley reached to check for a pulse and found a choke chain imbedded in her neck, and a dog leash curled next to her head. The woman made a whimpering sound. Ashley pulled the tape from her mouth. With caring hands, she unclipped the metal collar and pulled it gently from around the woman's throat. She placed the gray hands across a scarred belly and pulled the legs together.

The first attempt to lift the women failed. A plastic drop cloth streaked with body fluids stuck to her underside preventing a firm grip. The smell of human waste filled the air. Ashley, lifting and pulling, worked the plastic loose. With that gone, she searched for something to cover the woman. A man's bathrobe hung from a brass wall hook. She grabbed the robe and spread it over the body, then scooped her limp frame off the bed, and sidestepped through the narrow door of the bedroom. My God, she weighs nothing.

At the door, Ashley kicked it open and carefully backed out of the motor home. As she moved toward her car the woman raised her head and focused on Ashley. In a feeble voice she said, "Are you...Are you..." Then she slipped back into the void. Supporting the woman with one arm, Ashley opened the backdoor of her car and swiveled the lifeless weight onto the seat, allowing her to drop back into the car. She then dashed around to the other side, opened the door and pulled the young woman across the seat. She shut the door, and circled back to close the other door after carefully positioning the swollen feet out of harm's way. No one witnessed the rescue.

THE DRIVE TO THE Roswell Regional Hospital took ten minutes, but seemed longer. Ashley jerked to a stop at the emergency entrance, dashed into the reception area, flashed her badge and demanded help. Two orderlies pushing a gurney ran outside and transferred the victim, still covered with the robe, and rushed into the hospital. Within seconds the unconscious woman disappeared deep into the emergency care center.

The receptionist logged the time of admission as 3:03 p.m.

Ashley, emotionally drained, collapsed into a chair in the waiting room. Had she done everything she could do? Her mind raced through her actions these past fanatic minutes. Yes, she told herself–everything. Now this pathetic, tortured childlike woman's survival must rely on skilled medical care and a little help from a God she often took for granted. She touched the Star of David pendant she wore hidden under her shirt. Still clutching this emblem of faith, Ashley closed her eyes and for a few minutes drifted into oblivion.

"I'm sorry, Miss, but you have to move your car. It's blocking the entrance." A tall blond haired man, a nursing aid, stood over her. "Or I'll move it if you want."

Ashley woke with a start. "No, thank you. I'll move it. Sorry."

"That's okay, Miss, I understand. The doctors are tending to her now."

"That's good," Ashley answered with a hopeful glance at the man.

The car, the backdoor open and the motor still running, caused Ashley to focus. She pushed the door shut and got in. I've lost it, she thought. It's time I pull myself together. This isn't over. It's just beginning. She parked nearby.

Ashley waited in the lobby. Finally, a doctor dressed in green scrubs appeared. "Good evening, I'm Doctor Rader. I'm told you brought that young patient into the hospital. Your quick action may have saved her life." He nodded his head in approval. "You may see the patient now." They walked back into the intensive care unit where the woman lay behind drawn drapes.

The odor of disinfectant filled the area. A nasal cannula delivered oxygen and an IV bag hung overhead dripping a clear solution into a vein in the woman's hand. A blinking monitor next to her bed flashed numbers while a steady flow of spiked images crossed the screen.

"We've stabilized her," the doctor said. "She's weak and dehydrated. We got to her before gangrene set in, but I'm afraid there will be scars. I feel confident she'll recover. Do you know her name?"

Ashley saw her mutilated body was covered with clean white sheets and her face had regained some color. "No, not yet."

"Based on our examination, I am obligated to report her condition to the local authorities. Clearly this is a case of domestic abuse."

Ashley turned to the doctor, only now noticing his shock of red hair and faded freckles. "Doctor Rader, I'm Special Agent Ashley Kohen with the FBI. This woman is a party to an ongoing Federal investigation concerned with national security. I will need a report from you describing your observations and the medical treatments you performed." Ashley flipped her ID open for inspection. "This matter must remain confidential. No media coverage."

"I'm supposed to report this to the local police."

"I'll take care of that. We have jurisdiction in this matter. The Bureau appreciates your cooperation." She handed the doctor her business card. "Please send your report to the Albuquerque Field Office marked for my attention."

"I understand, Agent Kohen. I'll note your instructions and see that our records are sealed."

"Good. May I speak with her, now?"

"Of course, but not for long." Rader stepped out of the area as Ashley approached the patient, pulled a chair next to the bed, and leaned close to her.

The woman opened her eyes.

"Hi. I'm Ashley. I brought you here. The doctor says you will be all right. It'll take some time." She touched her hand. "What's your name?"

The woman studied Ashley's face. In a raspy whisper she asked, "You saved me?"

"I did what had to be done."

She repeated, "You saved me. God bless you." She squeezed Ashley's hand. "My name is Rita. Rita Durand."

"We can't talk too long, Rita. Tell me what happened, if you can."

Rita spoke with a weak and brittle voice. "I'm a good girl. I thought he was nice. We met in the UFO Museum. He asked if I knew about the UFO and did I think it was real." Rita paused a moment, drawing air into her lungs. "I said I did and that my great-grandfather saw it in the sky in 1947, and testified about it. I believed it happened, like grandpa said." She paused again. "Will I be all right?"

"Yes. It'll take time, but you will heal."

"The man said he liked a Mexican restaurant down the street and would I eat dinner with him. He smiled nice. I said okay." Rita eyes filled

132

with tears. "After dinner we left the restaurant, but I don't remember much after that." Her lips trembled. "I woke tied to a bed and he was on me." She started to cry. "He hurt me. He hurt me bad."

"I know Rita. We're going to get him. He'll answer for what he did to you." Ashley waited until Rita calmed down. "Did he ever talk to you? Tell you anything about himself?"

Rita's expression changed. Her face turned into a look of horror. The pace of her breathing increased. "Oh my God, yes, he told me what he wanted to do to us–to America. He is evil.

Between naps, Ashley listened as Rita talked for thirty minutes.

# THIRTY-TWO

JERRY CEBECK ARRIVED BACK at the trailer at three o'clock and immediately made a dual discovery. The motor home door across the road hung open and Ashley was gone. He checked his watch. The movie would end in a few minutes and it took twenty minutes to drive back across town. Unless the un-sub left the movie early, he could not have opened that door. He grabbed the microphone.

"Unit One and Unit Two, do you copy?"

"Jerry, this is Joe - Unit One. Where the hell have you been? The subject is on the move. He's headed your way. Where's Ashley?"

"She's not here. Have you been in contract with her?"

"No, not for an hour. We thought she might be with you."

"Negative. Hold on."

Agent Cebeck glanced back at the motor home door. Wide open. It didn't get that way by itself. Under his breath he said, "Mother of God, she did it."

"What did you say?" Joe asked.

"Okay, guys, we have a problem." He searched his tracking screen. "Where are you exactly?'

"Fred and I are following the subject. He's headed straight down Main Street toward you. Should be there in about ten minutes. What's going on?"

Jerry shifted into emergency mode. "Here's the deal, guys. The un-sub will find out he's under surveillance as soon as he gets back here. Can't explain why right now. You be ready to follow him. I'm calling downtown for back up, and the field office for orders."

"Are we talking arrest?" asked Joe.

"I don't know, but if I were calling the shots the answer would be yes." Jerry dropped the mike and phoned downtown. "I need two backup cars with tracking devices, right now. Move it." He then called the field office. "I need to talk to the SAC pronto." The operator transferred him to Dorothy Hogan.

134

"Special Agent in..." Jerry cut her off. "Dorothy, this is Cebeck. Transfer me to Mr. Kent–ASAP." She did. Kent picked up. "Mr. Kent, Agent Cebeck here. Our Bitty Smith surveillance is compromised. Subject most likely will flee. Do we arrest him?"

"Calm down Cebeck. What's going on?"

"Agent Kohen has fucked the operation. The guy will know we are on to him."

"Has he detected your presence?"

"No, he hasn't, but he soon will."

"Why?"

"Because the woman is gone."

"Woman? What woman?"

"Kohen removed a woman the subject had mutilated and confined in his motor home."

"Where is the woman now?"

"I don't know."

"Where is the subject?"

"He went to a movie and is on his way back. Be here in ten minutes."

"And you're sure he hasn't detected you?"

"Yes, I'm sure."

"There is no reason for him to link the missing woman with our surveillance. Since he doesn't know about us, he would assume someone discovered the woman and freed her. Maybe he'll think a bleeding heart saved the person or possibly a relative or someone in the RV Park heard something and checked it out."

Cebeck hadn't thought of that and hoped Kent was right, but his instincts told him otherwise. "So what should we do?"

"Do not arrest. Continue the surveillance at a distance, but don't lose the subject if he runs."

"Okay. You're the boss."

"What about Ashley?"

"Gone."

"Where?"

"Don't know."

A moment passed. "Keep me informed."

"Yes, sir." Cebeck then ran across the road, checked to be certain the woman was gone, and shut the open door.

IN THE DARKENED theater Abdullah gripped the arms of his chair. The action of *Crime Hunter* flashed in front of him. Lost in the make-believe world of the cinema, his body made involuntary jerks from side to side as his mind dodged the blows delivered by the hero. The sound and flashing lights engulfed him. In the final scene of the film, the mob boss lay dying with blood dribbling out of his mouth. Without realizing it Abdullah had rooted for the wrong character. He exited the theater by the side door, disturbed by the ending. His eyes narrowed in the bright daylight.

The Lincoln, heated by the afternoon sun, greeted him with hot leather seats and a steering wheel too warm to touch. Holding the door open, he waited until some of the heat dissipated. He noticed a man sitting in a gray sedan in front of him–the motor running and the windows up.

He headed south on Main Street and wondered if he needed to stop and pick up anything on the way home. Nothing came to mind. Abdullah sneered as he passed several signs advertising beer and liquor in the windows of two restaurants and a tavern. These Americans take alcohol into their bodies and cloud their minds. What fools. Never would an Islamic warrior like himself drink the devil's poison and take the ominous drugs that prop up those too weak to face reality. Many die of this indulgence. It is Satan's revenge on an immoral culture.

The RV park sign marked his turn into the campgrounds. He approached his site, and then backed into his parking space so his car faced the loop road. He inserted the key into his motor home door and turned the lock, but when he pulled on the handle, it didn't move. He tried again, this time turning the key in the opposite direction. The door opened. Had he left the door unlocked that afternoon? He must be more careful.

Abdullah entered and looked about. No sound came from the bedroom. He remembered she hadn't made much noise the past week. It would soon be time to dispose of her. She no longer held interest for him. All the fight had left her, and his needs were no longer met by her meager offerings.

If only he heard from Rome.

He lifted the lid of his notebook and booted up. Maybe an encrypted message awaited his attention. He quickly opened his messages and scanned them. Nothing. "In the name of Muhammad, the Messenger from God," he shouted, "why must I endure this trial? Am I not a true disciple of Allah the Majestic?" He slammed the lid shut.

Distraught, he stood and paced the long center aisle of the motor home, while mumbling prayers. As he entered the bedroom and started to pivot, he stopped. Then it struck him. *She is gone!*

Impossible. She is weak, a mere woman. She could not break her bonds–not possible. He slammed his fist against the wall. Someone violated his privacy. Someone took his wench–cut her ties and carried her off. Abdullah rushed to the front windows and moved the curtains aside. No one in sight. Everything appeared normal. He sat behind the steering wheel and peered across the loop road.

Who knew she lay at his disposal? Almost a week and no report on TV or the newspapers of a missing girl. The American press would pounce on a story like that. They feed on the misery of others. It earns revenue. Abdullah continued to stare out of the massive windshield.

If a stranger had found her, a report would have been made. The authorities would be here. There would be police with guns. He would have seen their marked cars before he drove to the campsite.

His eyes settled on the large trailer that had turned up yesterday. He had enjoyed isolation until its arrival. No one left or entered the unit that he could see. But then their door faced away from his vision. The front window, covered by a metallic material like the kind he mounted on the window of Smith Trading, reflected sunlight bright enough to make his eyes squint. Could there be a connection?

It doesn't matter. The woman, still alive, will talk. I told her fragments of my plans–plans I believed she would never live to repeat, but now she has escaped. Have I violated my oath as a warrior of Islam? I must assume the worst possible threat to me and my mission. I need to survive.

# THIRTY-THREE

EVERYONE KNEW DOROTHY HOGAN considered the people in the field office as family, and that she hated it when they fought. Monday morning she told Ashley about Jerry Cebeck's report of what happened the night before in Roswell. She warned her to be ready.

Walter Kent's voice blared over the intercom. "Dorothy, I need Agent Kohen, in my office right now."

"I'm sorry Mr. Kent, she's on an early lunch break."

"Is she in the cafeteria?"

"No sir. She never eats lunch. She's in the gym working out."

"Send someone down and get her up here now." He punched the intercom off and with the other hand gripped a pencil hard enough to snap it in half.

A few minutes later Agent Kohen dashed into Dorothy's office with a wisp of hair between her eyes. She wore a red tank-top damp with perspiration halfway down her back, and black gym shorts. Holding a towel in one hand, she clutched a folder in the other. Out of breath as she headed for Kent's open door, she asked over her shoulder, "Is he pissed, Dorothy? I mean really pissed?"

"Good luck, Babe. May the force be with you."

Ashley entered the doorway. "You asked to see me, Mr. Kent?"

Kent turned from the window. "Yes, I did, Agent Kohen. Sit down."

"I'm on my break. They told me to come right away. I didn't have time to change." She advanced to the center of the office. Her tank top didn't quite reach the top of her shorts revealing well-developed abs.

"I said sit down."

She sat.

As head of the field office Kent held final authority over matters of personnel. His authority had a downside. At times his position required him to take actions he didn't like. Kent noticed her still damp face, bright blue eyes and black hair in disarray. He cleared his throat. "This morning Jerry

Cebeck made his report on the former Roswell surveillance that ended late last night in a fiery explosion."

Ashley frowned when she heard the word 'former'.

"Yesterday Cebeck called and said you had removed a woman from the subject's motor home without authorization. He claimed you had abandoned your post during a critical period in the surveillance, and he did not know your whereabouts."

"I did not abandon my post."

Kent turned and began pacing behind his desk. "He called me yesterday and confirmed the woman was gone and advised me the subject might bolt as soon as he discovered it. I hoped that would not happen or if it did, we would keep in contact with the subject making an arrest possible if no other alternative existed. I was wrong."

If Kent had payed close attention, he would have noticed Ashley's hands tightly clasped. "Since you weren't there, let me tell you what happened. Yesterday afternoon, the subject returned to the RV Park after the movie. He remained in place and did not try to run. Our team stayed on high alert. The audio listening devices Jerry planted picked up the usual sounds inside the motor home. As the evening progressed, nothing out of the ordinary happened. Lights on inside and then lights off about nine o'clock. An hour later all hell broke loose. The motor home exploded and caught on fire. The firefighters arrived and tried to contain the inferno, without success. It burned to the ground with only the metal frame left standing. The park office and two adjacent homes were damaged including our rented trailer. One firefighter was hospitalized. After the fire, Cebeck inspected the site and found no human remains. He did find the rear emergency exit hatch in the grass next to the burned out shell and a hole cut in the chain-link fence behind the campsite. The fire was a deliberate act. Our man has vanished."

Kent stopped pacing and faced Ashley. He waited.

She looked at her boss. Her voice wavered a bit. "I hear Jerry got a nasty burn on one hand. Is he all right?"

"Yes. He's okay. He burned his right hand poking around in the debris before he discovered the escape route. The un-sub probably used a timing device to start the blaze. A perfect diversion. He walked away before anyone suspected it. The smart son-of-a-bitch had a Plan B that he carried out without a flaw."

"Sounds like it."

"Cebeck said if you'd come back and been a man, he'd of decked you right there."

"In the heat of the moment, I can understand that."

"Because of your actions, the surveillance failed and the subject escaped."

A spark of anger flashed in her eyes. "That's not true. This operation failed because obvious precautions were not taken."

"Are you saying the subject's escape is Cebeck's fault?"

"It's not my place to criticize, but yes that's what I am saying."

Kent began pacing behind his desk, faster this time. "I find it difficult to believe an agent of Cebeck's experience is the reason we lost this un-sub. I hope you aren't making a false claim that Jerry caused this disastrous outcome." He stopped pacing. "Explain yourself."

She started speaking in a slow and controlled voice. "When I decided I had to act to save that abused woman, I turned the surveillance cameras on so Jerry could see exactly how it went down." Ashley's words came faster now. "When he got back from downtown he had to discover my note stating I had rescued the poor unfortunate victim and for him to take defensive actions. It's obvious he ignored my note–obvious he panicked and lost control."

Kent frowned. "What are you saying?"

"I'm saying Cebeck sat on his ass surrounded by all of his electronic toys and let the un-sub slip away. He should have brought Joe and Fred on-site and armed them with night vision goggles. Then he should have posted them behind the RV and on the blind side of the motor home while he watched the front. Cebeck had mobile backups to replace Joe and Fred in case the un-sub tried to escape. He didn't do any of that. He ignored my note and screwed up."

"There's some truth in what you say. There's blame to go all around, but the fact remains your actions precipitated a downward spiral of events that resulted in mission failure."

Ashley did not respond.

Kent sat with his elbows on the desktop. Their eyes met. He waited for Ashley to say something. Ashley reached for the folder she held by her side, opened it and removed four photographs. She stood and spread the photographs on the desk in front of him. "I want you to see these pictures. I took them yesterday afternoon while Jerry went downtown to send his download of the un-sub's hard drive to Bill Johnson."

He glimpsed them briefly. "Cebeck told me about the woman."

Her voice urgent, Ashley controlled her anger. "Look at them."

Kent lifted each picture and studied it. One at a time. An expression of disgust spread across his face, and intensified with the review of each image. "Only a depraved barbarian would perpetrate these acts of brutality. Do you know how long he held her captive?"

"More than a week."

"Where is she now?"

"She's in intensive care. The doctors feel she'll pull through, but she'll have many scars, both physical and mental, the rest of her life. She's nineteen years old."

Kent pushed his chair back from the desk and stood. "I understand the dilemma you faced Ashley." He used her first name without realizing it. "But the fact remains you acted without authorization. You ignored agency protocol. You struck out on your own. That's not how we do business in the FBI."

"The doctors said she would not have lived another 24-hours. The man, this monster who kidnapped her and repeatedly raped her would have killed her just like he killed Russell Smith. I couldn't stand by and let this innocent woman die. Agency protocol is one thing–life and death is another."

"So you acted on your own."

Ashley, without hesitation and with renewed defiance answered. "Fidelity, Bravery and Integrity."

"I know the FBI motto, Agent Kohen, what's your point?"

"Our motto, Mr. Kent, defines Integrity as adherence to a strict ethical code, the reason we are an agency of the Federal government. Fidelity as faithfulness to moral obligations as a fundamental principle. And Bravery as the courage to do what has to be done when no other alternative exists. That's how the FBI does business and that's what I did." She stopped, when she realized her control had slipped. "I don't mean to preach, sir. It's just the way I see it."

They stood face-to-face,

Kent's expression registered sadness. He knew she was right, at least on a moral level, but she was also wrong in terms of the discipline needed to run a criminal investigation. "I'm taking you off this case, Ashley, and reassigning it to Cebeck. A Special Agent must not allow emotion to interfere with the conduct of any investigation. It endangers the agent and all those on the team."

"No. No! You can't do that."

"Of course I can."

"This is my case. I am meant to work this case. It's my life," she pleaded. "I have to do this work."

With a downturned mouth he said, "I'm placing you on indefinite administrative leave, with pay." Ashley held on to the back of her chair to steady herself. A sudden coldness hit at her core. "Most administrators in my position would terminate you. But I think you have potential and deserve a chance to..."

"If you take me off this case you might as well fire me."

"Of course that's an option, but that's not my decision, Ashley. My intention is to help you. You will learn from this incident."

"My job is my life. You are telling me the only way I can remain in the Bureau is to surrender my badge and gun and not work on this or any other assignment. That I must wait for an administrative process to take place while this un-sub is free to commit crimes I can only imagine."

"The investigation will continue. I'll bring every resource at my disposal to bear on this case, Ashley."

"Not every resource, sir."

"Of course every available resource."

"You won't have me, Mr. Kent, but you will have my resignation." Ashley stared at him holding back tears of rage, then made a military about-face and marched out of his office in a four cadence beat.

Dorothy caught Ashley as she quickened her step through the reception area. She spun her around, encircled her with both arms, and whispered, "I'm so sorry. You were right to save that young woman." She added, "If you need anything. I mean anything. you let me know."

Ashley gave her a squeeze, and then turned and left.

# THIRTY-FOUR

FOUR DAYS AFTER RASHID and Ike started working in earnest to crack the Key Code that barred them from penetrating the coconuts, Rashid neared the NSA office building for yet another night of work. He parked in an area reserved for guests of his status, which allowed him to enter and leave the building with a minimal security check.

As he did every night, Rashid carried with him a list of related data sets associated with Islam and the Middle Eastern cultures—groupings he hoped the author might have used as a foundation for a unique encryption. Each night they tried his ideas and proved them unworkable. As his list of schemes grew shorter, His frustration mounted.

Ike worked the joystick on his electric scooter to open the door of his private workspace and greeted his friend. "Evening, Prof, got something good for me tonight?" His optimism sounded forced.

"Yes, Ike. I have six possible data sets to try out." They moved to Ike's work station in the darkened room with the colorful blinking lights. Ike sat at his keyboard and Rashid at the table alongside. "You're going to be busy writing code, I'm afraid." He handed Ike the lists of options to read.

(1) Islamic Calendar and Gregorian Equivalent

(2) Sunrise and Sunset times in Mecca

(3) List of 25 recognized Prophets.

(4) The Five Pillars of Islam

(5) Primary Rituals of Islam

"Interesting," Ike said. "You'll have to explain this stuff. Let's roll."

Rashid reviewed the details of each item. Ike made notes, then assessed the research time and how much code needed to be written before Big Mamma could go to work. "Be lucky to get one of these done tonight. Which one first, Prof?"

"Let's start at the top."

The Islamic calendar is a lunar calendar based on the phases of the moon. The Gregorian or Christian calendar is based on the birth of Jesus

Christ using a solar system. Ike built a matrix of data, and then wrote code that allowed Big Mama to search finite parameters associated with each message. He lined up the six coconuts in a date received sequence. If Mamma broke through the first one she would automatically tackle the next using her successful findings. He then set her to work. "Let's get a cup of java, Prof. This'll take some time."

When they left the office, Ike locked the door to his private space. With a devilish grin he baited Rashid. "Race you to the elevator." He shoved the power lever on his scooter forward and bolted down the hallway. Rashid tried to keep up, but Ike reached the elevator button first. "Ain't technology wonderful," he said, as the elevator door opened.

They found a table in the corner of the first floor cafeteria. Ike loaded cream and sugar into his coffee. Rashid drank his black. They talked about family. Rashid explained his wife's bout with cancer and the toll it took on him and on their savings even with health insurance. Ike shared his experience after coming home from the war, and undergoing extensive physical rehabilitation that he endured for two years. He told Rashid how he lost his high school sweetheart to a car accident, and how coming to the NSA had changed his life. Without realizing it, they talked for an hour before heading upstairs.

When they got back, Ike checked Big Mamma's output. "Looks like we might have something here, Prof." Under Ike's Project ID number, Big Mamma had spilled forth data contained in four of the coconuts and started working on number five.

Rashid peered over his shoulder. "Appears to be Arabic, but I can't read it."

"I thought you knew Arabic."

"Yes, but not this–this is nonsense."

"Hey, man. Big Mamma's got 108 languages in her database. Forty percent of all the people on earth speak eleven of them–that includes Arabic. The rest of the world speaks the other eighty-seven."

Rashid eyed the letters scrawled across the screen. It contained the twenty eight letters in the Arabic alphabet. The letters didn't spell translatable words. "Can you print those out?"

Rashid sat in the corner and read the five information exchanges Big Mamma had cracked. Almost nothing he read made sense. Occasionally he identified an isolated word or phrase. Meaningless without a context. He spent an hour working without success.

Ike checked his watch. "It's gettin late, Prof."

"I can't read them," he said with desperation in his voice.

Ike focused on his friend, who looked like a kid who opened a Christmas present and found the box empty. "You know, Prof, I bet the Japanese felt the same way back in the second World War."

"What do you mean?"

"Ever hear about the Code Talkers."

"Yes. Native Americans used their language as the basis for an encryption. The Japanese never figured that out because they had no knowledge of the Navajo Nation or their language." Rashid leaped to his feet. "Damn it, I think you've hit on something!"

"How's that?"

Rashid explained. "Big Mamma has the Modern Standard Arabic form of the language in her database. The formal language I learned at the university. But stretching from far West Africa to the Sultanate of Oman in the Middle East there are four regional groups that speak a variation of Arabic. Each group has three or more dialects in it."

"How different are these dialects?"

"The differences are so great Arabs of one region often can't talk to Arabs from another part of their world."

"What do we do?"

Rashid paused. "We think like the author of the encryption. We search for a remote dialect within the Arab speaking world, and then make Big Mamma translate it into formal Arabic."

Ike's brows knitted. "That's not as easy as it sounds, old buddy. We got to find lots a samples of each dialect, assemble 'em, then digitize 'em into a new linguistic source, and then enter it into Mamma so it becomes a reference language. Once we have that language onboard, we can feed the data we just cracked back into Mamma. All that could take weeks for each dialect."

Rashid shook his head, "We can't afford that much time."

"How many dialects is there?"

"Sixteen."

"As my momma used to say, Lord A-mighty."

Rashid whispered, "We might get lucky."

"Say what?"

"The key is obscurity. We start with the most obscure and work up."

Ike thought about that. "Yea, that might improve our odds. He rolled his eyes to the ceiling. "I think we got a time problem, brother. While you and me is dick around with all this–somethin' terrible might happen..."

Rashid finished his sentence, "...leaving our country at risk."

"Right on, Prof. This aint no technical problem no more. It's something way above my pay grade. I'm takin this to my boss first thing tomorrow mornin'."

Rashid read Ike's expression of concern. "I don't agree with that, my friend. I think we should do it right now, tonight."

# THIRTY-FIVE

NORMAN MILLER'S REPORT TO NSA Director Smithy set off a chain reaction not the least of which was the Admiral's forceful and terse reaction. "Norman, are you telling me you've cracked the six coconuts?" Smithy pointed at the interoffice memo on his desk as Miller, Isaac Gunner and Rashid al Youris, stood at attention.

"Well, yes and no, sir," stammered Miller, his mustache less than its usual tidy self.

"What the hell does that mean? You either did or you didn't."

"Let me explain, sir. We have cracked the encryption, but not the code."

"That doesn't make any sense!"

Isaac Gunner, his electric scooter parked behind Miller, leaned to the side. "Can I explain, Mr. Admiral, sir?"

"Well I'd like someone to tell me something I can understand."

Ike maneuvered his scooter next to Miller facing Smithy. "The Prof, that's Doctor Youris, and me been working nights on these coconuts. We feed Islamic related datasets into Big Mamma and one of them recognized the Key Code, letting us open 'em up.

"Big Mamma?"

Miller interpreted for the Admiral. "Mr. Gunner refers to our super computer as 'Big Mamma', sir."

"Oh, I see. Go on Gunner."

"So we broke the Key Code, but not the data inside. It's got to be translated. The author double coded the messages."

Smithy looked perplexed. "Translated?"

Miller spoke again. "I think Doctor Youris might be able to clarify what we mean by translate."

Rashid glanced around the room. "Admiral, I see you have decorated your office with photographs of navy vessels including several famous World War II ships. I'm sure you remember the huge advantage our military had over the Japanese when it came to communications. We broke their codes, but they never figured out ours."

"You mean the Code Talkers? Yes, anyone familiar with the Second World War knows about that."

"What we have here is something similar. The messages we have cracked use the Arabic alphabet, but not the Classic or Modern Standard Arabic that I can read. We need to research the many dialects and compile each of them as a new language. Then we can apply our advanced decryption techniques and translate them. I'm sure we can do this, but it will need a massive linguistic assault requiring hundreds of work-hours, maybe thousands. We need your help, Admiral."

"You need my help? Hell yes. What do you want?"

"I think Norman has an estimate." Rashid faced Miller who produced a folder from his briefcase.

"Sir, there are sixteen Arabic dialects. They are all different. All must be assembled, compiled as a language, coupled with our decryption software and run through our system."

"How much time? How many people?" snapped the Admiral.

"Best estimate: two dozen language experts, working shifts twenty-four hours a day for two weeks might get the job done."

Smithy settled back in his tall leather chair and fiddled with a gold button on his coat. "Linguistic assault," he mumbled to himself as he swiveled his chair so he could see a broad expanse of a green manicured parade ground out his window. "I like the sound of that--linguistic assault. Reminds me of a military action, like our D-Day assault on the Normandy beaches." He turned back and faced them. His eyes sparkled. Everyone waited.

"Pat Fitzgerald over at Langley has a unit that deals with forensic linguistics. Doctor Ophelia Verbich heads the unit. She brings forty years of experience to her job. A true pioneer in her field. You might have heard of her, Doctor Youris. Her pen name is Otto Benjamin."

"Yes. A pioneer in the field of sociolinguistics."

The Admiral agreed. "I'll give Fitzgerald a call. If anybody can conduct this 'linguistic assault' it's Doctor Verbich at the CIA."

DOCTOR OPHELIA VERBICH had white hair, without a trace of gray. It framed her softly lined face in smooth waves with a neat bunch of curls nestled above her forehead, a hairstyle out of the 1940's. "Oh my. NSA sends three handsome men. My briefings seldom have more than one." She offered them seats at a small conference table in the corner of her office. "Director Fitzgerald said you boys need a little help." She hobbled to the table with the support of a cane.

The 'boys' waited until she took a seat and got comfortable. "We appreciate this opportunity to work with you," Norman Miller said, taking a chair next to her. "We have a project that is time sensitive."

"A little interagency coordination between members of the intelligence community can't hurt our reputation." Verbich paused. "As long as the word doesn't get around," she said with a hearty laugh. The crew from the NSA nodded approval and rewarded her humor with a polite chuckle.

Miller then reviewed the history of their effort to decode the coconuts and the problem of assembling the sixteen Arabic dialects. Verbich asked pointed questions during the discussion.

"So, there you have it," said Miller after completing his presentation. "If you think you could shave a few days off our estimated two-week project, it would be welcomed."

Verbich studied each of the three faces around the table. She produced an iPad and started tapping and swiping with quick movements, pausing briefly to gather her thoughts. Finally she raised her head. "With our involvement in Middle Eastern affairs soon after the Twin Towers incident, the CIA undertook extensive steps to understand the enemy. Despite these efforts, we still have much work to do in sociolinguistics." She hesitated while searching her iPad screen. "About your requests, I'm afraid I can't shave two days off your work schedule." The three men looked devastated. "But with a waiver of confidentiality from Director Fitzgerald, I can access my database catalog and give you what you want in twenty-four hours."

Surprise and relief broke out on the three faces. Ophelia Verbich enjoyed the reaction immensely.

TRUE TO HER WORD, Doctor Verbich sent a messenger with an armed escort to the NSA building in McLean the next day with sixteen fully articulated dialects using the Arabic alphabet. In his small enclave of blinking lights, Ike Gunner backed-up this data and entered it into Big Mamma. He programmed her to decode the remainder of the six previously cracked messages using the new languages as a reference. In less than a minute the six messages lay stripped of their encryption.

Rashid scanned the output, and then settled down to digest the full meaning of the material. Ike programmed Big Mamma to search for any subsequent incoming messages using the unique characteristics of this encryption. When finished, he turned to Rashid who was oblivious of his surroundings while scribbling notes on a Big Chief tablet.

"Hey, Prof. This is a paperless society. Whatcha doin writing on a paper tablet?"

Youris straightened his back and stretched his arms wide. "You're right, Ike. Old habits are hard to break."

"Well, are you finding anything?"

"No smoking gun, to coin a phrase," Rashid said with a straight face. "But I get the feeling something bad is about to go down."

"Could you be a little more specific?"

"The first message is by someone who goes by the name *The Sword*, probably a code name. Reference is made to the recipient as his 'brother'. I assume that means the writer is a male accomplice. Apart from the frequent Islamic titles, words of praise and religious connotations, he tells of his arrival in America through El Paso, Texas. He describes how he got a local identity, and that his work is financed by the Hawala network—an underworld banking operation. Finally, he speaks of gathering information on places 'ripe for destruction'. His words, not mine. It all sounds ominous, but nothing specific."

"Somethin' is cookin' on the stove and it's startin' to boil."

"The second message is more enlightening. It commands the Sword to come to Rome. Gives a specific hotel location and a date; about two weeks ago. No travel information. The third message is the Sword updating Rome on his plans to relocate. A reference is made to a motor home, and his researching of a suitable target. Message four is from the recipient and hints at expected developments. It complements the Sword on his dedication and skill. But doesn't say anything meaningful."

"Yea, but somethin is goin on, I bet."

"Number five is the Sword calling for faster action. He sounds like he's ready, but is waiting for further orders. While still respectful, he's a little pissed off, to coin yet another phase."

Ike pulled his keyboard over. "We got number five about a week ago."

Rashid nodded. "The last message, the sixth, sounds like actions are about to happen. It makes reference to assembling personnel, arranging transportation and asking for confirmation for the receipt of a shipment. Whatever that means."

Ike checked his watch. "That message is dated a day ago."

Rashid dropped number six on the top of other messages. "There will be more of these. Someone is directing the actions of an operative whose mission is not yet complete. Can you trace the origin and destination of these exchanges, Ike?"

"We can identify the computer the message came from by its unique Internet Protocol address–the IP, but its geographic location I can know only in a general way."

Puzzled, Rashid said, "I thought NSA could trace any email."

"Mostly we can. Let's say you send me a message from your computer at home and I receive it on my home computer. We can know those locations because you and I bought access to the internet from an ISP, an Internet Service Provider like the telephone company, who has your name, address and phone number."

"So what's the problem?"

"The problem is we are dealin' with computer savvy dudes. They use portable devises and move all around using different public Wi-Fi connections."

With an edge of frustration in his voice, Rashid asked, "What about servers, don't they show a location?"

"Servers, called Root Servers, are located worldwide. They all work on a demand and time basis."

"What's that mean?"

"Let's say we send a digital message from here. There's a server in Washington DC, but if it's overloaded or a faster routing is available the message will be picked up by another server. It might be only two or three milliseconds faster, but the system is design to follow the fastest route. That route may go through Canada, England, or Australia. The same message sent a minute later may follow a different route depending on system conditions at that moment."

"So servers can't give us specific origin and destinations?"

"You got it Prof."

Rashid tapped his Big Chief tablet. "So we're working blind at this point."

"No. The messages contain place names: El Paso and Rome. My guess is the Sword is located in southwestern United States."

151

"And the facilitator is in Rome?"

"Yep. Rome or at least southern Europe."

Rashid felt a shadow of dread. He thought of a time years ago when he used his language skills to earn money to pay hospital and cancer treatment expenses for his wife Hessa. He was paid a hundred thousand dollars for one night of work in Italy. The money was good and the job simple enough. Whatever went down that night seemed trivial at the time. Some underworld types working out a deal. Was there a connection? A shudder passed through him.

"Their conversation isn't finished, Ike. I think the next message, the seventh message, will tell us what we need to know." And, he thought, what I need to know, too.

# THIRTY-SIX

ASHLEY SPENT A MISERABLE sleepless night thinking about what she should have told Walter Kent during their heated confrontation in his office yesterday. Now she sat on the edge of her bed feeling more tired than when she went to bed six hours earlier. Her feet lay on the cold hardwood floor of her one-bedroom apartment, toes crunched together as if trying to keep warm. Where are my slippers? Where are my goddamn slippers?

She pushed herself upright still in a sleepy fog. Why am I pissed off at my slippers? They haven't done anything to me, at least not yet. The thought of her slippers, harboring ill will toward her feet, caused an uncontrollable laugh to break the silence.

Her clunky old alarm clock started its irritating clang across the room as if it was another ordinary day. With cold feet, she scuffled across the floor, snapped it off, and then put on a bra and panties. Now what? A five mile morning run? I don't feel like a five-mile run. Shit!

She found her slippers. They were like wool socks with a leather pad on the bottom. Squishy, but comfortable. She looked at her navy blue pantsuit flung over a chair in the corner. I won't be wearing that today or ever again. Double shit!

There she stood half naked feeling a tightness building in her throat. She fought the need to cry. I don't want to cry. Damn it, I never cry.

Ashley Kohen, the tough, determined fighter cried while standing nearly naked and alone in the middle of her bedroom. A loud sorrowful wailing echoed off the walls of her room while she stood head up and tight-fisted. A good cry. Like a snowdrift that melts after the storm has passed, her cry cleared away emotion she had stored up. It left her exhausted, but relieved.

Breakfast consisted of a blended smoothie of frozen strawberries, yogurt, diet orange soda and a scoop of protein powder. Today she indulged herself with a toasted English muffin - no butter. She cleaned up after herself as she prepared her food. The tidiness of her apartment testified to her obsession with keeping everything in order. She paid attention to details.

She knew details were like little flakes of gold. If you gather enough of them together you can make something of value that will endure, like catching a killer or stopping a terrorist. Ashley had many details on Case Number NM-1056 stashed away in notebooks, on scraps of paper and in her memory. She knew everything about the Bitty Smith Case. What she hadn't explored were the loose ends. That's where she would start.

One loose end concerned the un-sub's visit to Smith Trading on the west side of Roswell. Since the un-sub, also known as Russell Smith, had a key to the building of a company that had his last name, it was reasonable to assume he owned Smith Trading Imports and Exports. She wondered why he established a company in New Mexico and what he planned to import or export.

The second loose end that nagged her was the 1979 Ford pickup truck transferred to Russell Smith from someone named Allen Lee. Bitty Smith's profile didn't fit a guy who would own a pickup truck. His sister made no mention of his having one. She said he drove an old VW Bug. The DMV records showed the truck's title transfer from Allen Lee to Russell Smith occurred after Bitty's murder, making Bitty's ownership impossible. That meant the new owner of the truck was the person who killed Russell Smith and took his identity, and his truck. That person, the killer, had gone by the name of Allen Lee. Could that be his real name?

The 1979 truck had a Texas title registered to Mr. Lee with an El Paso address. She had copied the Bill of Sale on file in New Mexico. Someone in El Paso must know this Allen Lee and may be able to offer important information about the man Ashley now hunts.

Dealing with these loose ends posed a big problem. Officially she had no credentials to support an investigation. No longer a Federal agent or a cop, she had no legitimate standing. She checked out procedures to become a private investigator in New Mexico. The state made her take a test and pass an in-depth background check that took months. She could legally carry a handgun in the state, but not conceal it on her person. To get a concealed carry permit took ninety days. She didn't have time for all that.

As long as her actions were legal, no law prevented her from investigating on her own. She had access to public records, like any citizen, and could follow someone covertly, but she had no authority to compel anyone to answer her questions, to conduct a formal interview or to detain a person.

That left her with only one choice–bluffing.

Carrying out investigations within the framework of law enforcement required hard work. But working outside the mantle of law enforcement was much more difficult and dangerous. In her early days, before she joined the Chicago PD, she caused the arrest and conviction of two criminals. One a rapist and the other a would-be terrorist. Driven by her personal need to make a difference, she tracked down both felons using bluffing techniques, and then called in the police for the arrest. Illinois police officials honored her with a Citizen of the Year Award, which led to her being hired by police Chief Marvin Danforth. That old son of a bitch.

Bluffing meant she had to walk a thin line between acting as a concerned citizen and not impersonating a police officer. She had done it before. Ashley would find the bastard who killed Bitty and abused Rita Durant. The man who told Rita he planned an unspecified horrendous act of terror.

BEFORE GOING to Roswell, Ashley spent time planning a strategy. She gathered the tools of the bluffing trade, which included an assortment of disguises, fake ID's, a Ruger LCP .380 caliber handgun, and plenty of cash.

She drove to Roswell, parked next to the airport terminal on the south side of town and rented a small car that could not be traced to her. Dressed in cheap loose fitting clothes, wearing a blond wig and a pair of nondescript eyeglasses, she programmed her GPS and drove to the Westside Plaza. She found the surveillance teams' description of the place accurate. The first store had a *Rent Me* sign in the window. The next advertised vacuum cleaner repairs and shared a wall with Smith Trading which shared a wall with Jake's Ice Cream Parlor. All the units were old, but clean.

She parked in front of the ice cream store and went inside. Ashley lived most of her life on the east coast but had lived in New Mexico long enough to mimic the southwestern twang of the natives without sounding corny.

A chubby man stood behind the counter wearing a white apron and cap that read *Beam Me Up Scotty*. Cheerfully he asked, "Hi, I'm Jake. What can I get for you little lady?"

"Well now, let me see." She studied the menu posted on the wall overhead. "Everything looks pretty darn good." She noticed no other customers in the store. "I shouldn't,"–touching her padded skirt front–"but I'll have one of those banana splits." She pointed at the menu with a sheepish smile.

"Comin' right up!"

She sat at the counter and watched the construction of a calorie laden dessert through her plastic eye frames, "What's that place next door? I don't remember seeing it before."

Jake sat the banana split on the counter in front of her with a napkin and spoon. "Some kind a Trading Post, I think. Hasn't been there long. About two weeks or so."

"Sign says import and export. Maybe it's a front for drugs or something." She picked the cherry off the top of the ice cream.

"I don't know about that, but it must be something important. A big old semi-truck dropped off a trailer just yesterday around back. Kind of blocks the alley."

Ashley swallowed the cherry whole. She hadn't thought to drive the alley. "They must be doing a good business." She cleared her throat.

Jake agreed. "Must be, but I never see anybody over there since it opened. They probably do everything with computers and cell phones." He noted the ice cream had started to puddle. "Everything alright, little lady? Can I get you something else?"

"No. No, this is great, thanks." Ashley snipped off a piece of banana, and began to chew. A couple of teenagers dashed through the door behind her. Jake moved down the counter and took their order. When he returned, he found money and a generous tip next to the melted ice cream.

Ashley left the store and turned left, walked the depth of the building and turned again onto an alley pockmarked with potholes and scattered trash. Parked next to the back door of Smith Trading she saw a weathered cargo shipping container mounted on a truck trailer. The vacant alley allowed her to inspect the container box unobserved. She estimated it to be about eighteen to twenty feet long and eight feet wide. Made of heavy corrugated metal, its double doors were latched down and secured with hardened steel locks. She made out the faded letters CMC painted on the side of the container. A metal plate riveted down low on the door read *Container Management Corporation Sales and Rentals*. The unit had a serial number printed high on the right side of the door. She memorized it. With a rock she tapped all four sides of the shipping container. It sounded full, not hollow. She continued down the alley and around the building. In her car she wrote down everything including the license plate number of the trailer.

Ashley had a choice to make. Stakeout the shipping container and wait or take Dorothy Hogan up on her promise to help, which would free her to work on loose end number two. She remembered Dorothy's words. *If you need anything. I mean anything, you let me know.* Ashley fished her phone out and tapped in Dorothy's number.

"Good morning. This is Special Agent in Charge Walter Kent's office, how may I help you?"

"Dorothy, it's me."

She lowered her voice. "Ashley, where are you?"

"I'm in Roswell. Can you talk?"

"It's okay. Kent is downstairs in the conference room. How are you holding up?"

"I'm fine. Dorothy, you said to call you if I needed anything. I don't want to put you on the spot. So if you say no, I'll understand."

"Tell me what you need, honey."

Ashley let out a sigh of relief. "I need a trace on a shipping cargo container. Write this down. OWLU 202386. CMC Container Management Corporation. It's a smallish container parked behind Smith Trading in Roswell. It's on a semi-trailer with an Ohio license plate, number 779-542. Did you get that?"

"Got it. Why is this important?"

"Our guy has setup Smith Trading for a reason. I need to know where this shipment originated and what's in the container. I think it's important."

"I'll ask Bill Johnson to get on it right away. I know he'll pitch in and help." Dorothy paused a moment. "Ashley, what are you doing in Roswell?'

"I'm working the Russell Smith case."

"Honey, you're working without a net. You need back up."

I'm okay. I'll be careful. I'm going off-line the next couple of days. Got to go Dorothy. I'll check back with you. Thanks. I mean it."

Ashley disconnected before Dorothy could tell her the good news.

# THIRTY-SEVEN

MAGNIFICENT PATCHES OF SCENERY, isolated between long stretches of flat sparsely vegetated deserts, made little or no impression on Ashley as she drove the 200 miles between Roswell and El Paso, Texas. She used the early morning drive to plan her meeting with the occupant at South Estrella Street. Without arousing suspicions, she wanted to learn about Allen Lee and the buyer of the old Ford pickup.

Ashley had never been to El Paso. She knew it shared the border with Juarez, Mexico and had over half a million people. When she entered the outskirts of the city she found it looked like most large towns in the southwest with fast-food restaurants and big box stores.

After exiting I-10 she programmed the Estrella Street address into her GPS which led her to an old residential part of town. The dwellings were small and close together. When she reached her destination, she found a narrow unpretentious house on a corner that intersected with East San Antonio Avenue. Several houses on the block had *For Rent* signs in the yard. She parked one street over, and mentally, rehearsed her impending performance. She didn't know who currently lived at that address, but she would pretend the occupant at 3689 was Allen Lee and see what happened.

Ashley adjusted her blond wig and checked her makeup in the rearview mirror. She decided not to take her newly purchased ankle holster and Ruger handgun.

The house was freshly painted an unfortunate shade of purple with white trim, and stood on pilings two feet off the ground. Three wooden steps led to the front door. There was no doorbell, so she knocked. A dog barked. She knocked again.

The door opened and a man peered out. In an accent Ashley didn't place, he asked, "What do you want?"

"Good afternoon. I'm with Tri-State Life Insurance. I'm investigating a claim. Do you have a minute?" She extended a business card with a bright smile. "I'm not selling anything. This involves an insurance claim."

The man opened the door further, and took the card. He read, *Julie Pinzola, Claims Investigator, Tri-State Life and Casualty Insurance Company, Phoenix, Arizona.* "What does this have to do with me?" he asked.

"It concerns a hit-and-run accident involving one of our insured clients." Behind her a diesel truck rumbled by. "It's noisy out here. I wonder if we might talk inside. It will only take a moment, please?" Another bright smile.

The man pulled back, hesitated, and then opened the door. "You may come in." He wore a denim shirt and pants and displayed a full beard that matched his black hair. Around his neck hung a gold amulet. His slopping shoulders suggested a muscular build. "We will talk briefly. I have work to do." He walked to the center of the room, turned and remained standing. A large dog sat by his side wearing a spiked choke collar. Ashley recognized the breed–a Doberman Pincher. Its tail did not wag.

She stepped into a living room of well-worn furnishings. The walls were bare of decorations accept for a photograph of a man standing in front of a twin engine aircraft dressed in a dark suit with gold braid. A colored rug lay partially unrolled in the corner, and a computer monitor flashed screen-savers every few seconds.

"Thank you. This involves an injury claim made by our client. She is a victim of a hit-and-run accident involving a 1979 Ford pickup truck that fled the scene. She suffered serious injuries. A witness wrote down the plate number of the truck. Records show it is owned by a Russell Smith. We have been unable to find Mr. Smith. The Bill of Sale on file at the New Mexico DMV lists you as the seller of this truck to Russell Smith a little over two month ago. I wonder if..."

He interrupted her. "I sold no truck."

"But Mr. Lee, the records are clear you..."

"Who?"

She stopped short, acting confused by the question. "Alan Lee. You sold the truck that is involved in this claim. I thought you might be able to help us find..."

"I know no one by the name of Alan Lee."

"You're not Alan Lee?"

"No, my name is Bashir Hashim. You may leave now."

"I'm sorry Mr. Hashy, but..."

"That's Hashim," he said, irritated.

159

She spelled the name. "H-A-S-H-I-M?"

"Yes. Go now."

"Motor Vehicle records show an Alan Lee, at this address, sold the Ford pickup truck to Russell Smith two months ago."

The man fidgeted with his amulet and frowned. He drew back and spoke quickly. "There has been a mistake. I have lived here only one month. It must have been someone else."

"Oh, I'm sorry. You're a new tenant?"

Shifting his weight from one foot to the other he answered, "I know nothing of which you speak. You must leave now." He advanced on Ashley in a manner less than friendly, thrusting her business card back into her hand. The dog stood, poised.

She stepped back. "You're right, this must be a mistake. So sorry to bother you," Staying conversational, she added. "If you should come across Mr. Lee, I would appreciate a call." She moved to the door. "This claim is for a large sum of money. I'm sure we could arrange a reward for any information you might have." She stepped outside and turned back to face Bashir. He slammed the door shut.

Freaky son-of-a-bitch, thought Ashley as she walked to her car. She placed the bent business card in a plastic bag in her purse for Bill Johnson to check for fingerprints. Slipping behind the steering wheel, she closed her eyes and reviewed the facts. Fact one, the Bill of Sale gave the seller's name and address. With the seller living in Texas, the New Mexico DMV would have checked that against the title to verify it. Fact two, the address is a real place, not made up. She pulled out a notepad and listed three possible scenarios.

1. Hashim acquired the truck by some means and forged the title and bill of sale using the name of Allen Lee.
2. Allen Lee lived with Hashim when he sold the truck.
3. Allen Lee sold the truck and moved from the house over a month ago, as Hashim claims.

Forgery of the title is possible, but remote. The New Mexico DMV researches out-of-state titles to guard against fraud and odometer misrepresentation. Again, it's an old truck hardly worth the risk of forgery, which is a felony. She drew a line through number one.

In the second scenario two men named Lee and Hashim makes for an odd couple. Mr. Hashim is obviously a practicing Muslim. The amulet he clutched had two Arabic letters etched on both sides. The screen-savers flashed views of Middle Eastern religious shrines, and the small rug, partly unrolled in the corner, depicted a mihrab–an arched doorway to the Great Mosque in Mecca. Allen Lee and Bashir Hashim would be an unlikely pairing.

The third possibility that Hashim moved into the house on South Estrella last month suggests the previous occupant was Allen Lee. This claim may be true. But if his story was false, Hashim was lying. Liars are usually hiding something. She knew how to check the truth about how long Mr. Hashim had lived at that address.

First she called the El Paso Field Office and identified herself, confident her resignation had no yet been processed. She asked if they would run a Texas ownership profile on the 1979 truck. They agreed, and told her to call back in an hour.

In urban areas the County Tax Assessor keeps the public tax records. Ashley tapped her phone and quickly found the address of the Civic Center Plaza. She drove there, parked, and took the elevator to the second floor, where she found the door to the Assessor's office.

A young woman greeted her at the office counter. Ashley handed over her Insurance Company card. "I'm researching an insurance claim and need to know the name of the property owner at this address." She wrote it down. "I hope this won't be too much trouble?"

The young woman gawked at the address. "Gosh this is a street address. To match an address to ownership we have to use the computer. I'll ask my boss Ms. Holmberg about this. She does all that." The young woman turned and went to the back of the office. Ms. Holmberg made a face and looked at Ashley standing behind the counter. She then slapped the address down on her desk and began typing. A minute later a printer chugged out a single sheet of paper. She stepped over to the printer and wrote something on the bottom. The young woman snapped it up and ran back to the counter. "Ms. Holmberg says the property is owned by *Mid-Town Rental and Leasing Management.* She added the name of the CEO so you can contact him."

When Ashley got back to her car, she reviewed the information and found the name Pedro Rodriguez scrolled across the bottom with a telephone number. She selected a second identity out of her purse, and phoned Mr. Rodriguez.

The receptionist inquired, "May I say who's calling?"

"This is Carmen Pantano with the New Texas Employment Service." She waited.

A deep buttery male voice with a Spanish accent spoke. "Good afternoon. This is Pedro Rodriguez speaking. How may I help you Ms. Pantano."

"Thank you for taking my call this late in the afternoon."

"It is my pleasure."

"A Mr. Bashir Hashim is seeking employment through our agency. His resume states he lives at 3689 South Estrella Street and rents from you. I am verifying his information and credit status, you understand?"

"Of course. How may I assist you?"

"How long has Mr. Hashim lived at this address and does he rent or lease from your company?"

"You must excuse me, Ms. Pantano, but I own many properties and cannot recall this gentleman's name. If you will hold the line I will have someone assist you."

Ashley felt the tightness in her shoulders relax. This ploy was working. "You are most kind, Mr. Rodriguez. Thank you." She held the line and in a few seconds a female voice offered to find the information. Minutes later the woman came back on the line. "Ms. Pantano, the current occupant has rented from us the past twelve months. He always pays on time."

"Thank you for your cooperation. Have a good day." Ashley gave herself a thumbs up gesture. That confirmed Bashir Hashim was lying.

She called the El Paso Field Office to find out if the ownership profile of the truck resulted in anything of value. She experienced only a little surprise when she learned Allen Lee had purchased the truck, for one dollar, from Bashir Hashim who had bought it from *Happy Harry's Used Cars*.

Ashley's stomach growled, her body felt ragged and her head ached. Considering the going-home traffic in El Paso, she faced a four-hour drive back to Roswell. Apart from feeling miserable, she had a greater problem: she wanted to stakeout both the Hashim house and Smith Trading, but she could not be in two places at once.

She checked her watch: 4:45 p.m. Dorothy Hogan would be tidying up her desk in preparation to go home. Ashley tapped in Dorothy's number. Hogan picked up.

"It's me, Dorothy."

162

"Oh, Ashley." She softened her voice. "Where are you?"

"I'm in El Paso."

"El Paso? My, you do get around. You sound tired. What's up?"

"I don't want to do this, but I'm in a spot."

"Are you in danger?"

"No. Nothing like that. I need help."

"What can I do?"

Ashley's words came quick. "A couple of days ago I found this shipping container behind Smith Trading in Roswell."

"Yes, Bill Johnson already checked that out for you."

"So soon? What did he find out?"

"Bill said the container shipped fewer than four weeks ago from the Port of Dubai in the United Arab Emirates. Marked for General Delivery to Roswell. It was loaded on an oil tanker instead of a cargo ship."

"Why do you suppose that?"

"He says tankers are faster. Like a direct flight. It was received about four-days ago in Houston, and picked up by a trucking outfit out of Dallas. They delivered it to Roswell two nights back."

"Sounds like an expedited shipment. Did Bill find out what's in the shipping container?"

"Honey."

"Honey?"

"Yes. It's full of honey. Sixty barrels."

Ashley didn't speak for a few seconds. "That's bizarre. Who knows about this?"

"Bill, me, and now you, what are you thinking?"

"I'm thinking the shit is on the way to the fan."

"Okay. What do we do? Move the fan? Turn the fan off? How far do you want to go with this analogy?" Dorothy heard Ashley giggle.

"Thanks. I needed that. Here's the deal. I have to be in Roswell to stakeout Smith Trading. It's my chance to connect with our killer–the man who blew up his motor home and blew town the same night. I also have to be in El Paso. I need to watch a man who sold a pickup truck to whoever posed as Russell Smith. His name is Bashir Hashim and he's part of this whole mess." She took a deep breath. "Dorothy, I can't be in both places at the same time."

"Look, babe, you're way ahead of me on this, but I can tell you need help." A few seconds passed. "Ashley I know what I'm about to say will be hard for you to hear, but I think it's time you had a talk with Walter."

Ashley's voice sounded strained. "I can't do that, Dorothy. I don't belong there anymore. As far as the Bureau is concerned, I'm nobody."

Dorothy's rubbed the back of her neck. "This is difficult for me to say, but I didn't know any other way. Are you an American?"

"What?"

"Are you an American?"

"You bet."

"Do you love your country?"

"Yes, of course."

"Then it's time you swallowed your pride and came in out of the cold."

Ashley said nothing. Her mind searched for other options. Finally, she responded. "It's not pride, Dorothy. I don't fit in there anymore."

"Trust me. You are not the best judge of that. Tell me, when you want me set up a meeting with Kent." She waited for a reply. When it came, the tone was firm and deliberate.

"Okay. I'll meet with him, but it has to be on neutral ground."

"Where is this neutral ground?"

"This meeting needs to happen fast. I'm four, maybe five hours away from Albuquerque. I can be there tonight at 10 o'clock. You know the Best Western off 1-25 at Southern?"

"Sure. Why?"

"Book a room in my name. I'll check at the desk when I get there."

"So you want to meet the boss at a motel tonight?" She asked with a playful sound in her voice.

"Cut the crap, Dorothy. This isn't easy for me."

"Sorry, I couldn't help myself. I'll set it up, and I'll get Kent there if I have to pull him by the ears." A couple of seconds passed. "Ashley, I'm not going to get into this right now, but you will want to hear what Walter has to say to you. Good night, honey. You drive safe, you hear?"

164

# THIRTY-EIGHT

SMITH TRADING FACED WEST on Union Avenue, and received the afternoon sun. The reflective material Abdullah installed in the front window helped shield him from the heat. Still the temperature reached an uncomfortable 103 degrees inside the office he now used as living quarters. He planned to buy an indoor air-conditioner and vent it into the back half of the building.

Abdullah thought of his deluxe motor home and the event that brought him back to Smith Trading and this degraded existence. He had enjoyed the luxury of living in a magnificent RV with a woman to satisfy his needs. Then, within a few hours, he faced the likelihood of discovery and capture. He'd gathered his essential items, the bag of money, the Master Plan of Action, and his computer. He then assembled the cell phone bomb and attached it to the fuel tank. After walking a mile, he had detonated the bomb and viewed the orange glow of the explosion in the night sky. Two hours later at the Westside Plaza, using his duffel bag full of money as a pillow, he lay on the cold office floor, asleep by midnight.

The next morning he found a pay phone, and called Bashir in El Paso. The Russell Smith identity was compromised. He needed new credentials. Using Abdullah's photograph from the original Allen Lee forgery, Bashir got a new Social Security number and New Mexico driver's license from his longtime source in El Paso. The next day he sent them to Abdullah at the Smith Trading address in an overnight pouch.

Armed with a fresh ID, he walked to a pawnshop, and bought a bicycle. He rode it to a U-Haul outlet and rented a truck. After buying the air-conditioner, some used furniture and a mattress, he waited for the ice cream and the vacuum repair shops to close before he unloaded his furnishings into his unit, using the back door. Abdullah then returned the truck and retrieved his bike. He paid cash for everything.

When the shipping container arrived on the evening of day four, he signed for it and discovered heavy-duty locks on the doors. He tested the locks and found them resistant to any hacksaw he might have to cut them off. He entered the back door of Smith Trading, stored his tools. That's when he heard a banging sound out back. He hurried to the rear of the building and peered out of a small cobweb covered window. He watched a woman pounding on the sides of the container. She circled it and stared at the identification plate riveted to the door. She did not look like a homeless person. His first inclination was to go outside and confront her, but decided that would expose him to someone he did not know or trust. She soon walked away and didn't return.

In preparation for his need to hide that one important item from the cargo container, he bought a beat-up old panel truck from a private party he found on Craigslist. He did not intend to register the truck for the short time he would need it.

The next morning he again called his contact in El Paso and learned Bashir had received a key to the shipping container from Dubai with instruction to foreword it to Abdullah. It would arrive the next day by express mail. Bashir also told him of the strange woman who inquired about the old Ford truck he had bought from him. The one Abdullah later transferred to the Russell Smith identity. "She seemed legitimate, but when I searched on line for the insurance company name, I didn't find it listed anywhere."

Abdullah's asked what she looked like and Bashir described her. She didn't sound like anyone he knew.

Now he waited for delivery of the key on this, the fifth day. Late tonight he would open the shipping container and remove an item that would arm him with a powerful weapon. This meant that soon he would receive encrypted instructions from Rome. Finally, his need to serve Allah the All Powerful, and become a revered figure of Islamic history would be realized.

# THIRTY-NINE

EL PASO AND ALBUQUERQUE are connected by two Interstate highways. Considering Ashley's fourteen hour and 500 mile day, she needed the safety offered by a controlled access roadway. When she arrived in Albuquerque after dark, she pulled into the Best Western motel, parked under the portico and went inside.

The night clerk raised his head. "Evening Miss, do you have a reservation?"

She started to dig out a credit card. "Yes, in the name of Ashley Kohen."

The clerk checked his file. "Don't have one with that name."

"Check again, please. Maybe it's under Dorothy Hogan."

He went back through the fil again. "Nope."

Ashley frowned. "Try Walter Kent."

"Okay, I have one in that name." The clerk said, with a sly grin. She handed him her credit card. "The room's already paid. Government rate. Our tax dollars at work." He grinned and rolled his eyes.

Ashley glared at him and replaced the card in her wallet. "Room number," she demanded.

"Yes, ma'am–room 126. It's right down from the office–ground floor." He pointed over his shoulder. "Your Mr. Kent is waiting." He cracked a devilish grin. She took the electronic key, "Have a great night," she snarled and left.

Ashley inserted the keycard in the door and stepped into room 126. She noticed the usual queen-sized beds separated by a small table with a double light fixture fastened to the wall. A round table and two chairs sat in front of the window. A red ice chest on the floor, with a briefcase next to it, seemed out of place. Walter Kent lay stretched out on the second bed watching the evening news on TV. He immediately snapped it off, and stood. She closed the door behind her and returned his gaze.

A few seconds passed. "The blond hair is good, but I like the natural brunette better."

It took Ashley a second before she remembered the blond wig. She moved into the room and sat on the end of the first bed. "Guess I forgot about that." She pulled the wig off, tossed it behind her, shook her head and ran her fingers through her hair.

Walter walked past her and stood next to the round table. With a sympathetic expression he said, "You seem tired, Ashley."

She lifted her head and forced an alert expression. "It's been a long day." The lamp in the corner lit his silhouette, giving him a radiant glow. He was ruggedly handsome, and tonight seemed softer then she remember. Not the Special Agent in Charge, but more like a fellow human being.

Kent inspected Ashley's exhausted face with dark circles under her eyes and her hair in disarray. "You have an uncanny ability to look great even when you shouldn't. Not many people can pull that off."

A moment of silence, and then Ashley asked, "Did Dorothy tell you why I asked for this meeting?"

"She told me you've been working on the Russell Smith case."

"I haven't done anything wrong," she said, ready to defend herself. "I followed up on a couple of loose ends.

"Tell me about those loose ends."

Ashley expected a different reaction. She relaxed, then described the un-sub's visit to Smith Trading during the early part of the ill-fated surveillance. She said it seemed curious to her that he would be running a business. Today, when she discovered the shipping container behind the store, she became convinced of its importance and noted the serial number. "Now that I know the shipment came from Dubai, I'm sure he will show up, soon. I need to stakeout that location." She paused and waited for Kent to ask how she found out about the origin of the shipping container, but his expression of interest held steady.

Ashley described what she learned today—what she did in El Paso using the New Mexico DMV information, her interview with Bashir Hashim and his lie. "I think he's involved in this case and needs to be watched," She stopped and realized this all sounded speculative, but hoped Walter would get the idea. "I called Dorothy because I can't be in both places at the same time."

Walter took a seat at the table, and pointed to the second chair. "Sit here, Ashley. It's important." Unsure of what was coming, she moved from the bed to the chair. The lamp above him highlighted his thick wavy hair. He reached down and pulled the ice chest over and opened it. He set two Champagne glasses on the table, a chilled bottle of Asti Spumante, a smaller bottle of Triple Sec, and a carafe of orange juice.

Ashley marveled at the array of drinks displayed. "What are you doing?"

He ignored the question. "Dorothy told me you preferred the Italian version of Champagne." I find it a bit sweet, but with a delicate hint of brightness." Walter poured a scant ounce of Triple Sec in each glass. He then pulled the cork out of the wine, with the usual popping sound followed by a wispy spray of moisture. He partially filled the glasses with the sparkling wine, and then topped it off with orange juice. "The orange juice is domestic, I'm afraid." He tried to be serious while sliding a glass over to her.

Confused, she asked, "What is this?"

"It's a Mimosa."

Her hand went to the glass stem without thinking. "Yes, I know. I mean why...I don't understand." She swirled the drink. "It's nice, but..."

Walter lifted his glass. "A toast!"

Ashley lifted her glass, still unsure. "To what?"

The glasses clinked. "To your return to active duty!" He sipped his drink and made a *huuuuum*, sound.

Her glass remained extended. Active duty? Her brain scrambled to understand. Bewilderment showed on her face. "No," she said out loud.

"How can you say no, you haven't tasted it yet?"

She lowered the drink and took a sip, and then another. She hadn't eaten all-day. "That's good. Damn good, but I mean, no. I can't be on active duty, I'm not in the agency anymore. I resigned."

Walter chuckled. "You wrote a letter to that effect, but you forgot an important point. You can write a letter of resignation, but you can't process it. Only I can do that, and I didn't." He reached for the Asti Spumante. "Refill?"

Ashley stared at him. His face held a pleasant expression, as if he had just complimented a student on getting straight "A's" She sputtered, "This isn't right. The Bureau is an important agency. It does great work, but I don't fit in. I've tried, but I can't deal with the culture."

"The fact is, you can't deal without it." His manner turned serious. "You need a Bill Johnson to check out the origin of a shipping container once in a while, and you need Jerry Cebeck to conduct a surveillance on Mr. Hashim down south, on occasion." He leaned back and drained his glass and put it down on the table, gently.

Ashley remained silent.

"You should know about a few other loose ends that have advanced the Russell Smith case. The un-sub's computer download that Cebeck sent to Bill Johnson was forwarded to Washington. Turns out some of the download matched six encrypted messages the DC office and the NSA had deciphered a couple of days ago–messages that imply a terror operation is in the making. Washington didn't know the destination of the messages, but now they do. Director Delong feels they are important enough to trigger a Joint Terrorist Task Force. He praised you for your suspicion that a terror plot may be afoot."

Ashley listened. Her thoughts surged in several directions. A terrorist threat, as she had suspected. Agency resources coming together. A commendation from the Director? She had to ask about that one. "Why would Director Delong praise me?'"

"He asked for the name of the Lead Investigator on the case."

Ashley grabbed the Champagne glass and downed it. "I'll have another." Walter began mixing two more Mimosas.

Ashley's brain shifted into high gear. Clearly, he wants me back, and deep down, when he's not on-the-job, he's an agreeable man. A man to be trusted and depended on. She wondered if she could work within the traditions of the Bureau, and not screw up again. Ashley lifted the second drink and savored the sweet mixture. Maybe a better question was could she do without the backing of the best law enforcement agency in the world?

"You also have moral support a bit closer to home," he said, as he mixed a third drink. The day after you and I sorted things out, I experienced a near mutiny. Johnson came from downstairs with this in his hands." Walter leaned down and opened the briefcase and put out Ashley's gun and badge and placed them on the table between them. "Dorothy followed right behind him. These are two people I consider the best in the business, and my friends. I'm glad they shut my door, before unloading on me."

When she saw her badge lying on the table she took a deep breath and reached out and touched it. Then looked at a man she held in total respect. "You were right, Walter. My actions caused the surveillance to fail."

"Your actions also saved a life."

"Did you get the hospital recording I sent to Dorothy?" A mental picture of Rita Durant came to her mind.

"Yes, I listened to it this morning, good work."

Ashley felt a wave of sadness pass through her. "I feel bad about the way this turned out." Her eyes fixed on her badge. "Walter, I need to be honest with you. I need the Bureau, but if I come back, I can contribute more if I work undercover." She reached out and touched his hand. "That's what I want to do. That's how I can contribute the most."

He placed his other hand on top of hers. "That's a dangerous arrangement, Ashley. I don't want you working alone. I don't want anything to happen to you."

"Every step of the way the Bureau will be with me. I won't be alone. I know you'll see to that." Ashley studied Walter's face. He appeared conflicted. She didn't understand until he spoke.

"I've been in this business a lifetime. I started as a street cop, like you, and worked my way up. It cost me a marriage. A mistake I haven't repeated. Then law school, public defender, prosecutor, and finally I found a home in the Bureau. I've met many people in law enforcement over the years. Most are sincere and dedicated, but at the end of their shift, they go home to a family and live an everyday life. You're different. You work 24/7 and 365." He squeezed her hand. "No husband, not even a dog. What keeps you going?" Their eyes met. "What drives you, Ashley? What gives you the relentless strength to push ahead?"

She pulled her hand away from his, stood and turned her back to him. Maybe because this last week had been an emotional storm, and she was exhausted or because she sensed he cared like no one had ever cared before. She didn't know why, but she felt she needed to face the past and share it with him. That turning point in her life she hid from everyone. That terrible day.

She faced him. "It was Tuesday and the weather was clear. Mom went to work like she always did. She worked in the financial district long hours to pay the bills and keep me in school. That day, at 9:03 a.m. American Airlines Flight 11, bound for Los Angeles, crashed into the 60th floor of the South Tower. The World Trade Center was under attack. The North

171

Tower was already on fire. Mom worked on the 95th floor, above the impact zone. She called me at 9:10. I remember the time. I'll never forget it. She told me she loved me. I said I loved her. She said she would not be home tonight. She made me promise to be strong and remember everything she had taught me. She said there was a terrible accident and many people would not go home. Mom told me she had to try to save the good people around her and that I must save good people, too, and protect them from the bad people. I asked her why she won't be home. She said God had a reason. She told me to be strong. She wanted to be proud of me. I heard people screaming and I said I didn't want her to go. I wanted her to stay with me. She said, 'I love you, dear Ashley'. Those were the last words she said to me."

Walter jumped to his feet. He went to her and held her shoulders to steady her. She looked at him, her eyes glistened with tears that began to flow. He cupped her face with gentle hands and brushed the tears away. She felt unsteady. His arms encircled her. Ashley felt his warmth and needed his support. They stood, holding each other in silence. Then, with his hand, he lifted her chin and gently kissed her. She tightened her grip on him. He kissed her again. This time she responded.

# FORTY

SHORTLY AFTER THE WEEKLY meeting of the Terrorism Threat and Investigation Center broke up, Rashid and Mike Johansson drove back to their office via Connecticut Avenue. At the meeting they had explained the procedures used to crack the coconut encryptions. Leo Adornetto, Director of National Intelligence, and a regular member of the President's Council on National Security, had attended the meeting. Adornetto had a long and distinguished background in national security matters. He had served as chief investigator for the Chairman of the Armed Services Committee, CEO of the Cyber Security Institute, and most recently as a special adviser to the Chairman of the Joint Chiefs of Staff.

In the car, Mike asked Rashid's opinion. "What did you think of Adornetto's reaction to our combined efforts with the NSA?"

Not wanting to dampen the Big Swede's enthusiasm Rashid hesitated. "He seemed interested, but a little distant."

"Distant?"

"When you oversee the entire intelligence community, and speak to the President daily, our achievement may not seem all that important."

Mike pinched his eyebrows together. "Then he's missed the whole idea of our operation; interagency cooperation to heighten national security." As if to underline his point, when a taxi cut him off in traffic, he blew his horn, holding it down, "Damn taxies think they own the streets."

Rashid wanted to lessen his old friend's agitation. "Working across agency lines to break the coconuts is an important accomplishment, but we don't know their plan and when it will go down. We only know something is brewing."

Mike dodged another taxi, and said nothing.

Rashid felt a vibration against his leg. He pulled out his phone and read Ike Gunner's number. "Hey Ike, what's up?"

Ike talked fast. "We got it. We got number seven. Big Mamma just sent me the alert. She intercepted it. It's on hold, and it's somethin' big. Wait till you see what the turban-heads are up to now!"

Rashid covered the phone and turned to Mike, "It's Gunner over at NSA." Turning back he asked Ike, "What's it say?"

"You got a see this. These dudes are on the move."

"Are you in Virginia?"

"Yep, right here, Prof."

"Hold on."

Rashid turned to Mike again. "We have the seventh message now, and Ike says it's 'something big'."

The Big Swede wet his lips, blinked his eyes and asked, "McLean, right?"

"Right."

Mike swerved the car and headed for the Georgetown Bridge that crossed into Virginia. "Those damn taxies better get out of my way."

THE SECURITY GUARDS at the NSA building recognized Doctor Youris, did a quick check, and passed him through. Even though Rashid vouched for Mike Johansson, they did a pat-down of the assistant deputy director of the FBI. Once through security, they took the elevator to the fifth floor. Ike met them at the elevator in his electric scooter, and led them to his workstation in the Black Chamber.

Rashid introduced both men. Mike extended his hand and Ike shook it. With his other hand Ike, waved a sheet of paper over his head. "It come through minutes ago and it's decrypted." All three settled around Ike's worktable. Ike passed a copy of the message to each man.

Rashid read aloud:

*"In the name of Allah, the Beneficent, and Merciful.*

*Oh, Sword of the Great One, vanguard of the jihad and holy warrior, be it known to you, final preparations are at hand. In accordance with our supplier's agreement, three members of the Team of Deliverance will travel from different nations. They will rendezvous at the house of Hashim in our southern portal to America.*

*Know the team members and memorize their code names: Kassar Suri: (Khoon Baha), Alexander Kosloff: (Pasol), Danish Maloof: (Magister).*

*In the name of The Granter of Security, at full moon they will assemble and await your instructions. Secure a safe location. Your meeting must be*

174

*blind to all who would harm you. Guard against the great Satan. If it please Allah the Exalted, your training must be swift and complete for you have their expertise no more than 24 hours. Learn the skill needed to cause the culmination of our plans to force our enemies to their knees and free us of their interference. May the All Powerful One, reward you for your actions that will bring the Day of Resurrection and Sharia rule to the world. With the blessing of Allah the Divine,*
*Your Mentor,*
*AG"*

Mike Johansson rubbed his hands together. "Sounds like we finally have something to work with here." He held the paper. "They allude to a time and place. What the hell does 'southern portal' mean?"

Rashid reviewed the message, savoring each word. "El Paso, Texas," he answered. "In the first message we cracked, the Sword describes how he entered our country over the bridge from Juarez to El Paso. So that's where these people will first assemble.

Ike said, "The house of Hashim. Sounds like an international restaurant."

Mike shook his head, "I doubt it, but that's something we can check out easy enough. I'll get my people on it right away." He made a note on the back of an envelope. "What else can we deduce from this writing?"

Ike had a ready answer. "They will meet at 'full moon', that means they will meet this here Friday."

Mike asked, "How did you determine Friday?"

"I looked it up. There are 29.5 days in a lunar cycle, and eight phases of the moon in each cycle, which makes for about 3.68 days in each phase. Right now we is approaching the waning gibbous phase. The next full moon is Friday. That's five days countin' today." Ike appeared pleased with himself.

Mike quipped, "You computer guys never stop surprising me."

"Get use to it, Mike. Ike likes to show off." Rashid turned his attention to the words on the paper. "It says here, these men will come from different nations. That means they live outside the U.S. Let's assume a reasonable scenario. They have to come from somewhere in the middle-east or about halfway around the globe. If you consider time for preparations and travel, that's two of the five days, leaving us with about three days before this Team of Deliverance gets airborne. Not much time."

Ike tapped his keyboard. "I can't change the day of the meeting, but I can shorten the Sword's time to prepare for it by one day."

Rashid's eyebrows went up. "How so?"

"Simple. I programmed Big Mama to recognize their transmissions' signature, and programmed her to hold it in quarantine. I can hold it for 24 hours. I can't hold it longer because the risk of detection starts doubling after a day."

Rashid placed his hand on Ike's shoulder. "A smart move."

Mike appeared thoughtful. Standing, he stepped back. "We need a plan. A plan that will let us take control of this threat."

Ike, rubbed his hands together. "Find out where the house of Hashim is and arrest the bunch of 'em."

Mike shook his head. "That doesn't tell us what we're dealing with. This team will meet with our un-sub who, based on everything we know, works alone. He's a Lone Wolf controlled by an outside authority. Capturing this bunch doesn't erase the threat. It would simply delay their plans long enough to replace these assailants with new people and move on."

"Mike is right," said Rashid, who felt a tightness in his stomach. "We must infiltrate this team if we are to learn the nature of this threat."

Ike blurted, "Man, how we gonna do that?"

Rashid fingered the message. "Let's start with these three team members." He turned to Mike. Do you recognize any of these names?"

"No. Not offhand, but I can do a search of our IC databases and INTERPOL. That might turn up something."

Rashid studied the message. "One name on the team sounds familiar. Danish Maloof. Not a common name. I can't place it, but I know that name." Mike and Rashid looked at each other as if studying their memories. Then in unison they said "Iran."

Mike slapped his old friend on the back. "That's right. When we worked in that part of the world years ago, Maloof, a professor at the University of Engineering and Technology in Tehran, helped us with communications between Pakistan's FIA and Iran." Rashid agreed. Mike continued. "But why would he be a part of this team? He taught in the language department. He's not political."

"It's here in front of us." Rashid poked the paper with his finger. "*Three members from different nations*, it says. One name, Alexander

Kosloff, is Russian or Ukrainian. The other two speak a different language." Rashid ached an eyebrow. "Maloof is a translator."

Mike leaned his head forward as if to say—why didn't I think of that?

Ike backed his scooter a few feet to view both men better. "You speak Russian, don't you Prof?"

"He sure does," said Mike. And a couple of other languages, too."

Rashid crossed his arms in front of his chest in a defensive gesture. "Hold on, gentlemen. I don't like the tone of this conversation."

Mike edged over to the table. "You said it yourself, we have to infiltrate this team. It's the only way we can learn the nature of this threat. If I arrange an intercept of Professor Maloof before he gets to the rendezvous point, I can detain him as long as needed."

Ike's expression turned serious. "What if any member of this team, including the Lone Wolf, knows Maloof. Rashid would be in trouble. Big time."

Mike pushed back from the table. His face darkened. "You're right Ike. It's too dangerous. Forget I said anything."

All three men fell silent. It remained quiet in the Black Chamber for a full minute. Then Rashid spoke.

"So Danish Maloof gets deathly sick right before he boards his flight to points west. He sends a trusted associate, in his place, armed with the secret password and a note explaining the last minute change. He demands his payment for services not be reduced. What do you think?"

Ike grimaced. "It's dangerous, Prof,"

Mike moved back to the table. "Yes, but it could work. I'd make it work. My friends at the CIA would intercept Maloof before he gets to the airport in Tehran and detain him. We can forge a convincing note and an ironclad identity for Rashid."

Ike cleared his throat. "Lots of "ifs" in there, Mr. Johansson."

Both men stared at Rashid, and waited.

Until this point, Rashid had steered the conversation in the direction he wanted it to go. In his mind, he reviewed the choices he faced. *Hessa's cancer is in remission, but it could come back. If it does she will need me. Still, I know she would want me to do this because our beliefs support the saving of lives. She would say, 'If it pleases Allah, then it is ordained by Him.' She would be right, but it has value only if I can make it work. Mike doesn't know I recognize a name on this Team of Redemption; the Russian, Alexander Kosloff. He will remember me from that night years ago when*

177

*we stood shoulder to shoulder in the dark subterranean chamber in Rome. I must be myself, not some impostor or this plan will fail. If I do this, I will let Mike detain Danish Maloof, forge a note, and create a new identity. But, when I arrive in El Paso, I will be Rashid al Youris, translator, seeking the protection of Allah the Forgiving, with some invisible backup from the FBI.* He stared at his hands tightly clasped in front of him, and made his decision.

"Gentlemen, I don't think we can pass up this opportunity. I'll do it."

# FORTY-ONE

JERRY CEBECK DROVE SOUTH to El Paso in the smaller of the two available plain-vanilla surveillance vans from the motor pool. Lost in thought he didn't notice the sunrise colored clouds that formed a canopy over a nearly deserted Interstate highway nor did he see the morning light that cast long shadows and pink highlights on the countryside.

The events of the past week kept repeating in his mind. First he was assigned to conduct a surveillance of a subject in Roswell as part of a case headed by a new member of the staff, Ashley Kohen. Then, after she blew the stakeout, he found himself appointed Lead Investigator in a case he knew nothing about. Before he finish reviewing the case files, Walter Kent demoted him to Acting Lead. Now he was back to his old job of staking out suspicious characters. He didn't deserve to be pushed around like this, but at least one good thing happened. Walter Kent praised him for his site inspection of the burned-out motor home and his discovery of the subject's escape route.

With all that behind him, his new assignment was to watch a man called Bashir Hashim. During his early morning briefing he learned that Agent Kohen had survived the Roswell debacle and now worked undercover. In her new role, she had discovered that Bashir Hashim may be associated with the Russell Smith killer. Anyone in contact with Hashim must be identified and have background checks performed by the El Paso Field Office who offered staff support. Not an exciting job, but that's what he did for a living.

The subject, Hashim, lived in the old part of town. His narrow house stood on the corner of two intersecting streets. The local field office found a second story apartment in a diagonal position from the target's location. This gave Cebeck an excellent vantage point to view the comings and goings of Mr. Hashim. The next few days or weeks may not be stimulating, but at least he would not have to live in the van.

ASHLEY'S MEETING LAST night in the Best Western with Walter had turned out different from what she had expected. She thought about the less than professional interlude they experienced after she shared, for the first time, her most private secret: the tragic story of her greatest loss in life. A story she had promised herself to never tell anyone. She didn't fully understand what made her do it. Was it an undiscovered need she had suppressed all these years? A momentary weakness? She didn't know, but she suspected it had something to do with the man who cradled her in his arms when she felt most vulnerable. His warmth and tenderness comforted her, but at the same time sparked a fear that she might lose her independence–might need someone to lean on in the future. It was a strange, wonderful, scary feeling she could not shake. She told herself to compartmentalize, set these feelings aside, and deal with it later.

Working undercover she lacked the sidearm an active duty agent would carry. Never not ready, she strapped on her Ruger .380 semi-automatic and ankle holster to her left leg and pulled her pants down to cover it–keeping it out of sight, but available.

Today her work took her back to Roswell. She concentrated on loose end number one, knowing Jerry Cebeck would be in El Paso watching Bashir Hashim at the same time.

Based on Bill Johnson's follow up on the shipment, she planned to do a little surveillance work of her own. She would watch the shipping container and wait for the un-sub to open it and unload the perplexing cargo of honey. Shipping sixty barrels of honey from Dubai to New Mexico made no economic sense. The vast pecan groves that lined miles of roads surrounding Roswell supported beekeeping to pollinate the pecan trees. Imported honey could never compete with local suppliers. So why import honey?

Once in town she drove to the Westside Plaza, and searched the area for useful observation locations. That's when she made an unexpected and disconcerting discovery: the shipping container had vanished.

"Gone," she gasped. Thirty six hours ago the container sat parked behind the building fully loaded, and now it was gone. Walter was right, she couldn't do this alone. It required a team.

Pissed at herself, she wondered, what now? The obvious next step would be to check out the contents of Smith Trading. She drove down the alley behind the building, got out and tried the door. She found it secured with a heavy padlock. Without substantial probable cause, she needed a covert entry search warrant. She fished her phone out and called Albuquerque. Normally she would seek a warrant through their legal office, but sometimes they got fussy about details. She called Bill Johnson, the get-things-done guy.

"Johnson speaking."

"Bill, this is Ashley."

Johnson chuckled. "Ashley Kohen, a mythological creature that arises from her ashes. To what honor do I owe this call?"

"This mythical creature needs a favor from the gods. I thought I'd start at the top."

"You've come to the right place, my dear. What do you need?"

Ashley felt the tension in her body begin to ebb away. "I'm in Roswell. I need an entry warrant for Smith Trading Imports and Exports. It's Unit 3 in the Westside Plaza, on Union Street."

Johnson wrote down the location. "What's the purpose of the search?

Ashley thought of her talk with Rita Durant in the hospital and made a 'best guess' decision. "I'm searching for firearms illicitly imported. This is time critical."

"I'll pull a few strings. Go to our satellite office downtown and standby."

"Thanks, Bill. You're a dear."

"I prefer 'Stag', if you don't mind."

By the time Ashley drove to the Federal Building and climbed the stairs to the second floor, the warrant had been faxed and lay on the receptionist's desk with a note marked *Attention Agent Kohen*. God bless the old stag. She flashed her ID and picked up the warrant. On her way back to the Westside Plaza, she stopped at a hardware store and bought a long handled bolt cutter.

As required by protocol, she knocked on the front door of Smith Trading three times and loudly identified herself as FBI. She heard no answer. She went around back, where the sun cast a dark shadow, and knocked with the same result. The long handles of the bolt cutter gave her leverage, allowing her to sever the bold in a second. She made a mental note to tell the local chief of police about her actions and give them a copy of the warrant.

Ashley found herself in a dark area lit only by a small dirt-covered window in the far corner. A stronger light shone in the front of the building. Following that light source she found the morning sun filtered through the plate-glass window covered with a metallic film. The door glass was painted black. She tried the light switches next to the door and found they worked. The room, designed to serve as a reception area and office, was bare of furniture except for a portable air-conditioner and a twin sized mattress on the floor. A blanket lay crumpled in a corner next to a big plastic toolbox. She started for the back of the shop, then realized the toolbox was a treasure trove of fingerprints. Using the nearby blanket, Ashley opened the box and found a hacksaw and a package of assorted blades and tools. She closed the box, wrapped the blanket around it and carried it into the backroom.

Piled haphazardly about the room were stacks of wooden barrels much like the kind used to age wine, only smaller. After setting the toolbox down, she inspected the nearest barrel. Stamped on the side were the words, *Djeddah, Arable Saouite*. She recognized the name, Djeddah, a port city on the west side of Saudi Arabia. On top of each barrel the words *Al Shifa 100% Natural Honey* were stenciled in red paint. She tilted one of the barrels and rolled it a few feet. It felt like it weighed almost a 100 pounds. All the barrels had the same markings.

Ashley began counting the barrels. She counted them a second time, and got the same number–fifty nine. One less than the sixty listed on the cargo manifest. One barrel missing.

# FORTY-TWO

MIKE JOHANSSON LEARNED long ago in the FBI to be selective about what assignments he delegated. Routine administrative work or matters that did not affect life, he appointed other people to handle. Anything under his command involving a threat to life, he supervised.

Mike decided to craft all aspects of the plan to infiltrate the Team of Deliverance. He felt this effort would carry out two objectives: expose a dangerous conspiracy, and protect a longtime friend who had volunteered to put himself in harm's way. Nothing would happen to Rashid, he would make certain of that. Mike worked out details of the plan late into the night and named it *Operation Full Moon*.

The next morning, a Saturday, he met with Ed Delong and Leo Adornetto in the Director's office. "I want to thank you for meeting with me at such short notice. When you hear what I have to say, you will agree this matter is urgent."

He shared with them the highlights of the case, the content of the seventh message, the existence of the Lone Wolf, and how Mike planned to penetrate this conspiracy. "I've canvassed all of our databases both here and abroad. We're dealing with dangerous people," he told them. "First off, Alexander Kosloff, who also goes by the names of Boris Minsky and Anton Petrovich, is a ruthless international arms dealer wanted by us and a dozen counties around the world. He supplies mostly Russian arms to anyone with cash. We know he has sold arms to both sides of the same conflict. The fact that he is part of this team means a large sum of money is involved. The next team member is Kassar Suri a weapons specialist from Pakistan. One of the world's most skilled CBRNE scientists."

Delong said, "Chemical, Biological, and what else?"

Adornetto chimed in, "Chemical, Biological, Radiological, Nuclear and Explosive specialist."

Delong yanked his unlit cigar out of his mouth. "Holly shit! Why's a person like that coming to a clandestine meeting here in the U.S.?"

Mike took a breath. "That's what we're going to find out."

"Okay, you have my attention. What's your plan?"

Mike pulled a folder out of his briefcase and opened it. He placed it on Delong's desk upside down to be read. "The third member of this team is an Iranian named Danish Maloof. He heads the language department at a university in Tehran. We think his role is to translate what the other members of the team have to say. Two, maybe three languages are represented here. Professor Maloof is our link to infiltrate their team and take this conspiracy down."

Adornetto studied the documents on Delong's desk. "Give me the details."

Mike explained the plan. Maloof would be detained by U. S. Customs. Doctor Youris would take his place armed with the code word, a convincing letter of introduction and identity papers. He would act as the translator. His knowledge, skill and religion made him perfect for the job. He would play his part until the team broke up. Afterwards, based on his report, appropriate actions would be taken.

Adornetto rubbed his chin. "And Doctor Youris is willing to do this?"

Mike shook his head in disbelief, but reluctantly confirmed it. "Yes, he volunteered. He knows this is a risky undertaking. A damned heroic gesture, if you ask me."

Delong frowned. "I've been meaning to speak with you about this Rashid al Youris. I had a background check run on him and I have some questions I want answered before I approve his involvement in this or any other matter."

Mike felt a sudden coldness hit at his core. "Questions? I don't understand."

Delong pulled a report out of his desk drawer and dropped it next to Mike's folder. "Youris retired from our organization five years ago. His service record shows skill and bravery. He got high performance rating every year and quality step increases, but what about after he retired?"

"I'm not sure I follow you, sir. He did what everyone does. He took some time off. After a few years he accepted a position at the university, teaching."

"Yes, I know. Part of our investigation reviewed his financial affairs. The first two years, after he separated from service, he had no outside income beyond his retirement annuity." Delong thumbed through the report. "He paid out enormous sums of money far more than his income.

Where did he get that money? More to the point, what did he do to get that money?" Delong stared at Mike, tossed his well-chewed cigar in the wastebasket, peeled the wrapper off a new one, and jammed it into his mouth.

Mike remained motionless. He wondered what the hell his boss was getting at with such a question. His voice dropped a tone and his hands clenched. "I want you to know, Rashid saved my life at least twice and I may have saved his butt a few times, too. He's a brave, dedicated American who has served his country..."

Delong put his hand up. "Calm down, Mike. I know all of that. I'm not accusing him of anything. I am simply asking a legitimate question. We are about to send this man into a sticky situation. I want to be sure he's on our side all the way."

Forcing himself to appear relaxed, Mike answered. "He is on our side, sir."

"What about the money?"

Mike stepped back and clasped his hands behind his back. "After Rashid retired we stayed in touch. Soon after he separated from the Bureau his wife was diagnosed with early signs of acute liver cancer. He became her constant caregiver. He never left her side. Her treatments were extensive: radiation, chemo, surgery, and finally a transplant. I know the financial burden was staggering. Insurance paid most of the bills, but not all." Mike felt a tightness in his throat. He stopped long enough to regain his composure and plan his next comment. "I helped him with much of the cost not covered by insurance. He didn't ask for it. I did it because I felt I owed him my life. Because he's my friend." Mike swallowed hard. "I'd do it again, if I had too."

The ticking of an antique clock mounted over the fireplace was the only sound heard in the room. Stunned, Delong slowly extended his hand to Mike. "Well done," he said. "My apologies."

Adornetto shrugged his shoulders. "Now that that's out-of-the-way, let's settle the details before we approve this mission. Have you drafted orders to use selected agencies of the intelligence community? You'll need their help tracking the movements of the team members.

"Yes, sir. I have," Mike said.

"Do you have identity papers ready for Youris?"

"They will be ready within the hour."

"...and the letter of introduction?"

"Done. I've included a phone number for them to verify Rashid's assumed identity. One of my people will man it 24 / 7."

"What about the meeting location in El Paso?"

"I conferred with Walter Kent in Albuquerque this morning. Their Lead Investigator, Agent Ashley Kohen, tracked down a man named Bashir Hashim a couple of days ago in El Paso. He is the link through which our enemies will enter the country. He is under surveillance as we speak."

"Then we know where they'll meet?"

Mike paused, "We know where they will assemble. I think the meeting will be elsewhere. Albuquerque and El Paso Field Offices are standing by."

Delong asked, "What about Doctor Youris, is he ready?"

"He talked to his wife, Hessa. He says she is frightened for him, but will support his decision."

Adornetto rubbed his chin again. "If you say *Operation Full Moon* is ready to go, you have my approval. Delong nodded concurrence. "Have you forgotten anything?"

"I hope to God I haven't."

Mike searched each man's face while his mind reviewed every detail of the plan. There was much at stake, not only his friend's life, and national security, but his reputation, too. He had never lied to a superior in his entire career, until today.

# FORTY-THREE

EACH HONEY BARREL WEIGHED 110 pounds. At forty-nine kilograms they were easy for Abdullah to pick up, but he had to lift each barrel twice: once out of the cargo container onto a two-wheel dolly, and again inside the building. After hoisting the first twenty, he stopped to rest. Since his rigorous training on the Afghanistan border with Pakistan, two years earlier, he had done little strenuous work. His sporadic weight training helped keep him fit, but not in top condition. He continued offloading the honey, with occasional breaks, until all were moved inside. Abdullah secured the two wheeled dolly in the container, closed the doors, and latched them making it ready for pick up early the next morning.

Now to find that one extraordinary barrel.

He went to his toolbox, picked out an ultraviolet flashlight and began shinning it on the top of each barrel. He moved between the barrels searching for one painted with fluorescent dye, visible only to someone with a black light. Within minutes he found a barrel marked with the shape of the old Soviet Union's hammer and sickle. His next step was to load the barrel into the trunk of the old car he'd bought.

Bashir's story about the insurance woman with a company not listed online, and his experience with another woman pounding on the side of the shipping container with a rock, concerned him. These incidences may be unrelated, but why take a chance? He had unlimited money and must avoid making any error this late in the game, no matter how remote the possibility. He must find a hiding place for the barrel.

He solved that problem by renting a storage unit on the south side of town. The storage facility had hundreds of identical units distinguishable only by the number painted on each door. He paid in advance and stored the barrel in unit 169.

Smith Trading had served its purpose. Abdullah would leave it locked, and never return. He didn't need it anymore. He decided to take a motel room tonight, and secure more permeant quarters tomorrow.

The next morning Abdullah searched for an obscure and inconspicuous place to stay. He found it in a second story one-room apartment over the Up Your Alley Bar and Grill. A place that attracted some of its clientele from the Center City Bowling Lanes next door. The room, accessed by a flight of wooden stairs at the back of the building, smelled of stale cigarette smoke, beer, and cooking oil that wafted from below. The bartender, who owned the building and rented the place to him, warned the nights might be a bit rowdy with all the laughing, fighting and loud music from down below. In a more positive note, he pointed out the Wi-Fi signal from the bowling alley next door could be accessed without a password. No extra charge.

In his little apartment, he opened his laptop and checked his email as he did every morning. Since he only corresponded with Rome, he usually found his inbox empty, but this morning he discovered an encrypted message. Allah be Praised, finally a message from his handlers in Italy. Abdullah quickly unbuckled his pants and withdrew a small leather pouch he wore around his waist. From the pouch he extracted the thumb drive containing the decryption code and inserted it into his computer. He flicked a roach off the keyboard and with a few key strokes watched as his message from Rome spilled out on the screen. He read the message quickly, then went back and studied each word.

Many thoughts crowded through his mind. So they will meet in El Paso–Bashir's place, of course. These names–Alexander Kostoff, Kassar Suri and Danish Maloof–meant nothing to him. No matter, they are the experts that will make his mission a success. The team would be here at full moon. Abdullah checked his calendar. What? Only two days? Not much time to prepare. They want me to find a meeting place. Yes, yes, someplace safe, and remote.

Abdullah found his hands trembling. He needed to calm himself, and stay alert. Prayer would help him. He went to the black duffel bag where he kept his prayer rug, his money, and a handgun he had bought. Unrolling the rug on the cracked linoleum floor, be began his morning ritual. Thinking only of Allah, he felt the tension in his body dissipate.

The rest of the day Abdullah concentrated on work. He decided the meeting place would be at his house in Maljamar. Leased for the year, it was the perfect location. *Blind to all who would harm you,* as the seventh message directed.

He called Bashir to tell him of the new orders and to warn him of the arriving team members at his house on Thursday. "Bring them to Maljamar. You know the way. I will be at the house waiting to receive our guests. Speak to no one. Guard them. They will be with us for a day and one night."

Bashir acknowledged the plan and added some suggestions. "I will buy food for five people and prepare the meals, freeing you for more important matters. The menu must please their unique tastes, including the Russian. I must, also, rent a larger car. Mine is too small and unreliable. Do you know when these men will arrive?

Abdullah explained they were from 'many nations' and that they may arrive any time during the full moon, "When they have assembled, call me," he ordered, and Bashir agreed.

The house in Maljamar would have to serve the team of three, plus Bashir and him. He would need bedding, disposable tableware, and many other items. Wal-Mart, on the north end of town, would have most of what he must buy. Of course, he'd take the barrel to the meeting. This entire enterprise centered on the contents of the barrel.

He reviewed the actions he must take from now until the meeting ended. Every detail must be carried out with precision. The image of his motor home lighting the night sky with an orange glow reminded him he must prepare for every contingency and expect the unexpected. He added more items to his list of purchases, closed his laptop and opened his duffle bag. He counted out the money he needed, and left his dingy apartment to go shopping.

AS THE BARTENDER warned, that night the floor beneath his feet vibrated with loud music mixed with the hubbub of party goers down below. Enough of this, I must get my mind on something else. If it's not too late, maybe I will watch this game of bowling. He left his room and descended the rickety stairs behind the building. He stepped into the dark shadowy parking lot and started to weave through the cars on his way to the bowling lanes next door. That's when he heard voices. A man shouting and a child crying. Abdullah couldn't see in the dim light, but he followed the sounds. Lit only by a distant neon sign, he saw a man slapping a child– a boy child. The man's words were slurred, but the young boy's words were clear. "No, Papa. Don't hit me, Papa." Staggering forward the man continued slapping the boy, again and again.

189

Stunned by the act of beating a boy about the age of his little brother, Abdullah, seized with a sudden rage, reached for the man. With one hand he grabbed his neck and pulled him back, slamming him against a parked car. Then, holding his shirtfront with his left hand, he slapped him hard across the face with his right. He raised his arm and struck him again. The man, numb with drink, went limp. Abdullah raised his hand once more, then felt a tug on his pants leg. He glanced down. The boy, his face tilted up, cried, "Please don't hit my Papa again. Please don't."

Abdullah dropped his arm and let go of the man, who slid down the side of the car and fell on the ground. His anger subsiding, he turned and considered the boy, who was not more than six years old. He picked the child up. Blood trickled down the boy's upper lip. "You're bleeding."

"It don't matter. It goes away."

Abdullah felt the boy's small body in his arms and remembered when he was young and frail. "A man should not beat a boy child. It dishonors his name and his family's name."

The boy wiped away the blood with his arm. "He gets like this some nights. I'm glad you didn't hit Papa again." He put his arms around Abdullah's neck as if to thank him. On the ground the man uttered meaningless sounds and tried to crawl away. Abdullah, feeling uncomfortable with his role as savior, put the boy down and turned to leave.

"Will you take us home? It's not far."

"Home?"

The boy pointed down the faintly lit street that ran next to the Bar and Grill. "It's that way. I can't do it, please? Please?"

Abdullah studied the boy's pleading face. What if this young man-to-be was his brother? Would he want him left like this? Even though the boy lived in America, he was of the age of innocence—too young to understand the ways of the world. Abdullah knew leaving him in the darkness alone with a drunken father would shame him in the eyes of Allah the Merciful.

He lifted the drunk to his feet. Holding him upright, he put the man's arm around his neck and held him tight around the waist. The putrid smelled of alcohol assaulted his nostrils. The boy, holding on to Abdullah's pants pocket, pulled them toward the street. In less than a block they stopped near a streetlight. The boy said, "He needs to go to bed, please?" He pointed at an old house.

Getting the drunk up the steps of the broken-down house took some effort, but finally Abdullah got him laid out on a worn sofa in a living room cluttered with empty whiskey bottles and trash. He knelt down, faced the boy, and held him by the shoulders. "Where's your mother?"

"I got no Mama. Just Papa."

Abdullah reached into his pocket and gave the boy money. "This is for you. Hide it. Buy some clothes, some food. Go to a doctor." He stood and patted the boy on the head. He knew if the man found the money he would take it and buy whiskey, but he could not allow himself to become more involved. He feared he might have already let his discipline slip.

Abdullah walked back to his roach-infested apartment. As he walked, he cursed America. The richest country in the world. A country whose streets are not paved with gold, but filled with greed. A country so bent on power and control that it allows boys to live in squalor and poverty. A culture of depravity. With new resolve, his mission took on greater importance.

# FORTY-FOUR

IRRITATED ABOUT BEING IN the right place at the wrong time, Ashley mulled over yesterday's fiasco in Roswell. A chance to reconnect with her suspect had turned into a humiliating failure. If she had arrived a day or even a few hours earlier, she might have linked up with him. Clenching her teeth, she wondered how much had to go wrong before something good happened. Yes, she discovered one barrel missing out of a total of sixty. A positive discovery, at last, but why such an elaborate delivery system? What's so important about one small barrel or more to the point– what's in the damn barrel? She didn't know, but she knew it wasn't honey.

She carried the toolbox she appropriated from Smith Trading upstairs to Bill Johnson. It held tools that most likely had fingerprints on them. If prints were lifted from the tools in this box, she might finally experience that 'something good' she needed. When Ashley entered Bill's office, she found him with his feet on the desk, head back and eyes closed. Ashley dropped the heavy plastic toolbox in the center of his cluttered desk with a loud thump. Bill opened one eye.

"You know," Ashley said, "one of the few things you can get fired for in Federal service is sleeping on-the-job." She plopped down in a chair next to his desk.

"I'm not sleeping." He opened the other eye. "I'm thinking. That's what they pay me for. I'm too old to do real work."

"Real work? Like what?"

He let his feet fall to the floor and sat up. "Like putting the cuffs on some asshole who needs to learn respect for the law."

"Your cuffs are in the drawer, but you still make it possible for other agents to use their cuffs, often."

Bill removed his glasses and adjusted his hearing aids. "I hate people who pity old folks." He winked at Ashley and replaced his glasses. "So what the hell is this?' He pointed at the toolbox. "You taking up carpentry in your spare time?"

192

Ashley leaned forward, "Based on the warrant you sent me yesterday, I found this box and it got me excited. I'm sure our suspect has handled these tools. I have to admit my expectations are aroused."

A twinkle flashed in Bill's eyes. "I love it when you talk dirty." He then yanked a drawer open and pulled out a pair of thin rubber gloves. "I'll bag these items and have the print-guys go over them." He pulled his glasses halfway down his nose, and tilted his head. "Did you get the word about the videoconference downstairs? It has to do with your case."

Still enjoying Bill's 'talking dirty' joke, Ashley nodded her head.

Bill shoved his glasses back up his nose. "Old Ed Delong will run it. The director himself. I understand it has to do with an intelligence break-through."

Ashley stuck her thumb up. "Maybe things are coming together?"

THE PRESIDENT appointed Ed Delong to serve as the Director of the FBI because his background and experience proved his ability to manage a complex agency with evenhanded discipline, and little or no tolerance for failure. While politically loyal, when it came to law enforcement he was a lawman one hundred percent.

"Are we ready?" Delong asked.

The video technician answered, "Yes, sir. Albuquerque will come on line any second now."

Delong placed his unlit cigar on the table and regarded the assembled participants who sat in a semi-circle facing the wall-sized video screen. "Okay people, so I can move along, and not waste time here's my agenda for this morning. I'll start with introductions followed by a brief summary of our plan, then open the meeting for discussion. Any questions?"

Admiral Smithy asked, "How much do your people in Albuquerque know about this case?"

"They originated the case and made significant discoveries locally before we knew the true scope of this threat. Based on your work at the NSA, Admiral, this is no longer a murder investigation in the deserts of New Mexico. But to answer your question, they don't know about the seventh message or the infiltration plan. I held that back for security purposes."

Smithy nodded his approval.

At that moment, the video screen brightened showing four faces, well-tanned by the New Mexico sun. Delong straightened his tie. "Good morning, Mr. Kent. I'll introduce our panel, then brief you on our plan of action followed by a Q and A. To my left is Admiral Henry Smithy, head of NSA and Leo Adornetto, Director of National Intelligence. On my right is Mike Johansson and Rashid al Youris, who you know." Delong moved his notes to see them better. "Three days ago Admiral Smithy and his NSA team, with the help of Doctor Youris, received and decoded the last of a series of seven messages. As we speak I'm sending number seven to you on a secure line. Based on this new information we know three conspirators will meet in El Paso tomorrow, Thursday. The purpose of the meeting is to train your suspect to perform an act of terror. The nature of the act is unknown."

Delong eyed the Albuquerque crew. Except for Bill Johnson, they looked about as comfortable as a cat on a raft in white water. "We've identified these conspirators as technical experts. It's essential that we learn the nature of their mission. To do that, we have devised a plan to infiltrate this Team of Deliverance, as they call themselves. Johansson here," he pointed at Mike," calls our plan *Operation Full Moon*. You'll understand why when you read message seven...and, oh yes, Mike named your un-sub the Lone Wolf, for obvious reasons."

Walter Kent squirmed in his seat. Ashley's tried to appear calm, but failed. Dorothy Hogan adjusted her audio recorder, and Bill Johnson sanded his fingernails with a plastic file.

"What I'm about to tell you is confidential. Lives are at stake." He shoved his notes aside and looked at them through the camera lens. "Doctor Youris speaks several languages and is Muslim. He has volunteered to assume the identity of one of their team members. The details are in my report to you. This group of co-conspirators will gather in El Paso tomorrow, but the actual meeting will take place Friday somewhere else." Delong picked up his cigar, inspected it, then put it in his mouth. "Any questions?"

Finally free to speak, Walter Kent began. "First, I would like to thank you for the work you have done in support of this case. We knew we were dealing with a serious situation, but we didn't know the depth of this threat." Ashley started to speak, but Kent squeezed her hand under-the-table and gave her a quick shake of the head. "I understand a Joint Terrorism Task Force will be formed. What is the JTTF status?"

Johansson in DC spoke up. "I can answer that." He turned and addressed Kent. "Excellent question. I have formed a task force and will deploy it when needed. I'll keep you informed."

"Thank you, Mr. Johansson. Meanwhile I'll strengthen our team in Albuquerque."

Bill Johnson gazed at the DC panel. "Ed, a couple of weeks back I sent a human hair sample to DC for a DNA analysis. Today I'm sending you some fingerprints I believe belong to Mr. Wolf. Considering the importance of this case, could you speed the lab work for the DNA and the data search for matching prints?"

"Because this request comes from you, Bill, and because we used to work the streets together, I will personally see to it."

"Thanks, old buddy." Bill went back to sanding his nails.

At full attention, Ashley said, "I understand the need to keep tight security. Our suspect is not your everyday suicide bomber. He's brilliant, well trained and ruthless. He makes plans for every eventuality, and so far has stayed a step ahead of us at every turn. If we are to stop him, we need to know what you know when you know it."

Kent interrupted. "This is Agent Ashley Kohen. She's the Lead Investigator on this case. Very dedicated, sir."

Delong pulled his cigar out of his mouth and held it next to his face. "I can tell she's dedicated. Nothing wrong with that. Agent Kohen, I'm personally invested in this case. You will know what we know as soon as it's appropriate."

"Yes sir. I meant no disrespect. I'm still frustrated. I missed picking up his trail by only a few hours yesterday."

"A few hours. Tell me about that."

"The Lone Wolf received a shipment of barrels in Roswell. He unloaded the cargo container while I interviewed Bashir Hashim in El Paso. When I returned the next day, the container was gone. I discovered one barrel missing from the shipment."

Rashid perked up. "Excuse me. You said shipment. The sixth message referred to a shipment. This may explain that reference. Give us details about what you learned."

"In Roswell, a city with hundreds of beekeepers serving the pecan groves, the Lone Wolf received a cargo container with 60 barrels of honey. It originated in Dubai. I found only fifty-nine barrels off loaded."

"That's important," Admiral Smithy noted. "Dubai is a major port for middle eastern goods. Honey is a popular commodity. A clever choice if you want to smuggle something into our country. Sixty barrels would be almost impossible to inspect at the port of entry. It probably passed through with little or no scrutiny."

Adornetto, silent until now, asked, "The question is what fits in a receptacle that size and still poses a threat to us?" No one spoke for a few seconds. Delong drew a big question mark on his notes. Admiral Smithy's expression remained grim.

Youris glanced at Johansson, who gave him a thumbs up gesture. With a hopeful expression, Rashid looked around the room. "Perhaps I'll have an answer to that question come Saturday night."

AS SOON AS THE Washington briefing ended, Ashley downloaded Director Delong's report, and the seventh decrypted message. Both Kent and Johnson reviewed the information with her. "The background profiles of Kosloff and Suri describe them as men with menacing underworld ties," Ashley said. "Maloof is not in the same league with them,"

Kent crossed his arms. "Kosloff and Suri will never leave America, at least not alive."

Johnson agreed. "With our task force primed and ready, you may be sure we'll pounce on them after their meeting Saturday. The Lone Wolf is another matter. We'll watch his every move until he is disarmed or should I say—defanged."

Ashley grinned. "You do have a way with words, Bill. And, speaking of words, I must call Jerry Cebeck in El Paso and alert him to the arrival of our special guests tomorrow."

WHEN CEBECK RECEIVED the call from Ashley, he had finished eating the last piece of stale pizza left over from the night before. It had rained all morning, driving the humidity up. He needed a shower and clean clothes.

"Good morning, Jerry," Ashley said.

"What's good about it?"

"You don't sound happy."

"Happy? Happy is a one of the seven dwarfs. At least Happy had six friends."

196

Ashley heard frustration in Jerry's voice. She'd worked a few solo stakeouts in the past and understood the feeling. "Well cheer up, Snow White will rescue you. There have been some major developments."

Jerry grunted, "About time."

"I'm sending you Joe and Fred as backup. You'll need them. Three important bad guys are heading your way starting tomorrow. They'll arrive at Bashir's doorstep, most likely at different times. Our information says they will leave Bashir's house and go to an unknown meeting location with the Lone Wolf. You need to follow them and keep us informed."

"Who's the Lone Wolf?"

"He's the same guy who blows up motor homes. Do you have a secure connection?"

"Yes. The El Paso Field Office arranged that."

"Good, I'll send you details."

Jerry's voice sounded a bit brighter. "This explains it."

"Explains what?"

"Yesterday Bashir showed up with a new car from Hertz Rental. A Chevy Suburban equipped with two cargo carriers mounted on top. He must be planning a trip."

"It sounds like your special skills are needed. Is the Bug Man alive and well?"

"He will be...tonight."

# FORTY-FIVE

FROM HIS SECOND STORY vantage point, Jerry Cebeck watched Bashir's house as the Thursday morning sun cast its first rays of light. Like a well-trained sniper, he positioned himself at a 45 degree angle to the window and remained several feet back from the opening. No one directly across or on the street below could see him through the window. His digital camera mounted with a 600 mm telephoto lens allowed him sharp close up views, even in lowlight conditions.

The rented Chevy Suburban, parked in front of the purple house, had been violated last night by the Bug Man. Two tracking devices, one behind the grill and one under the right rear fender were attached and operational.

Earlier, that same morning at 3:00 a.m., a phone call from Joe and Fred promised their arrival within minutes. Cebeck had arranged parking behind the building and told them to enter at the rear. Right on time they knocked on his door and walked in. It was comforting to see familiar faces.

Cebeck briefed them on the layout of the surveillance. He explained the arrival possibilities. "There are three men coming to El Paso to meet Bashir today. Their arrivals will be random. Anytime Bashir leaves his house he must be followed." Joe and Fred checked their tracking equipment and declared themselves ready.

As promised, Ashley had sent details of the infiltration plans to the El Paso Field Office. A runner delivered hard copies to Cebeck before sunrise with three fast-food breakfasts and coffees.

At 10:05, Bashir exited his house and drove off in the Suburban. His usual grubby denims were replaced with a white shirt and gray dress pants. He wore shiny black shoes: a sign that this day would be different from other days. Joe tailed him at a discrete distance. With the two big cargo carriers on top, he was easy to follow.

A drive to the airport took thirty minutes in light traffic. The morning rush hour had peaked. Cebeck estimated Bashir would arrive back home about 11:35. His estimate was only a few minutes off. The Suburban parked on the corner at 11:40. Bashir and one man got out and walked up the front steps. Cebeck fired off a series of photos and made a few notes.

At 2:30 Cebeck watched Bashir descend the porch for the second time and head to his car. A dark blue tie complemented the white shirt. Since Bashir drove off alone, it was reasonable to assume he would return, as before, with one man. If he had two men, the surveillance would rise to the next level. This time Fred followed the Suburban.

Every few hours Cebeck checked with Ashley in Albuquerque. "Have you heard anything from Washington?" he asked.

"Kent's been on the phone with them all-day. He says the JTTF, the task force, is on its way and will need minute by minute info once the Suburban is on the move with everyone on board. I guess these Washington shadow operations work independent of standard procedures." Cebeck noticed Ashley sounded a bit peeved. "For all we know members of the task force could be across the street from you right now," she added.

He shared her frustration. "If they're across the street, I bet they're eating better than me."

"Hang in there Jerry. You're on the front line of the action now."

"I'm not impressed. This is trench warfare."

At 4:10 Bashir arrived back and parked in his usual spot. This time he ran around to the other side of the Suburban and opened the back door like a trained chauffeur. A big man, dressed in a black suit and fedora style hat, emerged carrying a large briefcase. He walked with a regal step as he entered the house. Cebeck's camera clacked like a fully automatic Uzi. Two down and one more man to go.

Jerry, Fred and Joe huddled together. They agreed that if Bashir left with his two current guests, he would get the third member of the team and probably head for the meeting location, without returning to Estrella Street. They also agreed tailing the Suburban in the dark would be tricky. Fred tapped his phone to learn what time the sun would set: 8:02.

Cebeck switched out the memory card in his camera. After uploading the card to his computer, he forwarded the images to Albuquerque and then called Ashley and brought her up-to-date on their progress.

Joe arrived back with an assortment of sandwiches and several big cups of strong brew. He served Cebeck first, then took the food down to Fred. It was after six o'clock when they finished eating. The sun settled near the horizon.

Fred took over the vigil so Cebeck could get some rest. Cebeck didn't know how long he slept before he felt Fred shaking him. "Jerry, wake up. They're getting in the car: both men, Bashir and a big black dog."

The Suburban eased away from the curb at 6:55. Joe backed out of his parking place behind the building and began following Bashir. Fred scrambled down the backstairs and joined the slow speed pursuit across town. Cebeck hurried to pack his equipment and lugged it to the white van. He knew Joe would keep Bashir within tracking distance, even in congested traffic, but he wanted to join the chase as fast as he possible.

Joe kept up a running description of locations and landmarks. After several turns, the Suburban drove east on Montana Avenue, heading toward El Paso International Airport. It turned on Airport Boulevard and entered the one-way circulation pattern serving passengers arriving and departing scheduled flights. Joe found a place to park, near the intersection of Airport Road and Airport Boulevard, and suggested Fred do the same on Continental and Airport Boulevard. Anyone leaving the airport would have to pass one of those two points. Cebeck caught up a few minutes later and drove into the airport watching for the Suburban. He circled the east and west terminals several times. On his third drive-by, he spotted a man getting into the backseat, but when he made one more pass, the Suburban had disappeared. At 7:30 Joe squawked, "Got 'em! They're heading south on Airport Road." He pulled out of the Guesthouse Suites parking lot and followed close behind. A few minutes later he announced Bashir had merged with Montana Avenue heading eastbound—the opposite direction from his house.

Cebeck, tangled in airport traffic, cursed at his predicament. As he maneuvered out of the airport and made his way to Montana Avenue, the Suburban neared the city limits of El Paso, entering State Highway 180. Joe and Fred traded trailing positions so different cars would be seen in Bashir's rearview mirror. Cebeck began to relax. The Team of Deliverance would not be meeting in El Paso; Highway 180 led into the flat, dry deserts of west Texas. The sun set at 8:02.

ASHLEY PACED ABOUT her cubicle. It had been three hours since Cebeck last contacted her. She knew she was doing what the Lead Investigator should do at this point in the case, but that inner drive to be actively engaged nagged at her. *Operation Full Moon* could break the case wide open. If successful, it would allow the Bureau to capture two international criminals, find out the nature of the threat to national security, disarm the Lone Wolf and arrest that slimy bastard.

Her last contact with Cebeck had been 7:15. He reported three men had left the house, but didn't yet know where they were heading. He reported they had a big dog with them. Ashley remembered the menacing Doberman Pinscher sitting next to Bashir in his living room.

She called upstairs to Dorothy, "Any news on the JTTF?"

Dorothy sounded as frustrated as Ashley felt. "Nothing new. Not a clue."

"What is this with Washington? Don't they know we're all on the same side?"

"Mr. Kent says they are like the Navy Seals. Covert, independent and decisive." She lowered her voice. "I think he's as perturbed as we are, but doesn't want to show it."

Ashley started for the break room for coffee when her cell phone sounded. Before she spoke, Cebeck blurted, "We're on Texas Highway 180 heading east. We have left El Paso. Bashir picked up the third man at the airport. It's dark now."

"I'll check our software." Ashley went to her computer, clicked on the Bureau's mapping service and entered location data. "Has it become a two-lane highway yet?"

"Yes, a few miles back."

She studied the map. "There are only small towns on 180. There's Salt Flats and Pine Springs, and then the New Mexico border. The meeting place could be anywhere. I'll relay this information to Walter who's in touch with the task force. Call me with updates, okay?"

"Roger that."

The surveillance team tailed the Suburban using all the tricks of the trade. Using three cars they rotated their headlight patterns, and varied the distance behind Bashir. This game went on for five hours. After two hundred and fifty one miles, it ended at Maljamar, New Mexico at 11:45 p.m.

# FOURTY-SIX

CEBECK CHECKED IN WITH Ashley as the surveillance caravan moved eastward through the night. He reported their progress when they passed Pine Springs about 8:30, and a half hour later when they crossed the Texas border into New Mexico. Ashley figured they drove by Carlsbad Caverns about 9:30 but didn't see the national park sign in the dark.

They continued north on Highway 285, passed through the City of Carlsbad and arrived in Artesia a little after eleven o'clock. The Suburban turned east on Highway 82, passing a brightly lit oil refinery. As Ashley traced their progress she recognized they were south of the general area of Bitty Smith's burial site. Could there be a connection?

A little before midnight, Cebeck announced the Suburban had pulled off the highway at mile marker 35, and parked in front of a house set back off the road about a hundred feet. He saw lights in the house on two levels as he drove by. Fred, who followed Cebeck, noted the exact distance from the Highway 82 turn off at 35.6 miles.

Using Google Earth online, Ashley found the intersection of Highways 285 and 82. She measured the distance from that point, and found an image of a sun bleached house on the south side of the road with a small building in the backyard. She also found a clump of junipers across the highway set back a 100 yards from the house–a perfect place to watch the meeting location. Cebeck agreed the trees would give him cover.

After passing by the house he drove out of sight, then turned around and headed back. As he approached the house he switched off his headlights and navigated by moonlight. He left the highway surface and worked his way to the evergreen trees in the semi-darkness. Once in place, he called Ashley and told her he could see the house and the Suburban parked in front. Minutes after the call, he nodded off to sleep.

ASHLEY TOLD WALTER the highway pursuit ended in Maljamar. He in turn called Mike Johansson in Washington, who directed the JTTF's undercover operation. Kent reported the details of the pursuit and where it ended. "I believe the meeting will take place tomorrow in this old house."

Johansson mumbled good work and cut the conversation short. Elements of the task force would control the area from places of concealment. Kent ordered Fred and Joe to return to the field office.

Based on Ashley's inspection of the daylight images online, Maljamar was less like a real town and more like a transfer point for oil field operations. She identified few structures that might be occupied dwellings. A short distance east of the faded old house she noted a fenced industrial yard that contained a row of fuel trucks and three rusty crude-oil storage tanks with a capacity of about 100,000 gallons each.

Her suspicions of the treachery about to take place in this ugly, remote outpost colored her assessment of the danger inherent in this operation. A shudder rippled through her body like a seismic tremor, a forerunner to a disastrous event.

EARLY FRIDAY MORNING, Mike Johansson continued work at the Command Center in the FBI building on Pennsylvania Avenue. He paced back and forth, his arms moving in animated gestures as he barked out orders over his wireless headset. Acting under emergency authority, he commandeered National Guard property needed to carry out this mission. The requisition included a reconnaissance drone, one helicopter, and an assortment of armored vehicles designed for desert deployment. He may not need all of these assets, but if he did, he owned them for the next forty eight-hours.

Overnight he flew his task force members and equipment to the Roswell airport, the nearest runway able to handling high-speed jets. They quickly assembled and began briefings.

Johansson divided the task force into two units led by experienced assault leaders. Alpha Unit flew to Lovington east of Maljamar in a Black Hawk helicopter, and Red Dog Unit drove west to a position outside Artesia, causing a dozen scrawny cows to scatter in a state of panic. When Mike learned of Special Agent Cebeck's close observational position in Maljamar, he ordered a voice link to him though the Albuquerque Field Office.

With his forces deployed in a flanking formation, the enemy's escape routes were sealed off. He planned to arrest Alexander Kasloff and Kassar Suri long before they tried to leave the country. He would hold off on Bashir Hashim until he could figure out his role in all of this. Based on what he hoped to learn from Rashid's participation in this secret meeting, he would deal with the Lone Wolf in a decisive manner.

Johansson closed his eyes. Had he overlooked anything? Would his friend Rashid be safe? Yes, he felt confident he had covered all the bases.

He didn't know tomorrow would be a day of ominous consequences.

.

# FOURTY-SEVEN

ABDULLAH GLANCED AT HIS wristwatch every few minutes. He had heard nothing from Bashir since 7:30. They should be here by now. Did Bashir get lost or stopped by the police? The man lacked intelligence, but he wasn't stupid enough to speed on the highway or drive recklessly. He shook his head in disgust.

Earlier that day Abdullah arranged for the big meeting. Chairs circled the dining room table located next to the kitchen. He distributed bedding in the rooms upstairs and had spent an hour straightening up the place so it was less like a man's place of solitude and refuge and more like an orderly house. He hid his black duffel with the money high on a shelf in the kitchen pantry–after removing the handgun. He felt the need to arm himself, at least for now.

The wooden barrel was a bigger problem. It actually had honey in it. A sticky mess that surrounded a container about the size of a standard suitcase. To avoid a protracted cleanup in the house, he disassembled the barrel in the backyard. He ended breaking the thing open with a hammer, and getting covered with the gooey stuff. After washing everything with a garden hose, including himself, he found a lead box inside the barrel. It had no handle or visible lock. The only opening he could find was a hinged cover, about one inch long. He picked it open and saw an electrical connection. Abdullah hid the box in the old hand-carved dining room buffet.

Now, hours later, he waited in a darkened room next to the front window. Headlights of a car came into view but passed by and drove out of sight. A few minutes later, at 11:45 more headlights. This time the lights slowed and the car turned into his gravel driveway. He watched three men lumber out of the backseats of the car, a large white vehicle with storage containers attached on top. Bashir exited the driver's side and retrieved a big dog out of the rear compartment.

205

Abdullah turned on the inside lights, opened the front door, and stationed himself about eight feet back, so he could inspect his visitors as they entered. He sensed an emptiness in his stomach and his mouth felt dry. He thought of his handgun behind him, tucked under his belt, and tried to relax.

The first man to enter was large, older, and carried a briefcase. Abdullah challenged him, "Stop. What is your name?" The man stopped, and spoke. The words meant nothing to Abdullah, but the sneer on the man's face radiated disrespect. A second man, behind the first, leaned to the side and whispered in the big man's ear, then said in Arabic. "This is Alexander Kosloff. He's Russian and does not speak our language."

Abdullah caught his breath. "I want him to tell me his code name." Without waiting for a translation, Kosloff spit out the word *Pasol* and advanced into the room. Abdullah pointed to the sofa for him to sit. The second man stepped inside. "My name is Rashid al Youris. My password is *Magister*. He moved to the sofa and sat next to the Russian. The third man entered. In Urdu, the common language of Pakistan, he said, "I am Kassar Suri, sir. My password is *Khoon Gaha*, and your name, please?" Before Rashid translated, Abdullah put his hand up. "No need to interpret. I understand basic Urdu having trained in a border region of Pakistan." He turned to Kassar. "My name is Abdullah al Jamal of the House of Prince Jamal. I am known as the Sword. Welcome, you may enter."

Outside, Bashir took his dog around back and tied him to the porch. Then returned to the car to fill a box with items stored in one of the cargo containers strapped to the roof of the car. He stumbled up the front steps with the box of food supplies, greeted Abdullah with a nod and asked, "Kitchen?" Abdullah pointed over his shoulder, walked to the center of the room, and stood next to Rashid. "I don't know you. Your name is not on the list of members of this team. Are you the translator?"

"Yes," Rashid rose to confront Abdullah.

"I will deal with you in a moment, but first everyone must be searched. No weapons are tolerated and no phones." Rashid repeated the demand and received mixed reactions. Abdullah continued, "Explain to them this is a necessary precaution. No offense is intended." He then shouted, "Bashir, come here. You must search our guests." Bashir scurried into the living room and began a body search of each man. He found no guns, but recovered three phones. The Russian objected to this invasion of his privacy. Abdullah shrugged his shoulders.

"Now for you." Abdullah glared at Rashid. "You are not the man I expected. Who are you and how do you know the password?" He dropped his hand to his side and thought of the handgun wedged in the small of his back.

Rashid, still standing, reached inside his coat for the Letter of Introduction. Bashir stepped forward as if to stop him. "Relax, I have a letter to show you," Rashid said quickly. Bashir looked at Abdullah who motioned him to back off. "I'm an associate of Professor Maloof at the university. Danish asked that I substitute for him. He has fallen ill and is in an intensive care unit in Tehran under doctor's orders." He handed the letter to Abdullah, who hastily scanned it. He noted Maloof's signature scrawled across the bottom.

"How do I know you are not lying? Not an impostor?"

"For many reasons. First, I could not be here unless Danish had directed me. Second I know the password because Danish personally gave it to me. Third the letter introduces me and is signed." With a bow of the head he said, "I am Rashid al Youris, at your service."

Abdullah considered the claim. "Yes, but maybe you are a spy and Professor Maloof has been tortured and forced to cooperate with you and your masters. Prove me wrong."

Rashid stepped back as if offended. "You have a great imagination, sir. If you read the letter you will see there is a telephone number for you to call to verify the truth. I would prefer you not disturb my friend who is sick, but if you have to...." His voice trailed off.

Abdullah's eyes narrowed. "You think because we are out in the desert that I cannot make this call. You are a fool. This is the *oil patch*. It is served by many phone companies who bow to the wealthy interests in America."

The Russian began to talk. He sputtered angry words gesturing at Abdullah, who asked, "What's he saying?"

"He thinks your manner is unnecessarily rude, and wants to know why."

"Then tell him. My suspicions are warranted."

Rashid explained the situation. Kosloff laughed.

"Why is he laughing?"

"Because he thinks, shall I say—you are a silly man. You see, he knows me from before. I translated for him when this deal originated in Rome."

"He spoke in Russian. You could be lying."

Rashid smiled and extended his hand to the Russian, who shook it as if greeting an old friend. "If you need further proof, you should call Danish."

Still suspicious, Abdullah nodded, "I will."

Kassar Suri asked how long they must wait. After a long day, he needed to sleep. The Russian stated flatly they would meet tomorrow morning at the earliest. Both turned to Rashid to translate.

Abdullah ordered Bashir to show the men to their rooms while he made the call to Tehran. He believed Youris to be legitimate, but he felt the need to confirm the truth, even if it meant disturbing a sick man.

The call lasted only a few minutes and confirmed Rashid al Youris was trustworthy. Abdullah accepted the authenticity of Youris, but doubt still nagged at him.


BASHIR CARRIED THE luggage upstairs. The Russian occupied one bedroom, stating he would not share a room. Rashid and Kassar took the second bedroom that had twin beds.

When Bashir returned downstairs Abdullah waited for him in the living room. "We must talk." He eyed the smaller man. Bashir glanced up, puzzled and said nothing. Abdullah slowly walked around Bashir as if inspecting spoiled goods. Facing him he asked, "How did you know this meeting would be indispensable to my mission?"

Bashir appeared confused and perspiration formed on his skin. "I...I don't understand."

"When I called you two days ago, I told you team members would arrive today, and you said this meeting was indispensable to my mission. How did you know that?"

"I didn't know." He pulled back. "I mean, I assumed it must be important for you to call me. Why would you need my support if it wasn't important?"

Abdullah frowned. "You said you would buy food for five people. How did you know how many people were on the team? I didn't tell you the number." He advanced on Bashir barely able to control his urge to shake him.

"I made a guess at the number. If I had been wrong you would have told me. There are only so many people that can fit into one car. Why are you threatening me? I am your friend."

"You said, 'including the Russian'. Abdullah grabbed Bashir and shoved him back. "Talk to me you slimy son of a whore! How did you know about the Russian?" He lifted his fist, his face flushed with anger.

Bashir raised his arm to protect himself, and in a shrill voice screamed, "Yes, yes, I knew. I knew. Let me go. I can explain." Abdullah released him and Bashir fell back against the wall gasping for air. "Please, give me a minute," he pleaded.

Abdullah stepped back and waited.

Bashir straightened up, closed his eyes and took a calming breath. "It was for you. To protect you and our mission."

"What are you saying?"

"The truth."

"Explain yourself."

Bashir moved forward and began. "The Americans are good at spying. They spy on everyone even their own people and their allies. Our encryption is unbreakable, but can we be sure? Completely sure? No matter what you think of our enemies, they are smart, clever, and relentless." Bashir moved to the sofa and sat down. "If they broke the code, no matter how unlikely that may be, it would lead them to the recipient here in America. If that recipient were you, our mission would fail, and our investment would be lost. That's a hundred million dollars in pure gold and an opportunity to shift world power to Islam."

Abdullah wondered how Bashir knew something he didn't know. A hundred million dollars in gold?

"So our leaders built a safeguard into our communication. All instructions would be sent to me, and I would relay them to you. If by some chance these godless capitalists penetrated our transmissions and followed them to their destination, our enemies would capture me. They would not know about you. You would be safe. Our mission would be safe."

Abdullah stood dumbfounded. How could he not know all of this? Why was he, the chosen one, kept uninformed? His mind raced to understand. What Bashir said made sense, in a strange way. "And my reports to Rome, are they routed through you?"

Bashir, relaxed now and in control, continued. "Yes. I am the information exchange agent for this undertaking. Please remember what is important, Abdullah. I am not important. You are not important. Only our mission is important. We are but a means to a necessary end: punishing the Americans for their sins against Allah, our Benefactor."

"So you have known everything all along, from the beginning."

"Yes."

"And if the Americans captured you, what would stop them from finding me?"

Bashir stood and looked into Abdullah's eyes. "My death would stop them."

# FORTY-EIGHT

THE FBI COMMAND CENTER had turned into a sleeping dragon, resting now but able to exert intense power when aroused. Like the dragon, Johansson sat slouched in his leather chair, his chin resting near his chest, an empty coffee cup wedged between his legs. Agent Ackerman hesitated to wake him, but knew the director would want to know. He touched him on the shoulder. "Director, sir. Sorry to disturb you. I have news."

Dazed, Johansson opened his eyes and raised his head. "What? News?"

"Yes sir. The call came in minutes ago. It went off pretty well."

"Pretty well?" He pushed himself upright in the chair.

"Yes. As planned, Agent Sharif answered the call. She had no problem with the language. She followed the script and forwarded the call to her husband, Mr. Sharif who pretended to be the sick Professor Maloof. They convinced the caller that Rashid was his substitute."

"So we pulled it off?"

"Yes sir, but there was one problem."

"Problem?"

The man who called asked to verify the identity of a Rashid al Youris, not Mohammad Faisal.

Johansson jumped up, fully awake. "Did you say Youris?"

"Yes, sir. Rashid al Youris, but Mr. Sharif went along with it. He vouched for this Youris guy. I hope that was okay?"

The Big Swede nodded. "Sure. Tell Agent Sharif and her husband we appreciate their help. Thank them."

Ackerman stepped away.

Johansson felt a slight chill pass through him. So Rashid has changed the plan. He's using his identity. He must have also forged a letter of introduction with his name in it. I don't know why he'd do that. Maybe he feared his real identity might be recognized, and he didn't want to take a chance of our being discovered. I don't know what's in his head, but he must have a good reason. I hope he had a good reason.

# FORTY-NINE

ABDULLAH STARED AT THE CEILING of his downstairs bedroom. The revelation that Bashir shared communications between himself and Caliph Abd al-Ghayb in Rome made his muscles tighten. He felt anger because his importance became weakened by Bashir's involvement. He, the Sword, no longer was the sole warrior for Islam's advancement. With an inferior acolyte, he must share the glory and recognition that will flow from his accomplishments. *This lesser man will stand in my shadow. A shadow cast by the bright light of my heroic deeds.*

He ran his hands through his hair. As much as he loathed to admit it, Bashir's intervention served a useful purpose. This insignificant person, who now sleeps on the sofa of his living room, will act as a shield against those who would do him harm. The American dogs would rip Bashir apart while The Sword stayed free.

Other members of the team also contributed to his sleepless night. The substitute translator, Rashid al Youris, who appeared to be a trustworthy replacement, still made him uneasy. But Youris didn't trouble him as much as the Russian. The pompous Alexander Kosloff, irritated him by his appearance and his manner. Sleep finally came to Abdullah in fitful periods of shallow rest and troubled dreams.

THE NEXT MORNING Bashir awoke refreshed and ready to begin his day of work. The house remained quiet as he set about preparing to cook a fine breakfast for the guests and Abdullah. He needed some items from one of the cargo carriers mounted outside. Slipping out of the house into the morning light, he opened the rear door of the car and reached for the roof container. He found several kitchen utensils and a canister of baking flour. As he closed the container he noticed a white vehicle parked across the highway in a grove of trees. It seemed like an odd place to park, since there was nothing around it: no pump jacks humming, no storage tanks or oil field equipment nearby. Probably lovers hiding their sins.

213

Last night he had parked in front of the house without thinking how visible the Suburban might be in the daylight. He entered the car, started the engine, and moved it further down the side of the house. Bashir noticed an old car parked in the backyard, which he assumed belonged to Abdullah. He returned to the kitchen and his breakfast preparation duties.

RASHID AND KASSAR Suri came downstairs at a quarter past nine o'clock. The smell of fresh bread baking in the kitchen perked up their appetites as they waited for the others to join them. At half past the hour Abdullah arrived a bit blurry eyed and unshaven. "Where's the Russian?" Rashid said that Alexander was still snoring when they came down earlier. "Well, we can't wait for him all-day. Someone needs to wake him."

An hour later the Russian descended the stairs, dressed in a dark blue silk suit and carrying his oversized briefcase. Light bounced off his polished shoes. "I'm ready for breakfast," he said in broken English. Rashid crooked his head to the side and wondered if Kosloff had understood their conversations last night. As if reading his mind, he said to Rashid in his native tongue, "I only speak a few phrases in English. Your job is secure."

Bashir had set the dining room table for what would now be a late morning breakfast. He began bringing out plates of food. He set before them a choice of pan-fried or fresh baked Pita bread. Then he arrived with bowls of black and green olives, turnips, pickles, tomato wedges, and hard-boiled eggs that prompted words of praise. White cheese made from goat's milk and fresh jams complemented this Middle Eastern feast. To satisfy the Russian, a generous serving of chicken Shawanna was placed in front of him. "What is this," he asked. Rashid explained that it's an Arabian sandwich—Pita bread filled with meat—rarely served for breakfast in the Arab world, but prepared for him on this special occasion. Wearing a pleased expression Kosloff caught Bashir's eye, and bowed his head.

The small talk during breakfast consisted mostly of comments on how difficult it must be to set a civilized table in the land of fast-food and endless frozen meals in a box. When breakfast ended, everyone complimented Bashir on his culinary skills. "Wait until dinner," he said with a flicker of a smile, something he rarely showed.

Abdullah, appeared annoyed by Bashir's morning success. "It is time we conduct the business that brings us all together."

Alexander Kosloff removed his coat and carefully draped it over the chair at the head of the table. Pointing to Abdullah he commanded,

"Produce the nuclear device." Rashid dutifully translated, softening the tone and sometimes the words.

Abdullah opened the dining room buffet and lifted the lead container onto the table. In silence, everyone stared at the somber gray box. Kassar Suri, the weapons specialist from Pakistan, sat at one long side of the table. Abdullah sat across from him. Rashid, at the end of the table, sat opposite the Russian. Bashir lingered in the background.

Rashid translated during the meeting as needed.

Kosloff unlocked his briefcase, withdrew a small black battery-powered appliance and reached for the lead box. "As you may have noticed, this box lacks a handle or a lock. There is a purpose for this design. Only someone with a coded device like this one," he showed the black appliance, "can open this box without destroying its contents. It will self-destruct if opened with force." The Russian inserted the appliance into the connector hidden under the small hinged cover on the side. He flipped a switch and the lid snapped up. He lifted the lid and set it aside. Everyone peered into the opening. The Russian laughed. "What do you expect, a Genie to jump out?"

Inside, a black metal box sat suspended on a bed of a dense gelatin. The same substance coated the inside of the lid. Kassar Suri, the weapons specialist from Pakistan, placed his hands on either side of the black box. "Gentlemen, you are about to inspect one of an estimated 250 Soviet made nuclear weapons designed in the Sixties. The USSR intended this to be a tactical weapon for use on a battlefield. Not a strategic weapon designed for large populations such as Boston or New York. This weapon can level a small city or inflict limited damage to a larger metropolitan area. The device, designated as a RA-115-01, was built in the late Seventies. It's one of almost a hundred that fell into private hands when the Soviet Union dissolved and the Cold War ended. No one knows how many of these bombs have survived. Many assume they are no longer operational. Of course officially they don't exist."

Abdullah hesitated to touch the black box. "Are we exposed to radiation?"

Perplexed, Kassar said, "Of course, but only a low dose, no more than you would experience from several X-rays." He lifted the lid of the black box and displayed the internal workings of the bomb. "Plutonium 239 is the neutron acceptor in this bomb. The construction of this bomb is quite simple." he pointed to various parts. "This is a long life battery. The system will fail if the electric charge is lost." With admiration in his voice he stated, "Alexander Kosloff has, shall we say, *nurtured* this device for many years so it remains in working order."

The Russian withdrew a charger out of his briefcase and attached wires to the battery. He handed the plug to Bashir.

Kassar continued. "This is a pure fission weapon using a gun-type assembly. Upon detonation a high explosive charge forces a bullet of Pu-239 down a tube and into a Plutonium target. You will note two neutron generators astride the tube. They serve as linear particle accelerators. The space between the bullet and the target is filled with gases that, when electrically charged, create hydrogen ions, which result in critical mass when the atoms of Pu-239 collide. This in turn causes nuclear fission—an explosion."

Struggling with the technical jargon, Rashid translated Kassar's explanation. Abdullah nodded his head to show he understood. The Russian appeared bored.

Abdullah found the technical description academic, and not useful. His interest lay in how to blow the damn thing up in a controlled way. "How do you trigger the bomb?"

"Yes, of course," responded Kassar. "Setting the bomb off is a two-step process. First arm it, then detonate it. You will notice this switch." He pointed to a red button on top of a stainless steel box in the corner of the unit. "Pressing this will arm the bomb," he said as he pushed down on the button. Abdullah, Rashid and Bashir uttered a sound of surprised shock and pulled back. A red light blinked next to the button. Amused by their reaction, Kassar grinned with satisfaction. "Don't be frightened. As I said a detonator must be added before the device will fire."

After a few moments, Abdullah lashed out at Kassar. "This demonstration is not entertaining. This is serious business, and is not a matter for theatrics."

"Forgive me, I didn't mean to frighten you," lied Kassar, still entertained by Abdullah's concerned expression. "The detonator is missing. A simple and effective precaution against a nuclear accident."

Rashid hastily translated as he, Abdullah and Bashir composed themselves. Bashir asked the obvious question, "Where is the detonator?"

The Russian stood. "I have it." He reached into his briefcase and took out two pieces of equipment, both slightly larger than a man's fist. He placed them side by side on the table.

216

Kassar thanked him. "If this bomb should fall into the hands of the enemy, it would be useless to them without these accessories." He positioned the detonators in front of him, then cleared his throat and straightened himself. "So far we have talked only of the mechanics of this weapon. We have not explored the effects the explosion will produce." He paused as if gathering his thoughts. "Explosive blast, ionized radiation, thermal radiation, and radioactive fallout are the four significant results from a detonation. Anyone living in this nuclear age should be familiar with these effects. I will not go into details." He checked the room, but no one asked questions. "The intensity of these effects are influenced by the manner in which detonation is delivered." He stopped and looked intently at Abdullah. "I must stress it is *highly* influenced by where detonation takes place."

Everyone turned to Abdullah, who felt he had become the center of attention, but didn't know why. He glanced from face-to-face and then responded to Kassar. "Are you making a point of some kind?"

Kasloff, the Russian, stood and addressed Abdullah. Rashid quickly translated between pauses. "You have told your handlers in Rome that you intend to attack a crowd of spectators in a small stadium not far from here in Mexico." Rashid corrected the Russian by saying *New Mexico.* "Yes, I mean New Mexico. You have estimated in your reports the maximum damage to life would not exceed thirty thousand Americans, and could be far fewer. Your plan," he continued, "is to hide this weapon somewhere in the stadium at ground level and explode it remotely when you are at a safe distance." The Russian stressed the words 'safe distance.' Rashid repeated what he said word for word.

Abdullah, his heart pounding, stood and faced the Russian, an aging hulk that he regarded with less respect than a pile of camel dung. "May Allah the Bringer of Death, damn you for your impudence!" Abdullah advanced on the Russian. "My plan is not made in haste. I have created a plan to uphold the values of my faith and the moral codes of Islam. Something a nonbeliever such as yourself cannot grasp—much less respect."

Rashid softened the translation to avoid further confrontation, almost to the point of misrepresentation. Bashir regarded Rashid with disapproval.

Kosloff pulled back, surprised at the ferocity of this verbal counterattack. Then he fired back, "I speak the truth as I have learned from your masters, who do not agree with you." With a curled lip he leaned forward, "Explain the merits of your strategy."

217

Abdullah, his hands still trembling with rage, moved away from his opponent. "I do not answer to you, but for the benefit of the others, I will put to rest your accusations." He turned to Kassar, Rashid and Bashir. "I have studied this opportunity to punish the Americans for their meddling in our affairs. I have determined I must get their attention without forcing them to bloody Islam with their great military power, which is known to be vast and invincible. Their stockpile of nuclear weapons would easily annihilate the Muslim world. No, this must be a measured attack. I have selected a target that not only reduces the possibility of killing Muslims who live in America, but avoids the slaughter of children within the age of innocence. My target includes Americans of ethnic diversity, mostly the young and the able bodied. This fool," pointing to the Russian, "would relish a holy war of worldwide proportions. He would become richer for it." The translation in both Russian and Urdu took several minutes. No one spoke when Rashid finished. The Russian shrugged his shoulders, turned away and sat down.

Looks were exchanged around the table. Finally, Kassar resumed the briefing. "If I understand this discussion, we have two scenarios to consider: limited impact versus maximum impact. Fortunately, detonators exist for either choice. In my right hand I hold a detonator that incorporates a radar altimeter to measure the height of an aircraft above ground. This altimeter is programmed in a special way. First the plane must arrive at an altitude greater than one thousand feet to activate it. When the aircraft descends below 500 feet the bomb will detonate. Five hundred feet is the correct distance above ground if the greatest effect is to be achieved. Once armed, it *cannot* be disarmed." Kassar paused a moment. "In my left hand, I hold a detonator that may be activated at any chosen time by a remote signal, produced by a cell phone. Entering a coded sequence of numbers is all it takes. Obviously this would be used for a ground-level explosion." He summed up. "In both cases, arming the bomb must be done manually, that is to say, by a human being."

No one spoke after the translation.

The Russian closed his oversized briefcase and placed in on the floor. "I will leave these accessories. How you use them is not my decision. I have met my obligations to the deal." He folded his hands behind his back.

Abdullah demanded further training in the proper procedures for attaching the detonators. He took notes, as Kassar explained the fine points. When the briefing ended and Rashid no longer needed to translate, he asked to be excused, explaining he needed a trip to the bathroom. Abdullah waved him off.

RASHID PUSHED HIS chair back and left the dining room. He climbed the stairs and headed for the bathroom that served both second floor bedrooms. He shut the door and quickly reached down and pulled his pant leg up, retrieving a compact phone. He quickly tapped in a number, and then a short text message. As he finished he heard someone stumping up the stairs. Bashir knocked on the door. "Don't you know there is a bathroom downstairs?" He asked in a loud voice. Rashid lifted the toilet tank top and dropped his phone in the water, then carefully replaced the top and flushed the toilet.

"Of course I know," he answered opening the door, "but what if someone else needs the facilities? We can't all fit in the same bathroom, now can we?" Bashir, wearing a pair of binoculars around his neck, peeked over his shoulder into the bathroom. "If you need to go, Bashir, help yourself. I'm done."

ABDULLAH REVIEWED HIS notes. The Russian left the dining room and stepped out on the front porch stretched his body and faced the overcast sky–his eyes closed and his expression blank. Rashid checked to see if anyone needed his services, but Abdullah again waved him off. Rashid flopped down on the sofa, picked out a six-month-old magazine and thumbed through it.

Bashir, after leaving the upstairs bathroom, deposited the binoculars on the dining room table, and joined the group. He eyed his watch, then started for the kitchen to prepare dinner. Everyone agreed they would stay a second night and make arrangements for morning flights out of El Paso.

The Team of Deliverance had met, talked, exchanged views and trained Abdullah in the use of his suitcase nuke. Except for dinner, packing up, and the flight home tomorrow, the day was over. Or was it?

# FIFTY

IN THE EARLY HOURS OF Friday morning Ashley grabbed her backpack from her cubicle on the first floor of the Field Office, and took the stairs two at a time to the third floor. She saw a dim light at the end of the hall in Kent's office and found Walter lying on the office sofa with his eyes closed and a phone on his chest. She sat on an adjacent chair two feet from the sofa, and made only enough noise to test how deep his sleep might be. His eyes opened.

In a soft voice she said, "Its one a. m. officially morning. Any word from DC?" Walter touched the phone on his chest with his right hand and took her hand with his left.

"Nothing new. The task force is in position. No word from Cebeck." He swung his legs around and sat up, dropped the phone next to him and ran his hand through his hair. "Johansson can't contact Cebeck."

Ashley nodded. "He's probably asleep. He put in a long day." She paused, then pulled at his hand to get his attention. "I've done everything I can do here. I feel the need to be down there, near the action."

"You're not alone. Johansson wants me down there, too. It's not that he doesn't trust his task force, he feels we should be in on the kill since we—that's you and I—opened this case."

"It's a long drive." She was pleased Walter included her.

"No. About ten minutes."

She looked at him and raised both eyebrows. "It's over 250 miles."

"More like five," he said with a sly grin, "to Kirkland Air Force Base across town." She didn't speak, but her expression asked—what? "Leo Adornetto has a long reach. He called the Secretary of Defense. That opens many doors. We have a Beechcraft Turboprop at our disposal."

"I trained in a Beechcraft years ago during my college days when I learned to fly and became a flight instructor."

"Are you still current?"

"Yes, but just barely."

Walter let go of her hand. "Time to move out." He stood, then walked to his desk and centered the phone on the seat of his chair. "Your old buddy Mark Ramirez will be here to take over communication in a few minutes. He'll find the phone because I know he'll sit in my chair."

KIRKLAND AFB OPERATES out of the Albuquerque International Sunport, a joint civilian and military airfield. Lieutenant Colonel F. Avery met them in the main lobby of the airport. "Special Agent in Charge Walter Kent?"

"Yes, Colonel Avery, this is Agent Kohen," he replied, reading the Colonel's nametag. "Sorry to disturb you at this hour, but I don't control the timing."

The colonel nodded. "No problem, sir. Follow me. The aircraft is standing by." The twin engine King Air sat positioned on the tarmac. Major R. Henderson, the copilot, stood by the aircraft, its door dropped to allow entrance. After brief introductions, they climbed aboard. Twelve minutes later, at 1:45 a.m., they were cleared for takeoff

With the cockpit door closed, Ashley moved next to Walter. He took her hand. "Better get some sleep, it will be a long day," She nodded and snuggled against his shoulder.

About an hour after takeoff, the King Air touched down on runway 12/30 at the Artesia Municipal Airport. Colonel Avery taxied to the general aviation building, and idled the aircraft. Major Henderson unlatched the portside door and dropped the stairs. "We radioed ahead," he yelled, over the engine noise. "There will be a ride waiting for you around in front of this building at three hundred hours–about now. Have a safe trip."

Walter dipped his head, "Give my regards to the Colonel. Smooth ride."

They walked around the darkened terminal building and spotted a Humvee with running lights on. It came equipped with a burly man in army fatigues who appeared half awake. "Are you Walter Kent?"

"Yes."

"Very good, sir. Hop in. Assault Leader Davis is expecting you."

They drove thirty-two miles east on Highway 82, then turned south on a dirt road. The Humvee bumped along for two miles then stopped at the temporary field center for Red Dog Unit–the western half of the Joint Terrorism Task Force. In the vehicle's headlights they saw a straight walled tent. When the driver killed his lights, a glow inside the tent became visible.

A man stepped out of the tent as they exited the Humvee. "Good morning, Mr. Kent. I've been expecting you. Who is that with you?"

"Lead Investigator Ashley Kohen."

"Come inside, please. I'll brief you on current conditions."

Unlike the old canvas field tents, this one was made of polyester and could be erected in five minutes. Assault Leader Davis stood lean and tall with a touch of gray in his hair. He offered them folding chairs. On a plastic storage box, he rolled out a mapped layout of the target house and the JTTF positions. "The subjects of interest are less than two miles from our position. We are well out of their sight. Both my unit and Alpha Unit, east of here, have forward observers with eyes on the two-story dwelling. Your man, Agent Cebeck, has the closest vantage point. So far he hasn't reported anything since midnight." Davis tapped his iPad. "These are infrared images of the house. Our drone took them. As you can see lights-out about one hundred hours."

Ashley and Walter studied the images and the drawing. She asked, "What's your plan?"

"Our orders are to report any movement or overt actions. We know there are four men inside and assume one or more people were already in place before their arrival Thursday night, a few hours ago. If they leave, we will close in on them when ordered."

Walter asked, "Any chance of approaching tonight and mounting a listening device?"

"We thought of that, but DC said no. Director Johansson doesn't want any chance of discovery until we know more about what's going on in there. I understand we have a man on the inside."

"Yes," Ashley confirmed, "An experienced man from headquarters."

Davis nodded. "It's a wait-and-see game right now. I don't expect any change until after sun up." He noticed dark circles under their eyes. "Sorry about the accommodations. Best I can do is a couple of sleeping bags. You're welcome to catch a few hours in the back of the Humvee parked outside."

Ashley gave Davis a tentative smile.

The clear night sky allowed the moon to cast faint shadows on the desert landscape. Bright pinpoints of starlight pierced the upper atmosphere like tiny snowflakes on a black canvas, their contrast sharpened by the clear dry air of the desert.

The choice between sleeping in the Humvee or on the ground was an easy one to make. The ground offered a flat surface and space for unrestricted movement, something the military designers failed to stress in their modern version of the Jeep. What the ground didn't offer was protection from the elements. Ashley scrunched her face into the sleeping bag to avoid the desert insects and debris.

With the sunrise came a low-pressure system that stirred the winds and brought scattered clouds that soon thickened into a gloomy overcast blanket, allowing temperatures to moderate. Ashley checked the time: seven o'clock. Walter lay asleep a few feet away. She took a long look at this man who held a strange attraction for her. Strange because she had never had this kind of warm feeling for any man.

Assault Leader Davis interrupted her contemplation. "Good morning Agent Kohen. I trust you slept well?"

From the ground she answered, "Like a baby."

"Must be the desert air."

Walter rolled over and squinted up at the tall lanky form of the leader. He immediately wriggled out of his sleeping bag and stood facing Davis. "Any new developments?"

"All's quiet on the eastern front," he answered with fake seriousness. "Agent Cebeck checked in a few minutes ago. No visible movement in or around the house. Our observers report the same." He offered Ashley a hand up. "I have some hot coffee in the tent. Doughnuts are on the way."

THE HARDEST PART of directing a field maneuver from Washington DC is having to rely on status reports before decisions are made. Johansson found the lack of activity in or around Maljamar an annoyance. He paced back and forth in his darkened Command Center while keeping an eye on all the large monitors displayed on the wall overhead.

At 8:30, Mark Ramirez relayed a report from Agent Cebeck to Johansson and both field units of the JTTF. His report said Bashir had exited the front of the house and removed items from the one of the cargo units on top of the Suburban. He then drove the vehicle around to the side of the house where he parked it, and carried the items inside. Cebeck's next report came later that afternoon at four o'clock. A large, older man had stepped out on the front porch and looked around a few minutes, then reentered the house. Johansson continued to scrutinize every scrap of intelligence.

In his pocket his phone rang. The first call was from his daughter. His brother in Maryland called an hour later. He didn't have time for personal calls. He turned off his phone. He had more important things to think about than family matters.

# FIFTY-ONE

BEFORE GOING TO MALJAMAR Bashir planned the dinner with great care. He wanted it to be appetizing for everyone so they would find the food irresistible. Considering the diverse backgrounds and nationalities, the meal would be a culinary challenge. He settled on Ottoman lamb, jeweled rice, tomato salad, and for dessert pistachio baklava. To shorten the preparation time, he had mixed all the dry ingredients at home and stored them in separate plastic bags, all carefully marked. Many of the wet ingredients were also stored in jars with tight fitting lids. At home he practiced preparing each dish several times to be certain the dinner would come off without problems. Now in this remote desert house, he proceeded with confidence.

Abdullah sat separate from the others, thinking about the conflicting opinions expressed around the table earlier. Except for Rashid, who remained neutral throughout the meeting, he felt alienated from Kosloff and Suri. The Russian's accusation that his handlers in Rome did not approve of his target selection, festered in his mind. How dare this relic from the Soviet Union take it upon himself to evaluate my plan, and claim it is not supported. He is delusional. My work continues to be sustained with unlimited funding from Rome. Suri's did not consider the level of retaliation each scenario would cause the Americans to take against my people. Our minimum attack will deter major U.S. meddling in our affairs and show the fallacies of America's foreign policies. A maximum attack would force retaliation of inconceivable proportions.

Rashid interrupted Abdullah's reverie. "There is much responsibility resting on your shoulders, Abdullah." He took a seat at the other end of the sofa. "Only a brave man would sacrifice his safety for the advancement of holy jihad and the love of his people."

Abdullah listened to these sympathetic words. Maybe he wasn't alone in his determination to do the will of Allah, the Omnipresent. He agreed with Rashid's comments. "They," he motioned toward the others, "serve only their own interests. I evaluate the consequences of my actions."

"Yes, you have a rare opportunity to serve Islam. Timing is important. When will the stadium attract the greatest crowds?"

Abdullah studied Rashid's face. His questions took him off guard. He thought about the football schedule and tried to remember when the rival teams of New Mexico State and University of New Mexico would play. Before he could sort that out, Bashir announced dinner would be served momentarily. Standing, he replied, "Soon, Rashid, soon."

The Russian took his place at the head of the table. Abdullah selected the chair at the other end, wanting to be as far from Kosloff as possible. Rashid and Kassar faced each other. No one noticed the absence of a place setting for Bashir.

Carrying a tray, Bashir served drinks to everyone–water for all and sparkling apple juice for the Muslims. Alexander Kosloff expressed pleasure when a bottle of vodka was set before him with a glass of cracked ice. The Russian touched the bottle and said aloud, "Not only a civilized drink, but *Snow Queen Vodka,* from Kazakhstan, magnificent!" He poured his glass full and raised it. "A toast. To all who seek a better life." No one needed a translation. Rashid and Kassar joined in, but Abdullah only touched his glass.

Bashir quickly left and returned carrying a tray of four plates of food with generous servings. Each plate was adorned with attractive garnish. He served Abdullah last. When he set the plate in front of him he whispered in his ear, "Drink, but do not eat if you wish to live." Abdullah froze and continued to stare at his plate. A ripple of fear consumed his body. He gripped his fork, and picked up his glass. His hand trembled.

In the kitchen, Bashir prepared a meal of lamb cut into small pieces for his dog who he respected only for his fearless aggression. The dog attacked the meat with zeal.

In the dining room the Russian eagerly ate his food starting with the lamb, which he washed down with a gulp of vodka after each bite. Kassar tried the tomato salad, tested the rice, and then sampled the meat. When Bashir brought in the pistachio baklava, he ate some of that, too. Rashid pushed the food around on his plate with little enthusiasm. Bashir had made such an effort to please everyone. The buttered rice, with nuts and berries, added color to the meal. He concentrating on that more than the lamb and tomato salad. Abdullah stared at his plate. It all smelled and looked delicious.

The first to feel the effects of the colorless, tasteless gamma-hydroxbutrate mixed into the food was the Russian. He went from a gregarious playful dinner partner to a listless and then silent man. When his head fell back and his arms dropped to his sides, Rashid and Kassar assumed he had drunk too much vodka. When Kassar's head dipped down, then descended into his plate of food, it was too late for Rashid to react. He tried to stand, but lost consciousness as he fell to the floor in slow motion. Abdullah watched this spectacle speechless, unable to grasp its meaning.

Bashir entered the dining room holding a semi-automatic 9mm handgun with a suppressor attached almost doubling the gun's length. Abdullah jumped up. "What have you done?" He screamed. "Why are you armed?"

"I am following orders," he answered perfectly composed. While he spoke, he fired a shot through the head of the Russian, rocking him violently to the side. Blood and brain tissue splattered against the nearby wall. "I serve the successor of the Prophet Muhammad, and Supreme Head of the Society of Rule by Sharia Law." He positioned the gun at the base of Kassar Suri's skull, and then fired a bullet that tore through his brain and split the top of his head, spraying a path of bloody gore across the table and into Rashid's food. Bashir walked around the table and stood over Rashid who lay on the floor unconscious. He never took his eyes off Abdullah when he fired two rounds into Rashid al Youris killing him instantly. He then raised the gun and pointed it at Abdullah.

# FIFTY-TWO

MIKE JOHANSSON ARRANGED a four-way call with Mark Ramirez, Leader Davis and his counterpart Leader Perry positioned east of the house. "It's five o'clock and nothing new," he said speaking with restraint through compressed lips. "What the hell is going on?"

Assault Leader Davis spoke first. "Not much, sir. My observers report to me every thirty minutes."

Perry, head of Alpha Unit added, "We did see a man exit the back door and untie a dog and lead it back into the house. Didn't seem important. I planned to mention it during our half hour check in."

"Untied a dog–took it in the house?"

"Yes, sir. A Doberman a few minutes ago. Been tied up all-day. Cebeck wouldn't have seen that, he's around front."

Johansson couldn't fault them for a lack of activity. He felt nervous about Rashid's continued exposure to danger. "If Rashid al Youris leaves– as soon as he's out of sight, you close in and rescue him. No gunfire if you can help it, but get him away safe. You understand?"

Davis answered for both of them. "Yes, sir. We have a plan. We'll intercept them before anyone knows what happened."

"What about Cebeck?"

"We're keeping an eye on him. Agent Kohen tried to figure a way to get food and water to him, but I didn't want to take that chance. He'll survive."

"Yes, he'll survive."

Davis waited a long second. "Sir?"

"Yes?"

"What if they leave during the night? It could be messy."

Johansson scrubbed his hand over his face. "This is a three-step operation. First you get Rashid. Second, you debrief him on the spot, and then tell me what he says. I'll decide when we take the house."

"Yes sir." Davis hesitated again. "What if we don't get Rashid?"

Dealing with this threat to national security had to be his first concern, even though his anxiety about Rashid's safety tormented him. He lowered his voice. "We'll do what we have to do."

# FIFTY-THREE

BASHIR HELD THE GUN with both hands, removed his finger from the trigger, and placed it against the trigger guard. His aim did not waver, nor did his intense eye contact with Abdullah, who held onto the back of his chair to steady himself. Only five feet separated them. "And were you told to kill me?" Abdullah asked in a shrill voice.

Bashir calmly considered the question. "That's optional."

Abdullah took a deep breath and struggled to take charge of himself. He waited to respond, hoping this might be a test and would end soon. Bashir's eyes did not flicker. "Optional? You dare to stand there pointing a gun at me and say my death is optional?" Abdullah's grip on the chair turned his knuckles pale. "There is nothing optional about my mission. I am the chosen vanguard of Allah the Exalted. The man who will change history." He tried not to look at the hole in the end of the gun barrel. "I will give new life to our holy jihad against the infidels of the west, who dare to impose their will on us." In a scathing tone he ordered, "Put down that gun before Allah strikes you dead."

Bashir ignored the order. "You may consider my warning to not eat the food laced with Liquid X a professional courtesy."

"A courtesy?"

Bashir slipped his finger off the trigger guard. "Yes, a courtesy not extended to our former associates who now lay silent around us."

Abdullah, who cared little for the others, now faced an immediate threat. Bashir was inferior to him in every way, but the gun gave him power. "You are my servant. It is not your decision to bring my crusade to an end."

"True, it is not my decision, and yes I am a servant, but not your servant. I spared you from my meal of death because you deserve a chance to redeem yourself."

"Redeem myself?"

"Yes, to fulfill your pledge to do the work of Allah the Magnificent."

Abdullah, stupefied by this contradiction, blurted out, "But I am fulfilling my pledge!"

"Our leader, Caliph Abd al-Ghayb, described it best. He said you have lost your way. You are influenced by weak morals and a lack of discipline–unwilling to sacrifice for Islam. Your plan would waste a rare opportunity to inflict monumental chaos among our enemies while allowing you to survive."

Abdullah fired back, "Untrue! My plan will save Islam from a catastrophic retaliation by the Americans. A calculated attack, as I plan to carry out, will get their attention and make them question their further involvement in our affairs. A reckless attack and loss of American life will force them to annihilate our people!"

Bashir sneered. "So you stand by your football stadium target in Las Cruces, and a ground level detonation?"

"My target will cause many thousands to die, you fool."

"Words, Abdullah. You speak many words that hide the truth: you are a coward. You plan to live, not die for Islam."

His face flushed, Abdullah shouted out his answer. "If necessary I will die a martyr, but I shall not commit suicide. The Quran forbids it, as you must know."

"Then, my misguided soldier of Islam, I will grant your wish of martyrdom." Bashir's finger pulled the trigger sending a hollow point 9 mm bullet into Abdullah al Jamal's chest.

BASHIR LOWERED THE GUN and watched the man from Saudi Arabia die. Abdullah lie on the floor, an expression of disbelief on his face, and eyes open wide as if straining to see a fading light. His hand covered the wound that oozed blood between his fingers. When he sucked in his last breath, it left his mouth agape.

His killer, standing in an-ever widening circle of blood, surveyed the room decorated with splatter patterns and fragments of human tissue. He studied the motionless bodies around him, each in a different grotesque pose as if in a wax museum of horror. A wave of satisfaction flooded through him. Phase one complete.

He moved into the kitchen.

The Doberman pincher lay next to his bowl of half eaten meat. Careful to avoid a damaging ricochet, he leaned down and fired a shot into the dog's head. Then he tossed the silencer equipped handgun into a metal garbage can and stepped over to the sink to wash his hands. The clock on the microwave oven read 6:15. He had much to do in a short time.

He opened a kitchen cabinet and removed the black duffle bag that contained Abdullah's money, and set it on the counter. He checked the bag for booby traps and found none. The bag contained tens of thousands of dollars and a handgun Abdullah had replaced last night as everyone slept. Bashir knew this because he had watched Abdullah's movements.

Next he retrieved the heavy lead container that housed the nuclear bomb. Abdullah had cleverly hidden it under his bed–who would guess? The oversized briefcase with the detonators and battery charger sat perched in plain sight on the living room coffee table displayed by the Russian who had considered it of no value to him after their meeting. Bashir gathered these items and made a pile on the kitchen counter. Then he went about the house turning on lights so the place would look lived-in tonight. He closed most of the window blinds and locked the front door.

Based on the range-finder readings calculated in his field binoculars, the man across the highway in the white van would not be a problem if he stayed put. Everything depended on the house appearing occupied and normal. Bashir searched his mind to be sure he had performed everything that needed to be done. Satisfied, he then returned to the kitchen and removed a plate of food from the refrigerator he had set aside for his dinner. He heated it in the microwave and sat down to feast on his delicious meal. When he finished eating, it would be time to leave, right on schedule. Life couldn't be better.

Bashir welcomed the heavy cloud cover that made the night exceptionally dark. It would allow him to slip unseen into the backyard and open the shed that hid Abdullah's old 1979 pickup, the one he had bought for Abdullah months earlier. He hoped the truck would start, but if it didn't he had an extra twelve volt battery in the Suburban.

Dressed in black pants and shirt, at 8:15, well after the sun had set, he moved catlike across the back porch. Crouching down, he took a few steps at a time until he reached the shed, a light rain begin to fall. Bashir opened the door six inches. The bottom edge scratched a shallow grove in the dirt. He lifted the door enough to clear the ground and slowly walked it open.

Back in the house he put the lead box under his left arm and held the briefcase handle and duffle bag straps in his right hand. When he got to the truck he opened its door and the dome light came on. Good, he thought. The battery still has a charge. He yanked the cover off and twisted the bulb.

It went out. After packing the briefcase, the bag and the box behind the seat, he inserted the spare key he had saved into the ignition, and turned it. The engine hesitated, cranked twice, and then started. "Bless Mohammad the Prophet and Allah the Merciful," he whispered and put the truck in low gear.

Bashir had researched his escape route. He would not drive on highway 82. His plan was to head south into the open desert, making slow progress in the darkness at about two miles an hour. He turned on the windshield wipers, but did not turn on the lights and didn't touch the brake pedal. If he had to stop he would use the emergency brake. Bashir dodged the endless maze of oil field pump jacks, work-over rigs and storage tanks. Often he avoided crashing into a fenced area by the sound of a pump motor straining against the lift cycle.

Ten miles from Maljamar lay state Highways 62 and 180. He hoped to intersect with those roads by midnight. At ten-thirty, when the odometer registered five miles from the house, he stopped and pulled out his phone. He entered a predetermined code.

Next to the house, in one of the cargo containers on top of the Suburban, he had stored 150 pounds of PBX plastic bonded explosives. Buried in this highly stable material, Bashir had planted a detonator complete with a tiny antenna. Even at his distance, the initial explosion lit the night sky, shattering the house, the Suburban, Abdullah's old car and everything within a hundred yards. The oil storage tanks on the east side ruptured and soon ignited, sending a fireball and black smoke into the night sky.

Bashir flipped on the headlights, increased his speed to five miles an hour, and never looked back.

233

# FIFTY-FOUR

THE FORWARD OBSERVERS SAW and heard the explosion first. For a brief second a brilliant white-hot light lit the countryside and the night sky. That stab of light blinded those closest to the blast, leaving them momentarily sightless. An instant later a thundering blast rolled through the darkness followed by a shock wave of heat swift enough to make the observers cringe while huddled flat on the ground–their hands clutching the dirt. As if alive with evil intent, a bulbous column of orange fury boiled aloft, writhing like a tormented beast. Those in the rear witnessed the ball of fire belch upward, encircled by a rolling ring of white smoke, lit by incandescent gases. Burning fragments of debris whirred over the landscape, some striking the surface with a thud. Large and small fires burned on the ground like scattered campfires.

Pressure from the blast opened a rusted seam on the side of a nearby crude oil storage tank, causing a steady stream of oil to flood its base. Burning embers from the explosion settled on the exposed fuel, igniting a new fire. Heat from this inferno caused the warped seam to split open, creating a fiery torch that shot up the side of the tank making more fuel gush out. Within seconds a massive fireball filled the air with billowing flames that created thick black smoke visible by the light of the fire that rose twisting and changing shape as it grew higher into the night sky. Glowing light from this hellish scene revealed the tortured land.

Ashley heard the first explosion as did Walter and Assault Leader Davis. They dashed out of the tent in time to see a bright column rise above the land and form a tornado-like funnel lit by the ruby red fire within the cloud of churning smoke. Ashley thought of Cebeck.

"Walter," she shouted. "I have to go." She ran for the Humvee, and jumped behind the wheel, with Kent right behind her. He didn't have to ask where she was going. "Hit it," he said, swinging into the front seat beside her. The tires tore through the sandy soil as they swerved onto the dirt road heading for Highway 82.

While they jerked over the rough terrain, several new explosions occurred in the distance. Once on the hard road, Ashley floored it, determined to make fifteen miles in ten minutes. Gripping the steering wheel her eyes never left the yellow centerline. As they approached the geyser of smoke and fire, it grew larger, swirling overhead like a blazing dirt devil.

Walter checked the odometer. "One mile," he shouted, as they neared the inferno. He searched south of the road for signs of the two story house, but couldn't find it. As they neared the site, a wall of heat engulfed them. Ashley slowed and left the highway on the north side. A barbed wire fence lined the right-of-way. "I'm going through," she yelled steering into the fence and hitting a metal post square on. "Tally-ho," shouted Walter with a taste of satisfaction in his voice.

They swerved back and forth covering a wide swath of land with the headlights, as they searched for that clump of trees amidst layers of smoke. The heat became suffocating. "Over there." Kent pointing to the right. The lights reflected off a white patch between several shattered junipers. Ashley geared down and pulled near the crumpled vehicle, its hood, bent back. Only bits of the windshield remained. Kent leaped out and ran as Ashley set the brake and jumped out, too. The van, its front end lifted off the ground two feet, sat pinned between several tree stumps bent at awkward angles. Ashley, holding back a scream, felt the scorching heat on her body from the nearby fire. Stumbling over debris in the darkness, she yanked on the driver's side door. The hot metal burned her hand. Wedged shut, the door didn't move. She heard Walter shout for her to come to the back of the van.

In the headlights of the Humvee, Ashley saw Walter pulling on the rear right door with both hands, one foot on the center of the left rear door. She grabbed him around the chest. "We pull together...now!" The door moved only an inch. "Again!" It moved two inches. "Again!" The door gave way and they both fell back crashing to the ground. They faced each other with grim satisfaction, and then leaped toward the open door.

Together they crawled into the van and began a frantic search for Cebeck. The fire created heat, but also light. Surveillance equipment lay scattered about the interior. Choking on the smoke, they moved forward. On their knees, they searched as much with their hands as with their eyes. Ashley pulled herself up with the back of the passenger seat. "He's over here." Walter moved to the driver's side. On the floor jammed between the dashboard and the seats lay a man–not moving.

Walter catapulted over the driver's seat and touched Cebeck. "He's alive. He's breathing."

From behind the seat, Ashley tried to open the passenger door, but couldn't. "Kick the door. Kick it hard," she shouted, then reached down near the floor for the seat release. Her hand scraped into the tiny space between the door and the seat controls. It touched a lever. She pulled it. The seat snapped back. Walter, with more room to maneuver, kicked the door, bracing himself against the steering wheel. He kicked with both feet. With an abrupt grating noise of metal against metal, the door cracked open. Another kick and it opened just enough. Kent jumped outside, turned and grabbed Cebeck by the shoulders. Ashley, now in the front seat, locked her hand under Jerry's belt and lifted. "We have to be careful, we don't know his injuries." Walter nodded and pulled with care, sliding Cebeck off the front floor, a few inches at a time. He got a better hold on him and pulled as Ashley lifted. The semiconscious man moaned when he slipped to the ground. Ashley vaulted out of the van. "I'll get the Humvee."

The headlights let Kent do a quick examination. No compound fractures. No profuse bleeding. Together they moved Cebeck onto the back floor and Ashley stayed with him as Kent drove east toward Lovington and the nearest hospital. Ashley called in their medical emergency.

Sprawled on the floor, she cradled Cebeck on her lap. He moaned and opened his eyes; one nearly swollen shut. "Jerry can you hear me?" she asked pulling his head toward her. He stared at her with a blank expression. Blood and dirt stained his face. She brushed his hair back and felt angular grains of glass from the windshield. "We're getting medical help, Jerry." His mouth moved, but no sound came out. "It's okay. Hang in there."

Cebeck focused on her face, and brought his hand up, but it fell back. In barely a whisper he said. "Ashley...Ashley."

"I'm right here," she reassured him.

He tried to lift his head. "I saw it."

"Yes, I know, a terrible fire."

His head shook slightly. "No. I saw it."

She cradled his head. "You're going to be alright."

With an expression of urgency he touched her arm and struggled to speak. Ashley knew he wanted to say something. She leaned near his face. "What is it Jerry? What are you trying to tell me?"

"I saw it...next to...the house."

"What did you see?"

His lips moved, but again no sound. She put her ear next to his mouth. "What did you see, Jerry?"

In a faint voice he choked out two words. "Explosion. Suburban."

Ashley straightened. Her face grew ashen as she processed those words. He nodded his head slightly. She nodded back.

# FIFTY-FIVE

EARLY TO BED AND EARLY to rise described Ed Delong's daily life cycle, but this Friday night it would be late to bed. The FBI Director had to attend the President's Council on Crime and Constitutional Rights. His major contribution to the meeting was chomping down on a cigar and staying awake. After the meeting, and a brief round of handshakes, Delong slipped out of the building and into the backseat of his car. He dozed off as his chauffeur drove him to his home in Arlington, Virginia.

After a hot cup of decaf coffee, spiked with a shot of Bailey's Irish Cream, he started for his bedroom upstairs. That's when his home phone alarm, wired to the emergency line at headquarters, sounded off. Frowning he reached for the downstairs phone. "Delong here," he barked.

The night desk chief answered, "Sorry to disturb you sir, I have a POISN alert. One minute, please, while I arrange a transfer of this call."

Delong hated that acronym. Someone, years ago, figured out a title for the Emergency Operations Manual, that would phonetically spell a word descriptive of the name: *Personnel Operations Information System Network* or POISN. How bureaucratic can you get?

He heard a click on the line and thought he'd been cut off, then a voice spoke. "This is Agent Ackerman, sir, Norman Ackerman. I...I'm calling you from the Command Center downtown about *Operation Full Moon*. There's been a God-awful explosion. I don't know who else to call. Sorry sir."

Delong leaned against the entry wall. "Calm down Ackerman and tell me what kind of hell broke loose."

"Davis and Perry both report a big explosion and a bad fire out in New Mexico. Real bad. Several observers got burned. Director Johansson is real upset. I'm not sure what to do. I'm real sorry I called you, but I hope I did the right thing. You know I just got assigned yesterday, and..."

As *Operation Full Moon* came into mental focus, Delong cut him off "Okay, I understand. Put Johansson on the line."

238

"That's just it, sir. Director Johansson he's, well, he's real upset right now. I mean he's–how can I say this–emotional, sir."

A chill came over Delong. No one in the Bureau had more resolve to get a job done then the Big Swede. This sounded wrong. "I need to talk to him. Tell him I'm on the line."

"Yes, sir. I'll tell him."

Distant background voices filled the void as Delong waited. He reviewed the facets of the operation and realized the potential dangers. Finally, a flat monotone voice, he did not immediately recognize, came on line.

"Ed, they tell me everyone is gone. Rashid is dead. The whole place got blown to hell. The meeting house has disappeared. I did everything to prevent this. I should have stopped him from going." Ed heard a sobbing sound. "Hesse will never forgive me for what I've done. I can't believe this."

Delong's hand tightened on the phone. "You had a solid plan. Youris volunteered. You knew there were risks."

"Risk, yes. But not this. Not my friend."

Delong focused. "I'm sorry for your loss, Mike. Collateral damage happens."

"Ed." A choking sound. "I know. I know, but Rashid was my partner."

"Listen Mike, I want you to go home."

A long pause. "I can't leave my post."

"You're not abandoning your post. I'm ordering you to step down, temporarily. You're in no condition to stay. I regret this happened. I understand your grief. Now go home. I'll take it from here."

Silence, then, "Yes, sir. Of course you're right."

"Is there anyone to take your place in the Center?"

Another silence. "No, sir."

"I need your recommendation for an On-Scene Commander."

Johansson thought a moment. "The assault leaders are in the field, but this situation needs executive leadership, not commando tactics."

Delong, losing patience, demanded, "Give me a name. Mike."

"Kent. Walter Kent. It's his case. His jurisdiction. He would be my pick for an OSC. A good man."

"I agree, now put Ackerman on the line, and you go home."

"Yes, sir."

239

Special Agent Ackerman had worked the communications console as his primary duty. He quickly forwarded Delong to Mark Ramirez in the Albuquerque Field Office. The director told Ramirez that he was appointing Walter Kent as the On-Scene Commander of the Maljamar incident and *Operation Full Moon,* effective immediately.

At 9:45 p.m. Mountain Daylight Time, Ramirez reached Kent as he pulled into the Artesia General Hospital Emergency Room entrance with Ashley holding Jerry Cebeck's unconscious body on her lap.

# FIFTY-SIX

WHEN WALTER AND ASHLEY arrived at the hospital, paramedics lifted Cebeck onto a hospital gurney they had shoved against the Humvee. Ashley followed the medical techs into the Emergency Room.

At ten o'clock Ramirez called Kent. "I got a call from Director Delong. He has appointed you On Scene Commander with full authority. He'll give you whatever you need to deal with this."

"What about Johansson?"

"No comment, but Delong will get back to you with an official declaration."

Kent paused to focus on his new responsibilities. He knew that as the OSC he had extraordinary powers, and that few agents were given this level of challenge during their career. "Okay, Mark. Write this down."

"Yes, sir."

"First, contact Leaders Davis and Perry and brief them on my appointment. They must keep the scene secure, and maintain its integrity. Only allow firefighters access. No media or local law enforcement. This is one big-ass crime scene and I don't want a bunch of people stomping around there." He stopped a moment to think. "Next, I need more personnel on the ground. Review staff assignments and send me everyone you can free up."

Ramirez, used his personal shorthand to get everything down.

"Call the SAC in the El Paso Field Office. Explain the situation and ask him for a dozen people—more if he can spare them. Stress that we have a large crime scene and need extensive evidence collection." Kent took a deep breath. "I want our forensic team with full gear. This will be a large area for documentation. It will need a photographic and video walkthrough. Finally, call Doctor Zumbeck in the State Medical Investigator's Office and invite his staff to join our search. Tell him there will be body parts. Any questions?"

"What about the State Police?"

"Call them. They can deal with traffic. Anything else?"

"How's Cebeck?"

"He's in the ER. I think he'll be okay."

"Agent Kohen?"

"She's with Cebeck right now, but I need her with me. I'm counting on you for all communications. I'm heading back to Maljamar. My estimated time of arrival is ten thirty. Okay?"

"Yes, ten thirty. I'm on it."

THE FIRE IN MALJAMAR painted the horizon pink. The night crew at the Navajo Refinery in Artesia reported what they saw to the fire department who scramble into fire engines and trucks equipped to fight hydrocarbon fires in the Permian Basin. Artesia's night dispatcher alerted Lovington on the other side of Maljamar, to the explosion. Both departments carried all the Class B foam possible.

The Joint Terrorism Task Force was overwhelmed. Assault Leaders Davis and Perry formed two six-member crews to search for trapped or injured people. The remaining personnel moved into position to cordon off the rural highway in both directions.

The Lovington Fire Department arrived on the scene first. They assessed conditions and determined the main fire uncontrollable, and would let it burn itself out. The lighting crew cranked up generators and erected floodlights. The fire suppression units built containment dikes and dispensed a blanket of Class B foam on the east side. Fifteen minutes later the Artesia firefighters arrived on the west side and made the same determinations. They attacked the fire using similar tactics. Both departments coordinated and settled in for a long night.

# FIFTY-SEVEN

THE SILHOUETTE OF A MAN in the doorway cast a long shadow into the bedroom. He advanced to the bedside of Ed Delong and put his hand on his shoulder. "Director Delong, wake up." He shook him with more vigor. "Wake up sir."

Delong moved barely conscious. "What?"

"Sir, you have a message."

He opened his eyes.

"Sir, you have another POISN call."

Delong rolled over to face the man. "Watson. What is it?"

"It's Mike Johansson," said Watson, Delong's personal assistant.

"What the hell time is it?"

"It's three o'clock, sir. He says it's urgent."

"Damn well better be." He rolled over on his back and reached for the phone in Watson's hand. "It's three in the morning, Mike. What's this all about?"

Johansson responded without hesitation. "Sorry, Ed. I wouldn't call if it wasn't serious."

"Okay, I'm awake now. What's so damn important?"

"After we talked earlier I went home, like you ordered. I kept thinking about Rashid. Then I remembered I got several personal phone calls yesterday while working, and shut my phone down. So I checked my messages and discovered Rashid had sent me a text about four o'clock in the afternoon."

With the mention of Rashid's name, Delong winced.

"It's a short message, Ed. I'll read it to you." A second passed while the director fidgeted. "It says, WMD RA-115-01."

Delong frowned. "That's it? That's all?"

"Yes, and it's more than enough."

Delong searched his mind for an interpretation. "Save me a little time, Mike. What's it mean?"

"WMD. Weapon of Mass Destruction. RA-115-01. That's the designation for a Russian nuclear bomb in a suitcase."

Delong bolted upright in bed. "Holy shit!"

THE WEST WING of the White House is the most secure patch of ground in the United States. Even well-known members of Congress and the administration undergo vetting by the Secret Service before entering.

Delong and Leo Adornetto were the first to be seated in the reception area next to the office of the President's Chief of Staff Edmond Pruitt. Pruitt, a craggy faced man with a prominent belly he hid with an out of fashion double-breasted suit coat, had entered the building minutes earlier. He asked Margret Madden, National Security Adviser to the President, to join him in his office. "It's six in the morning. What the hell is this all about, Maggie?" Pruitt asked.

Ms. Madden, who needed no make-up and wore a leather belted cowl neck dress, shrugged her shoulders and shook her head. "Something to do with national security and an undercover operation out west."

Pruitt continued, "We have enough damn politics around here without bringing in some cloak-and-dagger mystery. In addition to the men outside my office, I understand the Attorney General is sending his deputy, Aaron Perlman, over and Admiral Smithy of the NSA is coming, too. All this and I'm not included in the loop."

Madden stifled a smile. "What about President Steward, is he alerted?"

"Yes, of course. Secret Service took care of that."

By 6:15 Aaron Perlman and Admiral Smithy joined Delong and Adornetto. Pruitt led the procession down the hall to the Oval Office. Irked by the fact no one had briefed him on the purpose of this meeting, Pruitt waited until everyone had taken a seat before he unloaded. "I'd like to know who called this meeting. There is such a thing as protocol. All matters of importance to the President go through me." Before anyone answered, President Graham Steward entered the room and everyone stood.

The President headed for his desk and gestured for all to sit. "Good mornin'. Nice to see you all workin' overtime on a beautiful Saturday," he said with his down-home accent. Steward, a lean man with square shoulders and silver hair, stood behind his desk wearing a plaid polo shirt, and golf pants. "We have more than enough for a foursome here." He opened his arms to the group. "Of course if you play with me you can't have an average score of less than ninety-two." This comment caused a ripple of well-mannered laughter. "So, my fellow Americans, what's all the fuss about?"

The room remained silent until Aaron Perlman spoke. "I received a call from FBI Director Delong early this morning. I think when you hear what he has to say, you'll understand why we are here." All eyes focused on Delong, who stood.

The President assumed a false seriousness. "What is it Ed? Did you find a member of Congress stealing from his postage fund?" Another wave of nervous laughter.

"No Mr. President." His grim face caused Graham Steward to take on a serious expression. "I know this meeting doesn't follow standard procedures, but I think you'll agree this matter is of the highest priority."

Chief of Staff Pruitt interrupted. "That's right, it violates the chain-of-command. Now get to the point."

Delong never took his eyes off the President. "I have reason to believe we are in imminent danger of a nuclear attack by a militant jihadist."

The President leaned forward and planted his hands on his desk. Framed by the light from the windows behind him, he said, "Please say that again. I want to be sure I heard you correctly."

"An agent of the Bureau sent a text message before he died last night while working undercover." He handed a copy to the President. "I'll read it so everyone can hear me." He held his copy. "It says, WMD RA 115-01. We know what WMD means. The designation RA115-01 refers to a nuclear device designed by the Soviet Union in the late 1960's. They called them suitcase nukes. Don't let the term 'suitcase' mislead you. This is a six kiloton bomb with the ability to kill and maim upwards of a half a million or more people in the right hands and in the right place and time."

The President held a brooding expression. "Would you be so kind as to expand on that statement, Director Delong? You have my attention."

"Yes sir. Working with the NSA and other members of the intelligence community, we intercepted a series of encrypted messages that we decoded. The messages outlined a planned attack on America, but didn't give specific details. The seventh message, the last one, told us of a meeting of the conspirators. We devised a strategy to infiltrate their meeting and learn about their plans. Our man on the inside sent this message a few hours before he died in an explosion we are now investigating. We have reason to believe the explosion was not an accident. A person we call the Lone Wolf is suspected of the crime and is at large."

The President moved from behind his desk. "And the nuclear bomb, where is it now?"

Delong cast his eyes down. "I must assume it is in the hands of the Lone Wolf, but I don't know, sir."

Chief of Staff Pruitt blurted out, "What do you mean you don't know? It's your job to know."

The President put his hand up. "Calm down Edmond. Let's take this one step at a time." He faced Delong. "This Lone Wolf sounds more like the Leader of the Pack. What do you know about this jihadist?"

Delong glanced over to Adornetto who nodded his head in a gesture of support. "At the same time we broke their code, the Albuquerque Field Office in New Mexico was working a murder case that linked with our findings. I can tell you our suspect has operated in the U. S. for about six months. Five months ago he murdered a man and stole his identity. We tracked him down, but he escaped our surveillance about two weeks back. Based on excellent work by a field agent, we learned about a man acting as our suspect's local contact. This contact lives in El Paso. We staked-out his house. He was joined by an international arms dealer, a weapons specialist and our undercover man posing as their interpreter. Two days ago they met with the jihadist. The meeting took place in a house in rural southeastern New Mexico. We have kept it under close watch. Last night an explosion destroyed their meeting location and everyone in the house. I believe that was the work of the Lone Wolf. An extensive search of the area is underway as I speak."

President Steward moved from behind his desk and faced Delong. "So you don't know if the bomb survived the explosion or if it was even present at the site."

"We know the bomb came from a port in Dubai and arrived in Roswell, but we don't know where it is now."

"And you don't know, for a fact, if this terrorist perished in the explosion or if he survived it."

"Not for a fact, sir, but our observers believe the explosion was intentional. The Lone Wolf is a ruthless man who covers his tracks. Someone got out of that house and blew it up. I think he did it."

"Back on the farm, my Daddy use to say if the dogs are chasin' a varmint you don't know if they're chasin' a bear, a bitch in heat or some other critter until you see it treed or go to ground. For your sake, Director Delong, I hope your dogs on are on the right scent."

246

Leo Adornetto asked, "May I speak, sir?"

"Of course, Leo."

"I've been working with Ed on this investigation from the beginning. He's given you the recent highlights. Admiral Smithy will back me when I say this is a real threat to national security. It's well thought out, carefully planned, and professionally carried out. We have connected enough of the dots to know what we are dealing with. The next step is to learn the identity of the perpetrator and stop him." Admiral Smithy, seated next to Adornetto, nodded his head in agreement.

The President walked to his desk, turned his back on the room, folded his arms, and stared out of the window. After a few minutes he turned and faced the group. "This office got surprised years ago when the Twin Towers came down. I don't intend to let that happen again. Not on my watch." He singled out his National Security Adviser Madden. "Maggie, I want you to get smart on this threat and brief me daily, hourly if necessary. My chief of staff," he pointed to Pruitt, "will give you whatever you need."

The President then addressed everyone. "I don't want this conversation to leave this office. I will hold everyone here accountable for complete secrecy. No leaks. I don't want this coming out in the damn media. The last thing I need is panic in the streets."

His words were met with a nods of agreement.

The President turned to the FBI Director. "As for you, Delong, my Daddy also use to say if it smells like a skunk, it's a skunk." His expression hardened. "You and your boys let this skunk skip out on you. That's not the American way. I hold you personally responsible. You hear me?"

# FIFTY-EIGHT

BEFORE IGNITING THE MASSIVE Maljamar explosion, Bashir had traveled five miles in two and one half hours. Now, after detonation, he flipped on his headlights, increased his speed, and continued his escape. Even with the lights of the truck, progress was slow in the inky darkness under an overcast night sky.

He touched the lead box containing the bomb on the seat next to him and felt an inner joy, a contentment he had not experienced for many years. This box would give him the peace and satisfaction he yearned for. It would allow him to advance the cause of Islam and punish the Americans who hunt down his people and kill them. Also it would let him be with the one true God, Allah the Beneficent, the place all true Muslims aspired to be.

The truck lurched to one side as it rolled over a large rock. The metal case slipped off the seat and fell on the floor, its impact cushioned by the bag of money. A second rock jolted him back the other way and a few seconds later the motor cut out. Bashir depressed the clutch and turned the ignition key. The motor turned over but didn't catch. He tried several times, and then stopped to conserve the battery. The odometer read six miles from the house and his watch showed 10:45.

Bashir pulled a box of tools from behind the front seat and opened the truck's hood. A small flashlight from the glove compartment helped him search for the problem. Each time he attempted a fix, he failed. Finally at 11:30 he found a loose connection inside the distributor cap. He patched it with some electrical tape and tried the motor again. It started. Allah the Giver of Life must be with him. Bashir had lost forth-five minutes making the repair. He closed the hood, shoved the toolbox back behind the seat, and continued his southward trek. Twelve minutes later the truck began a choppy bounce as it rumbled over the ground.

What now? Bashir stopped, got the flashlight and walked around probing for the problem. He found it. The rear tire rim pressed down into a flattened tire. He leaned against the truck and said a prayer then noticed the flashlight growing dim.

A rage exploded within him. He stood holding on to the bed of the truck, and kicked the tire again and again. Breathing hard, he stepped back and forced his mind to deal with this new calamity. First he checked for a spare tire. Yes, under the rear of the bed. Then he hunted for tools to jack up the truck and remove the wheel. He found parts scattered around the passenger compartment, but no ground plate for the jack. Bashir explored every space in the vehicle and didn't find one. He needed it or the jack would sink into the sandy soil from the weight of the truck. Why not use a flat rock in its place? In the dark it took twenty minutes to find a suitable rock.

The flashlight gave out halfway through his work dismounting the spare from under the truck. He thought to use the headlights, but decided against it to save his battery. He worked in the dark feeling his way around like a blind man exploring the intricacies of a new machine. Finally, after an hour and a half, he tightened down the tire lugs and disengaged the jack. The truck settled down, and the newly mounted tire gave way under the weight. A useless spare with too little air pressure. Kneeling beside the truck a wave of desperation swept through him.

When Bashir got back in the truck he checked the time. The clock on the dashboard read one thirty-five Saturday morning. He had to go three miles to reach Highway 180. Bashir started the truck and put it in low gear. As he let up on the clutch the truck hobbled forward pulling to one side. He corrected the steering, but the truck continued to tilt to the left. He heard the tire flapping against the wheel-well and finally rip apart dropping the steel rim into the soft desert soil. He gunned the motor and the truck slowly spun around in a circle digging a hole that grew deeper with each revolution.

He rested his head on the steering wheel and wondered if this might be a message from Mohammad. Did this mean he was meant to fail? After a moment of reflection he renewed his determination. Allah, the Finder of the Unfailing, wanted to know if he was a true believer and a soldier of the jihad. He resolved to let nothing keep him from his oath to serve the cause and the holy mission given him to perform.

He gathered the bomb, the briefcase and the duffle bag. They totaled thirty-seven kilograms or eighty pounds. He must carry them three miles in the dark. He might make a mile in an hour. That would put him at Highway180 about 4:30 or 5 o'clock. Close to sunup.

Walking in the desert at night offers many challenges. One might stumble over or into the many varieties of cholla, prickly pear or barrel cactus. Each accident would inflict a painful wound from hundreds of barbed spines. Creosote bush and mesquite trees, with their brittle branches and random clumps of dry grass, all pose dangerous obstacles able to inflict hostile collisions at night.

Bashir crept across the rolling prairie ground as if hunted by an army of ghostly warriors armed with tiny daggers and picks. After many bloody encounters he realized that his goal of three miles in the dark was impossible. He sat down on the cold desert soil and waited for the sun to show him the way.

Morning light penetrated the darkness at 6:00 o'clock, turning unseen dangers into fuzzy silhouettes. He saw his arms were swollen and bloody from contacts with the desert plants. Bashir realized if he had continued walking in the dark, he would have traveled east into the vacant desert, not south toward the highway. He gathered his three items and started in the right direction.

By 9:30 the highway appeared as a straight line on the horizon. He trudged toward it, noticing only a few cars pass by. At 10:00 he stumbled into a roadside rest area. Exhausted, he almost fell on the concrete picnic table holding the bag, case and metal box. Wet with perspiration, his clothes stuck to his body. He welcomed the hard bench, and rested twenty minutes before preparing to hitch a ride. While he rested he noticed no cars passed him going south, and only two drove by heading northeast toward Hobbs or Lovington. Bashir glanced at his wristwatch–10:35. He had planned to be near El Paso by that time.

Years ago hitch-hiking in America allowed anyone a good chance to get a free ride in a short time, but not now. A lone man in disheveled clothes offered little appeal to drivers. Bashir found many cars speeded up when he put his thumb out.

That afternoon he got an idea. He reached into his wallet and pulled out a few dollar bills and started waving them at cars with his left hand while thumbing with his right. In half and hour a pickup truck slowed and then stopped. Bashir ran to the passenger side door. The driver lowered the window. A weathered man wearing a beat-up cowboy hat tilted his head back. "Where you headin' amigo?"

"El Paso," blurted Bashir.

"Carlsbad's as far as I go. Don't need your money, but you can jump in the back." He motioned to the open truck bed. "Ain't got all-day, amigo," he said as the window closed.

Bashir shouted. "I have a duffle bag. It won't take but a minute." He ran over to the picnic table, rushed back, loaded his baggage over the tailgate, and jumped in using the bumper as a step. He barely settled down when the truck lurched forward. The wind scattered his hair and cooled his body. The bed of the truck had deep scratches and dents from years of hard use. Bashir estimated he would be in Carlsbad by 4:00 p.m. He laid down in a corner and tried to sleep but couldn't.

Sometime later, he felt a change in the truck's movement that woke him. Laying on his back he discovered the man in the western hat glancing down at him. "Okay, amigo, this is where you get out. I'm headin' north now." Without waiting for an answer, the man turned and started for the driver's cab. Bashir gathered his things and barely jumped down when the truck's tires squealed, leaving him standing next to a sidewalk in the city's downtown. He moved out of the street onto the sidewalk.

Still confused, he became aware his clothes were dirty and torn in places. He saw several people stare at him as they walked by. He felt miserable, tired, disoriented and weak. This wasn't the way he planned it. An ornate bank clock on the corner read 4:35.

He moved down the street. It looked like the center of town. A sign pointed the way to the Royal Hotel and Suites. Bashir needed a hot shower and a rest. He shuffled down the street, and found the hotel that at one time had been an elegant place to stay. The lobby appeared dated, but clean and tidy. A plaque on the wall declared the structure a Historic Landmark.

He took a room and paid cash. Using the handrail he labored up the stairs. Once in the room he undressed, showered, and stood in front of the bed. He felt fatigued to the point of total exhaustion. It had been many days since he last performed his prayers. He knew he didn't have the strength now. He crawled into the bed, and pulled the metal box next to him and hugged it. "What's another day," he said, talking to the box, "one more day won't make a difference. He will understand." Bashir fell asleep.

251

# FIFTY-NINE

EARLY SUNDAY MORNING the third floor conference room of the FBI field office hummed with the sounds of orderly confusion. Mostly unfamiliar faces interacted in a growing frenzy of activity. Everyone fiddled with a laptop, a tablet or similar digital device. Three teams of people clustered around the room, some with whiteboards covered with words, phases, diagrams and crude maps. Others had photographs tacked on the wall in a random pattern. Ashley remained silent in the corner, sickened by the scene.

A stocky round-shouldered man peered down his gourd-like nose through thick eyeglass frames that appeared to contain bulletproof glass. He banged an oversized gavel, on a rock-hard sound block. "Listen up people. I'm not hearing from you. This is phase one—profiling. I want your input—pronto, you hear?" Heads turned in response to his demand. The speaker, Oliver West, appointed by the President to head a Special Strike Force Unit to catch the Lone Wolf, had a reputation for being a relentless taskmaster. Working as a freelance investigator for various Federal law enforcement agencies, he got his start in government as the chair of the Committee to Elect Graham Steward.

Ashley gave in to her compulsion to flee the conference room.

Ten hours earlier she had finished her work in Maljamar. Under Walter Kent's direction the entire crime scene had undergone a thorough examination. Evidence was marked, photographed and cataloged. The list of findings included fingerprints, document fragments, blood, hair, fiber, possible bomb parts, and chemical samples from select surfaces. The mobile forensic lab processed everything they could handle in the field. Some items needed study in a lab. A crew, headed by the State Medical Investigator, collected body parts that ranged in size from a small fragment of tissue to whole limbs. Within hours these samples would undergo DNA analysis.

At the end of that long, hot, and exhausting Saturday, Ashley had slept during the trip back to Albuquerque. The entire staff had to report to work the next day–Sunday. After a quick morning shower and her usual protein shake, she returned to her office and found it invaded by the Strike Force flown in from Washington to take command of the 'Maljamar Case.' They had briefed her, Bill Johnson, and Mark Rodriguez, on the suitcase nuclear bomb and its characteristics. She assumed that her position as lead investigator had evaporated.

Midmorning, after she left the conference room, Ashley went to Bill Johnson's office and collapsed in a chair. Bill was completing work on a paper glider he created out of an old file folder. He glanced up. "You look like someone ran over your cat. Why so glum?"

"It's called a Special Strike Force Unit, and it's not the FBI."

"That's S.O.P. Standard Operating Procedure for the Federal bureaucracy."

"Did you hear big nose Oliver West spouting off about 'things are going to get done around here now–did you?"

"Talk like that from Washington is also S.O.P." He put his feet on the desk. "When Delong learned of a possible nuclear threat, he had no choice but to go to the President. That's the fastest way to lose control."

"But why bring an outside unit into our field office?"

"Chief of Staff Edmond Pruitt hates Delong's guts. That goes way back. This a political slap in the face. They're here because this is where the data is."

"Bill, they're reinventing the wheel. Oliver West is trying to make fleas march in a straight line. We don't have time for this crap."

Bill made a tepee out of his wrinkled fingers and peeped at Ashley over his creation. "Anyone ever tell you how appealing you are when you get pissed off and frustrated at the same time?"

Ashley, not offended by the compliment, relaxed her tense expression. "You're right. What I think doesn't matter anymore."

"I didn't say that."

Her eyebrows came together. "What do you mean?"

"I mean we can't do anything about the Strike Force or Washington's inept meddling, but we don't have to stop doing our job."

"Doing our job?"

"Did anyone tell you that you don't work for the FBI anymore?"

"No."

"Did anyone tell you that you aren't the lead investigator anymore?"

"No, not straight out."

Bill dropped his feet, cocked his head to one side, "Well then, it's time you got off your well-formed ass, and get to work." He tossed the paper airplane. It glided in a smooth arc over Ashley's head.

She watched the four second flight. "Nice, but your landing failed to impress me. How many hours have you logged?"

"Thousands–all in experimental planes."

Ashley gave him a sideward glance. "I have more than three thousand hours in certified aircraft. Imagine what we could do if we became a team."

"A team?"

"You and I can accomplish more in a couple of hours than that bunch of Keystone Cops can in a couple of weeks or months."

"I suspect you're not talking about flying anymore."

Ashley stood and began to pace back and forth. "The President's involvement isn't all bad. Evidence that took weeks or months to process is fast-tracked now. It's available in hours. Findings are pouring in as we speak." She stopped in front of his desk. "I need your help to sort through all this stuff. What do you say?"

Johnson leaned back, put his elbow on the arm of the chair and supported his chin with a balled fist. "I thought you'd never ask."

THEY SET UP IN Johnson's office because it had a door. Only managers had doors, but Bill knew how to work the system. He dropped a printout from IAFIS on his desk. "I got this report on those fingerprints I sent in."

"The prints on the tools I found at Smith Trading Post in Roswell?"

"Yes. They belonged to an exchange student registered with the State Department and the U. S. Immigration Service. Abdullah al Jamal received a one-year student visa to attend graduate school at the University of Oklahoma four years ago. The genealogical database matched DNA samples from the coastal region of Saudi Arabia."

Ashley's eyes sparkled with enthusiasm. "That confirms the DNA report on the lock of black hair found in the shroud that wrapped Bitty Smith's body."

"That's right."

"Is there a photograph of our man?"

Bill flipped open the report. "Ever see the likes of him?"

Ashley studied the picture. "I only saw him at a distance, but it looks like the man in the trailer park. Does Oliver West know about this?"

"He will, if he ever stops pounding that damn gavel. I sent it to him."

"Do you think he'll go to the media with it?"

Bill made a face. "Do sharks like blood?"

Ashley shook her head and thumbed through her personal notes on the case. "So we know the identity of our subject and we know he met with an arms dealer and a bomb expert Friday night." She stopped and became calm. "But we don't know..." She paused again and worked out the question. "We don't know if he survived the explosion."

Bill ran his hand through his white hair. "Everyone assumes the Lone Wolf–I mean Abdullah al Jamar–set the explosion and is roaming around with a nuclear bomb under his arm."

"I'm not so sure. Have you studied the inventory report Walter Kent sent from Maljamar?"

"Sure. It's preliminary, but loaded with findings. Why?"

Ashley asked, "How many people died in that house?"

"They found parts of four bodies and the skull of a dog with a bullet hole in its head. They found Rashid al Yours's wedding ring, and passports belonging to Alexander Karloff and Kisser Suri. There's only two persons whose identity is unaccounted for. DNA studies will clear that up."

"How long will that take, under these circumstances?"

Bill raised his eyebrows. "Don't know. Hours, days, maybe a week. There are more than twenty body parts to examine. Our studies will go to the top of the list, but they take time."

"We have Abdullah's DNA. If they match it, he's dead and Bashir is our man. If they don't, Abdullah set the explosion and escaped."

Bill stroked his chin. "I get the feeling you don't think Abdullah escaped."

"Jerry Cebeck witnessed the explosion. He said it originated, not in the house, but in or on top of the Suburban that Bashir used to drive from El Paso. He controlled the Suburban, not Abdullah. That's a significant fact."

Bill Johnson fell silent as he thought over Ashley's claim. "Your hunch is reasonable, but based on thin evidence. Only DNA results will prove you right or wrong."

"Yes, but by then we may see a nuclear catastrophe in our country that will dwarf the Twin Towers."

255

Bill Johnson removed his eyeglasses and began cleaning them with a microfiber cloth. "What do you know about this Bashir Hashim fellow?"

"Based on his fingerprints lifted from my fake business card, and run through our system he's clean." Ashley thought of her visit to El Paso. "I met him one time. Grim little man. Had a Doberman Pinscher that probably has a hole in its head now. I know Bashir's a practicing Muslim and is here on a work visa. He bought and sold a truck to a man now identified as Abdullah. His role in the Team of Deliverance makes him an important link in this conspiracy."

"Anything else?"

Ashley thought about their meeting. She tried to remember details about the purple house, and the living room. "I can't remember, but I took notes. I'll find them."

Bill mounted his clean glasses over his ears. "Do you think Bashir destroyed the house and escaped with the bomb?"

Ashley nervously fingered the stainless steel Star of David she wore around her neck. "Everyone will be searching for Abdullah." Her voice dropped an octave. "I think I'll go shopping for a Bashir."

# SIXTY

AFTER HER TALK WITH Bill Johnson, Ashley reflected on the past forty-eight hours. She had lost touch with her mission, let recent events sidetrack her drive, and smother that inner voice that urged her to protect her country and its people. Bill, with his whimsical manner, had pulled her back to reality and set her on course again.

That course started back in her drab little cubicle with a review of her notes on the Bashir Hashim meeting fewer than two weeks ago. She remembered his threatening manner, the cluttered living room, the dog, the ugly purple house, and that she had caught him in a lie about the sale of the 1979 pickup truck. She knew she had to go back to El Paso, and had one more favor to ask of Bill. She phoned him.

"What took you so long?" he asked with a smile in his voice.

"I'm going to El Paso, Bill. If Bashir's our man, I must pick up his trail. His house is my starting point. I need a covert entry search warrant for the Estrella property, and a flight to El Paso today. Can you help me out?"

Bill didn't hesitate. "If I can bypass Oliver West, and I think I can, the answer to your question is yes. I'll get back to you."

Confident Bill would come through with both requests, Ashley grabbed the black duffle, issued to her the first day on the job, and loaded it with everything she might need. What have I forgotten? Walter Kent came to mind. He would be in Maljamar finishing the site investigation. She called him.

He answered on the first ring. "Kent here."

"Walter, do you know about Oliver West?"

"Yes, Ramirez briefed me. Odd turn of events."

"More than odd. I'm afraid they're making a mistake and chasing the wrong guy. Walter, I want you to trust me on this. I think our man is Bashir Hashim and I'm going after him."

"Are you playing a hunch?"

"Yes, I believe it's a plausible hunch. If I'm wrong, it won't interfere with the work of the Strike Force, but if I'm right then it's a whole different ball game."

"I don't like you going off on your own."

"I'll be all right. Bill is backing me up, and there's the El Paso Field Office if I need them. I'll be fine. Don't worry."

He lowered his voice. "Of course I'll worry. You're important to me and I don't mean as a member of my staff. I want you to check with me often–hourly if possible. You hear? Every hour. That's an order."

A warm feeling flooded though her. "Yes, as often as I can. I promise."

"That's my girl. Every hour, okay? Got a go now. Be careful."

Walter's words, 'that's my girl', brought a flash of emotion she savored for a moment, then pushed back to enjoy another day. The phone, still in her hand, sounded off.

Bill spoke. "Drop by my desk and get your search warrant, and then take a company car to the Albuquerque airport, and leave it there. I'll get it later. Major Roger Henderson is standing by

"Thanks Bill. You're a jewel."

After a quick flight to El Paso, the plane landed at two o'clock. At the airport Ashley signed out a government car provided by the local field office, in accordance with Bill's arrangements. She headed for the Estrella Street address. Ashley reminded herself that Bashir Hashim was a proven co-conspirator in a terrorist plot, and that she had probable cause to arrest him on sight. First, she had to find him.

Viewed from the outside, the purple house appeared deserted. She circled the block twice and parked in front. Dressed in street clothes and holding the search warrant, she approached the front door and knocked. No answer. She knocked again, and then tried the door and found it unlocked. Ashley stuffed the warrant in her back pocket. She drew her weapon and entered the house.

Ashley held the Glock straight out in front of her gripped with both hands as she quickly moved from room to room. The place was empty. She holstered the gun and went back to the living room. The same worn-out furniture remained in place, but she found no personal items; the computer and prayer rug were gone.

She searched the house again. This time she exercised greater care while examining the content of each room. As she walked through the house it looked like burglars had ransacked the place. She found trash in two wastebaskets, an opened book left face down, bedroom drawers pulled out partway with garments on the floor and thrown across the bed. In the kitchen she checked the garbage can and discovered a nearly full bag of dog food and a dog dish with the word 'Slayer' scrawled across the side. That discovery made sense. Why keep food for a dog you plan to kill? Dirty dishes lay everywhere, and a slightly warm half eaten frozen dinner sat on the counter. Clearly someone had left in a hurry not long ago. She checked the backyard and found it empty.

She needed something to connect her with Bashir. Ashley searched each room a third time without finding any clues. She ended back in the living room. Standing in the center of the room, she closed her eyes and thought of the day she bluffed her way into this house. She replayed in her mind all the words spoken and everything she saw: the religious screen savers flashing on the computer, the prayer rug rolled in the corner, the picture on the wall. *The picture on the wall?* She turned and found a photograph of Bashir standing in front of an airplane dressed in a dark suit with gold epaulets and a cap with a gold braided visor. She stared at the image a moment then screamed, "Oh my God, the son-of-a-bitch is a pilot!"

Ashley took down the framed picture, left Bashir's house and drove to the nearest commercial district. She hunted for a Starbucks or any place that offered Wi-Fi for her laptop. Spotting a Denny's Restaurant, she parked near the door and asked for a booth. Once seated, she opened her computer and went online. When the server arrived, Ashley ordered a cup of black coffee. She entered the URL address for the Federal Aviation Administration. Once on the FAA's web page she clicked on N-Number Inquiry, and then Aircraft Registry. In the request box she typed the N number painted on the side of the twin engine aircraft pictured in the photograph. Instantly the FAA's Registry file flashed on the screen. The plane, a McDonald Douglas DC 3 built in 1944, listed Keserwan Flight Services, Inc. as owner—found at 3887 South Estrella Street, El Paso, Texas. The physical location of the aircraft was listed as El Paso International Airport, Allen Aviation Limited. It only took seconds to learn the address of Allen Aviation. The privately owned aircraft would be stored in the general aviation section of the airport.

She picked up the picture of Bashir and tore off the backing, removed the photograph and left the frame on the table. When her coffee came, she gulped it down and realized she hadn't eaten all-day. On her way out she paid for the coffee and two giant chocolate chip cookies wrapped in clear plastic. Not health food, but another sacrifice for God and country.

She drove to the airport and turned south on Airport Road. When she saw small planes tied down in rows she knew she was getting close. At Pilot's Drive she noticed a sign pointing the way to the General Aviation Terminal. She parked near the main entrance. The digital clock on the dashboard read 3:45. She twisted the rearview mirror and looked at herself. "I hope to hell you're not too late, my dear."

# SIX-ONE

BASHIR AWOKE SUNDAY MORNING to find the metal case containing the bomb almost covered with a blanket next to him. As sleep faded, he stared at it and realized this object would soon be his pathway to paradise, the garden of eternity. Then his body stiffened with thoughts of yesterday, and how he had failed to keep to his schedule. He tossed the covers back, rolled out of bed, and stood piecing together his next moves.

In the bathroom he washed his face, ran his hands through his black hair, and studied his day-old beard in the mirror. He had deprived himself of facial hair since coming to America. Now it didn't matter.

Bashir found his dirty clothes scattered on the floor and his shoes under the bed. He dressed and snatched money out of the duffle. Bashir remembered seeing a small department store across the street and headed for it after putting a *Do Not Disturb* sign on his door.

In the store no one approached him. Bashir grabbed what he needed and attracted little attention when he paid cash for the clothing. Back in his room he changed clothes, and prepared himself to travel.

He scanned the hotel phonebook for a car rental outlet and found they were all at the Cavern City Air Terminal five miles southwest of downtown Carlsbad. He continued searching for car dealerships and found a used car lot only two blocks from his room. After shoving everything under the bed, he pulled bundles of hundred dollar bills from the duffle bag and headed for *Economy Pre-Owned Cars of Carlsbad.*

At the car lot, a chubby-faced salesperson, wearing a white shirt with a striped bow tie, greeted him and offered help. "I'm interested in a reliable car." Bashir swept his hand in a wide arc. "My car was stolen and I need a new one. I'll buy a car from you for cash, if it's quick. Any problem with that?" The salesman's eyes widened as he agreed. Within ten minutes Bashir picked out a car, an older model Subaru Forester, and paid the full asking price without hesitation.

Counting the money, the salesman held each bill to the light to check the watermark. "You'll have to sign a bill of sale, and pay the tax and title costs of about three hundred bucks."

Bashir signed the paper and laid four one hundred dollar bills on the desk. "Mail the paperwork to my address." He stood and demanded the keys.

At the hotel he loaded the bomb, the bag of detonators and the duffel in the backseat. The drive to El Paso took about three hours. Bashir arrived at his house shortly after noon. He filled a suitcase with the prayer rug he had used since childhood, his computer, dark glasses and everything he imagined he might need after rummaging through his house. Satisfied with his selections, he carried the suitcase to the Subaru parked in the alley. In the glove compartment he stored a handgun.

Bashir found his last frozen meal and heated it in the microwave. It tasted nasty–some American mixture he bought by mistake. He made a final check of the house that ended in the living room. Standing by the front window he noticed his photograph on the wall, and started to take it down, but stopped. He thought the world should know who had changed history and imagined his picture would someday be on televisions everywhere.

Bashir glanced out the window for the last time. That's when he saw a white car stop in front of his house and park close to a fire hydrant, something he knew would earn a traffic citation. A woman got out of the car, holding a paper in her hand, and started walking toward his house. She looked familiar. A handsome women with a good figure like that insurance woman he daydreamed about at night. She hesitated at the steps and tilted her head up. A sudden coldness hit him. It was the same woman. A few seconds later she knocked on his door.

Bashir turned and slipped out of the backdoor closing it carefully. Then he dashed to the Subaru, got inside and backed down the alley out of view of the house. While trying to collect his thoughts, he drove around the block slowing down as he approached the woman's car on the corner. It had a white license plate with the words *U. S. Government* printed on it. A chill rippled down his back. Bashir parked a half block away and waited until the woman came out. She held his framed picture in her hand.

His mind filled with questions. Who is this person? What does she want? Where did she come from? Why did she steal my picture? Questions, but no answers. He did know she worked for the American government. That made her a dangerous person. One he must deal with.

Bashir opened the glove compartment, pulled out his handgun holding a fresh clip of twelve rounds, and dropped it on the passenger seat. When the woman eased away from the curb, he followed her. She drove five blocks and parked in a shopping center in front of a Denny's and went inside carrying the framed picture and a black bag. He parked where he could see the restaurant entrance. Within ten minutes the woman left Denny's in a hurry without the framed picture, and drove off faster than before. Bashir found it difficult to keep up. She turned onto Montana Avenue and continued east. He followed this same path every day. When she turned onto Airport Road he gasped for breath. No, he thought, this can't be. It's not possible. But when the white car headed down Pilot's Drive he knew it was possible and that his life and mission would soon be at risk.

Holding back, he watched the woman park in front of the GA terminal building and walk up the steps. Gripping the steering wheel his heart rate doubled, causing his face to flush red. He had only a few minutes to put together a plan.

He drove to the controlled access gate in the perimeter fence a hundred yards west of the terminal. The entrance allowed authorized personnel to enter the airport grounds using an access code. He tapped in the numbers and drove the frontage road to a row of twelve gray hangers. Avoiding his assigned parking space, he left his car in the adjacent common area, and with the handgun hidden, he hurried to his hanger. Bashir noticed the hanger next to him had the door open with people working inside.

In his hanger he flipped the lights on and locked the door behind him. He barely noticed his gleaming McDonald Douglas DC 3 centered on the floor. Bashir stood rigid while figuring out his next step. Using the gun would attract the attention of the nearby workers. After a few seconds he relaxed, unlocked the door, put his gun down and began searching for a silent weapon. He found it, turned off the lights and positioned himself next to the door.

ASHLEY WALKED TO the glass doors of the GA terminal and found the lobby lights on and the glass doors locked. She could see no one in the lobby or behind the counter, but knew from her days as a flight instructor that even on Sunday someone had to be providing flight services. She tapped on the glass with her car keys. After a minute she tapped again, harder. Still no answer. Ashley assumed the attendant, most likely in a communication center on the second floor, didn't hear her. She woke her phone and Googled *Allen Aviation*, noted the phone number and touched the link. A man with a Spanish accent answered. "Allen Aviation, may I help you please?"

"Yes. This is Special Agent Kohen with the FBI. I'm at your front door. I need to speak with you about an ongoing investigation."

"The FBI. Yes, I am here the only one. It's Sunday. Tomorrow can you come back?"

Ashley closed her eyes and promised herself to be patient. "Who am I speaking with, please?"

"My name Emilio Ortiz."

"Mister Ortiz this is a police matter. I need only a few minutes of your time."

"Oh, police. Yes, yes I open the door, but I am only one. You understand?"

"Yes, I understand, Mister Ortiz. Thank you."

In less than a minute a man wearing wireless headphones and a leather vest over a plaid shirt entered the lobby. Ashley showed him her ID through the glass doors that he immediately unlocked. When Ashley stepped inside, Ortiz offered his hand, but didn't make eye contact with her.

Ashley shook his hand. It felt cold and damp. "I apologize for this interruption, Emilio. I have only one question." Ashley had clipped Bashir's photograph to her leather ID holder. She unclipped it, and handed it to him. "Do you recognize this man?"

Ortiz glanced at the picture. "No, Ms. Kohen, I don't see him."

Ashley remained pleasant. "Please look again. This is important."

Ortiz studied the photograph for a full minute. "Sorry. I don't know this man, but I know this airplane behind him."

Ashley smiled. "That's good, Emilio. Tell me about the airplane."

"You see it's a DC 3. Popular in my country." He stopped and fumbled with the picture. "I mean in all countries."

"You're right. It's a famous aircraft still used around the world. Have you seen this particular plane here?"

He again inspected the photograph. "Maybe this airplane. I don't know for sure, but there is one like it here." He paused. "Maybe I know this man, too. Not dressed like this." Ashley felt a heightened awareness. "I think he is the one with the DC 3 in hanger nine over there." He pointed toward the apron in front of a row of hangers. "Yes I see him. Not a happy man. Never smiles."

"Can you take me to hanger nine? I need to inspect it."

Ortiz shook his head. "Oh no Ms. Kohen. I cannot leave here, but you can go. We own the hangers. You are the police. I will give you the code for the gate and a key for the hanger. It is all right." He turned the photograph over and wrote four numbers on the back. He went to the counter and got a key and gave it to Ashley. Seconds later he looked over Ashley's head as if in thought, then pointed to the headphones. "I must go now. There is my work to do."

"Thank you Emilio. I'll see that your boss knows you've been helpful."

He brightened with a toothy grin. "Si, I mean yes, thank you, too." He turned and dashed off upstairs.

Ashley followed the perimeter fence and found the gate, entered the code and drove down a frontage road lined on one side with gray metal hangers. Each one had a number painted over the entrance door and four reserved parking spaces for owner use. As she approached hanger eight she saw three cars parked there, but no cars parked next to it. She took one of the empty spaces in front of number nine and checked the time. Four fifteen–she'd have to call Walter soon.

With her senses on full alert, Ashley approached the door of number nine. She realized what she might find on the other side could change her life and maybe the lives of thousands of Americans. At the door her hand shook when she inserted the key and turned it. The door didn't open. She turned the key again and the door unlocked. Ashley hesitated. Hangers contain expensive aircraft and equipment. No one would leave a plane unprotected. She withdrew her gun for the second time that day, took a deep breath and yanked the door open.

The afternoon sun cast an extended shadow of the building into the street behind her making the interior of the hanger dark. She moved over the threshold, her gun at the ready, and waited a second for her eyes to grow accustomed to the darkness. Then she stepped further inside. Her peripheral vision sensed a blur of motion, but too late. She felt a sharp pain explode in her head, then nothing.

# SIXTY-TWO

THE HANGER DOOR BURST OPEN. Bashir's muscles tensed as he raised the metal pipe gripped with both hands. A moment passed, and then the woman advanced holding a gun in front of her. A flash of panic seized him as he swung the pipe wildly striking a blow to the back of her head. She pitched forward, falling face down on the concrete floor. Her gun skittered into the darkness. Bashir jumped to her side and raised the pipe ready to hit her again. Her body remained still. He became aware of the daylight flooding through the open door. Turning, he switched on the lights and pulled the door shut.

Holding the pipe at his side, he studied the woman's motionless body. Blood oozed from the wound and stained the concrete. He poked her with the pipe. She didn't move. His eyes traveled from the bloody mass of hair down to her feet and back. He exhaled a heavy breath and began to relax. The pipe clattered on the floor when he dropped it.

Now he must find out who this person is–this chameleon that changed identity as easily as a lizard changes color. To be sure she remained unconscious, he kicked her twice, then knelt down, and turned her over. Even with blood covering the side of her face, she remained a beautiful woman. He unbuttoned her jacket revealing her rounded breasts under her blouse. He touched them and found them firm like ripe oranges. He moved his hands over her body exploring every curve. He had never seen such a woman—one so perfect. Aroused, Bashir became aware of his lust for this magnificent creature. He fondled her breasts again. She didn't wear a bra like most women. He grasped her blouse with both hands and ripped it open. His breath came fast and his heart thumped as his passion mounted. Her underwear gave way in his frantic effort to undress her. She was even more desirable than he had imagined. He touched her, massaging her soft pubic hair. *I must have this women!* With shaking hands he exposed himself and fell on her fumbling with clothing that got in the way. Her pants, wadded at the ankles, hiding her ankle holster, forced him to jerk her knees apart giving him entrance to her. Pulling on her shoulders, he forced himself into her. He grunted with savage satisfaction. Salivating, he licked the clean side of her face as he began an urgent thrusting motion that mounted until he could no longer control himself. Stifling a cry of ecstasy, his muscles gave way and he fell on her. With his face only inches away, his eyes focused on her Star of David necklace tangled in matted hair.

Still breathing hard he pulled back as if dodging the strike of a viper. A wave of nausea passed over him. What had attracted him seconds ago became a repulsive heap of flesh. He felt unclean. As he struggled to free himself of contact, a compulsion to flee overtook him. Still reeling from his discovery, he stood on unsteady legs while pulling his clothes up. Would Allah forgive him? Could he forgive himself?

He stepped back and finished adjusting his clothing, his eyes darting about the hanger. Of course, no one saw him. Bashir walked a tight circle around her. He picked up her gun, and tossed it aside.

First he must find out who this person is. Repugnant as she had become, he began going through her pockets searching for some form of identification. Inside her jacket, he found his picture clipped to the outside of a leather folder. Inside was an FBI badge, with a set of handcuffs. His mouth opened in disbelief. FBI. How could this be? He had always protected his mission by using Abdullah as a diversion. Bashir realized that if she found him, others would soon do the same. He felt beads of sweat form on his face as he pocketed the cuffs, stuffed his picture in his back pocket and replaced the badge back into her jacket. His action caused the woman to moan. He reached for the metal pipe, and raised it over his head—then lowered it. This body, he had ravished only minutes before, looked wretched, even pathetic.

If he killed her he would have to dispose of the body or leave her on the concrete floor. Disposal would take time and be messy. Leaving her would open the chance that she might be found too soon. Someone gave her a key to his hanger door, probably that idiot Mexican. No matter how slight the chance, he must protect himself from discovery. Bashir placed the pipe on the floor and walked around to her head, reached down and grabbed both arms. Walking backwards, he created a path of blood as he dragged her almost naked body over to the plane centered in the hanger. Getting a better hold under her armpits, he pulled her up the portable steps on the port side of his aircraft. Her pants, still crumpled around her ankles snagged on the steps. Once inside he cast about trying to decide the best place to put her. A ghost of a smile creased his face.

Bashir had received the measurements of the case containing the nuclear device months earlier. He had built a metal platform designed to hold the bomb, and bolted it to the floor of the aircraft. He added clamps to the platform to guarantee the metal box would remain in place, even in turbulent weather. He would handcuff her to the base of that platform. Bashir enjoyed the irony of an FBI agent becoming a victim of what she had hoped to stop.

He snapped the cuffs on her wrists, made sure they were tight, and then pocketed the key he had found attached to them. He noticed her head wound had stopped bleeding. Good, he thought, I won't have to step in her blood.

Bashir suddenly realized that in his haste to deal with this woman he had left the bomb, detonators and money unprotected in the car. He dashed to the hanger door and quickly made his way to the adjacent parking lot where he gathered everything. Back inside, he carried his essentials into the plane, avoiding the trail of smeared blood on the concrete floor.

Bashir loved his DC 3. He had shipped it from his homeland because he had flown this plane for many years from Beirut, Lebanon to cities in Syria and Jordan as a commercial pilot. Later as a private pilot for the leadership of Hezbollah, he flew it to locations throughout the Middle East.

Restoring this Douglas DC 3 had consumed his life in recent months. With unlimited money he hired technicians to overhaul both engines, refurbish the plane with avionics including communication, and navigation controls. Now he faced the final step in his plan to carry out jihad in America. He must mount the nuclear device and assemble the detonator.

As he stood in front of the metal platform holding the bomb, he heard a gasp for air come from the woman sprawled on the floor at his feet. Good. The Jew bitch is waking up.

# SIXTY-THREE

TIRED AND DIRTY, WALTER KENT returned from Maljamar mid-afternoon Sunday. Because of the terror threat, it became another workday. The field investigation reminded him of the war he had fought years ago and tried to forget every day. He considered going by his home for a quick shower and a nap, but his concern for Ashley forced him to head straight to his office. He hadn't heard from her since she promised to check with him hourly.

When he entered his office he startled Dorothy Hogan. "You look beat and smell like smoke," she said.

"And I feel like..." He caught himself from saying a four letter word..."well, you can guess." He stopped in front of her desk. "Have you heard from Ashley?"

"No, Mr. Kent. Bill Johnson arranged for an early flight to El Paso for her this morning. Should I have?"

Kent remained expressionless and shook his head. "No. No, I just wondered. Ask Bill to come up, would you, please?"

Johnson got the call from Dorothy and headed for the third floor. He entered her office and raised an eyebrow as if to ask Dorothy what was up. She raised a shoulder, shook her head in response, and pointed to Kent's open door.

"Afternoon, Walter. You look like you've been dumpster diving."

"Thanks. I needed that assessment." Trying to hide his anxiety, Walter asked, "Have you heard from Ashley?"

"No. Not since she left for El Paso."

Walter motioned for Bill to sit. "I asked her to keep me posted on her investigation, but she hasn't called. I don't like her out there alone. There's too much going on all at once."

"Oh, she'll be all right." He then leaned forward. "But I know what you're saying. How about me giving her a call. She'll probably chew me out for becoming a mother hen, but I'll take the chance."

269

"Okay, do that. Let me know what you find out." He shuffled papers on his desk. "Fast-tracked preliminary DNA results should be in today. The more I think about her hunch, the more I fear she might be right about Bashir. Those lab reports will confirm who survived and who didn't." His face hardened with concern. "If Bashir's alive, Ashley will have plenty of company whether she wants it or not.

# SIXTY-FOUR

IN THE SHROUDED DARKNESS of Ashley's unconscious mind, an undefined existence flickered. It grew like a pinpoint of light that increased in brightness. This light, her awareness, flooded the emptiness with a blood red pain that seared the core of her being, forcing consciousness to surface. Her eyes opened.

She floated on a bed of agony. Amid this misery, her mother's sweet face appeared. It comforted her when life became cruel and unbearable. She heard her mother's words from faraway. *Ashley, when they knock you down and kick you, reach up and grab their foot and twist it until it hurts.* Yes. Yes, I must fight back. But the pain is so great, Mamma. Only then did she realize the meaning of the pain. It was a sign that told her she was alive.

The blinding light faded as Ashley focused on an object in front of her. A black object. Not far away. She strained to make it out. She closed her eyes, then tried again. Finally she realized—it's my coat sleeve. Fear swept through her as she questioned how wounded she might be. She began to test her senses. First, she moved her head. That hurt, but she could turn it in every direction. Then her left arm. It moved only a few inches. She studied her arm and found a handcuff around her left wrist and another cuff around her right arm. Ashley became aware that she was lying on a hard surface that vibrated along with a distant roar. The pounding in her head eased as she focused on her surroundings that were dimly lit by rows of square windows. The hard metal floor tilted back and forth slightly. It led to curved walls and a concave ceiling. The sound, the vibration—she knew that combination, but couldn't place it. Then it came to her. She was in an aircraft. An aircraft in flight.

She moved her legs—they responded. Bunched around her feet were her pants. She rubbed one leg against the other and felt her ankle holster still in place. Did it hold her revolver? She rolled over onto her side. Her breasts and most of her lower body lay naked. A coldness gripped her.

271

Naked? She concentrated on how she felt in her most private parts, and sensed a rawness that shouldn't be there.

The handcuffs dug into her wrists when she tried to sit up. The chain that linked each cuff hit against a steel rod bolted to the floor. Her vision began to clear. The rod, part of a four-legged structure, had a metal box clamped to the top. She squeezed her eyes shut, trying to clear her head. At that moment a shaft of light struck her when a door opened and a man's form advanced toward her. She rolled flat on the floor in an effort to protect herself, and turned her head, glancing up.

The man knelt down on one knee, grabbed a handful of her hair and jerked her head, causing the pain to intensify. "I see you are still alive," he said without expression on his face. He let go of her and wiped his hand on her sleeve. "I want you to live so you can die with me." On the floor he sat cross legged only inches away. "My name is Bashir, but then you know that, don't you?"

Ashley made no response.

"How do you like my plane?" He waved a hand over his head. "I call her *The Awakening*. Allah the Bringer of Death has allowed me to prepare her so I can advance His will. You shall share in this great deed." A flicker of sadness crossed his face. "It's unfortunate that no one, other than you and I, will know of your sacrifice." Ashley believed his sincerity, ridiculous as that sounded.

"Oh yes, I have bad news." He reached into his shirt pocket and took out a smashed phone. "Right after we took off 15 minutes ago, you got a call, but before I explained your predicament," he mouth twisted into a hard line, "I stepped on it." Bashir dropped the smashed phone on the deck next to the platform and continued. "Since you will join me in this monumental endeavor, you should know what is about to happen." He placed each elbow on his knees and clasped his hands in front of his face. "Above you I have mounted a bomb. It is small, as atomic bombs go, but I plan to maximize its potential. I understand it will kill at least a quarter of a million Americans in Las Vegas, Nevada, maybe more and hundreds of thousands over the next few weeks and months. That will happen five hours from now. Nothing can prevent it. The bomb is already armed. A radar altimeter, measuring our distance to the ground, is integrated into the detonator. The bomb, activated a few minutes ago, when we climbed above 1000 feet, will detonate when we descend below 500 feet. Even I cannot disarm it. But then I suspect you know nothing of altimeters."

Ashley remained silent.

His eyes traveled up and down her body. "You don't look like a Jew." His forehead wrinkled. "But then what does a disease look like until you learn about the plague it causes?" He leaned forward and slipped his hand under her breast. "Oh, by the way," he said showing yellow teeth through curved lips, "as you Americans like to brag, you were a great piece-of-ass."

From deep within her stomach an uncontrollable spasm forced a projectile of vomit to spew forth splattering Bashir face. He recoiled, instantly rolling away from her and then crawled to a crouched position. Crying out in horror he dashed to the rear of the plane to wash himself. Her reaction may have been caused by his touch, his words or as a symptom of her concussion. Whatever the reason, she felt pleasure for the first time.

When he returned, Ashley stiffened expecting his anger. She waited for him to kick and beat her, but it didn't happen. Instead Bashir skirted her as if avoiding a source of deadly radiation. He slammed the cockpit door behind him.

Ashley rested her head on the cold hard deck. She had no idea a cup of coffee and two chocolate chip cookies could smell so bad, but then she didn't know she would be knocked unconscious, raped, and chained to an atomic bomb either.

Time to reach up, grab a foot and twist it.

The handcuffs. They were her cuffs: the Model 100 made by Smith and Wesson—standard equipment used by most law enforcement agencies in the country. Years ago the Chicago PD issued her a shiny new set of cuffs with a looped key that locked them. Fearful she might lose the key, she had studied the locking mechanism and taught herself how to pick the lock. All she needed was a bobby pin, and about 30 seconds to bend it into the right shape.

She didn't own a bobby pin and suspected few people of her generation knew what one looked like or that they were used to hold hair in place. She must improvise. Maybe a small nail or wire.

Ashley lay still and concentrated while fighting the urge to panic. She did an inventory of everything within her reach. The smashed phone proved useless. Her blouse had buttons, and her pants at her feet contained a few coins—no help. Under her armpit she felt the leather folder that held her badge. The badge had a flat metal clip. Worthless. She pictured the folder in her mind. Aside from the badge, it held her ID card. The last time she used it she had shown the folder to Emilio Ortiz through the glass doors. She had, also, shown Emilio the picture of Bashir clipped to the outside. Her thought froze. *Clipped to the outside.* A paper clip. Yes, a paper clip is a wire about the size of a small bobby pin. She had to get the folder out of the inside pocket of her coat and get that clip. If still there it might be possible to get free.

She positioned herself to dislodge the folder. By lifting her body forward, and then dropping down and back again, she worked the inside pocket around in front of her. She saw a corner of the leather protruding. Using the side of her right leg she shimmied her body up, forcing her head under the metal platform. The jacket lapel snagged on the floor-bolt, blocking the pocket from her reach. With her teeth she bit the upper lapel of her coat and pulled up. On the third try the pocket slipped off of the bolt and past the metal leg. As she forced her hand down toward the folder, the handcuffs dug into her wrist. Her thumb made contact, but she needed a finger to grasp it. Her thumbnail slipped and pushed the edge deeper inside.

Ashley rested a moment, then brought both legs up and arched her back. Straining with all of her strength she nudged the folder with a knee. Each time she pushed, it edged out a fraction of an inch. Totally pissed, she hit it hard enough to reach it with her left hand, grip it and pull it free. Hoping to see a paper clip, she turned it over. The clip contrasted against the dark brown leather. Ashley dropped her head down on her arm and said a silent prayer.

Almost there.

She slipped the paper clip off the folder and straightened it. Then inserted one end halfway into the lock and turned it to a 90 degree angle. Next she bent the clip in the opposite direction creating an S shape. She then opened the handcuff on her left hand. In seconds she unlocked the right handcuff, sat up, and rubbed her wrists. That effort caused her to feel dizzy and her eyes to lose focus. It passed after a few seconds.

I'm free.

She buttoned her blouse, stood and pulled up her pants. The ankle holster held her Ruger handgun. What to do now? Ashley examined the bomb Bashir had described. It appeared too small to be so deadly, but at least five people had died to make this flight possible and two more will die in a few hours along with thousands more.

Ashley determined the plane must have hauled cargo because there were no seats. Seven small square windows lined both sides of the fuselage.

She looked out and judged they were at twelve thousand feet which meant the aircraft was pressurized allowing flight at higher altitudes.

Bashir had warned no one could set off the bomb, but if she could, would it be high enough to be harmless? She remembered reading about the two atomic bombs dropped at the end of World War II, but didn't know how big they were or at what altitude they detonated.

Ashley stepped over to the platform and studied the bomb. Like her mother that September day in New York, she knew she would die, but wanted it to mean something. Bashir said it was armed and would explode at 500 feet. The only way to be certain the bomb killed no one was to fly this aircraft to an uninhibited place. There was only one way to do that. She had to kill Bashir.

Ashley moved her gun from the ankle holster to her pants pocket and walked to a spot next to the hinged side of the cockpit door. She must think this through. Bashir was a slimy bastard, but also smart and determined. She would get one chance. She had to get it right the first time.

She leaned against the bulkhead and imagined the layout of the cockpit she had to enter to kill Bashir. Ashley had never been in a DC 3, but she had flown many twin engine planes. She imagined two seats with power controls between them, instruments arrayed in front of the pilots, and communication equipment overhead. Bashir would be in the captains' seat, port side. She had the benefit of surprise on her side, but she'd have to get to him fast and shoot him in the top of his head. A side shot might compromise pressurization and destabilize flight. The corners of her mouth turned up. No holes in the plane, babe.

At that moment the cockpit door opened, Bashir walked into the cabin, looked down and froze. Ashley's right hand went into her pocket. He turned. She brought up the gun. He screamed and lunged for her. She fired without aim. A great howling sound engulfed them. He grabbed her arm. She fired again. His head jerked back. Disbelieving eyes widened. Ashley shoved him with her left hand. He fell at her feet, blood gushing from his head. The cabin depressurized. Ashley's ears plugged–all sound disappeared.

She sidestepped and aimed at his head. Her finger pressed on the trigger. With tight lips she whispered, "what's one more bullet between friends?" He lay motionless, but still breathing. She hesitated then stepped to the feet of the body, took aim and kicked him in the balls, hard. No reaction. She tucked the gun in her pocket.

275

That first bullet–the wild bullet–had pierced one of those square windows causing it to disintegrate. Air shrieked out through the shattered glass. She pinched her nose and blew hard. With a whistling sound, her ears cleared.

Ashley pulled his foot over to the platform and handcuffed his ankle to the same metal leg she knew so well. While he probably wasn't the bobby pin type, she knew she had to immobilize him in a more permanent manner.

In the rear she found three locked compartments across from the restroom. She opened one with a well-placed kick. Inside she found tools, a coil of electrical wire, duct tape, and a length of 2 x 4 wood.

She tied Bashir's arms to the wood as he lay on his back and his other ankle to the opposite platform leg. With the tape, Ashley reinforced each body part and slapped a hunk of it on the head wound to slow the bleeding. Bashir now resembled a nonlethal crucifixion. Tying Bashir in a spread-eagle position gave Ashley guilty pleasure. It almost made her plight worth it–almost. She considered cutting his pants off, but decided it would not be lady-like, and would in fact be disgusting. She did carefully slip Bashir's cell phone out of his pants pocket in case she needed a communication backup. After checking her handiwork, she felt satisfied Bashir Hashim would stay put right under his beloved bomb.

When she stood, a pain stabbed her head and she felt dizzy again. She grabbed the platform and held on until it faded. The cockpit door swayed as the plane reacted to a change in wind velocity.

Time to go to work.

# SIXTY-FIVE

BILL JOHNSON LEFT WALTER'S OFFICE and called Ashley three times on the way back to his desk in the field office. The first two tries ended with her cryptic voicemail response. "Kohen here. Leave message." Most people call once and give up or leave their number. Bill figured she would answer if he kept calling. Three calls should prompt her curiosity, a trait he knew she had. His tactic worked or did it? On the third call he heard noise. Bill said, "Ashley, time to check in." He heard a droning sound in the background, and something like the phone hitting against a hard object– then nothing. Several recalls were unsuccessful. He waited a few minutes for her to call back. She didn't.

When Bill got to his office, he added it up. She promised to check in, but hadn't. She finally answered her phone, but didn't speak. Her phone no longer rang. In a game played with a terrorist capable of a horrendous attack, that's one, two, and three–you're out.

Bill called the telephone service provider, identified himself, and asked to speak with a managing supervisor. Straining to keep his voice level he gave her Ashley's phone number and the time of the answered call. "This concerns a matter of national security. I need to know the location of that call, and if this number is still active. I will hold your company, personally responsible for any delay answering my questions. Do you understand? "

"Yes, sir. I understand. We always cooperate with the police. I'll have my technicians trace the call in our cellular network. Stay on the line."

Bill plopped down in his chair. He didn't know Ashley had promised to call Walter and hadn't followed through. His concern mounted. Hell, she could be my daughter or even my granddaughter. I should have checked on her myself.

The supervisor came back on line. "Are you still there?"

"I'm here. What'd you find out?"

277

"We ran a check on our frequency reuse patterns. We have pinpointed your receiving cell within our numbered location area." Bill's hand tightened on the phone, "and determined the mobile unit was on or next to the El Paso International Airport, and that number is no longer active."

Bill bolted upright in his chair. "Are you sure?"

"Oh yes. All usage is tracked and recorded for statistical and billing purposes. I'm sure."

"I mean are you sure it's no longer connected?"

"Not currently online or maybe turned off."

Bill thanked her and called upstairs. "Walt. I tried to call Ashley. Her mobile picked up, but she didn't speak. All I heard was background noise. The next time I called, her phone was dead."

"Dead?"

"Yes. Ashley never turns her phone off. The phone company confirmed it is off. "They traced the call to the El Paso Airport. She planned to visit an address on the other side of town, not the airport. I think you better call the SAC in El Paso and get his people out there right away. Our girl's in trouble."

Walter called the El Paso Field Office. FBI agents flooded the airport within minutes. When an agent shoved a picture of Ashley in Emilio Ortiz's face, and asked if he had seen her, Emilio didn't hesitate. "Oh, yes, the pretty policewoman. She went to hanger nine." The agents discovered her government car parked in front of the hanger and entered. They found the hanger empty and a smeared trail of blood that started inside the door and ended in the middle of the floor. The Douglas DC 3, tail number N-149L was gone and so was Special Agent Ashley Kohen.

278

# SIXTY-SIX

THE COCKPIT OF *THE AWAKENING* sparkled like a restored classic car. The rich scent of freshly conditioned leather smelled sweet to Ashley. This seventy year old plane was refurbished in every detail. She shared little with the brainwashed fanatic sprawled on the deck behind her, but as a former flight instructor, she understood the pride a pilot takes in his aircraft. She closed the cockpit door and locked it.

The aircraft shifted suddenly. She felt unsteady on her feet. Ashley grabbed the pilot's seatback for balance. A sharp pain reminded her of the swollen head wound now throbbing. She gripped the seat and fought against the growing concern that her injury might degrade her abilities. When the pain cleared she felt a new fear descend over her. Can I do this? It's not only my wound. Can I remember my flight training well enough to fly this plane? She closed her eyes, tilted her head up, and without forming words asked for support.

The sun, low in the sky, reflected orange light though the cockpit windows. She buckled up, and studied the instrument panel. All the necessary items were there, but arranged in an odd pattern unlike a modern aircraft. This would take some getting used to.

With the loss of pressure the cabin temperature had dropped to near freezing. Ashley disengaged the autopilot and descended to a lower altitude. She noted the current flight configurations. The indicated airspeed read eighty-four knots. That explained why the plane was mushing through the air and the stall horn sounded off intermittently. She increased power to 120 knots. The current altitude was 2500 feet, well within uncontrolled airspace. Ashley noted a heading of 315 degrees NW. The fuel gauge read full. Not knowing the size of the tank or fuel consumption, she couldn't calculate the aircraft's range. The autopilot controls were antiquated. Probably original design. She found the switch for the external red and green wingtip lights, and turned them on. Shocked, she saw the transponder turned off, which meant this aircraft's identity was blind to Air Traffic

Control and other aircraft in flight. She would deal with that shortly. First she must find her position.

Mr. Spread Eagle said he was going to Las Vegas. The 315 degree heading pointed in that direction. She had glanced out of the cockpit window every few seconds hoping to spot an identifiable landmark. When she saw an interstate highway bisecting urban sprawl she pictured a highway map of southwestern New Mexico. This early in the flight, the only location that fit that description was Las Cruces. She estimated the distance between there and El Paso to be about fifty miles.

She searched the cockpit and found three sectional flight charts. She spread the charts out, and using the map's scale, measured the distance from El Paso to Las Cruces—forty-four miles. Close to her estimate. To get an idea of how much fuel she had she then measured the distance from El Paso to Las Vegas, and found it to be 727 miles or 633 knots give or take. Maintaining 120 knots and factoring in the distance already covered, it would give her five to six hours of flight time depending on weather and headwind conditions. She had serious planning to do and needed all of that time.

Faced with many unanswered questions, she wrote down what she knew.

(1) The aircraft appeared reliable.

(2) Bashir carried enough fuel to reach his target plus ten percent: standard operating procedure.

(3) No transponder signal probably meant no flight plan had been filed, and there was no record of this flight.

(4) Based on the charts, they were in uncontrolled airspace flying under VFR, visual flight rules, often described as 'See and be Seen'.

(5) At some time she would enter controlled airspace, and should contact Air Traffic Control–ATC.

(6) She could not disarm the bomb.

(7) The bomb will explode at an altitude of 500 hundred feet.

(8) She had to find a location where no harm would come to anyone.

The Pratt and Whitney engines emitted a steady hum as the ground below faded into twilight. The pinpoints of light down below grew in number and intensity. Towns and cities formed cluster patterns. Widely spaced lights suggested suburban or farm and ranchland where people lived. Ashley felt a tightening in her chest—there were so many lights. They were everywhere. Everywhere.

If only she had followed protocol, this could have been prevented. She should have called for backup, not burst into that hanger alone. But no, she was so damn smart she could handle anything. Right? Well, Special Agent Ashley Kohen, what are you going to do now? She shut her eyes and clamped her teeth shut. She knew if she didn't fix this mess, people would die.

She had to find a place where no one lived. A place that is off-limits for humans. She grabbed the flight charts and searched for restricted areas. The third chart displayed Las Vegas. Then it hit her like a divine revelation. Right there on the chart in big letters were the words Nellis Air Force Base— the bombing range where atomic bomb tests occurred in the forties and fifties. Tears welled up as she bowed her head and clasped her Star of David. It's a way forward, Mom. A way forward.

The bombing range had five separate off-limit areas. In the middle of this spiraling complex she discovered what she wanted: a small centered restricted area far from human habitation. Area R4807 would became her target. It would be the safest place to detonate the bomb. Any radioactive material would be carried aloft and dissipate over a large and remote landmass.

She knew such a small area would force her to design a near perfect decent approach. It would be a tricky maneuver even for a pilot checked out in this aircraft. Without knowledge of the plane's basic configuration and flight characteristics, she could fail. Failure was not on her list of options.

She needed a *Pilot's Operating Manual,* usually stored in the cockpit of every plane. When she found the charts she didn't see a manual. She'd have to make assumptions, a fancy word for guessing. There was too much at stake for guessing. Her other choice would be to contact ATC and have them talk her through the approach. If they agreed to do that, she would become dependent on them. Not an acceptable alternative, at least not yet.

Time to examine the rest of the plane for the pilot's manual. She checked the autopilot and the charts to be certain she was on course and clear of near objects. She felt for her gun and unlocked the door. Bashir began screaming obscenities. "You Jew bitch! Untie me you whore of the gutter or Allah will strike you...." Ashley ripped off a foot of duct-tape and slapped in over his mouth. If only everything was that easy to fix.

In the rear of the plane she found three large cabinets and overhead bins. She had kicked open one cabinet earlier and now did the same to the last two. They were full of miscellaneous junk: assorted parts, control cables, a dirty flight jacket, tools, a battery box, and Bashir's rolled prayer rug. In the bottom of the last compartment she found a pile of books and magazines. With a tremor of excitement, she sorted through them but found no flight manual. Crap. The bastard has been flying this make and model for so long he doesn't need one.

Feeling the urge to relieve herself, Ashley opened the nearby rest room door and stepped into the small space fitted with a stainless steel sink and toilet. A metal cabinet supported the tarnished sink. Overhead a cracked mirror vibrated. Ashley finished and reached for toilet paper and found none. She opened the small cabinet door under the sink, and spotted two rolls of paper on the floor. She leaned forward and got one. Under the second roll lay a tattered pilot's manual. She snatched it up like a kid who found her lost puppy.

Clutching the manual, she started forward. Suddenly her vision blurred and she braced herself against the bulkhead near the shot-out window. The cold wind screamed though the opening, chilling her body. When her vision cleared she realized it would get colder every hour. She returned to the open cabinets and recovered the dingy jacket she had found minutes earlier. It smelled of aviation fuel, but it would keep her warm. With the flight manual she moved past Bashir, whose eyes bulged with anger.

Back in her seat, with the door locked, Ashley searched through the manual for the information she needed. Could she trust the manual? Did Bashir alter this aircraft so it no longer conformed to these standards? If he had, her planning would be off. She remembered the picture of Bashir wearing a ton of gold braid standing in front of this DC 3. Ashley deduced from his history he would have stayed with what he knew and not make significant changes. She decided to go with the manual.

She set about noting the critical information she needed: cruising speed 120 to 158 knots; fuel consumption 100 gallons each hour at neutral cruising speed; fuel capacity 810 gallons.

Ashley calculated how much fuel it would take to reach the restricted area that was eighty miles north of downtown Vegas. She had enough, but only enough. She could conserve fuel if she slowed her current speed and gained altitude. A steady 100 plus knots would reduce fuel burn, and a higher altitude would lessen drag. But with the loss of cabin pressure, she flirted with oxygen depletion and the chance of blacking out if she got above 10,000 feet. She would climb to 6,000, and hope the western headwinds were weak.

The soft glow from the instrument panel offered a haven from the black night. Patches of mist slipped between her and the twinkling lights below. The mist thickened and obstructed her view. Visual Flight Rules no longer applied. It was 8:20–time to contact ATC.

A flip of the switch turned on the transponder. Now her aircraft became a tiny beacon showing itself as DC-3, N-149L. Ashley turned on the radio equipment overhead and studied it. A weather screen lit showing bands of clouds moving northeast. She mounted headgear and plugged in. Her hand shook as she reached for the frequency dial. Ashley realized she couldn't remember the frequencies. She rubbed her hand over her face. Think. You know this stuff. She began turning the dial hoping to hear chatter. Then she remembered the radio frequencies were on the sectional charts.

Based on the charts she calculated she might be nearing Tucson's Class B airspace. *The Awakening* bounced when it entered a thick cloud formation. The twinkling lights down below disappeared.

# SIXTY-SEVEN

THE DARKENED ROOM at the Terminal Radar Approach Center bustled with a low hum of activity. Everyone from the controllers to the weather staff spoke in small voices, almost a whisper. This ATC unit served aircraft within fifty miles of Tucson International Airport. Compared with weekday traffic loads, Sunday offered an easy two-hour shift and extra time for controllers to confirm aircraft movement within their airspace.

Julia Ramos worked aircraft passing through or landing in her sector. She noticed a blip enter her radarscope moving NNW at 6,000 feet. The blip did not broadcast a block of data. It was nordo—out of radio contact. She checked traffic in that area and found it clear, but that wouldn't last. Ramos watched this slow moving blip every few minutes. Controllers know it's not uncommon for fair-weather pilots to forget to switch on the transponder.

When the blip's data block lit up at 8:15, Ramos tried to make contact without success. She continued switching radio frequencies, every few seconds. At frequency 123.675 she caught a transmission fragment. In a flat even voice Ramos called, "DC- 3 November-One, Four, Niner squawk ident."

Ashley pressed the identification button on her transponder which flashed her flight information.

Ramos replied, "November-One, Four, Niner this is Tucson Approach, confirmed. One hundred knots, heading Three, One, Fiver, level at 6000."

"Roger that Tucson." Ashley waited for instructions.

"Maintain heading Three, One, Fiver, increase speed One, Two Zero, ascend and level at 10,000."

Ashley turned the autopilot off and answered. "Tucson. Ascending to 10,000. Permission to maintain current speed."

Ramos showed no emotion in her voice. "Negative. Increase speed One, Two, Zero knots."

"One, Two, Zero knots, affirmative." Ashley pushed the throttle, and watched the airspeed indicator crawl to 120 knots. This would use valuable fuel, but there was no help for it. She knew ATC could see everybody and she could see no one, until it would be too late. She needed ATC at night, but she didn't have to stay in a heavy traffic patterns.

Ashley checked the charts and plotted a course that would skirt most congested areas on her way to Vegas. After clearing Tucson, she would have to head due north twenty minutes then assume a 310 heading. She zipped the flight jacket and cupped her hands in front of her face and blew on them. Damn cold at 10,000 feet.

She keyed Tucson. "DC-3 One-Four-Niner request heading Three Sixty."

Tucson Control: "DC-3 One-Four-Niner turn right heading Three, Six, Zero. Ascend 12000."

"DC-3 One-Four-Niner, affirmative 12000."

With the mike off she shouted, "My fingers are stiff with cold and you want me to climb to 12000?" A chill rippled through her as she searched the instrument panel for cabin temperature control. She found it under the throttle assembly, and turned it up all the way. She pulled back on the yoke and watched the altimeter edge toward 12,000 feet. It got colder, and she started to breathe faster. A sharp pain behind her eyes increased.

Ten minutes later the radio chirped, "DC-3 One-Four-Niner. You're leaving my airspace. I'm handing you off to Albuquerque Air Route Traffic Control Center, radio frequency 125.025. Have a safe flight."

Ashley switched frequencies and within seconds she heard a male voice welcome her, "Good evening DC-3 November-One, Four, Niner–this is Albuquerque Center. Confirm."

"Albuquerque Center, confirmed." Ashley knew the Air Route Center, always referred to as the 'Center', would check for the required flight plan. She didn't have a collision-avoidance-system which would have allowed her to fly at night in uncontrolled airspace. Ashley had to fly in controlled airspace. She needed to rely on the electronic eyes of ATC for her flight safety and everyone else's. The controller at the Center didn't take long.

"November One, Four, Niner. Flight Services has no, repeat, no Flight Plan for you on file, over."

She decided she would tell them the truth or at least part of the truth. "Albuquerque I want to file an inflight-plan, over."

"One, Four, Niner. What's your destination?"

285

"Destination LAS, McCarran International direct. ETA 2400."

"One, Four, Niner. Roger that. Estimated time of arrival 2400—midnight. I'll forward to Flight Services."

Ashley did not plan to land at Vegas. She would deal with that when the time came. She requested a course change and a decent to 8000 feet, and got it. After setting the autopilot, she noticed the cloud cover had faded and she was able to see the lights below again. She knew the hard part lay ahead: planning the decent profile.

The pain behind her eyes became a dull ache and she felt physically weak and mentally exhausted. Ashley leaned back and closed her eyes. She remembered how her mother would sing her a soft song while rocking her back and forth when she came home from school crying. She let the tears flow now. No one could see her. No one would hear her sobs.

The sound of the engines, steady and smooth, comforted her. At the lower altitude warmer air eased the cabin temperature. She'd set the autopilot to take over, and checked the weather screen: all clear for now. Ashley had a little time to rest—needed to rest, but only for a few minutes. She fell asleep at 2100—nine o'clock Mountain Standard Time.

# SIXTY-EIGHT

THE CALL FROM THE EL PASO Field Office came in at 5:45 Sunday afternoon. Dorothy Hogan forwarded it to Walter, then went into his office and watched his face grow pale as he listened to the report. Walter learned of the trail of blood in the hanger, and the bitter news that Ashley had disappeared. Staring down at his hands, Walter bent over and his eyes appeared moist. Dorothy tried to comfort him with a hand on his shoulder. "Get Johnson and Ramirez," he said, unable to look at her.

Earlier that day he had received the DNA reports confirming Abdullah al Jamal had perished in the Maljamar explosion and Bashir Hashim survived. Ashley had been right, Bashir was the surviving terrorist and now both were gone.

Bill and Mark ran into his office minutes later. "What's up?" Bill asked a bit out of breath. Walter, his expression now grim with anger, told them what he'd learned. "That madman Bashir has Ashley, and he's gone off in a plane registered to his address in El Paso."

Mark stood at attention. "Gone, what's that mean?"

"She tracked Bashir to a hangar at the El Paso airport where he had a plane stored. I have the tail number. There's blood on the floor of the hanger. The plane took off at 5:30."

Bill steadied himself against the doorframe. "If there's blood it has to be Ashley's, otherwise she'd have him in custody."

Walter tried to stay centered. "All they know is that Bashir contacted Clearance Control at 4:45, and the Tower cleared his plane for departure at 5:20. Fewer than thirty minutes ago."

Mark shook his head. "Can they track him?"

Walter looked at Bill who shrugged his shoulders and said, "There's a big FAA building over on Louisiana Boulevard, not far from here. We could call them."

Walter stood. "This needs a face to face. Let's go."

On their way out, he told Dorothy, "Call the FAA. Tell them we have an emergency and I'll be there in minutes. Then call Director Delong. Fill him in on the situation. He'll know what to do."

"Yes, I know Delong's secretary. I'll get through to him. Count on it."

CODY ROGERS, Director of the Albuquerque ATC Center got Dorothy's phone call. He left orders for the security guard at the entry gate to escort the FBI personnel to his office when they arrived. Ten minutes later, Walter Kent, Bill Johnson and Marcos Ramirez entered his office on the first floor of the building.

Rogers stood, introduced himself and offered his hand. "Some kind of problem?"

"Yes." Walter shook his hand, showed ID and made brief introductions. "This is what I can tell you. We have identified an armed terrorist flying an aircraft out of El Paso. This man kidnapped one of our agents. Our agent and many American lives are at risk–thousands, maybe more."

Cody Rogers gasped. "Are we talking another 9-11?"

"Not if we can stop him. We need to find that plane."

Rogers straightened. "We control airspace in this region. If he's in our system we'll find him. Can you identify the aircraft?"

"Yes. It's an old DC 3 with a tail number N-149L.

Rogers nodded. "Follow me, upstairs." He took the steps two at a time. When the others caught up, he took them into a dark cave-like room, put his finger to his lips to signal quiet, and then walked to a nearby corner to consult with a tall man wearing headphones. The man's badge read *Floor Supervisor*. After a brief conversation, the man moved into another room filled with rows of men and women staring intently at green illuminated radarscopes.

"That's Ryan Simpson," said Rogers to the FBI crew. "He's a good man. This center controls aircraft at low, high and ultrahigh altitudes. He will start with low and high targets. Given the age and type of aircraft that's where it'll be found." Rogers pointed to an alcove off the main room. "Stay there, I'm going to check Flight Services for a flight plan."

Rogers left them and disappeared into the semi-darkness of the control room. Minutes later he returned. "Flight Services has no flight plan on file for our aircraft. I've sent out an alert to all towers and approach control facilities in the region. They will be on the lookout for this aircraft."

Ramirez shook his head in disbelief. "Don't you know where all the planes are?"

"We control only aircraft we can identify and talk to. Sure we have safety rules, but if a pilot wants to fly blind to us, he or she can do it. Right now our DC 3 is only a blip with no ID on someone's radar screen. Mr. Kent, I'm going to call the National Airspace System in Virginia. They conduct traffic flow management for all flights occurring in the United States. The Command Center needs to know about this threat. Can you be more specific?"

Walter stared at Cody Rogers, who appeared to be a competent and sincere man. "That's top secret. Details must come from Edward Delong, FBI Director, but I can tell you this aircraft is armed with an explosive device capable of inflicting massive loss of life, if set off in a populated area."

"Thank you. That's what I needed to know." Rogers turned abruptly and dashed back into the darkened control room.

Walter Kent had no control over events confronting him. Powerless, he had to wait, hope, pray, and depend on others. He thought of Ashley and felt a lump in his throat. This can't be happening—not to my Ashley. Please. Not to Ashley.

# SIXTY-NINE

ASHLEY FELT A STRONG GRAVITY TUG on her body and woke up. The engines whined at a high RPM. *Oh God, how long have I been asleep?* She checked the altimeter and discovered she had dropped two thousand feet. She heard an urgent voice in her ears.

"DC 3 November One, Four, Niner, do you read my transmission? Over."

Ashley checked the time–9:30. She had lost 15 minutes. She overrode the autopilot, adjusted her power settings, and pulled back on the yoke. The engines labored at a climb rate of 500 feet a minute.

Again an urgent voice. "DC 3 November One, Four Niner, this is Albuquerque Center, acknowledge?"

Ashley answered, "DC 3 One, Four, Niner, affirmative Albuquerque. I've experienced a sudden drop in attitude due to Clear-air Turbulence."

"One, Four, Niner, is this C. A. T. an emergency?"

She reviewed the weather screen. It displayed isolated turbulence in her immediate area. "Negative, Albuquerque. I experienced an air pocket. Returning to 8000. Over."

She had been out of touch with ATC for too long. They probably had to reroute aircraft for avoidance purposes. When she reached altitude she reported: "Albuquerque, DC 3 One, Four, Niner, 8000 and level. Sorry about nordo."

She waited for confirmation. A different voice responded.

"DC 3 November One Four Niner, radio frequency change to One, Two, One, Point Fiver, repeat frequency change to One, Two, One, Point Fiver, confirm." Ashley confirmed the change and adjusted her radio to transmit on the Universal Emergency Frequency. This frequency was never used for communication. It was reserved for extreme emergencies. Did they know more than they were saying?

Explaining her mission to ATC this early in the flight complicated her strategy. She had hoped to delay this until after Las Vegas. By then there would be little they could do to interfere with her plan. The Air Force would have limited options, too.

After turning the dials to the assigned radio frequency, she announced, "DC 3 One, Four, Niner. Tag-up Albuquerque."

The Center wasted no time. "DC 3 One, Four, Niner, who is piloting this aircraft?"

Ashley's thumb trembled as it hovered over the response key. She could lie. Make up a name. Try to confuse the situation. But no, she must do her job. This frequency was off the working network. She dropped the formal nomenclature. "Who's asking?"

"This is Ryan Simpson, Floor Supervisor for this center, identify yourself."

"Special Agent Ashley Kohen, FBI, sir."

"Confirm your identity, Agent Kohen. What is your badge number?"

"FBI agents don't have badge numbers. You can confirm my ID with Special Agent in Charge Walter Kent. Albuquerque. Field Office 555-480-1000, over."

"We know you filed a flight plan terminating in LAS and that you are carrying an explosive device on board. What is the purpose of your flight?"

Ashley closed her eyes for a moment. She was about to say words never before exchanged with any air traffic controller. Every muscle tightened as she spoke. "I have on board one disabled terrorist and one enabled nuclear bomb. It's locked down. I'm going to a location where no one lives and detonate this device."

Communication with ATC is rapid and concise. It is rare to experience dead air. Ashley waited 15 seconds before a response. "Say again."

"I have a nuclear bomb locked down. I can't defuse it. Over."

Ashley's heart rate quickened when she heard, "Stand by." Hold a minimum altitude of 8000 and navigate to the nearest landing point: Love Field coordinates N 34.39.29 by W 112.25.15". Over."

"Negative, Albuquerque, I can't do that." Ashley imagined the turmoil her response caused. You almost never refuse an air traffic control command. You might question it, but you comply.

"This is an aviation imperative. Proceed to Love Field immediately. Bomb experts will be on hand for your landing. Over."

"Sorry, Albuquerque, I'm signing off. I have work to do." Ashley started to remove her headphones when she heard a familiar voice.

"Ashley, this is Walter, I'm here at the center." His words came quick and sounded strained. "What's going on? Are you alright? Are you safe? Talk to me. "

Ashley brought a shaky hand to her forehead. She was willing to deal with the inevitable, but this was too much. She gripped the yoke. "I'm sorry, Walter. I messed up again, but I can't turn back. If only I could." She choked out those last words.

He sounded frantic, now. "Whatever it takes. I want you back. Tell me what you need. I'll make it happen."

She drew in a breath and expelled it slowly. "I know, but you can't help me. There's a nuclear bomb on board that will explode below 500 feet. I can't disarm it. No one can. Tell them. Explain it to them." Her voice trembled with awareness and fatigue. "I'm going to the bombing range north of Las Vegas. That's a safe place. No one will be hurt. That's the only way. I'm sorry Walt. I'm so sorry for everything.

"What do you mean no one will be hurt?" He screamed, "You will be hurt!"

Ashley felt a tear slip down her cheek. Her voice cracked when she said, "If only you could be here, but you can't. I have to do this alone." Ashley switched off the radio.

# SEVENTY

WHEN SHE TURNED the radio off her hand quivered, and she felt a deep fatigue. The pain in the back of her head started again. She felt like throwing up, but a dry heave was the best she could do.

The engines, invisible in the clouded night sky, labored against the buffeting winds. Until now, fear, and the adrenalin it produced, had given her energy. But at this moment she felt lost in a nightmare of hopelessness.

She leaned back, closed her eyes and thought of the people in her life who had real meaning. She thought of her mother, who remained her guiding force in time of stress. Ashley sensed if her Mom was watching she would be proud of her. And then there was Walter. She finally admitted her feelings for this man who clearly cared for her. Ashley opened her eyes and realized she was grieving for the loss of companionship she would not live to experience. Life was a gift filled with setbacks, and this would be the hardest to accept.

Feeling sorry for herself wouldn't fly this plane and get this job done. People's lives were at stake. She checked the charts and airspeed. Fuel looked marginal. NOAA weather showed a low-pressure system moving in with winds 20 gusting to 35 mph, light to heavy rain, and mostly cloudy.

Based on the coordinates ATC gave her, she was crossing Prescott, Arizona's Love Field right now: the time 10:35. Vegas lay190 air miles or about two hours away. Once she cleared McCarran International it would be less than an hour to her target. She had to plan a descent profile that ended in the middle of R4807-B.

To fly over Las Vegas airport, one of the busiest in the western United States, she had to drop down into uncontrolled airspace: below 1200 feet. That would keep her out of the busy air traffic pattern. Once past that point she must climb, then begin her slow controlled descent. She didn't know how high she must climb or how long the descent, but she knew the outdated autopilot in this plane would be useless.

Ashley began her calculations with the aid of the flight manual and aeronautical charts. She had to determine the precise power settings, manifold pressure, and engine revolutions per minute to make this work. Maintaining a speed of ninety knots allowed her to travel one point four knots every minute. She knew that once past North Las Vegas, she had only sixty-five miles to complete this maneuver.

She wrote down numbers, then scratched them out. She calculated several altitudes to begin her descent and found them too low. Finally, she settled on a design that worked–on paper. As soon as she left uncontrolled airspace, she had to climb to 12500, level out for two minutes, and then begin her descent. She must lose altitude at a rate of 500 feet each minute for twenty-four minutes. Her aircraft would travel thirty-three point six knots before terminating over the restricted area at an altitude of exactly 500 feet. *Terminate at 500 feet.* She realized the word 'terminate' had several meanings. End of flight. End of life.

Ashley knew her plan would work in a perfect world, but she also knew the world wasn't perfect. With a front moving through, winds would be unpredictable. She would also have to endure cold thin air at 12500 feet. How long could she endure that environment? And then the fuel. Would it last? The distance she had flown already exceeded her earlier calculations. Running out of gas would be an ever-present danger.

She checked the time. One hour from Vegas. She must contact ATC. They were tracking her and probably frustrated by her silence. She hoped they would be cooperative, whatever the hell that meant. Short of shooting her down, which would end badly for everyone, what could they do? Yank her pilot license?

To avoid Las Vegas controlled airspace, Ashley started her decent as she approached the city. Sometimes she would break out of cloud cover and see lights below, but most of the time she lived shrouded in the blackness of a cloudy night.

USING HEADPHONES plugged into the audio circuit Cody Rogers and Ryan Simpson, in the darkened room of the Albuquerque Center, listened to the conversation between Walter Kent and his special agent. Finally it made sense. She couldn't land at Love Field or any airport because the bomb was rigged to go off in midair. Cody's expression turned to horror. "Jesus Christ, Ryan, we have a disastrous situation here."

Ryan's face drained of color. "My mother lives in Las Vegas."

Cody didn't hear him. He yanked the headphone off and ran to his office downstairs. His mind raced through the choices that confronted him. This might be worse than 9-11. More people could die. He had to take action. How much time did he have? It's the middle of the night. He searched his computer for bookmarked phone numbers. "National Airspace System," he muttered as he speed dialed the System Command Center in Virginia. Someone had to be on duty. They worked 24/7.

THROUGH PUFFY, WATERY eyes Alex Borkowski saw the red light blinking on the console. After thirty-two years with the FAA he'd seen all the red lights he wanted to see the rest of his probably short life. He ran his hand over his hairless scalp and stretched the other out to get the phone. It didn't reach, so he scooted his chair a few inches to the left and snagged it. In a slow southern accent he said, "Traffic Flow Management, Borkowski speakin'."

"This is Cody Rogers, Albuquerque Center. We have an emergency. We're tracking a target carrying a nuclear bomb."

Borkowski frowned. "It's too damn late for this kind a bullshit. Balls of fire, Cody. This ain't funny."

Cody sounded hysterical. "Wake up you old fart. This is real. A DC 3 is approaching Las Vegas flown by an FBI agent with a terrorist and an A-bomb locked down. She can't land because the bomb is rigged to go off below 500 feet. She can't stay in flight and we can't predict what's going to happen."

Borkowski staggered to his feet. "Okay. Gim'me the data block info and the flight plan. Are you in active contact?"

A moment of silence. "Not right now."

"What in blue blazes?"

"We're tracking her. She's planning to go to a restricted area at the Nellis bombing range north of Vegas. She's going to explode it there."

"Mother of God. We can't know what might happen, so I'm gonna assume the worst. First, I'm gonna curtail operations at Las Vegas Approach Control and McCarren Tower. I want ya to reroute all aircraft, commercial and private, away from Vegas airspace. Tell 'em to land at the nearest feasible location. I'll get ahold of Los Angeles and Salt Lake Centers, same deal."

"What about Nellis?"

"I'm puttin 'em on alert.

Cody rubbed the back of his neck. "Grounding this many planes will disrupt the entire continental system."

"You got that right."

"And scare the crap out of everybody."

"Better scared than dead."

# SEVENTY-ONE

HEAVY RAIN SPLATTERED against the cockpit windows, setting off a choppy cavalcade of sound as Ashley neared McCarran International. She continued losing altitude to avoid the heavy flight traffic serviced by that airport. She knew Vegas Approach Control would see her on their scopes when she crossed the 50-mile radius in only a few minutes. She opened her emergency radio frequency to ATC. "DC-3 November-One, Four, Niner-Lima. Do you read me Albuquerque, acknowledge?"

She received an immediate response. "One, Four, Niner, yes we read you. You are below your assigned altitude. Climb and level at 8000. Maintain speed and heading."

The stabbing pain behind her eyes persisted. The instrument panel became a blur. She reached out to touch the bulkhead–a solid and stationary object giving her balance. Come on old girl get it together. You only need two hours, maybe less.

Her headphones squawked, "One, Four, Niner. Do you copy?"

"Sorry Albuquerque. Is this Ryan Simpson?"

"Affirmative. Talk to me."

"I'm descending into Class G airspace to avoid McCarran traffic."

"Negative, Ashley. Central Control Center in Virginia has cleared all McCarran traffic both into and out of LAS. You have a clear sky."

Ashley, still holding on to the bulkhead, felt her focus return. "Read back?"

"We know about the 500-foot detonation and your plan to reach restricted airspace. All flights in and around your sector have been grounded or rerouted. Nellis Air Force Base is Code Red."

Stunned by this response, Ashley squeezed her eyes shut and drew a deep breath. This meant ATC approved of her plan and would aid her as she carried it out. Thousands of people, who will never know the danger they faced have a greater chance to live now. "How can I say thank you?"

A moment passed. "You just did."

The altimeter read 4000. Ashley began a slow ascent, which would conserve fuel by slowly gaining altitude this far out. While checking her instruments, she explained to Simpson the details of her controlled descent starting at 12500 and forty six miles from the designated termination point. She asked for confirmation that this approach profile would put her 30 miles west and 40 miles east of any human habitation. After a minute, Simpson came back online. "Your calculations are correct. You are to be commended." Ashley bowed her head in relief and at the same time felt a touch of pride in her accomplishment.

A half an hour later her altimeter read 8000 feet. The rain had stopped and clouds started to dissipate. Clearly the weather front had passed this point. To her amazement the moon came into view, and minutes later it shown bright and clear. This change in conditions gave her confidence that weather would no longer be a factor. She continued her slow ascent.

At 12:28 she glanced out of the window. It offered her a grand sight. She saw the sparkling multicolored lights of the Las Vegas strip and thought of her only visit to Vegas years ago during happier times.

When she crossed over North Las Vegas she started her final ascent to her target altitude of 12500 feet. In five minutes she would level out for two minutes and begin the final approach.

Suddenly two sets of blinking lights appeared on either side of her aircraft. Sleek jet fighters with aerodynamic swept-back wings shot by her window, and swooped up and out of sight in seconds. She could feel her plane shudder from their wake turbulence. In less than a minute they reappeared, flying much slower this time. She immediately switched to frequency 122.750 for air-to-air communication. A man's voice spoke to her.

"Good morning, little lady. My buddy and I thought we'd escort you for just a bit. Courtesy of the United States Air Force." A second voice chimed in, "Yes, ma'am it's our privilege, to say the least."

Surprised, Ashley said the first thing that came to mind. "Thank you, gentlemen, it's not every day a woman gets two escorts on short notice."

"We can't stay long—orders you know, but we want to recognize that your bravery will save thousands and prevent a bloody world war. It's an honor to salute you."

Ashley watched as both jet fighters moved ahead and dipped their wings in an aviator's gesture of respect for a superior comrade. For a few seconds she didn't breathe.

That persistent pain behind her eyes brought her back to the real world. She tried to ignore it. The altimeter read 12000. One minute and she would level out.

A jumble of thoughts crowded Ashley's mind. She thought of Bashir, who she had cheated out of his evil goal to murder a million Americans. She thought of her mother and hoped she would be pleased with her little girl who would soon sacrifice her life, so others would live. A sacrifice much like the one her mother made on that terrible day in New York. And she thought of Walter. There was so little time. She had to talk to Walter.

Ashley switched back to the emergency frequency and keyed her mike. "Albuquerque, is Walter Kent there?"

"Yes, here he is."

She braced herself. This would be hard, but she owed him.

Walter started out, "Ashley isn't there some way..."

She spoke softly. "Walter, I want you to listen. Don't talk. Just listen. I only have two minutes." Ashley felt an ache in her throat that hurt. "I want to tell you I'm sorry. That night when I told you about my Mom and cried in your arms, I didn't have the strength to tell you what I felt. What my heart knew and my brain refused to admit. For the first time I found someone I wanted to share my life with. I knew it then, but didn't say it. I want to tell you now. You are the only person I have ever and wanted to be with. I tell you this because I want you to know. I need for you to know even though I'm afraid it will hurt you. I 'm sorry for that, too." Ashley struggled as tears flooded her eyes. "Forgive me Walter. Please forgive me for what might have been."

Ashley shut down the radio, sat back and screamed at the night. A long, loud wail of bitter anguish and emotional pain. At that moment she wanted to live. Wanted to be a normal woman, a wife and a mother. Wanted to share the intimacy of a loving partnership and feel the warmth of a baby next to her heart. But that was no longer possible because her life would soon end.

It was time. Ashley adjusted the power settings, manifold pressure and engine RPM's to begin her final descent. With care she positioned, and then immobilized the yoke. She had twenty-four minutes to live.

# SEVENTY-TWO

THE RADAR ALTIMETER READ 12500 feet. Ashley tapped the Time App on Bashir's phone and started the stopwatch. Seconds flashed on the screen until they equaled one minute. She shot a look at the altimeter; it read 12000 feet. The *Awakening* was flying hands free exactly as she had planned. She waited another minute–11500 feet. Twenty-two minutes to go.

She wondered if she would feel unbearable pain when the bomb exploded or would she evaporate instantly, like a suicide bomber. Thoughts of suicide made her think of Bashir. She felt obligated to tell him what was about to happen. Ashley checked her gun, grabbed a flashlight, and unlocked the cockpit door. It would be dark and cold on the other side. Bashir was tied down, but what if he had gotten free and lay waiting for her?

With the small Ruger handgun ready, she unlocked the door and kicked it open. A blast of cold air hit her as the beam of light cut through the darkness and revealed Bashir tightly bound on the deck next to the platform. Her nostril's sensed he had soiled himself. His face was drained of color, and his body trembled. She knelt down.

"We cleared Las Vegas minutes ago," she said in a level voice. "We're headed for a desolate patch of uninhabited desert where only you and I will die." She glanced at the stopwatch, "in twenty-one minutes."

Bashir's eyes opened wide darting back and both as if to find a place to escape. He tried to speak, but only a garbled sound came out. He raised his head a few inches and tried again. This time in a hoarse whisper he uttered words Ashley didn't understand.

She moved closer. "Speak English, Bashir."

He again raised his head. "Quran."

She frowned. "I don't have a Quran."

Bashir turned his head and pointed with his eyes to the rear of the plane. His voice cracked as he shouted, "In the bin."

Ashley shook her head in disbelief. This man, this evil man who would murder innocent people, wants a holy book before he dies, as if that will give him salvation. Trying to understand, she realized that in his mind he was on a holy mission to convert the world to a radical form of Islam. He didn't understand the Islam he would die for was based on a twisted and perverted version of the Muslim faith. A distorted view which would meet the needs of men who would dominate the world with their self-serving interpretation of the Quran. Men who used a clever selection of words and phrases to give them power over others.

She looked at Bashir's pleading eyes and saw a wretched and pitiful man. A misguided believer who thinks he's failed his beloved Allah. Ashley touched her Star of David medal, bowed her head, and using the flashlight, made her way to the rear of the plane.

The constant drone of the engines barely registered in her mind while the icy stream of air howled through the shattered window.

Across from the rest room were three overhead bins. She opened the first bin, pointed her light inside, and found it empty. The second held a khaki colored cloth bag. Under one side of the bag she saw a flash of gold color. She directed her light back to that object. It was a book with gilded edges. She stretched and tried to grasp the book, but it stayed lodged under the cloth bag. Frustrated, she put the small flashlight in her mouth, pointed it at the bag and pulled hard with both hands. The bag tumbled out and fell on the deck. Ashley snapped up the book. It was a copy of the Quran. Only then did she examine the bag.

Holding the book in her hand and the light still in her mouth, she ran her other hand over the oddly shaped bag that struck her as something purposeful, not random in shape. She pulled it open. It had straps and buckles protruding. She released the book and grabbed the bag and searched it with both hands. When she discovered its purpose, her body froze. She collapsed on the bag, hugged it, and almost cried with joy.

Quickly she snatched up the book, ran back to Bashir, and shined the light on the Quran so he could see it. She placed it on his chest. He raised his head and showed a flicker of appreciation. His shaking had stopped and he appeared at peace.

Her stopwatch read six minutes, leaving eighteen minutes to ground zero. Converting knots to statute miles, she calculated the distance to be thirty-one miles at this point. Not much time. She must move fast.

301

With the flashlight she examined the port side door. It turned out to be two doors: one for cabin entrance and another for cargo. The cabin door opened from left to right making it impossible to open against the airstream outside. The cargo door opened from right to left. Once unlocked and pushed out a few inches, the wind would catch it and slam it open maybe ripping it off its hinges.

Seventeen minutes to go.

Ashley ran to the rear and grabbed the bag—a standard Ram Air parachute with a reserve chute attached. Years ago, during flight training, she had made one jump under controlled conditions. It scared the crap out of her then. She knew it won't get any better this time, but the alternative was unacceptable. Ashley put the flashlight in her mouth again and studied the only thing that stood between her and certain death. At the center of the chute container, a small tag caught her eye. It read 'descending canapé–minimum deployment 3500'. It took her two minutes to figure out the harness design, strap it over her shoulders, and buckle the reserve chute pressed across her belly. She cinched all the connections.

Fourteen minutes, now.

One last check. She moved forward to the cockpit. The altimeter read 6700 AGL—above ground level. Right where it should be. She headed back, hesitating briefly to check on Bashir. Strangely, in the dim light, she saw him smile at her. No time to figure that one out.

Twelve minutes left.

She moved to the portside cargo door secured in place with a locked lever. To open the door she had to turn a screw assembly, swing it aside, and lift the lever out of its cradle. All manner of dire results flashed through her mind. What if the maelstrom sucked her out of the plane and knocked her unconscious? If she cleared the door she might collide with the tail assembly? What if the force of the wind threw her back into the plane?

Ten minutes.

Ashley turned the screw, a giant wing-nut affair, and shoved it down out-of-the-way. Then she gripped both hands on the lever. The door parted two inches from its frame, and then slammed open against the fuselage, catapulting Ashley Kohen into the cold dark void five thousand feet above the bleak Nevada desert.

# SEVENTY-THREE

AT THE FAA COMMAND CENTER Alex Borkowski forgot his nagging arthritic right hip when he learned of the airborne nuclear bomb approaching Las Vegas. He shut down McCarran airport, then ordered the Los Angeles and Salt Lake City Centers to reroute or ground all flights.

Nellis AFB lookouts reported a huge fireball over the Nevada test site at 1:32 a.m. Nevada time: 4:32 a.m. EST. The Air Force observers were not alone. The American News Network, ANN, started getting reports from the field about a big explosion out west.

The President had already initiated a National Security Council (NSC) meeting. While there was notable confusion, mostly because of the time zone changes, President Graham Steward learned the details of the imminent disaster thirty minutes before it happened. Starting with the Nellis AFB Commander and ending with the Chairman of the Joint Chiefs of Staff, his control and command structure functioned as the system was designed to do. He wanted to assure the NSC no significant loss of life had occurred and that he would rank this incident as Top Secret.

The primary members of the NSC gathered at 5:15 that morning in the Cabinet Room of the White House. Present were the Vice President, the Chairman of the Joint Chiefs, the Secretaries of Defense, State and Treasury, plus Margret Madden, National Security Adviser, Edmond Pruitt, the President's Chief of Staff and Leo Adornetto, Director of National Intelligence.

President Steward waited until everyone settled down. "I know this is an early hour, but I want to brief you on an incident that has happened out in the Nevada desert. A small nuclear bomb was harmlessly detonated in a remote location with no loss of life. It occurred over a restricted area of our Nellis Air Force Base bombing range many miles north of Las Vegas. I wanted you to know this before the media started churning out their usual speculations and predictions of Armageddon." Steward eyed the council members arrayed before him, and noted Leo Adornetto squirming in his chair. "Some of you know a few days ago I appointed a Special Unit Strike Force to investigate a possible infiltration of a terrorist armed with some kind of nuclear weapon out west. I'm not happy with their performance, but at least no collateral damage has occurred."

"Amen to that," said the Vice President nodding his head. Others around the table uttered similar approvals.

Leo Adornetto, unable to remain quiet, put his hand up and spoke, "Mr. President, there might be a little more to this incident then you've been told."

The President ignored the comment. "All of this could have been avoided, if the Strike Force had acted sooner. Unfortunately, I became aware of this terrorist plot too late."

Adornetto tried again. "But Mr. President..."

Steward cut him off. "I'll get to you in a moment, Leo."

The Director of National Intelligence clasped his hands in front of him, and gritted his teeth.

"As I was saying, if we had captured this jihadist only a few hours earlier, none of this would have happened. As you know, we have spent much political capital and billions of dollars to beef up our national defenses. If the word got out about this breach, the public would become alarmed. We would have a lot of questions to answer. Since no real harm has been done, I consider this matter closed. For purposes of national security, I declare this matter Top Secret as defined by law."

Adornetto no longer remained silent. "Mr. President that means no one will know the tremendous success we have accomplished."

"I think you mean tremendous failure, Mr. Adornetto."

"No, sir. I have been involved in this case from the beginning. The intelligence community has worked as a team and saved our country from a catastrophic event far greater than the 9-11 attack."

"That's nonsense. A terrorist has successfully exploded an atomic bomb on American soil. That is hardly an accomplishment I want aired in the public arena."

"That's not supported by the facts, sir."

President Steward's face reddened, his eyes grew hard, "Mr. Adornetto, may I remind you violation of any information classified as top secret carries with it fines and imprisonment. Do you understand me?"

Silence prevailed. Everyone around the table bowed their heads and glanced over at Adornetto. Finally he answered, "Yes, sir. I understand you completely."

"Good. Now if you all will excuse me, I am scheduled to speak to the nation." Everyone stood as the President left the Cabinet Room.

# SEVENTY-FOUR

BEFORE THE SUN CAST LONG SHADOWS across the east coast, the airways sizzled with un-substantiated claims and speculations, led by a popular TV news show host of the American National Network

"Good morning. This is Tom Neumann broadcasting to you from our ANN newsroom in the nation's capital. At this hour reports of a strange happening are pouring into our newsroom. Only a few hours ago something occurred in the desert regions of Nevada that have many observers wondering if the United States Government has broken the long-standing Nuclear Test Ban Treaty signed nearly fifty years ago. Our correspondent Mindy Logan is live at the scene. Mindy, what can you tell us about this event?"

A young blue-eyed woman with blond hair and high cheekbones appeared on a split screen with streetlights glowing in the background. "Nothing official yet, Tom, but I'm hearing from sources that a large explosion occurred shortly after 1:30 this morning. Witnesses in North Las Vegas say they heard a distant explosion and saw a red glow low in the night sky earlier this morning. Over that horizon behind me."

"Thank you Mindy for that live report. Joining me is the former head of the Government Accountability Office, Daniel Santana. Daniel what can you tell us about this strange sighting?"

A dark haired middle-aged man with a carefully crafted beard stared straight ahead. "As you know, the Test Site has been off-limits for many years. Only authorized personnel are allowed on-site. I can't speculate, but if an atomic bomb exploded last night it was either top secret or possibly a terror attack gone awry."

"A terrorist attack of this magnitude, Daniel, would be a serious threat to national security. Could you elaborate on that point?"

Daniel shifted his position. "Nuclear testing ended years ago. It would take an act of Congress to reauthorize testing. No such act has been approved. That means only an unauthorized detonation occurred or something is going on the public should know about."

"That's an intriguing idea. Thank you Daniel Santana for your thoughts. Moving on, we are following events that occurred early this morning in Nevada. I want to bring in our panel for an assessment. Joining me is Gabriel Lloyd, a former State Department official, Zoey Chapman, a national security analyst with the Hawkins Institute, and Gavin Taylor, president and CEO of Global International Studies. Zoey, I'll start with you. There are indications that a bomb has exploded. What do you make of this?"

The screen split into four windows. A woman with tightly curled gray hair spoke. "I'm disturbed that we have not heard from the military. This incident has occurred in restricted areas under their jurisdiction. The public has a right to know what's going on. Are Americans in imminent danger from a foreign power or does this signal a change in our policy dealing with nuclear proliferation?"

Gavin Taylor interrupted. "I disagree. If the military is performing exercises in the desert, there is no reason to believe it poses any threat to Americans. In fact, this might be the government's way of showing we mean business when it comes to national defense."

Tom Neumann turned to Gabriel Lloyd sitting across from him in the studio. "Gabriel, do you think there is a link to terrorism?"

Gabriel shook his head. "No. Acquisition of a nuclear weapon is far too sophisticated for the terror operations at large today. Even if they got such a weapon, creating a delivery system would be difficult, if not impossible."

Neumann faced the camera. "I want to thank my guests for their informed opinions." The camera angle changed and he turned his head. "Here in our studios, Bryant Smith has a special report for us."

A slim gray haired man stood in front of a giant map of southeast Nevada. "Thank you, Tom. As you can see the test site covers almost 1,400 square miles. Based on what we know," he pointed to the map, "the explosion was about here, in the middle of this vast area. The fact that there are no towns anywhere near suggest this was a planned experiment."

"Thank you Bryant. That's good information for our viewers. I've just been handed breaking news. The President will address the nation on this mysterious explosion in the southwest. Our White House correspondent Rina Nankato is standing by to report on President Graham Steward's forthcoming appearance. What do we know, Rina, about the President's sudden decision to speak to the country?"

The face of an attractive Asian woman standing in front of the White House flashed on the screen. "It was announced a few minutes ago the President will address the nation. He will make a short statement and will not take questions from the press at this time. Sources close to the President say he's been thoroughly briefed, and is in control of the situation."

"Have you heard any talk about this being linked to a possible terrorist threat, Rina?"

"Right now there is no confirmation that this development is connected to terror activity, but no one is ruling out that possibility."

"Thank you, Rina. It will be interesting to find out what the President has to say about a subject that is on everybody's mind. The fact that he's speaking directly to the country and not dealing with the subject in a White House Press Conference underscores the importance he must place on this strange occurrence." Neumann paused. "Here is the President of the United States."

A full-length podium with the President's Seal filled the screen backed by four American flags. President Graham Steward stepped up, faced the camera and assumed a serious expression.

*"Good morning my fellow Americans. Today I come before you not to spread an alarm, but to spread the word that America is strong. America is safe.*

*"Safe from all those who might think we are not ready to defend ourselves, if defense is needed.*

*"Safe from those who would do us harm, if harm is intended.*

*"Safe from the insidious forces that lurk within and without our borders, if these forces underestimate our resolve.*

*"Safe because we value every citizen of this great country and can and will protect them with the most powerful military force in the history of the world.*

*"Because we have the duty to purge ourselves of the dark forces that stand ready to invade our way of life–our family values and basic freedoms earned by the blood, sweat, and tears of our forefathers and the sacrifices of our brave men and women of the armed forces. We resolve to remain the shining example of what the rights of men and women mean to society at large, I can assure you, all is right in the America we love.*

*"I can tell you this because our constant vigilance demands that we never fall behind in the endless struggle to maintain our defenses. That vigilance was demonstrated early this morning in the vast deserts of the great state of Nevada where a top secret experiment was conducted. An experiment that furthers our constant research into a strong military presence in the greatest nation on the globe: the United States of America.*

*"I know there are those among us who would speculate with theories of conspiracies. Let me assure you our goal is to preserve the freedoms we cherish and preserve the security of the nation. God bless all of you and God bless America."*

The President remained standing, his head high and displayed a thumbs up gesture. The camera pulled back and a commercial for sexual enhancement flashed on the screen.

# SEVENTY-FIVE

THE GROUND CAME UP FAST. She hit hard. A sharp pain seized her left leg when her body struck the packed soil. It jolted her. A gust of air filled the grounded parachute, dragging her across the rough desert surface. Ashley yanked on the cords trying to pull the yellow nylon canopy flat, but the chute skittered across the land dragging her like a fallen rider caught in the stirrup of a runaway horse. Ashley grappled with the harness buckle, but couldn't break it loose. Seconds later her movement across the rough ground stopped.

In the dark Ashley fought to free herself. She felt blood on her right hand cut by the parachute cords. It made the buckle on the harness slippery. When it gave way, she rolled free and lay motionless on her right side. In the dim moonlight she saw the parachute snagged on a stand of prickly pear cactus, portions still billowing in the wind.

The smoky clouds parted showing a splendid array of stars scattered across the sky. Her breathing slowed and her heartbeat tumbled back to something close to normal.

Suddenly a blinding flash of light stuck her eyes. She covered them with her bloody hand. A thunderous roar assaulted her ears, then a gush of searing hot air knocked her flat. When the shock wave passed, she rolled forward facing the horizon. A ball of flame grew like a fiery fountain shooting out of the ground unfolding upwards–a magnificent and horrifying sight of deadly fireworks. Then the glow faded, and finally evaporated leaving a smudge of graying smoke, trailing off into the distance. She had witnessed what should have been her death.

Ashley became aware of the cold desert soil beneath her and countless pricks of pain and soreness. Her left ankle throbbed, announcing a new serious injury.

She tried to sit and look at her leg, but the effort taxed what little strength she had. She fell back on the ground hitting her head. That brought back the persistent ach she had lived with this long day and night. Staring at the sky Ashley saw tiny star lights begin to spin in circles. She lost track of her place in time and space. As darkness drifted over her, she thought of her mother and of Walter.

CAPTAIN MIKE PORTER pulled himself into the cockpit of the aging Kiowa reconnaissance helicopter. Much like the aircraft he was about to fly, he had been around a long time, starting with the first Iraq war. Today his gray hair still stood in a close-cropped buzz cut, but his airman's uniform fit a bit tighter than it used to. The sun, still below the horizon, cast a hint of daylight across the shrouded land. Not enough light for Mike to see his instruments clearly, but he didn't need to see them. He knew them like a doctor knows his surgical procedures. The copter fired up, and the twin blades began beating the air, producing that familiar pounding sound. He checked with the base tower, than lifted off, veering north into the Nevada desert.

His mission was to fly a pattern over the terrain north from Nellis AFB to restricted area R4807-B while searching for any anomalies. When he approached ground zero he would check for elevated radioactivity levels and report his findings. As he climbed to an altitude of a thousand feet, he glanced over his shoulder at the lights of North Las Vegas. He always marveled at how abrupt civilization ended and the ancient desert claimed the land.

Sunlight spread across the flat countryside causing the stark features of the ground to come alive. Mike began flying his east-west pattern with each pass, covering a swath of land about five miles wide. He worked his way north, nose down to give him an open view. On his fifth pass he saw a bright yellow patch off to the right. He swerved toward it and dropped down to 500 feet, then 200. His first pass proved it was not a natural feature. On his second pass he spotted what looked like a human form lying near the colored spot. He circled and then landed, shut down the engine, and unbuckled. The rotation of the blades slowed. Mike kept his eyes on the object while he strapped on his sidearm and jumped to the ground. As he walked forward, he saw a movement and started to run.

Mike Porter had seen plenty of blood in the past, but never got used to it. The woman sprawled on the ground reminded him of those bad old days. He glanced up and spotted the parachute pinned to a clump of cactus, and then knelt down and touched the woman gently. "Can you hear me?

A vacant stare slowly focused on him. She spoke with a weak voice, "Is that you, Walter?"

Mike took his flight jacket off, folded it, and put it under her head—a head matted with dried blood. He saw cuts and bruises all over her exposed body, and a foot bent at an odd angle. He paused for a second, but couldn't think of anything more to do, except get help.

He ran to the chopper, leaped into the cockpit, and turned on the radio. He immediately identified himself, gave his co-ordinances, and called for a medivac unit. "Make it quick. She needs medical help right now." Mike grabbed a bottle of water and ran back, hoping the medics would get there in time. He offered the woman water, which she drank in small sips when she drifted into consciousness.

Fifteen minutes later the Black Hawk set down ten yards away and two medics hit the ground hunched down under the whirling blades. Mike got out of their way fast. Both men assessed Ashley's condition and motioned for a portable gurney. Two more medics arrived and the four lifted her onto the gurney and dashed for their helicopter. Mike timed the operation. Landing to lift off took fewer than six minutes. The Black Hawk headed for the base hospital.

ASHLEY BECAME AWARE that people were helping her. She heard the steady sound of the chopper blades beat the air and felt strong hands moving her. Her pain eased, and then disappeared. Voices shouted over the noise. She felt a thump when the chopper set down. Men in desert khakis lifted her. She felt cool air. A hand touched her shoulder, and a man's voice said, "You're in the base hospital. You're going to be okay, Miss."

Base hospital. I'm in a hospital—they can help me?

Awake now, she raised her head. There were plastic bags of fluid hanging from metal hooks above, tubes dangled down, feeding an IV taped to her left hand. She watched white walls roll by her and felt the vibration of movement. A woman, a nurse or doctor in a white coat, leaned over. "The commandant has ordered a private room for you. Colonel Myers is waiting."

Ashley tried to make sense of what was happening to her. Her pain had vanished so she must be all right, but if she was all right what was she doing in a hospital? And, why a special room? She felt the sheet under her move. Two nurses pulled her off the gurney onto a stationary bed; then they transferred the plastic bags of fluids.

A man, a uniformed officer with colored ribbons pinned to his chest stepped to her side and smiled down at her. "Good morning, Ms. Kohen, welcome to the Nellis Air Force Base Hospital. We have prepared for your arrival. I'm Colonel Myers, Deputy to General Brunel, the base commander."

Ashley looked up. "How do you know my name?"

"Oh, we know all about you, Ms. Kohen." He said with a faint smile.

She turned her head to the side. "Then you must know I'm with the FBI."

"Yes, of course. Of course. That's why the general has assigned you this room and will post two guards at your door."

"Guards?"

"Yes, Ms. Kohen." Myers dropped the smile. "The general has asked that I place you in protective custody."

"Protective custody?"

"Yes, for your protection."

Ashley's eyes widened. "Protection from what?"

"General Brunel feels it's in your best interest that you be kept safe for now. We'll take good care of you. You've had quite an adventure." Myers face remained passive as he backed away. As he left the room, he mumbled something to the guards. They exchanged salutes.

What the hell is going on? She lifted her head to see if her "guards" were facing the hallway. The nurse came into the room. "Okay, my dear. We have to get you out of those dirty clothes and clean you up." She started to pull off the sheet.

"I need a drink of water. If that's possible, please?" Ashley assumed a pitiful expression.

"Why of course, dear. I'll be right back–don't you worry."

Ashley watched as the nurse left, then went for Bashir's phone lodged in her right pants pocket. She pulled it out, woke it up, and then tapped the Settings feature. It searched for a Wi-Fi signal. Her hand trembled while she waited. Come on, damn it. The fan shaped icon lit up. She tapped quickly with her thumb, and held the phone up to her face.

When the nurse arrived with a cup of water, the phone was back in her pocket.

# SEVENTY-SIX

WITH HIS EYES FIXED on his open hands, Bill Johnson couldn't stop thinking about this awful night that had now turned into a Monday morning. He sat at his desk unable to concentrate on anything except the loss of Ashley. It was so horrible, so shocking, and so sudden his mind didn't accept the truth. He covered his face with hands that soon became wet. His shoulders shook. It wasn't right.

On the floor he saw the paper airplane he'd made to tease her. He picked it up, crushed it into a ball, and threw it in the wastebasket. Ashley represented the best of the young people of today—smart, dedicated, determined, and able to take whatever came her way and keep going.

The cell phone in his pocket vibrated, alerting him to a call. He decided to ignore it, then thought it might be Walter, cloistered in his office upstairs. Bill touched the home-key and the phone came alive. The telephone icon had a number one circled in the corner. He tapped it and a picture flashed on the screen. A face smeared with dried blood and many wounds looked at him. A familiar face. *Ashley's face*. A rush of adrenaline surged through his body. He screamed, "Ashley you're alive!"

His pulse raced as he checked the send-date and time: today one minute ago. He stared at that battered face. The eyes were red rimmed, but he felt they talked to him. They said, I'm here, come get me.

Johnson bolted from his office and climbed the stairs faster than he had in many years. Out of breath, he rushed into Kent's outer office. A somber Dorothy Hogan turned toward him. Kent's door, always open, now stood shut.

Between gulps of air he asked, "Is he in there, Dorothy?"

"Yes, but don't go in. He's hurting and needs his private space right now."

Without a word, Johnson leaned over her desk and placed his phone in front of her. Dorothy braced herself. "Is that Ashley?" She clutched her throat. "You mean she's alive?"

"Yes. That's Ashley as of," he checked his watch, "four minutes ago."

She moved her hand from her neck to her mouth. "Oh my God, look at the poor thing." She touched Bill's arm. "How bad is it?"

"We're going to find out. Let's go in." She nodded. They both walked to the door, knocked, and then entered. Bill Johnson had never seen his boss so wretched and distraught as he appeared at that moment. After the explosion in the Nevada desert, Walter controlled his emotions as he would at any crime scene. But that brave front was gone now, replaced with slumped shoulders, puffy eyes and a face full of pain.

Bill and Dorothy glanced at each other, then Bill moved forward. "Walter, I have some good news. I received a selfie."

Walter squared his shoulders. "A selfie?"

"Yes. I got this a few minutes ago." Bill showed him the phone image.

There was a moment of silence. Walter raised his head. "This is Ashley." Bill nodded. "When was this taken?"

"Time dated six minutes ago"

Kent pushed his chair back a few feet as the reality of Ashley being alive took hold. "How did you get this?"

"It popped up on my phone. Someone we care about sent it to me...to us I believe."

Kent came alive as if waking from a bad dream. With a nervous laugh he said, "This is a miracle!" Their faces brightened and all three gathered in a group hug followed by an awkward, joyous celebration that lasted a full minute.

Walter calmed down. "Let's see that picture again. Ashley looks like she's gone through hell. Do you know where she is?"

Bill shook his head, "Not yet."

Dorothy studied the image. "My sister's a nurse. That's a monitor for vital signs like blood pressure, and heartbeat in the background."

Bill agreed. "A hospital. That makes sense, considering the shape she's in. The question is, what hospital? I'll trace the call." Within minutes he learned the call originated from Nellis AFB.

Walter felt convinced Ashley sent the picture from the base hospital. With the speakerphone on he got through to the Nellis operator a few minutes later, and asked to speak with the commanding officer. The operator switched him over to General Brunel's administrative assistant, who asked the nature of his business. He explained it had to do with an FBI investigation that affected the General.

"Good morning, this is General Brunel. How may I help you?"

"I understand you have one of our agents on your base. FBI Special Agent Ashley Kohen."

"Who is this?"

"Special Agent in Charge Walter Kent, Albuquerque Field Office."

"What makes you say I have one of your agents here?"

"It's not a guess, General Brunel. I know she's there." He winked at Dorothy. "I need to talk to her about a current investigation."

The general didn't answer.

"General Brunel, I'm waiting."

"I'm not at liberty to discuss this matter with you, sir."

"Agent Kohen is a federal law enforcement officer, and I'm her superior. I expect your full cooperation, General. It's urgent."

Another moment of dead air.

"I have my orders, Mr. Kent. I suggest you take this talk with your superiors. That's all I have to say. Have a good day." The line went dead.

Bill Johnson screwed up his face. "He didn't deny she's there, nor did he confirm it. That's a no denial confirmation."

Kent agreed. "It's time to call Director Delong."

# SEVENTY-SEVEN

IN HIS CONFERENCE ROOM in Tysons Corner, Virginia Leo Adornetto surveyed the faces of his closest associates who, technically, answered to him on all matters of national security and intelligence. Admiral Henry Smithy of the NSA, Pat Fitzgerald, head of the CIA, Ed Delong, FBI chief, and Mike Johansson, his Assistant Deputy, had assembled on short notice. They gathered to view the President's message to the nation, carried on every major TV channel. At the end of the speech Adornetto snapped the TV off to avoid the inevitable post analysis by the media.

Everyone sat silent in the wood-paneled room lined with photographs of former Federal officials who used this space to protect the country from its enemies of the past. CIA chief Pat Fitzgerald spoke first. "What the hell was that all about?" His comment caused a snicker and a few head shakes.

Johansson, with a strained voice, answered. "That's Graham Steward skipping the eulogy for two FBI agents who, in the past forty-eight hours, have fallen in the line of duty: Rashid al Youris and Ashley Kohen."

"Please forgive Mike, he has good reason to be bitter." Delong placed a hand on his friend's arm. "Youris was a longtime friend and partner to Mike, and Kohen was a bright young agent new to the service. Both heroes in my mind." He jammed an unlit cigar in his mouth. "But I agree. The President is playing politics with the truth."

Admiral Smithy snorted, "Our leader has proven, once again, he knows how to lead–in the wrong direction."

Adornetto leaned back in his chair, crossed his arms and rolled his eyes. "You don't know the worst of it. Earlier this morning I came from a meeting of the National Security Council. The President not only refused to recognize the greatest national security success of our time, he smothered it with a top secret classification, essentially banning it from public view."

"Doesn't he know the system worked exactly as we have designed it to work?" said Fitzgerald. "Because of our mutual cooperation we have averted a terrorist attack that, if successful, would have murdered thousands of Americans and plunged us into yet another bloody war." He slammed his fist on the conference table. "We have diverted a tipping point in world affairs. The country needs to know we have protected them from our enemies."

Adornetto's mouth turned down. "I tried to explain that to him this morning, but he cut me off. He listens to the advisers who tell him what he wants to hear. The President has supported draconian cuts in our budgets and piled more work on the intelligence community. Now that we have something big to prove our worth, he shuts us down."

Delong straightened his well-worn brown sport coat. "I think we can agree the President left us out in the cold. We also have to agree there's not much we can do about it."

The conversation continued with everyone trying to control their disgust and soften their opinions of Graham Steward. A man entered the room unnoticed and whispered in Mike Johansson's ear. Mike turned around in his chair, and then followed the man into the next room. Three minutes later he slipped back in, took his place next to Delong, and handed him a cell phone while rapidly speaking to him in a hushed tone.

Delong studied the phone in disbelief and a quick shake of the head. "Incredible," he whispered, and then got everyone attention clustered around the table. "Gentlemen, I think we have a way out."

THE PRESIDENT'S SECRETARY, a mousey little man with scant hair combed over a prominent bald spot, stood at attention when he recognized four of the most important members of the President's administration enter his office. He straightened his tie and shirt cuffs to be certain they were properly visible. "Uh...good morning, gentlemen." The name plaque on his desk read Eugene Petit.

With thick black eyebrows arched together, Adornetto looked down at Mr. Petit. "We're here to see the President."

"Oh, I'm sorry. I don't have an appointment listed." He checked the calendar on his desk. "I have an opening next week on Tuesday. Would ten o'clock be all right?"

"No."

"How about 10:30?"

"No." He reached over and closed Eugene's calendar. "Our business can't wait. The President should be the first to know."

"To know what?

Mr. Adornetto tilted his head to one side, and shouted. "Why we are here, of course," he said loud enough to be heard in the next office only six feet away–the Oval Office.

Petit backed away from his desk. A voice from the adjacent room asked, "Who's out there, Eugene?"

Petit went to the door leading to the President's office. "It's Mr. Adornetto and, and..." The four men brushed Eugene aside and entered.

Seated in his high-back leather chair, Graham Steward suddenly stiffened his posture and dropped a gold pen he held in his hand. He looked at each of the sober faces standing before him. "My. My. What a serious bunch." He spoke in his down-home drawl and forced an amused expression. "Have the Russians declared war on us?"

Adornetto ignored the question. "I'm here to offer you my resignation." He placed a letter in front of the President.

Admiral Smithy scowled at Steward. "I too plan to resign, sir. He put his letter on top of Adornetto's. "With some regrets, Mr. President," said Fitzgerald, sliding his letter onto the desk. Ed Delong, dropped his resignation on top of the pile and said nothing.

Steward's eyes widened and he reached out to touch the letters, and then withdrew his hand as if they might burn him. "You boys aren't serious?"

Adornetto became spokesman for the group. "We are serious, Mr. President."

"But why?"

"It is customary for heads of Federal agencies to resign when the President no longer approves of their performance."

"There must be some misunderstanding here. In no way do I have a problem with your work."

"We don't see it that way. With my support, the NSA, FBI, and the CIA, along with other agencies in the intelligence community, have worked as partners to foil a major terrorist attack that you saw fit to ignore."

"Oh, if you're referring to that blunder out in the Nevada desert..."

"That blunder in Nevada was an attempt to kill hundreds of thousands of our people, an attack that would have plunged us into a massive and extended war. An act of terror designed to brand your administration and leadership incapable of protecting the country and the citizens who elected you."

319

"I stand by my position, gentlemen." Steward used a sharp tone. "An enemy able to explode a nuclear weapon on American soil..."

"No enemy exploded a weapon in Nevada, sir–that was a controlled discharge of a nuclear bomb by an agent of the FBI, *not* a terrorist. Your speech today was a blatant distortion of the truth–a cover up."

"That's one-way of looking at it."

Ed Delong stepped forward. "The question is, how will the voters of our country, look at it?"

Steward's eyes narrowed, "What do you mean?" He shot to his feet as if to defend himself physically. "This matter is classified as top secret. If any of you utter one word about this, I will see that you are prosecuted under Title 18, Section 789 of the U. S. Code"

Delong acted as a teacher correcting a student. "That's Section 798, sir. Not Section 789."

The President glared at Director Delong. "I'm serious."

"We have no intention of violating your orders, sir. The others nodded support for Delong's promise.

Admiral Smithy took over. "Sir, do you recall the last time four well-known agency heads, such as ourselves, who often appear on popular Sunday morning talk shows, simultaneously resigned during a President's first term in office?" The admiral suppressed a smirk.

"I'm not a historian, Admiral."

"I am, and it is unprecedented. Never happened. We won't have to say a word. Our resignations are a matter of public record. The media will have a field day."

The President frowned. "If you think you can come in here and bully me, you are mistaken. I have two years left in my term of office. Let the media speculate. I will claim I was misinformed. It will blow over. Simple as that."

Adornetto reasserted himself. "You may be right, Mr. President. You, and former holders of this office, have much power and influence, but that power is not absolute. Remember, things didn't work out for Nixon or LBJ."

Graham Steward plopped down in his leather chair and clasped his hands behind his head. "That was different. They didn't have all the bases covered, did they?"

"That's right." Adornetto pointed at the four letters of resignation. "You have four of the based covered."

"I'm glad you understand." Steward winked at him.

"...but the umpire can still call you out." Adornetto dropped a print of a picture of Ashley on top of the stack of resignations.

"What's that?"

"That's the fly in the ointment. The monkey wrench in the machinery. The David that slew Goliath."

The President held the picture and studied it. "I don't get it?"

Ed Delong leaned over and gazed at the picture, along with the leader of the free world. "That battered beauty is Special Agent Ashley Kohen who survived the recent disintegration of a DC3 carrying a suitcase nuke over Nevada. She is an eyewitness to the fact that our intelligence community averted a catastrophic attack on the homeland–under your leadership."

"Where did you get this picture?"

Enjoying the moment, Delong answered. "After your address to the nation it popped up on my phone this morning. It's time dated earlier today."

Adornetto nodded. "I got one, too."

""So did I," said Fitzgerald.

Admiral Smithy arched his eyebrows and held his phone. "I downloaded mine from YouTube."

President Graham Steward's hand trembled as he held the photo. Beads of sweat formed on his upper lip. "You mean this is in the public domain?"

"Hey, we had nothing to do with that," replied the Director of National Intelligence. "But I'd bet its widespread discovery is certain."

The room was silent. No one moved. Eugene Petit could be heard humming *God Bless America* outside the Oval Office. The President slumped forward. "They'll eat me alive."

"Who'll eat you alive?"

As if mortally wounded, the man behind the desk groaned, "The press. The Congress. My enemies."

Adornetto moved in for the kill. "It doesn't have to be that way, Mr. President."

With a vacant look in his eyes he asked, "It doesn't?"

"No, sir. You can turn this to your advantages. We can help you."

"How can you protect me from this?" He shook the picture in their faces. "It's on the internet. Living proof of the attack."

"It's not too late. Embrace it. Make it part of your legacy. This brave young woman will become a symbol of your leadership."

Steward tipped his head back and gazed at the ceiling. In a defeated voice he asked, "What do I have to do?"

The agency heads glanced at one another sharing a look of triumph.

"Lift the gag-order. Take credit for fending off an attack far greater than anything ever seen in the nation's history. You'll be a hero, and so will we."

Steward stared into the eyes of this man who dared to challenge his authority, the ringleader of a bureaucratic rebellion. He propped the picture of Ashley on his desk and reached for the pile of resignations. He lifted them as if to discover their weight. Then, in a loud voice he shouted, "Eugene, get in here. I have some paper for you to shred." His expression morphed from hopelessness to one of renewed confidence. "And get Press Secretary Mark Ward in here, too. I have to call a press conference, right now. The country needs to know I'm doin' a heck of a job!"

# SEVENTY-EIGHT

A CLEAR PLASTIC BAG of fluid hung over Ashley's head. At the bottom of the bag a tube fed the watery substance into a tiny glass cylinder. She watched a steady drip appear inside the cylinder, then drop methodically into the delivery tube letting it enter her bloodstream. She calculated a drop formed every 10 seconds.

Peggie, a petite, slightly overweight, round-faced nurse hovered nearby. Ashley pointed at the bag, "What's that stuff?"

"Don't you worry yourself about things like that, my dear. It's medicine."

Ashley took a deep breath and exhaled. Whatever it was, it made her feel good. Not good like a drug induced euphoria, but good like in 'feeling no pain'. She touched her partially shaved head. Still numb and a bit bumpy around the sutures, she tried to count them. Eight altogether.

"Now dear, don't touch those stitches, you don't want to get them infected, do you?"

Ashley shook her head. Peggie was a bit of a magpie, always chattering about something or someone, but good-hearted and eager to please. With a little encouragement she'd tell you everything she knew. After lunch she told Ashley those nice men outside her door wouldn't be back because the general was sure she would be safe now. That meant Ashley could hobble out the door if she had a mind to, which she didn't. Hobbling would require her to drag a Frankenstein sized boot that protected her swollen ankle. The doctor who treated her foot called it a malleolar fracture. Whatever that was, it still hurt and she was content to stay put for the immediate future.

Peggie left the white hospital room, and then returned ten minutes later. "Oh, Ashley. You have a visitor," she announced. "It's Colonel Myers."

Ashley raised her head. Myers stood in the doorway with a genuine smile on his face. He moved into the room. "Agent Kohen, I have good

323

news for you." She didn't respond. "General Brunel is transferring you to the Los Vegas South Springs Rehabilitation Hospital downtown. We've done all we can do for you here."

She couldn't resist, "Will I have an armed guard?"

"Oh, no. That was only a precaution. You'll find the folks at the rehab center highly professional." He stepped closer and lowered his voice. "It's been an honor to serve you Agent Kohen." The colonel snapped to attention, saluted and then made a smart about-face and left the room.

It took a few seconds for Ashley to react. She shut her mouth and put her hand to her forehead. What in the hell was that?

Peggie fidgeted with a stethoscope hanging around her neck. "Isn't Colonel Myers a nice man, and handsome, too." Ashley considered several answers and rejected them all. "All right dearie, we have to get ourselves dressed and ready to go."

"Go where?"

"Why to South Springs, like the Colonel said. I have all your things in this bag and some fresh clothes for you to wear." She held a zippered desert khaki bag and an arm full of matching clothes. Peggie split open the Velcro straps on the orthopedic boot. "There, we have Mr. Black Boot off, how let's put our pants on. You be careful with your ankle, now." The dressing operation took longer than necessary because Ashley offered minimal cooperation.

Soon she found herself dressed and sitting on the edge of the bed when a burly male nurse rolled a wheelchair in and positioned it by her side. He offered a muscular arm and assisted her into the chair. Peggie handed her the zippered bag and a pair of green and tan crutches. Ashley felt relieved the wheelchair wasn't camouflaged, too. They loaded her into an unmarked white van.

South Springs Hospital was a 30-minute drive across town. It felt good to get out into America again. The glittering hotels, flashing lights and cascading fountains made her feel right with the world. She thought about what it might have looked like today if the terrorists had been successful in their plans.

The walls of the two story rehab hospital were made of reflective glass that sparkled in the sunlight. Two staff sergeants dressed in airman-blue helped her out of the truck and wheeled her into the back entrance. Two security guards met them at the door. The airmen, with young eager faces, saluted Ashley. She thanked them with an uncertain tone in her voice. They marched back to the truck as the guards wheeled their patient into a small waiting room a few feet off the lobby. One guard stood by as the other left the room. Ashley turned to the man, "What's going on?"

The man cut his eyes toward her. "Don't you know?"

"Know what?"

Before he could answer, Walter Kent and Bill Johnson walked into the room. Breathlessness overtook Ashley. Because her Frankenstein boot got trapped in the footrests of the wheelchair, she stumbled when she tried to get up. Walter caught her in his arms before she fell. Ashley climbed up his frame and locked both arms around his neck. Tears surged over her cheeks as she burst into a radiant smile. He kissed her lightly, and then pulled her close.

Over Walter's shoulder Ashley saw Bill Johnson and extended a hand to him. Bill took it and bowed as if meeting the queen. He then turned to shield this tender greeting from interruption. That's when he saw a blond-haired man, impeccably dressed in a white suit and black tie, waiting patiently nearby. He signaled to the man and they met halfway. "Yes?" Bill asked.

"I'm Kevin Weber the hospital administrator. I can see this is…a private moment, and I don't mean to interfere, but I have a hospital to run. You must understand." Weber motioned for Bill to follow him into the lobby.

When Bill returned with Weber in tow, Walter was helping Ashley back into the wheelchair. "I don't need this thing," she complained.

Bill whispered in Walter's ear, who nodded. "Call Ramirez, he'll know what to do."

Ashley perked up. "Ramirez? Mark is here?"

"Yep, I've brought half the field office." Walter grinned. "Well, not half, but enough to do the job."

"Do what job?"

Walter leaned down, found a spot where there wasn't a bandage, and kissed her. "That will have to hold you for a while, Ashley."

She spread the palms of her hands out with a perplexed look. "What?"

"I'll show you." Walter guided the wheelchair into the lobby and stopped behind the two glass front doors. Ashley leaned forward, squinted her eyes, and then recoiled. "God almighty, what is all that?"

"It's your fifteen minutes or maybe fifteen years of fame waiting for you."

Ashley gripped the arms of the wheelchair and straightened her body. Arrayed outside was a hoard of journalists holding microphones. They stood pressed against a rickety barricade hastily thrown-up. Photographers leaned forward holding every kind of camera. Reporters jostled to get the best position for an interview. Mobile trucks and vans with satellite dishes were parked behind the crowd of eager broadcasters. They waited like hungry piranhas eyeing their prey.

Ashley stared into the eyes of Walter. "I can't go out there."

"Don't worry, I'll protect you. I have a team of agents ready to manage that bunch. You'll be safe."

Ashley shook her head. "No Walter. I mean I can't go out there like this. Look at me. Bandages, hair a mess, baggy clothes that don't fit. This bad-ass boot. I look ridiculous. No way am I going out there."

Walter held on to the wheelchair as he laughed hard enough to make him unsteady. When he recovered, he bent over and tilted her face up to his. "You couldn't look bad no matter how hard you tried." She smothered a grin. "Your assignment, Special Agent Kohen is crowd control. I've got your back."